BATTLE RING EARTH

MEGASTRUCTURE
1

JON FRATER

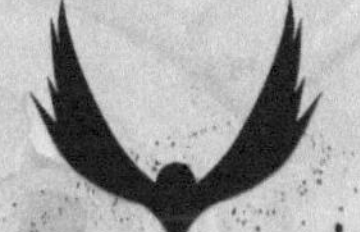

aethonbooks.com

Megastructure
Colony
Grand Reversal

PROLOGUE

A RING IN SPACE.

It was clearly insane, even as its bulk confronted Zluur's research vessel. More than a kilometer away and it still filled his bridge's viewing surface, stretching apparently into infinity. In fact, it stretched around the far side of the planet and met up with itself, a solid band twelve kilometers wide and two thick, studded with weapons, defenses, and docking bays which held countless fighting machines.

In theory, a Battle Ring was a brilliant way of managing the defense of a developed world. Take a cable, spin it around the equator of a planet, and allow it to orbit there. Surround it with magnets and it produced electric current. Surround the magnets with structures and you could stand on it, reinforce it, build maglev tracks that could zip around it. Fill it with all the resources of a battleship, arm it with weapons, install power plants, buttress it with armor. Suddenly your ring was a defense base that encompassed the world. Omni-directional defenses. A military station like none other. You could even drop lines from the ring to the surface of the home world in order to ferry cargo and passengers from surface to orbit. Plenty of room to store weapons, ships, and cargo.

With these built across the Two Thousand Worlds, the thought went, the Sleer empire had no more need to support a fleet of thousands of ships to patrol a million cubic parsecs of space. Now every planet could have its own dedicated defense ring.

Simple. Breathtaking.

And too little, too late to save them.

Zluur, the closest thing the Sleer High Command had to a Chief Scientist, had seen the military projections. They were losing. Time was something they had little of, even as they publicly proclaimed their resistance to Skreesh migration. The six-armed, blue skinned three eyed monsters from further up the galactic arm hadn't merely encroached on their territory: they were swallowing up whole worlds now. If the Sleer were lucky, they'd have another century to figure out how to survive. If not...well, these Battle Rings wouldn't save them. A revolution was needed, in construction and deployment.

Zekerys, Zluur's former student and a current favorite of the military, claimed such a revolution in the offing. Zluur was here to see the proof. This battle ring was a new thing, developed by Zekerys, who had apparently named the monstrous design after himself. Of course he had.

"Docking procedure begins."

Doors parted and the great ship slid against clamps inside the even greater hangar bay. When metal met metal, the entire vessel vibrated with contact, a muffled echo like the door to a tomb closing for the final time. Zluur wasn't given to fits of anxiety, but he couldn't keep his hands from shaking when he heard that sound.

"Docking procedure complete. Welcome to Battle Ring Zekerys."

The control tower's voice was surely a reproduction of a Sleer female long since dead. Zluur wasn't given to despair, but he was tempted by it now.

He shook his head as if to clear it of evil spirits. No. What he'd done was to make plans and follow through with them. Over the past centuries of Skreesh incursions, the Two Thousand Worlds had dwindled to a mere handful of outposts and colonies. The empire was gone. The fleets were being consumed in battle. The object now was to protect the Sleer race. Nothing could be allowed to interfere.

It was far too late for self-doubt. Except...it clearly wasn't.

Zluur stood on the bridge of his research vessel, Genukh, a repurposed gun destroyer that had had its middle section completely remodeled and converted into a launch-capable cargo delivery platform. Where decks and crew quarters once lay were now situated rows of cylindrical objects each half a kilometer long. Twelve of them, so tightly packed with equipment that he couldn't imagine how to increase their mass further or squeeze out more efficiency from their mechanisms. The DNA synthesizers they contained were loaded with everything they needed to crank out as many colonies of bacteria needed to guarantee survival on whichever world they were deposited on.

Miracles of science, every one of them. Each one contained thousands of parts, they could duplicate every twenty minutes, and were considerably more reliable than nano machines. All they needed was a suitable environment to inhabit and they would do the rest. In a million years, the Sleer's genetic code might give rise to something far more interesting than its present form.

Or perhaps not. At any rate, it beat extinction at the hands of the Skreesh.

Together they represented a chance for redemption. Considering how much he had damaged the universe, it was about time he helped bring some life into it.

"Genukh," he said.

The ship's computer picked up on the summons. "Genukh answers."

"When is this infernal meeting going to begin? Do admirals and statesmen have nothing else to do but lounge around, making small talk?"

"It already has begun," answered the ship. "Ring Zekerys's command tower is the designated meeting place. I am being signaled by Great Fleet Lord Sselanniss. Are you sure you won't be attending in person?"

Zluur hissed. The last thing he wanted to do at this point was to leave his ship unattended. As of now, it was just himself and Genukh and no one else. That was how Zluur wanted it. He despised distraction, and the chance that someone would want to examine his ship's cargo hold was too great. They would ask questions. He would have to answer. If he lied, they would suspect him. Better to avoid a confrontation. "No, contact the command tower. I'll be there. In holographic form."

"Of course. Placing the call now."

Zluur retreated to his ready room, a spacious meeting chamber meant to house a staff of twenty, complete with holographic attendance if needed. There were wide, comfortable chairs along the walls. He chose to pace from one end of the room to the other and back again while he waited. He knew they were being petulant...keeping him waiting on purpose. Finally, he sat and gave another order. "Genukh, put up a schematic of this ring. Make sure you note the ship's position as well."

"Should I note the positions of the orbiting coalition fleet as well?"

That was unexpected. And alarming. Genukh hadn't mentioned a fleet on their approach. "Which fleet? Where?"

A new display appeared. Zluur could see the allied vessels clearly, each notable by its hull design. A Dec task force, a dozen ships of varying sizes and functions. A squadron of Rachnae cruisers. A Vix space control ship. A Movi super-carrier.

Movi. Which meant Cycomm advisors aboard their ships. Which meant Cycomm SenseOp agents. He felt the bottom of his stomachs fall out as the implications rolled through his mind.

They knew. Somehow he'd been incompetent. He'd left a tell-tale sign, like claw marks on a scratched surface. They knew he'd stolen their AI's innards.

A deep breath. No. They didn't know. If they had, the Movi wouldn't be just hanging in space with their allied races. They'd be demanding payment. Justice. Revenge. And they'd get it, too. The Cycomms were few but they wielded influence, and the Movi would back them up.

At least now Zluur had a good reason to be nervous. Genukh, for all his capabilities, wasn't shielded against SenseOp telepaths, teleports, or scramblers. If there was such a thing as shielding in that way. Perhaps the Movi had a way to do it. The Sleer did not.

He breathed more easily as a chime sounded and a dozen new images flickered into view. The Allied Fleet High Command. He recognized Sselanniss, whose plumage was in full bloom, easily identifiable. His eyes passed over the Sleer admirals not knowing their names, nor caring. The Dec rested in its tank, its arms slowly swaying with the currents produced by its aerator. The Vix stood to the side, their race's renowned patience on full display: attentive focus crossing their features. The Movi admiral and her Cycomm scientist wore frowns of intense concentration. It looked to Zluur as if they were passing signals. He'd never seen an agitated Cycomm before. Their faces cleared as they closed their hurried, intense, exchange.

Sselanniss spoke to him first. "We appreciate your prompt arrival, Zluur," she said.

He nodded at her, and raised his hands slightly to indicate that he was including all of them in the gesture.

"Home Fleet Master, you are too courteous. Forgive my not being physically present. Genukh developed a fault in his reactive furnace, and I wanted to be on hand should the ring's facilities not be able to repair it."

He could imagine Genukh frowning electronically at the lie. There was no faulty mechanism and they both knew it. But none of these people would care. They wouldn't even check the ring's readouts. They trusted him. Seven decades of loyal, fruitful service to the empire would do that. And this was Zekerys's moment in the sun, not his own.

Sselanniss motioned to the scientist to begin. "Your briefing, please, Zekerys."

The young scientist commanded the room's attention. He was everything Zluur was not: bold, vibrant, resplendent in his plumage. His crown feathers had a way of dancing as he addressed his audience. And he was confident nearly to the point of arrogance. "Battle Ring Zekerys is a revolution in the construction, deployment, and operation of the venerable ring design of warcraft," he began. While the nestling regaled the group with the technical details of his project, Zluur hung back, bringing up a viewing surface of his own to examine the megastructure. After some time, Zluur had to admit that the ring was impressive. He looked up to see that Zekerys waving his arms in front of a holographic tank. Taking his guests on a virtual grand tour of the facility he proposed to build.

"The first difference you'll notice," Zekerys was saying, giving Zluur a moment's distraction from his personal troubles. "The ring floats freely over the host planet. No elevators physically touch the ground. The spokes however still maintain lift and drop platforms which allow any aircraft access to the structure. Additionally, the ring itself no longer utilizes a static single-form construction. The centermost section uses a hollow routing corridor that allows the ring to shift structural modules from one location to another in a dynamic fashion. With this new development, any defensive or offensive module can be switched out for any other across the entire length of the ring within an hour. Think of the implications! No matter from which direction an opposing fleet might approach, the ring can concentrate its full fighting ability to the point of contact."

There followed a series of visual aids that showed the audience exactly how the ring could be deployed. It was a brilliant idea, Zluur had to admit, with peerless engineering.

Sselanniss frowned. "If the spokes are not physically anchored to the world, how will materials be delivered to it during construction?"

"There is no need. This ring is meant to be deployed over a developed world. The airlift limitations would be minimal." Zekerys displayed a toothy grin as the other considered it.

"Construction time?"

"It's built. Complete. Nine years and three months, an odd number of days."

Silence. Shock. No orbital ring had been produced in less than twenty years, ever. The admirals looked at each other, at Zekerys, at Zluur as they wondered if he wasn't exaggerating his success. "When and how are you to test it?" one asked.

"I have made arrangements for a full demonstration," Zekerys beamed. Zluur recognized the look. He'd seen it on countless young faces. Look what I've done! Aren't you proud?

Zluur wondered if Zekerys had truly expected them to fawn over him. He could tell them about his new ring design, but he couldn't tell them the truth. That battle rings wasted more time, lives, and resources than they saved. That each new ring represented a tactical success but a strategic loss. A ring would draw the Skreesh to it like a magnet. Could Zluur say such a thing here? No. He had spent a decade building them his own solution. An answer to dwarf all previous answers. It had taken time. A great deal of time, years of time. And commitments - plural, the kind that came in deals and bargains. The head researcher on Catalog, the greatest storehouse of knowledge in the known worlds, had been clear on that. Zluur was free to use their facilities but only if he gave them the new weapon. Defending Catalog was essential. If every world in the galaxy fell to the titans, Catalog would revive them given time and effort. If Catalog remained safe.

He said yes. Of course. He'd had no other choice. And in fairness, he would help them. Eventually.

There were the years he'd spent among the Cycomms. Introducing himself to their ruling machine intelligence, the Malkah. Three years gaining her trust, three years learning their language, attending their rituals, recording their secrets. Three years studying their computer science.

And three minutes to violate every trust he'd built with them, to snip out a segment of the Malkah's code to refashion for his own purpose. Perhaps they'd forgive him for that. But the virus he'd loaded into her matrix to confuse, confound, and wreck their society to ensure his escape? No. They would kill him on sight. Perhaps they were preparing to do so right now. He wouldn't blame them.

But without her code, Genukh would still be no more than a discarded gun destroyer, forgotten in some barely remembered shipyard on Home Nest, waiting for the day that it would be disassembled and its parts recycled into other, more modern warships.

Was it worth it? He needed to know. For now, he had to keep still and watch.

He concentrated on the proceedings. The presentation complete, now it was time for Zekerys to defend his thesis. One of the admirals in particular was not happy with the presentation. "The problem is that we can't risk developed worlds to mishap during construction. Another is that battle rings are stationary and have a tendency to attract attention."

Finally, Zluur thought. One of them understands!

"With this dynamic design, we lure them into one trap after another. We hold the initiative in every engagement. It will give us a chance to dictate terms," Zekerys insisted.

The admiral's posture changed to one of contemplation. He was falling for it. He was actually thinking about going along for the sake of propriety.

Zluur had had enough. "No, the problem is that battle rings are labor and material intensive projects. It takes a million laborers two decades to deploy one, and then if it is discovered in progress then it's no great feat to destroy it before it can be completed. That means they can only be built and deployed on worlds with the populations, and resources to build them. Populated worlds. Developed worlds. Worlds we cannot afford to lose. It has nothing to do with the chance of mishap." Pause. Let the bomb drop, now. "I have a better way."

Silence, as if the audience had been waiting for this moment. Zekerys made a strangled sound of rage but kept his fury to himself. The Movi admiral and her Cycomm officer stared intently, and Zluur understood that his life was now forfeit. They knew what had happened to their Malkah and now they knew he was responsible. Sselanniss approached Zluur, her crown feathers swaying in the air currents as she passed beneath a vent. "And yours is different?"

"It is."

"How?"

"A combination of machine intelligence, automation, and nanofabrication. I took a biological approach to…"

He never finished. Alarms sounded as the lighting changed from a bright white to a muted red. A mechanical voice drifted down from the ceiling, but seemed to be everywhere. Ring Zekerys was speaking to them.

"Gravity wake detected. Skreesh fold-space energy signature detected. Vectors are being evaluated...plotting...plot displayed."

A new hologram appeared, showing the expected point where the Skreesh vessel would appear. Barely a full light-second from the battle ring itself, if he was reading the scale correctly.

Zekerys screeched with glee. "Ha! Now, you will see! My machine will defend the world!"

And then it clicked. *This* was Zekerys's demonstration. He'd called the Skreesh here. Just to show them how successful his ring would be at repelling a titan in real time.

Zluur turned and headed back to his bridge. He could almost feel the thundering footsteps of two million soldiers and sailors rushing to their battle stations, boots pounding against myriad decks. Behind him he could hear Sselanniss ending the meeting, ordering all defenses into place and declaring launch windows for all the allied ships. Even now Sleer naval vessels were receiving final checks by the ring's automated systems, ensuring their crews were ready to fight whatever battle was being thrust upon them. Drowning out the screams of enraged protest from the Movi officer for the moment.

"It's not about machines!" Zluur bellowed. "It was never about machines...it's about *life*!" He took a deep breath, slowed his rage. It served no purpose. And time was running out. "Genukh."

"Genukh answers."

"Plot a departure. We need to leave."

"I understand."

Zluur winced at the smugness he heard—or thought he heard —in his computer's response. "Do you? Do you really?"

Genukh hesitated as it compiled its response. Two seconds,

then three, then four...he was truly taking his time about it, wasn't he? Ten seconds. Twelve.

Finally a sound that strangely resembled a sigh emerged from the speaker. "I believe I do. The cargo pods' DNA synthesizers are capable of creating bacterial cultures almost immediately upon deployment. But I rescanned the schematics for the cargo pods I carry." Pause. "Your intention is to release the resulting bacterial cultures on another world and spur the development of new life forms which will be genetically linked to the Sleer genome, isn't it?"

And there it was. His only friend saw into his soul far more deeply than any Sleer ever had, and he wasn't even strictly alive. "It is."

"And you believe that by helping to defend Zekerys's orbital station, we might be destroyed before such an opportunity can arise."

"Yes."

"And that by leaving now, we will preserve your project and successfully deploy the Sleer genome elsewhere?"

"Yes. I believe that."

"The genome will not produce copies of Sleer or any other form of life on Home Nest. It may not produce anything beyond basic multicellular flora and fauna for millions of years. Do you still believe that this experiment is worth pursuing?"

Zluur didn't believe in time travel per se...and no, he would never set eyes on what happened to whatever world the computer selected. But what would the Skreesh be in a million years? Still marauding, was the answer he came up with. Genukh had the chance to bring a dead world to life. If it worked, then over the eons new ships might be generated and sent back out past the ruined worlds the Skreesh left in their wake. In a billion or so years, perhaps a new swath of creatures would arise. They would be very different, but genetically nest-mates.

"I do," he said.

Another pause. When Genukh spoke this time, he sounded confident and decisive. "I am in communication with the ring's computers. We are being assigned a defense location. The reactive furnaces are already at full power, and I am preparing to charge the reactive weapons as soon as we clear the launch bay. We can be in position with weapons deployed within minutes."

That was Genukh's history as a warship coming to the fore. Even with the new programming, he always opted for violence as a first reaction to any perceived threat. "Open the hangar bay door and take us unto a rotational orbit ten kilometers from the battle ring," Zluur ordered.

"Understood. Umbilicals detached. Docking clamps released. Maneuvering thrusters operating at one-tenth power. We will be in position in three minutes."

The disturbance exploded into light and radiation as the titan emerged from fold-space. A massive ship well over one hundred kilometers long, with a flaring bow and oblong body, with space-warping vanes protruding from its tail like the roots of an incredibly huge tree. How many worlds had been swept clear of life and surface mantle to build it, Zluur absently wondered. What was that world's name? What manner of life had it birthed? No one would ever know.

Comm channels opened and chattered with a multitude of voices as orders were handed down from Sselanniss and her admirals in the ring's control tower. Genukh drove through the open bay doors and angled itself upwards, pointing its bow towards the attacking giant. The allied races deployed, creating a wall of metal between themselves and the Skreesh. On numerous screens, Zluur could see how Zekerys's design was working to reform itself, bringing defenses to bear as enormous weapon bays opened firing ports, pointing at the titan.

Then the titan attacked. Its nose glowed briefly and a blue

beam of energy a mile wide blasted through space, striking Battle Ring Zekerys directly. The structure held for a moment...then the beam passed through the structure to strike the planet beneath it. A flurry of activity as clouds of atmosphere burst out of the gaping hole in the ring, then snuffed as bulkheads closed off the damaged area. Secondary beams sliced and scarred the ring further, tearing a mile-wide gap in the structure.

Genukh's sensors zoomed in on the planet. A crater half a mile wide lay beneath a mushroom cloud. The landscape around the strike zone lay in flames.

The allied fleet took advantage of the lull between shots to respond as the workhorses of the Sleer fleet formed up. They formed a ring of their own as the fleet orbited the planet, deploying into coherent groups, flying above the plane of the ring. More clouds of warships appeared over the planet's pole, clearing the way for return firing solutions.

Zekerys's ring shifted, moving new modules into place in an attempt to repair the damage. Even now the ring was buckling, twisting as inertia worked to pull it apart. A hundred clouds of long-range missiles burst from open firing bays, streaking toward the Skreesh. Giving the assembled fleet time to lock their weapons on target and maneuver into optimal firing patterns. The missiles struck the titan head on, igniting into a flurry of bright specks against the thick hull. Another cloud followed, and another.

Zluur blanched. "Damage report?"

"The titan's armor is weakening. It is still at 98 percent strength." Pause. "Primary weapons are coming online all over the fleet. The ring's computer is requesting that we lock our weapons into their Integrated Planning Operation System. Shall I join them?"

Clearly the ring could organize the fleet's weapons better than individual captains could. "Yes. Hardly makes sense to hold back now."

The ship opened its main gun's firing port as displays appeared, showing the status of the weapon. "Main gun charging. Locking weapons batteries on primary target," it announced. Massive armored panels swung outward from the ship's nose, exposing a weapon mount that gaped, crackling with arcing power like a maw filled with electric fangs. After a minute of rising power levels the countdown presented itself. The titan's bulbous snout loomed in the observation bubble, a warning of what would come if they failed. "Firing."

On the display, Zluur could see the fleet's response. it made an imposing sight. One thousand main guns charged, flared, and fired as a single unit, striking the titan in its bow, tearing a ragged hole through its heavy armor. Secondary weapons joined the fight, throwing kinetic shells, terawatt lasers, and particle accelerators against the hull of the approaching ship. Explosions lit up the sky as fireballs peppered the gargantuan vessel.

"Titan is still approaching," Genukh confided. "Their armor is down to seventy percent."

"Great maker," Zluur murmured. "If we live through this, remind me to apologize to Zekerys. He may have actually known what he was doing after all."

A new combined strike blasted another piece of the titan into space, and another. Its armor was down to fifty percent, and still the fleet fought.

The titan's nose re-aligned and blasted another wide energy beam. This one was aimed at a swath of the Sleer fleet, wiping out entire squadrons as it cast its aim across an arc above the ring. An entire section of the tactical board turned from green to red in an instant. Before the explosions even died out, countless hatches all over the titan opened and millions of new units spilled into space.

"They're launching shock troopers. I am … just a moment. I am receiving a message for you on the command channel."

"Play it."

Home Fleet Master Sselanniss's face appeared before her. She was plainly enraged but terrified as well. "Zluur!" An explosion in the background threw her to the side. She recovered quickly, "The Movi fleet lord commands me to arrest you and deliver you to their ship. Why did she make this demand?" Another explosion, this one pixilating the hologram for long seconds until new channels could take up the connection. "Zluur, what have you done?" The connection blinked out and Zluur blinked at empty air.

New alarms sounded. "The Movi super-carrier is refusing to launch her fighters. In fact, she appears to be leaving the formation. The Dec and Vix ships are following. All of them have disconnected their ship's weapons from the ring's firing control system." Pause. "We are being ordered back to the docking bay," Genukh said.

"We're not following the order. I have another plan for you." Zluur's hands swept from one end of his console to the other as he picked out codes and instructions, building a program from component parts long since written and stored. Countless squadrons of Skreesh shock troopers were even now descending on the ring, ripping it apart with their armored claws and firing at crew who tried to defend. The titan unleashed another energy bolt against another section of Sleer vessels, wiping them out in seconds. "We need them to chase us," he said.

For the second time, Genukh hesitated. A lengthy pause, then, Genukh asked a question of his own. "Why are we not following the order?"

Zluur considered answering. But what could he say? The answer wasn't to build more rings. It was building rings in a fraction of the time with no wasted time or resources. To take the biased decision making out of the equation. Maximize efficiency. His ring, Batte Ring Genukh...would build itself. Powered by Sleer reactive furnaces, defended by reactive weaponry, weaponry, guided by modified Cycomm machine intelligence, supplied by reverse-engineered Skreesh recycler tech, and assembled according to Movi engineering principles. The twelve modules in Genukh's cargo hold would unpack in low orbit as each component module sought out its neighbors and linked up. Filaments would stream between the units to share data and power while deep within each, a reactive furnace would come to life. Fabricators would deploy. Recyclers would unfurl. The nascent on-board intelligence would sweep up any detritus in orbit and incorporate the harvested material into itself. Once the ring solidified and established a stable orbit, it would drop tethers down from the skies, anchoring it to the surface of the target planet. More raw materials would be ladled up from the oceans, the dry land, or whatever lay in between the two extremes. It would grow as a living thing grew. Tethers would evolve into elevators for cargo and passengers. The surfaces would expand into weapon turrets and shield generators, as the skin of the ring grew armor plating. The DNA synthesizers would deploy and spread the Sleer genome through bacteria, potentially giving rise to a new race of beings, Sleer in genetics, but utterly different in origin.

But living hands would not touch its controls. That was the point. Millions, hundreds of millions, perhaps billions of soldiers, civilians, scientists, refugees could be saved. All defended from the Skreesh titans that even now carved wide swaths through Sleer space. Self-building. Self-maintaining. Self-defending.

It would be magnificent.

"We're in danger here, Genukh," Zluur said. It was no lie. Even now the gravity wake dissipated and space beyond the ring began to glow. Zluur could smell smoke in his nostrils now, imaginary or not. The burnt flesh of the dying. "We need to attract their attention. Draw them away from here. They need to chase us. Make sure they can detect our presence from one fold-space engagement to another."

"How far should we travel?"

"As far as the fuel lasts. Multiple jumps and re-jumps."

"Very well. I am disengaging from the fleet and plotting a course down this arm of the galaxy."

"Excellent. Let's give them something to remember us by. Charge the main gun and the fusion drives. We'll hit the lead titan with the gun, and then wash the fusion flare across their bow as we turn to align for the first jump."

"I'm sure that will get their attention." Genukh almost sounded smug. Zluur couldn't decide if he liked the fact that his research ship was developing a distinct personality. In the end, he doubted it would matter. Genukh was a good servant, and that made everything else possible.

"Engage," he ordered.

The ship's huge fusion drives flared to life, driving the vessel forward on a kilometer-long plume of high energy plasma. Warning lights danced on the bridge as the machine worked to fulfill its orders. The main gun's capacitors filled and the gun port's focussing elements made adjustments. "Firing."

The beam poured forth in a torrent, blasting through the bow of the titan, ripping a hole in its hull and bursting out the other side of the ship. The beam held for long seconds and then dissipated, the damaged hull oozing sparks and white-hot slag. Flaming specks flew out of the damaged hole as unfortunate crew and equipment were carried away on escaping atmosphere.

Genukh turned the ship about, braking sharply across the titan's bow and coming to a new heading, facing the titan's stern. The plasma tail from the fusion drive was already irradiating the titan's outer hull.

"Full power," Zluur ordered.

"Full power...engaged." Genukh accelerated away even while the titan was struggling to turn and follow.

In ten minutes the titan was barely visible. In twenty, the ship was a speck, to be joined by additional specks. "Zluur, I'm picking up signals from the ring. Home Fleet ships are being ordered to intercept us. Shall I warn them off?"

Zluur bristled. He was already a traitor to the allied races...escape from the attacking titan or the defending ships remained uncertain. There was one more betrayal to propose. "Cut the drive. Flip us one hundred eighty degrees. Charge the main gun one more time. Target the—"

"Too late." Genukh's tone became somber, disappointed as a barrage of beams flew past. Three of them struck amidships, blasting chunks out of its thick armor. One more scored a solid hit on the drive section. The Fusion plumes sputtered and died as alarms sounds throughout the bridge. The force of the hits threw Zluur against the far wall, sharp pains in his back and head threatening to swallow him. He lay there for a moment, awash in sound, white light turning red, threat indicators demanding that he do something.

He staggered to his feet, leaning on any object to support himself as he climbed back into the command chair. "That couldn't have been the titan...we wouldn't be here if it was."

"That was Home Fleet Master Sselanniss. She has apparently sided with the Movi and the Cycomms. They are ordering your arrest and the disabling or destruction of this ship." Pause. "Shall we return fire?"

"No. Wait...yes! Arm every long-range missile battery we have, plot as many near hits as you can, tune the warheads for wide proximity bursts. Then fold us away."

"Zluur, we cannot navigate while nuclear missiles are exploding close behind us."

"Can we restart the fusion drive?"

"Not immediately."

"Then escape requires a fold. Plot a random direction and distance. Somewhere the Skreesh aren't likely to follow." He paused. "Off the star maps. You can take your bearings and re-jump if need be."

Genukh's question was plain. "'Will you not be accompanying me?"

"I won't. I will be taking the command shuttle back to Sselanniss's ship. She wants me to answer for my crimes, and I might as well not disappoint her."

"Zluur...you'll be killed."

"I expect so. But you will escape. Find a world where you can deploy the cargo pods. Get those DNA synthesizers running. Those are my orders, Genukh."

"Very well. You have five minutes to get to the shuttle. Good-bye, Zluur."

"Goodbye, Genukh.'

Zluur saw the blast doors opening to his right. Genukh was facilitating his demise. He couldn't have asked for greater loyalty from anyone, and likely only a machine would show him such. He stumbled through corridors, and around turns, the way growing dark with fewer red lamps to illuminate his way. The final blast door closed with a thump as he seated himself in the small craft. He punched an actuator stud and acceleration pressed him into his seat as the small ship was blasted away. He waited until his weight normalized and then turned the sensors onto his great ship. With a flash and a glimmer, it vanished into fold-space.

His great work, gone somewhere in the universe. Sselanniss wouldn't know where because he didn't know, and one couldn't divulge secrets one didn't have.

The shuttle shuddered as alarms sounded. The Movi carrier

was closing in, and fighters were even now bracketing his tiny ship.

There was only one last thing to do. He set the anti-hijacking program in place. It would flood the compartment with as much nerve gas as needed to ensure his death. It was a stupid way to die, but he refused to trust his welfare to the Sleer legal system. The High Command would never believe he didn't know where Genukh was headed and Zluur would just as soon not endure their interrogation.

He closed his eyes, pressed the button, and the gas enveloped him. "Goodbye, Genukh."

"Goodbye, Zluur."

[1]

OF THE TEN TIMES TEN THOUSAND THINGS THE MILITARY HAD
taught Technical Specialist Simon Brooks, the most important
was sleep. Get enough of it and all would be well. Not that there
had been enough of it the past sixteen weeks. Not with eighteen-
hour days of exhausting routine and two more hours of gear prep
wherever the NCOs could sneak it in. Four hours of sleep a night
was little enough to make a man wish for death but too much to
actually grant it.

Brooks had, over his first months in the Unified Earth Fleet,
learned to catch sleep when and wherever he could. It was the
sacred truth of his existence. But with the sleep, came the
thoughts, the anxieties, which coalesced into dreams. Or, more
correctly, The Dream. The only dream he'd had for a year.

The camping trip. Uncle Ray, his dad, a bunch of friends. A
fusion stove that doubled as a campfire due to federal environ-
mental laws that meant something in national parks but were
haphazardly enforced. A belly full of real meat, bug juice, and
marshmallows. Talk of girls, football, and Ray's life in the navy.
All of them fighting sleep.

The flash in the darkened sky. He could hear the voices of

those around him: Uncle Ray, Martin Touro, a few others whose names he didn't remember.

Martin slowly lowered his arm from his face, scanning the horizon. Looking for a mushroom cloud. "What is it? Nuke?"

Ray kept his eyes on the glowing ball of fire, raising his open hand to gauge its speed and distance. "Can't be a nuke, we're still here."

"What then? Meteor?"

"No, a meteor would drop out of the stratosphere. That thing is coming down low, over the horizon. That's a re-entry pattern."

"Re-entry? It's a spaceship?"

"Not one of ours. Too big."

"Brooks?"

"But you told us about the platforms, right? The orbital factories. Maybe one of them—"

"Yeah, maybe. But the public channels would tell us about that weeks in advance just to make sure everyone knew to get out of the crash zone. This is something else—"

"Brooks!"

"Up! I'm up." The squawk of his comm, buried in his right ear, snapped him back to reality. Stiff joints, a cricked neck. Surrounded by too much stuff, crammed in among bodies and equipment.

It wasn't fair. The Raven pilots, the royalty of the UEF, got to fly their ships straight over from air bases all over the South Pacific and Australia as well as the carrier Icarus to South Pico Island, while the technical specialists and officers got to fly coach. Again. You'd think that the U-Fleet could arrange for all of the air wing's equipment to head over at the same time, but no. Specter and Nightmare squadrons had been over there for weeks. The Yellowjackets had joined them five days ago. The Battler strike and support units, too. First Section of the Hornets were all Raven pilots, a dozen highly skilled and slightly nutty individuals who had been over there for three days. Even "Skull" Skellington, the Hornet's intelligence officer, had hitched a ride to AMS-1 in a two-seat Raven two weeks ago. Meanwhile this KS-17 transport plane was the last of the bunch, the tail-end Charlie, meant to deliver Second Section, the mechanics, system engineers, and other assorted nerds who kept the flyers in the air. They'd be expected to make sure everything worked once they unloaded their gear and boarded *Ascension*, the spanking new U-Fleet Flagship, three days from now. They'd have one more day to get the cargo and crew settled and then: launch day. If it all worked.

God damn navy.

Lt. Commander "Uncle" Ray Fairchild's voice rang in his ear. "On the boost, Brooks. Come forward. Bring your kit."

Brooks blinked himself awake. His body jerked as the abrupt message from his comm brought him back to his surroundings. The rear of the KS-17 "Kitchen Sink" transport plane was cold and crowded, and after six hours in a too small seat wedged up next to a pallet of secured gear, Brooks could barely feel his hands and feet. They'd shoved him in with the cargo. Not even the luxury of being shoved up next to squad mate he liked, like Judy Reagan. No, they paired him with Bob Norton, the unit weapons nerd.

He tapped the comm. "Brooks, coming forward." He undid his seat harness, pulled himself upright, took a moment to orient himself. As the newest man in Hornet Squadron he got the honor of using the rearmost jump seat while the rest of the squadron lounged in standard crash couches along the sides of the fuselage. He tried to pick out faces from beneath helmets. Nothing about this bunch made sense. Even the word "veteran" was wrong. None of these people had seen combat, except in simulated training missions. In that respect, yes, they were veterans. Survivors of eight weeks of boot camp and another eight weeks of MOS training. They'd all survived those. They all had their

Specialist stripes to prove it. But only "Uncle" Ray Fairchild and his exec, "Saint" Joanne Arkady actually carried the distinction of being under fire. As a veteran of the U-War, the global war of unification fought after the arrival of the great ship, and the attempt to unify the world in the face of potential invasion, Fairchild had shot down over one hundred aircraft and pilots. The man knew combat. Arkady had seventeen kills to her name, a proper ace. She'd only been fighting for a month before the war was declared over but she'd taken the call sign "Saint" from somewhere.

He caught snippets of conversations as he picked his ways past his squadron mates.

"I know it's illegal to burn wood in national parks. I just can't figure out why. We burn every damn thing else."

"Fusion is a misnomer, nothing actually fuses. It's just a battery. The big plants in Montana and the Dakotas, those are proper fusion plants. All the clean and nearly free power in the world and none of it doing a damn thing to help us make the world a better place."

"It was a good idea. Share the wealth. Eradicate poverty. Keep the predators at bay. Build a better tomorrow. Except their tomorrow is our today, and it looks a lot like a crappy yesterday with better gadgets and gizmos. I don't know. Maybe feeding, housing and handing out spending money to everyone really is the best we can come up with."

"There's a scary thought."

"Yup."

"I'm telling you there's no way those new multi-format planes work. Even with new AI tech. It's a scam to suck taxpayer money out of government pockets. God damn navy."

"But the spaceship is real. Right?"

"Well, yeah…you can see it from the air."

Simon wondered about that as well. Ray had mentioned the

new military R&D project, something called Avalon, years ago. Only a year after the fireball crashed to Earth…on top of South Pico Island. The Brooks family didn't believe in coincidences. Like it wasn't a coincidence that Ray had enlisted as the call went out and the U-War got into full swing. Two years of international hell, and then peace. America, Russia and China all sharing the wealth with the rest of the world pitching in as best they could. The peace dividend. Combining their strengths to build a brand-new military. Or something.

All because of a fireball from space. Words like *alien* weren't inappropriate but phrases like *Alien Megastructure-1* scared him. It suggested the first in a series. He tried to keep the anxiety at bay by reminding himself that an alien invasion was above his pay grade. He preferred to call the thing *Ascension* like so many others.

The flight deck was crowded. Three seats for pilot, co-pilot, and engineer. There wasn't enough call for a comm guy on the bridge during flight to warrant a full couch, just a crappy little jump seat. Then Brooks remembered. He was the comm guy.

Fairchild wasn't done with him. "Specialist Brooks, how nice of you to finally join us." Brooks knew sarcasm when he heard it. Simon was falling behind the class. Again. "If you strap in and tell me why the comm panel blew up when I tried to contact South Pico Island flight control, I might let you keep all those stripes on your sleeve."

Brooks took the hint. He'd get a proper chewing out after they landed and got settled at the base. For the moment, he had work to do. He turned down the jump seat, strapped in, and began looking over the console, searching for a port to plug the analyzer into while Fairchild ran through his position check. Chief Petty Officer Richard "Grandpa" Frost busied himself at the engineer's station across the narrow aisle.

Arkady turned her head, Simon could feel himself under the

squadron XO's peripheral gaze. "You seemed comfy back there, Brooks. What were you dreaming about?"

"Honestly, Lieutenant. Nothing."

"You don't dream? Sounds fake."

Fairchild broke in. "Just tell her, Brooks."

"I was dreaming about the AMS-1. Arrival night, ten years ago. It scared the crap out of me."

"How do you know to be scared of it?"

"Because he was there," Fairchild said. "So was I. A U-Scout camping trip if I remember correctly."

"That sounds like a helluva coincidence."

"Not really. Simon here was one of the nerd kids with stellar GPAs who were offered U-Fleet scholarships if they signed up after high school. I've been watching him ever since."

Frost harrumphed. "That doesn't sound creepy at all. Not even a little."

"I choose my recruits carefully is all."

Arkady stared. "You hand-picked this kid? This. Kid?"

"This kid won amateur signal conversion contests three years in a row."

"Excuse me, Uncle. It was five years in a row."

"My mistake, Specialist. Now tell me why the comm net is down and kindly repair that set."

Brooks plugged into the panel and flicked a switch. The analyzer had a bit of the U-Fleet's wacky new AI algo in it as well. In fact, every piece of equipment he could think of did. Thank you, AMS-1. No—thank you, *Ascension*. As a result, he didn't have to hunt through dozens of circuits. "Blown fuse in the main panel. I'll fix it." Ten minutes later, he flicked another switch and the lamps glowed a frosty green. "You're on the air, Uncle."

"Good job. South Pico tower, this is Hornet 126 heavy, requesting instructions for final approach and landing."

The chatter came through perfectly. Brooks put it on a speaker so they could all hear. "Roger Hornet 126. I'm instructed to ask you what your cargo is."

He saw Fairchild and Arkady share a look. "Hornet Squadron out of Air Wing 27, UNS Icarus. I'm carrying sixteen AMS-1 crew and support staff so new they still have the plastic wrap on them. Associated equipment and supplies for the squadron as well."

"Roger that, Hornet 126. You are clear for landing on air strip four. Come to course 216 and altitude of ten thousand feet to begin your descent."

"Roger, tower."

Static on the general channel and then lights began to flash across Brooks' board. He switched from one band to the next, scanning for key words and phrases. He blanched at what he heard. "Sirs? Trouble."

Fairchild snapped to. "What?"

"Uuuuuuuuhhhhhhh…"

Uncle raised his voice. "Spill it."

"Sirs, the whole Micronesian Defense Sector just went on alert. There's an announcement on the general channel. A bright flash of light and a flurry of gravity waves was detected near Mars."

Brooks noticed the look that Fairchild and Arkady shared. "Well, what does that remind you of?" she said.

"Reminds me of when the AMS-1 arrived. Light, gravity waves. One boy thought it was a nuke."

"With respect Ray, we all thought it was a nuke."

"I stand corrected. Brooks, are we patched into the command channel server?"

Brooks double checked his connections. "Yes, sir, full permissions are implemented. You have access to the entire island comm network."

"Good job. Get your ass back in your seat and tell the others we're heading in for an emergency landing."

"Yes, sir."

Brooks unbuckled, ducked down through the hatch, and moved back to his seat. He did the math as he walked. These days the red planet and Earth were about one hundred and forty-six million miles apart which meant that the spatial phenomenon had taken about thirteen minutes to reach them. If something had popped into the solar system, it had happened at least thirteen minutes ago. There was no telling how much time had elapsed between the event and the report of it reaching his ears.

He didn't know how fast they might travel but even the fastest ships the UEF had would take weeks to cover that distance. An enormous improvement over the two years Viking had taken to get to the red planet back in 1978, but still. A vessel that could travel one-tenth light speed could fly from Mars to Earth in less than two hours.

The clock was ticking.

He could feel the effects of Fairchild's approach as the aircraft banked and dove to a new course. The plane banked left then right then left again before finally straightening out. But the downward tilt of the nose sent them all a message: they were on their way down. Fast.

"Guys, I'm gonna hurl!"

"Dammit, Carson use the...Damnit!"

"Dude!"

"Gahhh!"

"No!"

"Gross!"

"Carson, here. See if you can pour it into this bag. No, not on me!"

"Serves you right, Reagan. You know Carson can't shoot for shit!"

"Does that count as a kill?"

"Counts as a splash."

"Gah! Gimme that. Carson, you gross son of a—"

The plane titled to the right and now the contours of South Pico Island were clearly visible through the tiny windows in the plane's side. "Dances With Gears" Reagan twisted in her harness, craning her neck to see the island. "Where is it?"

"It's down there. Pride of the fleet."

"Oh yeah."

"Can you see it?"

"All I see is Carson's barf."

Finally, a shriek rang out from the front of the cargo bay. "There it is. I see it!"

Brooks and Norton stepped over cargo and each other to get a look. Difficult through the porthole, made worse by their attempts to shove each other out of the way. Brooks gasped as South Pico Island came into view.

Alien Megastructure-1, the interstellar fortress referred to by the general public as the spaceship *Ascension*, but noted by the military simply as AMS-1—looked like a segmented oblong, a bulbous middle joining an angular, wedge-like bow and flaring stern. Its size became apparent as they cleared a layer of clouds. The ship, which measured nearly a mile long, ran nearly a fifth of the island's length and lay at an angle to its widest point, open water caressing its tail section. The huge machine had apparently tumbled out of the sky, struck the island squarely, then burrowed into the bedrock before sliding to a halt near the shore. The ship was easier to see than the buildings around it. In every way, it commanded the narrow blot of land. The city that had sprung up in the behemoth's shadow over the past decade had been a care-fully planned project, a product of human ambition and construc-tion. Brooks couldn't imagine how the crazy spaceship had even been salvaged.

Brooks stumbled back to his jump seat, pulling his slate out. The red icon was blipping, and it would keep flashing until he dealt with it. He swiped and found himself looking at a registration screen for the newest military-tech: the Situational Occupation Recovery Table, Expanded, Revised: SORTER. The idea could only have come from an Overcop wonk. Have every soldier, sailor, and officer enter their credentials and MOS into a giant database that tracked everyone across all operational theaters and recommended assignments when a unit needed help.

He entered his information, leaving nothing out. He needed the distraction and figured it was more useful a thing to do than merely sit and stew in his anxiety. Just another enlisted communications nerd. Good luck with that, guys.

On to other matters. A few minutes of searching found what he wanted: the archived photos of the salvage operation. The truly interesting images had never been posted online, but the declassified images were enough for him. The oldest ones showed the crater the ship formed on impact, its buckled, ragged hull open to the elements. He swiped through the collection, fast-forwarding a decade of work in only a few minutes. The army units flown in for security; the first barracks erected, then expanded to house battalions of laborers and engineers; the myriad scaffolds put up to shield the craft from the elements; the remodeling of the hull; finally, the finished product which bore only a limited resemblance to the crashed hulk.

Nothing interesting, though. No interior photos. No ideas what the inside of the craft really looked like. The general rule was that the ship had indeed been adapted to human use, with new equipment installed to supplement the original systems, or what had survived the landing. The hull had to have been heavily armored to even survive that exposure. Surely the engineers had added new armor and defenses.

Who built the damn thing and why? And why land here? Not

as an invasion. If there had been a crew on board they'd either died on impact or fried during its approach. But something had controlled its descent. There was no way any human machinery could have lifted it up and deposited it in a preferred resting spot.

Some intelligence had directed it here and guided it on the way down. For all they knew it lurked unseen and unknown inside the machinery, waiting to re-emerge and—

Norton punched him on the shoulder. "Brooks!"

"Gah!"

"You alive? Come on, final approach. Let's get ready to bail."

A hiss of static dropped from the overhead speakers. Uncle was planning to get this flying house on the ground, he figured. "Attention Hornet Squadron," he said, "You've all gotten your first look at South Pico Island, your new home for the next four days. Once we put down, we'll be loading all our gear and cargo onto trucks at the airfield and moving everything directly to the barracks. All section leaders need to be on the boost today. Nothing gets lost, no one gets left behind. We move as a unit. Two minutes for a final gear check. We're down in ten. Go!"

The entire plane transformed into a brief but intense knot of activity as a klaxon sounded and the deployment light swapped from an angry red to an eager yellow.

Brooks shook the thoughts of alien intelligences out of his head as his training took over. To some degree he still felt like an outsider in this outfit. Hornet Squadron was a mixed unit: mostly airmen who would one day fly advanced fighters, with a support group attached. Brooks had two stripes on his arm and certs to run all manner of communications gear, and a week of simulator training to drive a Challenger, the simplest of the UEF battler models. And that was where he stopped.

Habit took over. Check the equipment cases first. His pack, his gear, a small bag of personal effects he'd thrown together at the last moment. A quick check of his person, pockets and dog tags: spectacles, testicles, wallet, comb. His father had told him that. He wondered what his old man would think of him now. Easy enough to guess: he'd nod, smile, tell Simon he was proud. No. That was what Simon wanted him to say. Benjamin Brooks would have nodded and smiled all right, then walked away wordlessly. Despite his long friendship with Ray Fairchild, he had no patience for the military and nothing good to say about the U-War. Managing three thousand square miles of national parkland was more his speed.

Not that it mattered. The U-War had not been kind to the American northeast. Albany Crater and Lake Cayuga's red nighttime sheen were proof enough of that.

Brooks' ears popped as the cargo plane dove for the runway. He nudged Norton in the ribs. "Uncle is taking it a little steep, don't you think?"

Norton frowned as she craned his neck to look out the window. "Something's up. He wants us on the ground ASAP." His head snapped up and his eyes popped wide as he leaned over Brooks to look out the tiny window. "Dude, planes. Must be an air show going on. The tower probably—"

All at once, a bright flash of light poured through the windows. Brooks and Norton slammed their eyes shut and turned away. When Brooks opened his, all he could see were spots. A thunderous roar accompanied the spots and his colon loosened as he wondered what was going on and feared he knew.

At the same time, the plane dropped like a stone. As the seat left his ass hanging in the air just a bit, he hung on to his harness and leaned against Norton. "Nuke?" he asked.

"No. If it was a nuke, we'd be dead now. But something just happened. Christ, I can't see a thing."

All at once a female voice squawked over the speaker as Arkady gave orders. "Crash positions, people! We're heading in."

The silence of the inside of the cabin was deafening. The

engines had shut down. Brooks began to shake uncontrollably as he realized they were going to die. There was nothing stupider than dying in a plane crash, with your nose touching your knees and surrounded by cargo crates. No honor, no glory, no—

"Down in ten seconds!"

Frost joined the fray, his voice trailing over an open flight deck microphone. "Hang on to your beads, kids!"

Brooks tried to count down in his head but couldn't remember how long it was since the XO had said "ten seconds." Had it been ten? Five? Or—

The squeal of tortured metal met his ears as the plane's gear hit the landing strip, and then the floor dropped as the tires burst, the gear gave way, and the aircraft's belly skidded along the tarmac. He could feel every inch of the landing strip as the plane skidded and bounced down the length of the runway.

Finally, they stopped.

For a brief second no one did or said anything. Then the world erupted into motion as explosive bolts gave way and the rear cargo door popped away from its hinges. A whine sounded as the plane's rear hatch began to split in two as the squadron unbuckled their harnesses and fought to evacuate the aircraft.

Arkady burst out of the flight deck and gave orders while pulling on her own pack. "Squadron! Disembark to the rear, by the numbers! Into the terminal, on the double! Go!"

Norton shared another look with Brooks. "We're not dead! Come on!" He ran out the partially open exit with a huff. Brooks followed.

[2]

BROOKS STRUGGLED UNDER HIS PACK AND RAN, CHASING NORTON as the sky exploded and rained shrapnel on the island.

South Pico Island's air base was a military transit hub meant to serve as the lifeline between the nearest U-Fleet base at New Darwin, but maintained the capacity to handle civilian traffic as well. That was before. Now, the air terminal, a series of wide, blocky structures, stood in a shambles with blown out windows and shattered concrete littering the space around it. An air control tower still stood further down the tarmac but an explosion had taken a bite out of the radar dome at its peak. None of its windows remained intact.

Brooks led them, hanging on to his gear with both hands and not even daring to look behind him. One thing he'd been good at in training was sprinting. Good at short dashes, not so great at marathons. Fear and adrenaline kept him moving, pushed to his limits by the determination to not fall behind anyone. When he finally reached the terminal, he swung himself around a low barrier, and hyperventilated. The rest of the Hornets joined him in turn, but to Brooks it seemed that no one was gasping quite the way he was.

The soldiers took refuge beneath an overhang that an hour before had been an arrivals zone. Brooks could hear the screaming of terrified civilians inside the structure as another round of bombs fell across the air base, popping in orange and white bursts as the Hornets ducked down behind the wall, waiting for orders. Finally, Norton punched him in the shoulder, and Brooks inhaled. The noise stopped: the only one screaming was him.

Embarrassed, he looked back at the aircraft they'd abandoned. Black smoke poured from the outermost engine on the starboard wing, but besides that, the craft seemed intact. They might get their equipment out with a winch and a forklift or two but that was for later, preferably after the enemy stopped shooting at them.

Within a minute the others achieved the relative shelter of the terminal. Fairchild took a few breaths to oxygenate his blood and started giving orders. "Gentry! Allen! Get your gear out and scan the feeds. Gentry, find me whoever is in charge. Allen, talk to somebody in the control tower and find out if anyone else is expected to land."

Brooks nodded to the city in the distance. Streamers of black smoke rose haphazardly from the skyline. "What the hell is going on, Uncle?"

"That's a damn fine question, Specialist. But as a basic assumption I'd say were being attacked."

"By who?"

Fairchild poked his head above the shield barrier and stared at the alien behemoth. Five miles away and it still dominated the landscape. "Layne's Brigade maybe. If I wanted to project power, I'd destroy a symbol. That warship is the biggest symbol the U-Fleet has."

Brooks turned his eyes toward the AMS-1, the pride of the Unified Earth Government, the flagship of the newly formed U-Fleet. It looked almost benevolent lying in its gantry on the ground. From the air, Brooks could have looked at it abstractly, like the photos he'd viewed

online. Up close, it was a metal wall of spaceship, three quarters of a mile long.

Brooks opened his mouth to ask another question but Arkady got there first. She crouched, popped her head up for a second, then dropped back down. "How the hell would Laynies hit something that big?" she asked. "There's six thousand crew in that ship and nine thousand civilians on island who spent the past decade repairing it. They can't all be brigade lovers." Pause. "Hornet Squadron present and accounted for, but the way."

"Good. Crazier things have happened, Lieutenant."

"Like what?"

"Like a mile-long spaceship just falls out of the sky one summer evening in 2066 and out of a trillion or so square miles of ocean, happens to land on this tiny island."

Gentry ran up with a satellite comm, eyes twitching excitedly. "Got something, Uncle."

"Well?"

"The OMP Commandant, sir. Colonel Hendricks."

Fairchild grabbed the phone. "Colonel Hendricks. Lieutenant Commander Fairchild, Icarus Air wing CVN-27, Hornet Squadron. We just landed, and were supposed to be stationed at… sir, my people are here to fly Ravens. No…no, the pilots and their planes were transported days ago. Yes, on the AMS-1. But my technical people are…Yes sir. Yes, sir!" He handed the handset back to Gentry, a disgusted look crossing his face. "Well that's that. Bloody Overcops."

The Saint swore under her breath. "New orders?" she asked.

"Standing orders. The AMS-1 is prepping for an emergency launch in five minutes. Anyone not already aboard stays behind and herds civilians to the designated shelters. That's our job."

"Yes sir. Squadron, fall in!" In seconds they crowded around her. "Reagan, Darcy, Carson, Rodgers, sweep the terminal for civilians, get them down to the shelters. Don't take any guff, they need to go now. Norton, head to the control tower, tell those people to clear out. Go!"

Brooks winced as the comm filled his ear with static. A hurried voice followed. A nearly panicked Allen, Brooks thought. Allen wasn't prone to panic attacks.

"Uncle! Tower controller says that they have too many targets to track. The sky is filled with aircraft and they're heading this way. Seventy klicks out and closing fast."

"Any news about ground forces?"

More static. "Approaching from the beach, sir. Ten klicks and closing."

"Understood. Get back down here."

"Yes sir."

"Air attack and a coordinated ground assault?" Arkady asked. "Doesn't sound like any terrorists I've heard of."

"I concur. This is something new." He tapped his comm to switch channels, the broadband this time: "Squad leaders, report in."

"Rodgers, reporting. The basement shelters are closing up now. We're doing a quick sweep to hustle any stragglers along."

"Norton, reporting. Power failed in the control tower two minutes ago. Staff is taking shelter now."

"Copy that. Finish your sweeps and meet us in the main terminal."

They filed back to their impromptu shelter one by one, all looking harried and scared. Brooks had taken the time to dig into his pack and don his so-called "rain gear." Tac-3 ballistic armor: a lightweight ballistic vest, helmet, and an M-099 autopistol with one clip of armor piercing rounds. It wasn't much…not compared to the gear they'd have had with proper armory access…but better than nothing. Comms, of course, as well. Always comms. That done, he pulled out a set of binoculars and popped his head above the barrier, scanning in the directions that he remembered hearing Allen report.

After a minute, they heard explosions sounded in the distance and Brooks could just make out a series of floating objects, like beach balls bobbing on the waves. "We got armor approaching. I think."

"You think? Is it armor or not?"

He adjusted the frame rate and could now see details. They rolled along the surf in groups and he couldn't figure out how the damn things moved or even how their crews might enter or exit. "Sir…spherical in shape with multiple turrets. Take a look."

A number of them did, Fairchild and Arkady included, peering around a concrete column beneath the terminal's overhang.

It wasn't a vehicle they recognized. It had a spherical body and rolled along the ground with no obvious means of propulsion. Three hemispherical gun turrets sat atop it, floating on a magnetic field. Twin cannons emerged from opposite sides of the topmost turret and an armored sensor sat between them, a weird cyclopian arrangement that swung in all directions as it hunted for prey. Worse, the contraptions towered over them, standing at least thirty feet tall.

In a moment, it was joined by another, then a third. Brooks swung his eyes over the horizon. They came up from the south, rolling smoothly over hills and sweeping the area. Beach landing. It had to be.

The rollers began firing at will, blue beams of energy flying from their guns, blasting whatever targets of opportunity they could find. Buildings, vehicles, they didn't seem to care. Brooks couldn't stop watching them, trying to imagine how they moved, what their power source was, how their weapons worked. He ducked down as pieces of the control tower shattered and rained down around them. He could hear Norton grumbling as the roller's turret tracked toward the tarmac. "No! Not the plane, not the plane, not the—"

A jaw-grinding screech of energy and a bright blue beam flew from the turret guns and smashed the aircraft. The explosion blossomed skyward, ensuring their gear was now gone. "Dammit."

Warning sirens blared, drawing the squadron's attention back to the alien battleship. The great ship shuddered and shook, trembling in its cradle. Slowly and inexorably it lifted, rising on alien propulsion systems. It rose silently, smooth as a still pond.

Reagan gawked. "Holy shit, it works," she breathed.

"There she goes."

"Son of a bitch."

Brooks saw it first. A smoke trail from the rear section. Then a telltale wobble, like a spinning top that had begun to slow down and tip over. "Uh-oh."

"What?"

"Trouble in the stern."

"Where? I don't see—"

"Wait for it…"

Rodgers sniffed. "Greatest restoration project the human race ever took up and you have to spit on it."

Brooks pointed at the rising shape. "I mean it. Something's wrong."

About three hundred feet up, the AMS-1 shifted in the air, listing to port while the bow rose more quickly than the stern. The upward motion stopped completely as the ship wobbled, then tipped. Another smoke trail appeared near the bow. Now they could hear pops, and the ship lost its fight with gravity. It slid to starboard, bursts of shrapnel peppered the sky as rents erupted from its hull. The great ship came crashing down, slamming into its gantries, crushing them heavily beneath its stupendous weight with a monstrous *whump*.

"Well, fuck!" Reagan snarled.

The rolling gun pods stopped and rotated their turrets toward the ship, cannons twitching like antennae scenting the air. Then they crowded into a wedge formation and drove toward it.

Arkady's voice came over comms. "Do we pursue?"

Fairchild frowned. "Not on foot we don't. The car park is covered in debris, so that rules that out."

Brooks turned his binocs to the east and spotted a beer party on the horizon. Like a gaggle of teens with hunched shoulders and heads askew. "What about in battlers?"

Arkady sniffed. "Battlers'd be great. You got one?"

"We got at least a dozen, sir. Challengers and Archers. Right there." Brooks lowered the binoculars and pointed. Half a mile away a crowd of thirty-foot tall armored suits stood unoccupied. Some were clearly unusable, with torsos or limbs open to the elements, but others looked serviceable. "Looks like a repair and resupply depot."

Fairchild grinned. "Show of hands, who can drive a battler?" Nine hands went up. "Eighteen crew, nine pilots, nine passengers. Okay, new plan. Battler drivers will follow me, suit up, and pursue. We can still make our ride. Gentry, talk to Col. Hendricks and tell him the civilians are under shelter. The Hornets are going to link up with the AMS-1."

"Yes, sir."

Fairchild edged around the corner while the squadron packed their gear and Gentry navigated the comm net. "Uncle? Hendricks' office acknowledges. They're taking time to fuel the conventional lift rockets. Liftoff is in fifty-six minutes."

Fairchild bobbed his head. "Troops who cannot drive, team up with someone who can. Two crew max per unit. Half mile sprint, boys and girls. Ready? Go!"

The word held the force of a starter's gun. Brooks set his pack and ran for it, sprinting across the field on will power and endurance training. He sucked air into his lungs hungrily and blew it out through his lips, making noises like a freight train within a minute. He didn't allow himself to feel anything but the blood running through his veins, the pounding of his heart in his chest. The armored suits loomed above him, and he made a line for a nearby Challenger, a relatively humanoid model that looked worn but wore a ten-foot long gash in its right leg.

He shouted happily as his hand clung to the ladder build into the battler's rear right leg; handholds and footholds cast directly into the armor. He pulled himself up, his energy flagging after his run, the straps from his pack digging into his shoulders, heat and sweat making him vaguely nauseous. At the top of the leg he swung off to find more hand holds leading up to the mechanism's chest. At the top of the torso he found an open hatch, where he dropped down, unslung his pack, stowed it behind the pilot's chair, and settled in.

It took a moment for his experience in the simulator at New Darwin to kick in. It had been a while since he'd driven one of these monsters. The battlers were the ground forces equivalent of the Raven Variable Response Fighters, transformable planes that had battler-like ground capability but were meant for air to air combat. The battlers couldn't transform, but could supposedly out-shoot any of the VRFs in Battler mode.

Supposedly. That was the word that never left you alone. The twenty- and thirty-ton walking behemoths were only made possible by a scientific breakthrough, a revolutionary type of machine intelligence that had been discovered in the years after the AMS-1's arrival. No one ever spoke about it, probably because no one really understood it. The only thing the line troops understood was that the two events probably hadn't been coincidence. It wouldn't be the first time that scientists and engineers had harnessed a force they hadn't truly understood, but still...

Power: on. He buckled himself into the seat as lights came on and display boards glowed with electronic life. Communications. Locomotive systems. Point Defense. And…weapons. He toggled an ammo counter, saw that there were no rounds loaded for the chest-mounted autocannon clusters and only a few short-range missiles left in the shoulder launchers. That would help.

"Look out below!"

He snapped his head up at the new voice and flinched as another heavy pack dropped down into the compartment, half onto him. He shoved the item out of the way and a new person slithered into the seat next to him. Even if the flaming red hair didn't give away Judy Reagan's identity, her soprano voice did. "Specialist Simon!"

"Dance? What the hell are you doing here?"

"Uncle said people who can't pilot these crazy things team up with the ones who can. Just following orders. This bot was closest is all."

"Blah. Fine, you can handle shooting things."

"Roger that," she giggled, and settled in.

He set the comm on his head, adjusted the frequency, and heard Fairchild giving orders. "Everyone put up a status check. If you can't move and fight with loaded guns, call out, now."

Brooks adjusted his controls for a Level 2 status check. The onboard computer would check the status of every combat system and use a coded radio burst to link up to the battle computer aboard Uncle's own battler. When in status check mode, the captain would be able to monitor the power levels, life signs, and ammo loads of each member of the platoon. "Jesus," Fairchild growled. "I think every one of these tin cans was in for major repairs. Brooks, that's the last time I listen to you about anything."

Brooks toggled his comm. "I'm a comm specialist, Uncle, not a mechanic."

"And now we all know why. Very well, squadron, report in."

Brooks heard the channel click then Uncle's voice loud in his ears. "Specialist Brooks, I'm making you the commo engineer on this op. Find the closest battle net that incorporates telemetry from airborne units. Local squadron feeds, bursts from the tower, updates from the satellite ring, I don't care, as long as they cover the whole island and they're recent. Defend yourself but do not engage unless attacked. And keep up with the rest of the unit. Got it?"

Brooks frowned but answered. "Acknowledged." He swapped status displays. No long-range engagements for him, then. Fine; it would be one fewer thing to keep track of, and he'd have his hands full maintaining the electronic intelligence connection for the platoon, anyway.

"It was a solid idea," Reagan murmured. He turned to look as she busied herself. Finally their eyes met. "There's no way we could have walked to the ship, not with rolling armor driving all over the island. So. Battlers." She shrugged and got back to work, the sounds of grinding metal sweeping through the compartment as she tried to use the autocannon. "On the other hand, Uncle has a point, too. These beasts were in the depot for a reason. Gah, no rounds for anything except the small arms. Machine guns, the grenade launchers. Seven missiles. That's something."

Brooks said nothing as he set up the requested connections and the squadron finished sounding off. He used Fairchild's military ID to designate the formation as "Hornet 01/09" and then used his own to designate himself as the primary contact for the feeds he'd locked on. He had access to the gun cameras from a dozen different VRF fighters flying combat air patrols above South Pico Island as well as the exterior cameras mounted on both the control tower and the Ascension herself. The biggest problem for the Hornet would be…

His display lit up with new targets. "Uncle, there's a new formation of rollers approaching from the western beach and there's a wave of hostile aircraft incoming from the north. Locking you into my feed…now."

"Good job, Brooks. Keep up. Hornet Squadron, move out, double column formation, on me. Go!"

There was an artistry to handling a Battler. It wasn't so much the trick of co-ordinating the legs with the arms and keeping the torso upright, although all were important. The cockpit incorporated a dozen gyroscopes that could sense the pilot's position in his couch. Eventually you learned to twist your body, angle your seat, and feel out the position of the thirty-foot tall behemoth as it moved through its surroundings. A really top-rated Battler pilot could handle their suit like a second skin, moving and maneuvering as easily as they might their own body.

Brooks wasn't in that category. He'd mastered forward, backwards, and turning. He knew how to fire the weapons and could handle the electronic systems. But he was no pro. He relied on the automated systems to keep his Challenger upright and moving forward, syncing the pedals to the hand controls and tried not to give in to the temptation to watch every system every second. If you lost yourself in the details, someone else who was more focused would smash you from behind. He'd gone through that lesson many times in the simulators during training. But in a real sense his jam was figuring out how to talk to friends and strangers with the help of complicated equipment. Not combat.

He had to trust Uncle. Trust his mates. It's all there was.

"Sync up with your element buddies, people. Ground crews are fueling the AMS-1's conventional lift rockets now, and they are taking fire. We have forty-six minutes to catch our ride."

The paired columns broke into a trot, then into a run. Brooks did his best to manage his Challenger but he couldn't seem to keep from jostling his element buddy, who turned out to be Rodgers.

"C'mon, Brooks, turn the freaking autogyros on. Driving in

manual is no job for a basic."

Reagan grunted in disgust, reached over him, and made the adjustment. It worked. The cabin bounced like the back of a pickup truck struggling down forty miles of rough road, but now the towering machine stayed on course. "De nada," she said.

"Thanks."

The main road out of the airport quickly gave way to the bottom of a valley, hills rising on either side. When the squadron emerged, they could see the expanse of South Pico Island laid out before them. The bulk of the AMS-1 lay like a ridge across a meadow while the island's skyline broke up the monotony. Even a decade after its birth, the cityscape that had grown around the great ship's landing site had a raw, unfinished look to it. Ten story housing complexes erupted in discrete blocks between the big box warehouses and rows of factories. Everything surrounding the ship's immediate proximity was open, devoted to construction zones and storage depots. The area had been completely cleared for her impending launch. From what Brooks could see on his display, all that meant in reality was more room to fight.

Even grounded, the AMS-1 was fully active. Even now Brooks could watch as automated missile launchers popped up all along her hull, swiveling as they found targets then and launching their payloads skywards. The rockets disappeared into the clouds and every now and then he could see a bright brief flash as one of them connected. The sky was filled with aerial combat as well: Ravens swooped and dove overhead, chasing targets he couldn't even see.

The rollers, still in their wedge formations, closed in on the giant ship from all over the island and the air war was becoming a ground assault. VRF fighters were in battler mode themselves, ducking behind buildings to snipe at rollers. Some Ravens burst into the open, reverted to Walker mode and blasted into the air, hoping to come down behind their enemies and shoot from behind. Sometimes it worked,. Brooks watched one fighter and his wingman try to pull off the maneuver and come down on top of a tall building. A squadron of six rollers surrounded the building and launched a flurry of beams, melting the structure from the top down. When the planes finally switched back to Battler and tried to crawl out of the rubble, the rollers blasted them into pieces.

Brooks concentrated on sticking with his unit. Who were these guys and where did they come from?

Explosions in the column's midst cut off his train of thought as the squadron scattered. Brooks followed Rodgers behind a dome-like structure that housed building materials. Or so he assumed.

Rodgers triggered his com. "You go left, I'll go right."

"Got it. I mean Roger, Rodgers. Or—"

"Just shoot anything that rolls, Brooks."

"Dance, you hear that?"

"I did. We have seven shots. I won't miss."

Brooks followed instructions, maneuvering so that his battler poked its head above the building. Dance picked out a roller, pickled the target, pulled the trigger, and stared in horror as nothing happened.

He saw the problem immediately, this time slapping a stud on her panel. "Open the launcher doors."

"Fuck!" She tried again. "Missile away!" The missile arced upwards and saw its target, streaking into it and exploding in a flash of red and orange flame. The roller spun on its axis, as all three turrets trained themselves on their Challenger.

Dance triggered the launchers again and again, finally remembering to breathe as the enemy exploded. But where the target dropped, four more converged on their position, grouping into a semicircle, blasting their Battler without getting in each other's line of fire. Dance triggered her last three missiles, emptying the magazines as Simon tried to dodge. Finally, he tried to run, only to trip and fall as the Challenger's gyros failed.

A variable fighter dropped from the sky landing heavily in front of him and brought up its GU-22 gun pod, a self-contained, 45mm, rotary barreled horror. Armor piercing rounds tore into the rollers mercilessly, a single long burst that showered the rollers with destruction. The roller stopped as pieces flew off its hull. Another burst and the alien machine finally lay still.

Brooks and Regan looked up at their savior. The fighter had been modified slightly. Instead of a typical paint job its head was bright pink. He sat there stupidly wondering how that had gotten past the quartermasters office when a new display caught his attention. He flicked channels to hear a contralto urgently yelling at him to leave. "Join your unit, recruit. Now!"

The order rattled him, but brought him back to situational awareness. Rodgers had already moved well ahead of him. Brooks rolled the big machine onto its knees, then got its feet beneath him and stood. He goosed his battler into gear and strained to keep up.

"Come on, Brooks, pull the plug out!" Reagan chided.

Finally, the gray and blue hull of the AMS-1 loomed before them like a wall rising from the earth.

"All aboard, ladies," Arkady's voice ordered. "Any open hatch. Go!"

Brooks went. He pushed the battler to its limit, pumping the legs and straining to keep his balance even with the autogyros working for him. He found an open hatch, saw that the warning light was on and leapt forward. He landed badly, rolled to take the brunt of the damage, and came to a stop, half kneeling. The hatch closed, Brooks lost his balance and his battler fell on its side.

The huge ship rumbled and shook beneath him. Brooks understood they were on their way into orbit.

Hopefully it would work this time.

[3]

TALL FLEET LORD NAZERIAN, OF THE 269TH SLEER
Expeditionary Fleet, stood on the bridge of his flagship, hands
clasped behind his back, counting down seconds.

Any time now. They'd transition back into normal space,
verify their position, and then work from there.

One thought rang in his head: Zluur may have been the
greatest scientific mind the Sleer had produced, but if the scientist
were standing here next to him now, Nazerian would have happily
driven his bare claws into his eyes far enough to rend his brain.
That majestic brain which had given the Two Thousand Worlds so
much…and finally, taken much in return.

Ten years, they'd been looking for him. One fold after
another, and the process was wearing his crew down. The crew
was edgy, anxious. Bored, mostly. He and Edzedon, his chief
science officer, had broken their brains to find ways of keeping
them occupied. There was only so much attention to ship maintenance and combat practice one could work with. Ironically, if they
succeeded in their mission, combat would be the least of it.
They'd locate *Genukh*, recover the ship and any surviving crew,
and return home as heroes.

Three hundred plus folds operations later, his eyes felt ready to fall out of his head.

"De-folding in ten seconds, Lord Nazerian."

"Acknowledged." Maybe this time…

Bright light and flashes of the energy spectrum and they were out. He didn't recognize the constellations, but the navigator would already be working on getting a fix on their location. This arm of the galaxy was long, if sparsely populated, and the Sleer navigators had extensive star maps to work with.

"Lord Nazerian, I am pleased to announce that we have reached the end of the fold chain."

Nazerian stood a little straighter. "That is good news. Where exactly are we?"

Edzedon read off a string of co-ordinates. "A single yellow dwarf with nine planets. The third planet has an oxygen-nitrogen atmosphere. We've adjusted course to approach, one-half speed."

"Good work. Send two scout ships to orbit the planet. We'll want to identify likely landing sites as quickly as possible. We've spent ten years on this ridiculous chase. I want it over as quickly as we can arrange it. Understood?"

"Of course."

"Good. Arrange a series of long-range scans of the entire system. There's no reason not to bring back a proper survey to the Home Nest on our return."

"Agreed."

As the time passed the readings began to fill viewing surfaces scattered across the bridge. Oceans, continents. An old world with a young civilization, its residents still in their technical infancy. The blue-green sphere sat within a globe of electromagnetic distortion.

"Whatever else is going on, this system is inhabited. There's definitely a technological civilization here."

"Tell me about it."

"Massive electromagnetic activity from the third planet, for one. They seem to use it for all manner of signal transfer. There are sources on the fourth, fifth, and sixth planets as well but that activity is far more localized."

"Colonies? Have they just begun to populate their solar system?"

"Very likely. There is a band of artificial satellites in low orbit around the third planet. Some are huge. They could be warships or supply platforms."

"That's problematic. If these people are technically literate to the point where they've built a space industry…"

"Commander! We have a sighting!"

The sensor officer zoomed in onto a section of the global map. "We set an initial scan to detect magnetic anomalies on the presumption that they would identify any large metallic mass. It turned out that this planet is covered with such readings. Surface vessels, I'd guess. This one stood out so we refined the settings on our instruments. We found Zluur's battle fortress."

It became clear that the huge renegade vessel lay on the surface, nestled in a corner of an island in the northern hemisphere very near the equator.

Edzedon shook his head. "On a planet that's seventy percent water, Zluur's ship lands on a tiny island. Does anyone here think that strange?"

"Only if you think it's coincidental that the ship ended up in this star system as well. If it had crashed on a mountaintop or beneath the ocean, I'd think differently. I'd guess Zluur made very specific requirements when he set the computer's orders."

"Indeed."

"Commander! The scouts report high energy bursts from the surface."

Oh, no. "Show me. Direct all scans to their location."

The *Zalamb*-class scouts were the smallest in his fleet but they weren't small ships per se. Each held a crew of one hundred Sleer troops and all their equipment. They were built to skim over a planet in a low orbit and provide visual and signal intelligence for a much larger landing ships to utilize during a full-scale invasion. Alternately they could serve as orbital pickets or system patrol ships.

The bridge filled with additional viewing surfaces. It only took a few moments for Nazerian and Edzedon to realize any hope of a quick mission and speedy return home was done for. The scouts skimmed the planet in low orbit, transmitting radar maps of the world's geography and pinpointing hot spots. Several clear radar images of a massive vessel came through. Nazarian stared at one of them. "That's Zluur's ship, all right. What happened to it?"

Edzedon used a set of control gauntlets to maneuver the display to focus on particular details across the images. "The cargo drop section has been entirely rebuilt. The forward section has been remodeled. And the rear section is longer than the specs indicate. If it did crash, then the natives very likely managed to rebuild it."

"What about the crew?"

"I'm not sure Zluur had one on his last voyage. There. That's the energy burst. Zoom out."

The next scene from orbit showed a wide green energy bolt skewering each of the scouts and blasting them from within. The ships exploded as they watched.

"No crew. And yet two direct hits with that level of precision," Nazerian hissed.

"They have reactive weaponry, which means reactive furnaces," Edzedon concluded. "Maker knows what else that ship carried."

"Set combat alert throughout the fleet," Nazerian ordered. "We have a ship to recover and hostile aliens to contend with."

Standard operating procedures were now in effect. That *Genukh* had fired on the recovery fleet could only be attributed to two possibilities. One, Zluur's ship had fallen into alien hands, which made no sense. Zluur had reported a full crew for that portion of his travels. Even if Skreesh had attacked, some of the crew would have remained. Sleer soldiers, not to mention the ship's computer, would never have allowed aliens to infest the vessel, much less lay claim to it. Two, Zluur had ordered the ship's computer to resist any attempt on the Home Fleet's part to recover it.

The outcome was the same: they had to neutralize any defensive capability the converted gun destroyer maintained. Damage to the ship would be minimized if possible. Destroying the ship was out of the question. Nazerian did not intend to bring back pieces and parts and then claim victory.

In any case, establishing a beachhead was their next step.

"I don't know who these people are, but they have no concept of modern warfare," Edzedon said. He projected a new set of schematics on a viewing surface. "This is the full scan of the island where the ship came down. Notice these structures here, surrounding the ship."

"Construction site?"

"Not even that. This ring of towers is the landing zone. You can see the radar towers and these are probably communication sites. These are the gantries that are holding the ship in place. But these—" he pointed to a field of blocky structures—"are simple shelters. Probably to manage the work crews while the ship was repaired and serviced."

"Work crews? Barracks? Next to a landing area? If they ignite the fusion drive that whole island will be irradiated."

"Exactly. You see this area on the other side of the island? It's a city. It has to be. There are no hardened shelters, no dampening screens, not even shielded sections in the infrastructure. The entire city is given over to the air base's use. They have no idea what that ship can do."

"Let's use their ignorance. In fact, let's plan around it."

Nazerian used his control gauntlets to plot locations and movement orders. "A dozen amphibious drop platforms should make a promising beginning. Four here, near the ship, the remainder scattered across the other side of the island. They'll deploy their assault craft and meet at the ship. Assign one squadron of air superiority fighters to fly combat air patrol over each landing platform. I want nothing to come within striking range of that vessel. Once they've destroyed all targets in the landing zone, the troops will board the ship and secure the ship's computer. The boarding crew will fly it into orbit, we will synch its navigation system to our own, and that will be that."

He thought a bit more. "I think we'll start off with a laser bombardment from orbit. Clear the area of vermin before the drop ships arrive. Helm! Establish a synchronous orbit over that island. Stay out of the gun destroyer's established firing solution. Approach from above and behind."

"Understood."

Nazerian allowed his hopes to rise as he watched his crew do its job. All along the length of his flagship, armored ports opened and turrets rose to the surface, training their barrels to taking aim at the planet's surface. He watched the gunnery officer work, as he supervised his own crew, micromanaging the aims of the various weapons. Nothing could be allowed to damage the renegade ship. But flattening the city around it? Simple.

"All batteries ready to fire, my lord."

"Fire!"

Bolts of searing energy blasted out of the gun barrels and burst through the sky over South Pico Island, incinerating everything within a mile of the great crashed ship. In minutes the ship's sensors showed nothing but rubble and ruin in the blast zone.

Nothing moved. It was enough to clear the way for his ground forces.

"Very well. Cease the bombardment. Maintain telemetry from all fighters and ground assault units. I want as much information about these animals as we can collect."

The ground assault was more complicated. The drop ships and aerospace fighters blasted away from hangar bays to descend into the target area to be met with surprisingly primitive weaponry. Surface to air missiles and small caliber kinetic weaponry, mostly.

Nazerian found himself thoroughly engrossed in the data that came through as each of his ground assault units and fighters fed its own stream of recorded data to the mother ship. The natives were regrouping, using vehicles he'd never seen before. Bipedial symmetrical figures, built of metal and standing upright were being used as foot soldiers, while aircraft that could somehow reshape themselves into similar shapes covered them. They didn't seem to have any coherent plan of attack, however. They responded to Nazerian's troops but other than closing toward the great ship, there was no plan. They merely reacted. Interesting. And it meant that his fleet still had the initiative.

"Order the next barrage to focus on the city. Let's give them something else to worry about."

"Changing barrage co-ordinates. Firing, now."

Nazerian hissed in satisfaction as he watched the buildings and barracks melt into their component parts beneath the barrage. The defenders didn't seem to notice but new groups were starting to rise from shielded hangars he hadn't noticed before. His operations officers organized the Sleer ground troops to counter them. But ultimately, the natives kept moving toward *Genukh*.

Why?

"Sir," said one officer. "Power levels are spiking on *Genukh*. It looks like they're using their anti-gravity lifters." They watched as the great ship shuddered in its cradle, rose several hundred feet into the air and then slipped and slid, to come crashing down back into its gantry.

Nazerian has to stifle a laugh. "What was that?"

Edzedon, however, was deep in thought, staring at the displays without even blinking. "Some lifter damage they couldn't repair properly, I'd guess. They have plenty of power…"

"So their engineers are good, but not good enough. Excellent. Let's finish this. All ground units and fighters sweep the island."

"Right away, sir."

The watched as the shape of the battle changed but the outcome was never truly in doubt. The Sleer fighters reduced the defenders in the air even as the natives scored numerous hits of their own, and the ground troops did the same below. But the primitives kept retreating toward *Genukh*.

"New readings. The ship is making another attempt at flight, and this time they seem to know what they're doing. Rising now. One thousand feet. Twenty thousand. Thirty thousand."

"We can outrun them?"

"No question. They're using simple chemical rockets."

"Chemical rockets…they built a backup lift system in case the anti-gravity lifters failed. I can understand not igniting the fusion drive, it's possible they understand the danger to themselves."

"I suspect they are cognizant of just how many chances they're taking with Sleer technology," Edzedon said. "The best we can guess at this time is that multiple systems aboard *Genukh* were damaged in the crash beyond their ability to repair…or they attempted to repair them and failed to do so. We can assume that they supplemented his own designs with some of their own technology. In any case, we have a clear advantage in speed and maneuverability."

"Good news. Recall our remaining fighters and ground units. Once we've collected our aircraft, we'll orbit the planet, match velocity and course with *Genukh* and force the aliens to land."

"Yes, sir."

Nazerian watched the plotting vectors update as his bridge officers adjusted his flagship's course and speed. His fleet was not designed for the rapid response and overwhelming force that a major planetary invasion would require. Nazerian had been at Battle Ring Zekerys when Zluur had taken his former student to task in front of the allied races' delegations and the Sleer High Command. Battle Rings were immensely powerful weapons, capable of defending entire worlds, but incredibly costly in terms of time and manpower, as well as resources. Decades to build and one could theoretically be destroyed in hours.

Zekerys had beamed as he described his work to his superiors. When Zluur interrupted him, the young scientist had gloated that a test of his battle ring was imminent. He was right: a Skreesh titan appeared and attacked. To this day, Nazerian wondered if Zykerys had called the Skreesh to attend the meeting…but officially, Zluur was the traitor.

The Movi and Cycomm representatives had demanded Zluur, and Nazerian had taken his orders. Track down and retrieve Zluur. At least Zluur's ship. And here they were, years later, twenty ships in his task force, presenting a moderate attack force, even against untutored and unknowing native races like this one. Nazerian shook his head as he realized he didn't even know what they looked like. That wasn't important. Edzedon would find out. He was good at that.

He called up his task force's details. A single Navurness-class space control ship, his own; six troop carriers, packed with soldiers and delivery vehicles; a dozen fast destroyers and three more of the relatively tiny scout cruisers. One hundred eight thousand assault troops and all their gear. Enough to raze a city, but not enough to control a planet.

And not enough to even pretend to repel a Skreesh titan. With any luck at all, the Skreesh would never show their purple and blue insectoid carapaces here. These primitives had no idea how lucky they were never to have encountered them. Unless…

"Edzedon…is it possible that the natives know about the Skreesh? That they salvaged *Genukh* specifically to manage an expected incursion?"

The question brough the science office up short. He blinked rapidly and flexed his claws, his posture indicating furious thought. "I don't see how…we have no records of the Skreesh ever sweeping this far down the galactic arm…but—"

A report from the tactical station interrupted the thought. "Sir. A large fleet of ships are approaching from behind the planet. *Genukh* is likely going to attempt a rendezvous."

Nazerian snorted, his concern forgotten. "We can't let that happen, now can we? Gunnery Officer! Arm all missile batteries and prepare to fire. Make sure all warheads are set for proximity bursts. We want to avoid destroying them. At least, today."

The missiles flew from their tubes and Nazerian was rewarded with a wealth of orange and yellow fireballs. More waves of missiles flew from the launch tubes to similar effect. "All too easy," he murmured.

Suddenly a new wave of targets appeared. "Sir, they're firing on us."

"Excellent. There's no glory in shooting the weak and stupid. Set the missile batteries for full barrage, continuous fire, and let the warheads choose their own targets. No need to make it too predictable for them."

The natives' missiles flew through their ranks, exploding into his ships. They were sizeable but none of his warships took more than superficial damage. "Nuclear weapons," Edzedon noticed. "Crude, but somewhat effective."

"Commander. Something new is happening."

"Show me."

"*Genukh*'s cargo pods are deploying."

Nazerian peered intently at the display and cursed his lack of preparation for this mission. Ten years in transit and he hadn't studied Zluur's history sufficiently. "Edzedon, go into the archives. Find me the blueprints of that ship and every log and manifest that describes her crew, equipment, and cargo. Everything. Go."

"Right away, sir." The science office skittered away while the reports continued to arrive.

"There, another pod. That's two…three…four…"

They followed the smaller ship across the orbit of the planet and noted as each pod deployed. Time to get their bearings. "Where are we exactly?"

The bridge officer checked his console. "We've followed *Genukh* through a single complete orbit. The ship is climbing now. Possibly to move into an attack position. Several of the large orbiting craft have broken orbit and are adjusting course. It looks like they're still planning to rendezvous with Zluur's ship."

"Of course they are. What happened to the cargo pods?"

"There are twelve in all, and they're moving into their own orbit three hundred miles above the surface. They seem to be powered. Certainly they can maneuver on their own."

"Sir! The cargo pods are changing."

"Display it."

On the viewing surface the image zoomed in and clarified as the pickups translated what the external sensors were registering. Each cargo pod was a cylinder, long, wide, and dense, no mere empty shell with myriad contents. These were practically solid slugs of metal and who knew what else.

As Nazarian watched the modules began to slip apart, panels and segments unfolding, as if each cylinder were made of countless smaller pieces, opening like a nestling's puzzle. And every cargo pod underwent a similar transformation as it broke away from the mother ship.

"What are you up to, Zluur?" he wondered aloud.

The tactical officer spoke again. "Reports from the gunnery crews. Most of the small ships have been wiped out. Four large orbital platforms have been destroyed while a fifth has sustained critical damage. We are ready to pursue the gun destroyer, my lord."

Nazerian took the stance of acknowledgment. "Very well. Continue with the operation. Let's recover that ship and go home."

$$[\ 4 \ ]$$

Simon Brooks was lost.

Part of that was his fault. Well. All right, it was *all* his fault. He'd popped the emergency escape hatch on his Challenger as the tall battle suit collapsed just outside *Ascension's* inner door airlock. He'd unlocked his straps and Dance's and then unceremoniously shoved her and her pack out the hatch while he dug around the enclosed cockpit to locate his backpack. While climbing out of the giant armor construct, the AMS-1 rumbled and groaned, and shook hard enough to rattle his teeth. Lights had gone out, and the interior emergency lights had taken long seconds to kick in. By the time Brooks gained some inkling of where he was, an interior blast door the size of a cargo truck was crushing his battle suit's feet and Brooks needed to be somewhere else. He hadn't seen Dance leave, but she and her pack were gone and he didn't see her anywhere. Granted, crew were rushing both ways down the corridor; too easy to lose track of her. She was smart; she'd sort herself out.

Part of the problem was the ship itself. There were no directional signs posted, no illuminated strips along the floors, ceilings, or walls to point the ways to the various sections. He had no clue where his unit was and couldn't see any other battlers in the assembly point where he'd arrived. The enclosed space was nothing he recognized and wasn't a proper staging or recovery area for mechs. Yelling produced nothing but noise and a sore throat and his squadron comm was dead. His slate refused to synch with the ship's wireless network and didn't even have a ship's floor plan on it.

He walked. Up and forward, where he imagined forward to be. If he saw a staircase, he climbed it. Soldiers and sailors rushed past him on their ways to action stations. Since the Hornets had never properly arrived, and he had no orders to speak of, he had nowhere to be. He resolved to keep out of the way.

Finally, a hand grabbed his shoulder. He spun around to see a thick, bronze-skinned woman, a petty officer's insignia on her lapel and no sense of humor on her face. Her shoulder patch designated her as a member of the bridge crew. "Specialist! You're a communications MOS?"

"Yes, sir."

"Can you operate a class-4 comm console?"

"What? Yes, sir. Definitely. But my unit is—"

"As of now, I'm your unit. Follow me!"

"Where are we going, sir?"

"Bridge. I need a commo jock. You're it. Come on!"

He followed her down corridors, bobbing and weaving around crewmen, slipping past checkpoints and through compartmented hallways. After the third turn he was hopelessly lost. Even having seen the ship from the outside, he couldn't quite grasp the scale of this vessel. It was immense. Not a single ceiling was less than twenty feet high. "Is it the damage from the anti-grav system?" he asked.

"What do you know about that?"

He spent a few tense seconds wondering what to tell her. The truth seemed simplest. "I'm with Hornet Squadron, Icarus Air

Wing 27. Our flight landed just as the AMS-1 tried to lift off an hour or so ago. We pulled some damaged battlers out of a repair yard and followed Colonel Hendricks' orders to board the ship. Here we are."

She eyed him suspiciously. "Are you even supposed to be on board?"

"We are, sir. Just…with more equipment."

"I see. Sounds like you had an exciting afternoon."

Brooks hustled to follow his new officer up three flights of stairs and into an armored elevator. Once inside, she paused to take a breath as unseen motors whirred to life and the car began to rise. He finally looked at her name tag. Amir. "No, it wasn't the damaged flight systems. During the exchange of fire, we had a short in the console. It's fixed, but now the specialist who had comm watch is in sick bay with second degree burns. His designated relief never showed, so I had to hunt for a replacement. Turns out that SORTER gadget actually worked and alerted me to the fact that you were close by." She pointed to his air group patch, the MOS bar right below it. "I know a comm spec when I see one."

"Crappy first day for everyone, sir."

"Agreed. Here we are, and don't 'sir' me. Petty Officer First Class Amir is a mouthful enough for anyone."

Brooks hesitated to cross the threshold when the armored door slid open to admit his new handler. The wide room with high ceiling was very different from the rest of the ship. It reminded him of old photos he'd seen of warship bridges. Well-lit, functional, and crowded with displays.

The bridge had taken damage: he could smell the ozone and cordite. Melted insulation, burning circuits, and blackened paint. He turned to his right and found the damaged console: a wide tear in the casing ran from the top of the station to the floor, spewing occasional torrents of sparks until he turned the panel's circuit breaker off. He scanned the other bridge stations, all manned by harried and nervous enlisted men and women. Brooks got the notion that his handler had been pulling any competent bodies she could find to the bridge. Then he remembered her using the phrase "exchange of fire."

Just how bad off were they?

She led him to a crew station on the far side of the chamber. "This is your station. Get yourself settled." She turned to the center of the room, where the big chair sat. "Captain Rojetnick. The ancillary flight operation communication console is manned. All bridge comm stations are now staffed and functional. Request permission to return to my station."

"Mr. Amir, you may do so. AFO, report?"

Brooks plugged his headset into the open port and swept his eyes over the readouts, figuring out which channels were which and what conversations were going on. The switchboard of any warship was a busy place and none of it was particularly alien to him. But there was so much of it…

"Ancillary Flight Ops! Status report!"

The order jolted Brooks back to the here and now. He ran his hands across the controls and made sense of the mess. "Sir! Engineering is reporting full output in the lift rockets. Damage control stations report the hull breaches created by the anti-gravity system failure are sealed. And all deck action station officers are reporting in, ready for action."

"Thank you. Now tell me about the flight operations, which is what I asked you for."

Brooks punched himself with a mental fist. He was looking at the wrong display. "Sir. Portside recovery control reports that Air Wings 29 and 31 are recovered and the hangar is being secured. Starboard recovery control reports that Air Wing 25 is recovered. Air Wing 27 is being recovered now. Moderate damage to the port launch tubes, no damage to recovery stations. All surviving aircraft are entering the refuel and re-arming queue." He blinked as peered at the display harder. He couldn't take his eyes off the word, "surviving." How many survivors were there? How many Hornets from First Section were still alive?

"That's better." Brooks noted a shift in position in the Captain's chair. He was being examined. "What's your name, soldier?"

Brooks froze, his eyes locked on his console. His mind pulled a complete blank. His name? He had a name. What the hell was his name? He swung his chair back towards Captain Rojetnick, a mountainous, swarthy man with a dense mustache and eyebrows a stage magician could pull pigeons out of. If the captain had any expression other than a frown, Brooks couldn't imagine it.

"Specialist Simon Brooks, Icarus Air Wing 27, Hornet Squadron, sir."

Rojetnick bobbed his head once. "Welcome to my bridge, Mr. Brooks. Lieutenant Hart is running the flight operation console up front. Make sure she gets all the support she needs."

"Yes, Captain."

"Carry on."

Brooks eyed Hart from across the room. A tall, unfazed brunette near the front of the bridge, she never took her eyes off her station readouts and never seemed to stop issuing orders through her microphone. He tapped a selector and brought up a schematic of Hart's flight board. He could see that she was sucking bandwidth away from the rest of the ship. A look at the display told him why: eleven squadrons were in the air, one hundred and eight pilots talking to her, to each other, to the ship. More channels were devoted to the airbase at South Pico Island's control tower. Somewhere nearby there would be an Air Boss and Mini Boss managing the details of the aerial ballet around them, but the mission instructions and objectives came from up here.

Again, the scale of the operation flummoxed him. He'd get used to it.

Wouldn't he?

He stayed focused on his job. Conversations came through his headset, which he relayed as appropriate. He listened to the bridge activity with his other ear. Over time he learned how to pay attention to the cross-conversation, the orders and acknowledgments, and learned the bridge crew's names. Hart was easy, the spit and polish Flight Ops officer up front. Stationed on her left was the helmsman, a Lieutenant Spalding. Lt. Matheson served on weapons and tactical, Lt. Meng on Navigation, and Amir was acting as the ship's Communications department head. Commander Cobb, the ship's XO, had apparently died early in the fighting when an explosion in the Combat Information Center took him and two dozen others, most of them comm staff. That explained why his console was getting traffic from all over the ship. Brooks never learned the names of the enlisted people. They watched their screens and whispered updates into their headsets and Brooks felt certain they were happier that way. He would be, in their positions.

The thought reminded him that he was a bit of an imposter here. He switched feeds, scanned the ship-wide bulletins and found no mention of Hornet squadron or any of its members. He did see an update from a senior chief petty offer logged thirty minutes earlier about ground troops being pressed into service as damage control teams. The Hornets might well be fixing leaks, pulling wounded out from under wreckage, or even bagging corpses from one end of the ship to the other. Fairchild and Arkady would sort it out, that much he knew for a fact.

There was even a work order that someone should move a Challenger battler that was blocking airlock 364-B. He sent that one on its way to the maintenance section with a bit of a red face.

He'd have parked the stupid thing properly if he'd known where to do so.

Speaking of which…Hornet squadron's first section wasn't in the air, so who was? It took him a minute to figure out how his console shared channel information with Hart's flight operation station. He could pull up links between the squadron commanders and their private and shared command channels, too. The Nightmares were engaged in the re-fuel and re-arm queue, as were the Specters and Yellowjackets. Eight other squadrons, associated with air wings 25 and 31, were listed as reserve units. The Hornets weren't even listed: there was no entry in the computer. That made sense, as they'd literally only just arrived. It would take time to put them into the system. He touched a stud to find out more about the active units, and a bank of green lights became blood red.

"AFO," Hart yelled. Brooks froze, hands above his console, wondering what the hell he'd just screwed up. "I've lost contact with Nightmare squadron. Re-establish contact at once!"

"Yes, Ma'am!" Brooks undid his mistake and verified that the new channel was both on the board and accessible to the Flight Ops console before he responded. "Contact re-established. You have voice and visual."

"Good. Carry on."

Suddenly the ship lurched, sending a shudder through the deck plates. The entire bridge crew felt it; they looked around wondering what happened. Rojetnick spoke for everyone. "What was that?"

Spalding called out a response. "Captain, we've reached an altitude of three hundred and six miles but we're coming to a new course. Equatorial."

"Get us back on the course I ordered, we need to rendezvous with the defense platforms."

"I'm trying, sir…helm isn't responding."

"Fix it, Lieutenant, that's an order."

"Yes, sir."

Displays winked out as others appeared, and a baritone voice that sounded like a gravel crusher emerged from a grill above them. "Geologi elberblik. Erbit Kalkualeydad. Dasplaken ferbrukn."

No one spoke until Rojetnick broke the silence. "What the hell was that?"

Brooks' station blew up with new alerts and messages from various sections of the ship. Crewmen shouted into grills in panicked voices, while others reported new circumstances. He knew he couldn't hope to relay every one, and waited for a calm moment for him to interject his news. "Captain. I'm getting bulletins from all over the ship. Crew are reporting that parts of the midsection are…changing."

"Changing how? Be specific."

"I can't sir. Bulkheads are sliding into place, corridors are closing off, partitions are extending across entire compartments. It's like the interior of the ship is redesigning itself."

Hart's contralto voice added to the confusion. "Wonderful ship, *Ascension*. We should have gotten a warranty before launch," Then she cleared her throat. "Captain, some of the escort pilots are reporting that the ship's midsection is altering its shape. I have live feeds available."

"Show us, Commander."

Screens lit up with exterior views of the AMS-1. The midsection had once been a rough ovoid, but now massive exterior doors were opening and mechanisms within the bay were reconfiguring to maneuver extruded pods to the hull of their strange vessel. Cylindrical and giant, nearly a third as long as the ship itself. In minutes, *Ascension's* midsection was surrounded by a collar of twelve cylinders.

As they watched, the pods pivoted on their endcaps, angled

outward, and broke away from the ship, trailing thin streamers of plasma. In minutes all of them had successfully launched and moved into new orbits. Sets of heavy doors closed over the gaping holes in the hull, sealing off the apparent cargo bays.

"Where are they heading?"

Meng spoke from navigation. "They're adjusting their trajectories…moving into equatorial orbits. They are not heading downstairs. I repeat, they are not angling toward Earth. If anything, they're accelerating to higher altitudes."

Rojetnick turned his head. "Comm, alert defense platforms that they should not fire on those objects."

Brooks tried. "I don't think that will be an issue, sir. Platforms 1 through 5 report they are under attack. They're taking heavy damage. Casualties are high."

"Lt. Spalding, are we still locked on course?"

"Negative, sir. I have control."

"Good. Match velocities and set a course for the Defense Platforms 1 and 2. We can take some pressure off them. Lieutenant Hart, what's the status of Nightmare and Specter squadrons?"

"Both squadrons are re-arming and re-fueling along with Yellowjacket squadron. Air wing 29 is being prepped for launch. Air Wing Leader 31 wants permission to launch."

"Permission granted. Lt. Matheson. Have you corrected the mishap from earlier?"

"All weapons are armed and ready to fire. Sir, with respect, the meson cannons did not fire due to a mishap. The system activated, targeted two near orbit objects and fired on them, all on its own."

Amir spoke up. "I'm sure they did, Captain. Just like *Ascension* realigned itself to launch its cargo without Spalding's control."

Rojetnick closed his mouth, gave a curt nod and settled back into the big chair. Brooks logged a nugget of respect for the man.

A commanding officer who actually listened to his bridge crew had to be worth something.

A coherent message played in his ear. "Platforms 1 and 2 are coming up over the horizon now, sir. Estimated time of rendezvous is twelve minutes."

"Very well. Light up the active scanners. Let's find some targets to shoot at."

"Scans are in. Fifteen targets bearing 337, twelve more bearing 361."

Feeds lit up on Brooks's console. Several images from the airborne fighters were available. They were long, cigar shaped, and ugly as sin, bumps and ridges and bristling with gun turrets. "We have visual telemetry coming in from fighter groups; switching to main screen."

The bridge crew stared while Rojetnik leaned forward in his chair, studying his prey. "If we have visuals at this distance they must be gigantic."

"The biggest measures more than four kilometers long; smallest is five hundred meters."

"Prepare to fire heavy missiles and railguns on my mark. Mark!"

The screens lit up with interference as flight after flight of missiles, each one large enough to be a proper ICBM back in the bad old days of mutually assured destruction, flew out from launch tubes. Four massive railguns blew streams of projectiles at the enemy, each shell big as a car. As weapon crews traded information, Brooks could see that the *Ascension* was covered with smaller weapons, too. Nothing big enough to do much damage to something four klicks long at a thousand miles distance, though. Just what the hell had he gotten himself into?

The screens flashed again as eighty aircraft launched long range missiles, joining the attack. Minutes passed before new information came in: flashes of light like miniature suns appeared ahead of the *Ascension*.

Matheson blanched as the displays shifted. "Direct hits… proximity hits. Minimal damage."

"We can do better," Rojetnick thought aloud. "Move us into a parallel course. We'll broadside them with the rails and lasers as we pass. Then we'll—"

Two bright spots on the display accompanied by a veritable hail of shrapnel. "Platforms 1 and 2 are gone, sir. That was them."

"Survivors?"

"A few shuttles and drone fighters is all."

Rojetnick hesitated for half a second. "Recall all fighters and small craft. Reload missile launchers. Rails and lasers, continuous fire."

Now the alien ships were regrouping, figuring out what came next. Forward laser batteries shone with brilliant, deadly illumination as they directed their aim to the AMS-1. The ship bucked and rocked as beams heated and pierced the outer hull then ignited the interior compartments.

Brooks relayed damage reports as he received them. There were so *many*. The smaller laser and missile turrets evaporated under the onslaught while compartments near the outer hull popped open like popcorn kernels. The hangar decks weren't doing much better as fighters narrowly avoided hitting each other or the landing bay walls as they rushed to get aboard.

"All weapons, fire!"

The small turrets opened up joining their bigger cousins and then *Ascension* unloaded on its attackers. If they were making any difference, Brooks couldn't see it. He could see the comm net and telemetry feeds go dark one after the other, however. Not a good sign.

"Lt. Meng, where are we?"

"We've completed one full orbit. We're just about over South Pico Island."

Apparently Rojetnick came the same conclusion. "Lieutenant Hart," he ordered, "close all hangar bay doors once the fighters and auxiliaries come aboard. Lt. Spalding, make your course for Moon Base. Lt Meng, signal engineering to prepare for a spatial transition. Our target is Mars."

He turned to Brooks. "Comms, ship-wide alert. We will make a space fold in three minutes."

That, Brooks knew how to do. He toggled the general channel and spoke into his mic. "All hands prepare for a space fold in three minutes. Three minutes to spatial transition. All stations report in." The reports trickled in then came in a flood. He logged each one and finally was able to update his information. "All stations reporting ready, Captain."

Hart turned to look over her shoulder. "Sir, CAG signals all squadrons and auxiliary craft are aboard."

"Thank you. Secure landing bays. Mr. Spalding, let's give ourselves some room to maneuver. Ignite the fusion engines."

Spalding's voice wavered as he answered. "Sir, the fusion drive has only been tested in simulation. Shouldn't we…?"

Brooks' ear-piece erupted in noise. "Sir, fires in launch tubes one and two. Damage control parties are being directed to the site."

"So much for simulation," Rojetnick said. "Textbook says those drives can accelerate us three kilometers per second. Helm take us up, half power. We'll hover one mile above the lunar surface and execute our spatial transition."

"Yes sir."

"Comm, contact Mars base and alert them it is my intention to de-fold ten miles directly above their air space. Please don't shoot us down."

Brooks made the call. He spoke to an almost unnaturally calm female voice with the habit of emphasizing every third word. "*Roger* AMS-1, *confirming* your plan to rendezvous in *Mars* airspace at an *altitude* of ten miles. *Standing* by for your *orbital* insertion."

Brooks decided that at some point he needed to put a face to that voice. "Roger, Mars base. Captain, we are expected."

"Very good. All stations stand by for space fold."

The ship jolted and shuddered. New rows of warning lamps flashed for attention. "Sir, the fusion drive is misfiring. Output rising to sixty percent. We are accelerating."

"Can anything work properly today? Very well, shut the drive down. Slow us down with the conventional rockets."

"The drive won't shut down. Output at ninety percent."

"Put us ten degrees positive pitch. Let's not make a hole in the moon. Comms, signal engineering, pull the plug on the fusion drive."

The image of the Moon grew in the viewing screens so quickly they could see the disk expand as the seconds ticked by. The ship swerved beneath them and the image teetered and tipped. Brooks understood the problem. Once you start going that fast any tiny change in angle of approach turned into an extreme variance in direction. Eventually a new voice spoke into Brooks's ear. "Captain, engineering reports the fusion drive is off."

"Good. Activate fold drive."

Spalding and Meng played their consoles like musicians and suddenly the world stretched and snapped. Brooks' vision blurred as he felt himself weigh nothing, then less than nothing as the gravity in the ship disappeared. His heart raced in panic, his blood burned, and suddenly the universe came back into focus. They were still here. He was all there. He felt his chest and legs to be sure.

Slowly the bridge crew resumed its awareness. "Lt. Meng, please confirm our location."

Meng spoke slowly. "The constellations are correct. There's a massive object ten point two miles off starboard bow and closing."

"That's Mars you're seeing, Lieutenant. Widen your navigation beam."

"No, sir. It's far too small for that. Orbital velocity is wrong, as well."

"Six miles and closing."

"Spalding, correct your course."

"Too late, Captain…"

"Collision alert!"

The ship thudded hollowly as the object, an asteroid by the appearance, collided with the bow of the *Ascension*. The ship's prow broke through the edge of the asteroid scattering rocks and assorted materials over the hull and into space.

"Spalding, hold position. Meng, where are we?"

"Ten thousand miles off the planet Nix, sir."

"Nix? That's one of Pluto's moons."

"Yes, sir." Meng projected an orbital schematic onto a viewing surface. "Nix, Charon, Pluto. The other two moons are on the planet's far side."

"What did we just crash into?"

"The moon. Or the piece if the moon we brought with us when we folded."

"Amir?"

"The fold drive engaged just a mile above the moon's surface. We were passing directly over Moon base when we transitioned."

Rojetnick stood and blinked owlishly. "That's moon base out there?"

Meng and Spalding shared a look. "Not all of it, sir."

"Spalding, put us into orbit around Nix. Hart, organize rescue flights. All personnel and equipment are to be recovered as soon as possible. Meng, prepare to fold us to Mars."

Brooks turned back toward the bridge. "Sir. Engineering is reporting massive damage to the fold drive. They're saying its unusable. The fusion drive is damaged, but they believe that it can be made functional within twenty-four hours."

A shocked silence settled over the bridge like a weighted blanket. Finally Rojetnick sighed. "It's going to be a long trip back then. Begin rescue operations. Let's bring the surviving base personnel aboard."

[5]

Tall Lord Fleet Master Nazerian stood immobile in his command bubble on the bridge of his flagship. He stared unflinchingly at the displays arrayed before him, showing him everything from the disposition of his fleet to the current position of Zluur's battle fortress. His sensor technicians had, after much work, located the fortress on the furthest reaches of this solar system. Nazerian couldn't imagine what was out there that warranted their attention to the micro-system of dwarf planets they were currently orbiting. Spectral analysis had confirmed a fusion plume at that position so they were definitely there. He understood using a spatial transition to gain some maneuvering room, but why so far?

The images coming to the ship's sensors from the main planet held his attention. They'd retreated to a geosynchronous orbit, carefully hovering over the tiny island that Zluur's ship had launched from. From this vantage point, the flagship could monitor seven of the twelve cargo pods that ship had deployed. The equipment had undergone considerable changes in the past twelve hours. And they were not yet finished.

Each of *Genukh*'s cargo pods deployed its own array of

mechanical units which orbited their casing like a miniature solar system. Streams of metal scattered throughout the spaces between each module to link them up. They formed an embryonic orbital ring even now. More filaments had already descended to the surface. A proper science ship could have collected more data but the strategy was clear to Nazerian: a battle ring was being deployed.

In hindsight, he should have known this would happen. He should have stayed and dealt with the problem while the pods were still being launched out of *Genukh*'s cargo hold. He'd been on Battle Ring Zykerys's bridge while that insane scientist nattered away, describing how his new ring design would revolutionize modern space warfare while Zluur had hung back from the attendant crowd, nodding and smiling, apparently paying attention while the high command oohed and aahed.

Zluur had his own plans and they were not what the great lords wanted to see.

And now they had no recovered gun destroyer, and a ring building itself around an alien world at a frenetic, almost unimaginable pace.

He'd tried to take action against the nascent ring two days ago. He'd ordered a barrage of short-range missiles to blast one of the cargo pods. The weapons had been destroyed long before any had ever gotten close. Edzedon found out the reason: a battery of defense satellites orbited each cargo module. Deploying laser turrets hadn't yielded any better results. The defense platforms might be small but they were effective. His ship's main gun would probably wipe the growing ring out of existence…but his mission orders didn't include that possibility and his request to Home Fleet for additional orders had gone unanswered. For the moment, his judgment prevailed. And he wanted to see what this new megastructure grew into.

So he stood, and watched as the ring expanded and developed, almost like a living thing. He'd never seen one under construction. He doubted any living Sleer had. Battle rings were intensely expensive to build, both in terms of labor and materials. An entire sector fleet could be built and deployed in less time than would go into constructing a single ring. But the rings were essential to defending the integrity of the Sleer empire during a Skreesh incursion and the Home Fleet's intelligence division swore that such an incursion was on the way.

Zluur had apparently done the impossible: devise a way for a ring to build itself without Sleer needing to be physically present. Beyond the knowledge that this technology would, if it worked, change everything about how, when, and who the Sleer fought, Nazerian wondered about how the new structure would impact the blue world's environment. On planets with existing battle rings the geology hadn't changed much at all. Geological time moved slowly compared to civilization. But decades of work being compressed into days or months? Edzedon was trying to find out now.

In the meantime, the Tall Lord and Fleet Master watched and waited for new orders.

He barely heard Edzedon as his science officer approached. He was small for a Sleer, less than two meters tall, and light on his claws. Edzedon could retract his talons on command and skitter up behind any opponent, no matter how watchful. Silent, quiet, not one to draw attention to himself, until you needed him…then he appeared at Nazerian's elbow. If Nazerian didn't know better he'd swear Edzedon was part primate.

"News?"

Edzedon saluted. "Of a sort. We've completed some observations and projections about the planet's geology. Whatever else Zluur's technology is doing, it's stirring up the planet's weather patterns fiercely."

"Really? Show me."

A radar map of the planet appeared on a viewing surface. Twelve red dots marked the locations where Zluur's modules had dropped tethers to the surface and begun burrowing into the planet's mantle. "You can see the heat exchange ratio is very high around these points. There are tectonic adjustments and tidal waves forming all across the equatorial zones and hitting several coastlines. It turns out that the coasts are where roughly two thirds of the natives live."

"Too bad for them."

"Any race that can restore a gun destroyer to partial functionality can probably manage in the face of a disrupted environment with some warning. Not in only five days, however. Imagine a windstorm on Home Nest that covered half the planet and lasted for a month and you can see their problem."

"What about tectonic activity?"

"No major changes yet, but that's just a matter of time. Within perhaps one year, every active volcano on this world will be in full eruption. Dormant ones, as well. Some new ones will likely form. The tidal waves will sweep millions of them into their oceans."

"It should be quite a display." Nazerian swept the viewing surface away with a flick of his control gauntlet. "Is *Genukh* still on course back to their home world?"

"It is. Although its exhaust plume is dim and we're picking up a localized dust cloud in its wake. I think I can tell you what happened, though." Another display appeared, this time of the planet's large moon. A sizable crater loomed in the display. "The ship's fusion drive ignited and they executed a spatial transition very close to the surface of this body. You can see where the expansion field gouged out part of the surface."

"You think they carried the lunar deposit with them to their destination, then destroyed it? Why? As a hazard to navigation?"

"I'm not sure, but that's certainly possible. In any case, at this distance the dust is obscuring our sensors. They are heading back in this direction, though. That we can confirm."

"Let's meet them halfway. Send orders to three destroyers to maintain orbit around this planet and destroy any spacecraft if further launches are detected. They'll need to monitor developments in the nascent battle ring as well. Plot a heading for the largest moon of the planet with the stupendous rings and make your best acceleration. That will give us a few days to plan a blockade for Zluur's ship."

"We're going to attack?"

"We're going to recover that ship, one way or another."

$$[6]$$

"RELIEVING YOU."

Simon Brooks disconnected his comm headset from the main panel and rose from his command couch. He winced, his legs filled with pins and needles as circulation restored itself. He snapped to as the new console jock, a petty officer first class, moved around him.

"I stand relieved."

Amir nodded sagely as she rose from her own station and waved Brooks off the bridge. Once outside she punched his shoulder and said, "You did good. If you ever need work, I can probably hook you up somewhere else."

"Thank you. I'd prefer coffee, though."

Her expression faltered just a bit and he belatedly realized that his comment might have sounded like asking for a date. Finally, she bobbed her head once. "I'm in the general mess on deck five every Thursday night at seven. They have coffee. Let me know how Hornet Squadron is doing."

"Yes, ma'am. With respect, how do I find my unit?"

"First time aboard the AMS-1?"

"Isn't it obvious?"

"Brooks, I got here a month ago and I still get lost sometimes. You have your slate? Log on to the ship's network and you'll find a digital map. If your unit has been logged aboard—and your CO should have done that as soon as you boys arrived—then you'll find directions to their quarters. If you get really desperate you can pick up a paper map of the deck plans from any ship service store. If you know the alphabet and can count to one hundred, you have all the tools you need to find your way. And thank you again for your help today. Dismissed."

"Yes, Ma'am." He saluted and turned away, hurrying down the corridor.

The digital map wasn't complete. There were omissions and additions to manage and the small problem that the central third of the ship's layout was entirely different to deal with. But he found his squadron's billet, a barracks listed only as 10-75-4-L-J298. The legend told him that meant Deck 10, Frame 75, 4th compartment out from the ship's centerline, Port (left) side, living quarters, room assignment J298.

He stumbled into a small office to see a furious Ray Fairchild glowering at him from behind a desk that resembled a folding card table. A frazzled Skull Skellington hovered nearby, trying to navigate a slate of his own. "Where the hell have you been, Specialist?"

"The bridge, Sir!"

Fairchild snorted. "Tell me another one, you little shit."

"I'm deadly serious, sir. Petty Officer First Class Amir pulled me out of the airlock, found out my MOS was communications, then set me minding a console on the bridge for thirteen hours. The relief comm watch showed up and I made my way down here."

Fairchild gave a curt nod as he accepted the information. "Down is right. Well. You did better than the rest of us. We were all shanghaied into damage control. People have been trickling in all day. I haven't seen Arkady in hours. Hooks is in sick bay with second degree burns."

"Gah, what happened?"

"He tried to be a hero and forced open a twisted crash door without checking the fire signal on it first. He took a face full of flame for his trouble."

"Gah."

Fairchild nodded. "He'll recover but I'm out a section leader for the moment. I moved Norton into his spot, mostly because I wanted to see how good he was at taking charge. But you…I'm thinking we need another section in this squadron. "Skull, we can make Brooks leader of Third Section, can't we?"

Skull Skellington was a strange kind of soldier. Older than any Hornet except for Grandpa Frost, he was tall and painfully thin, the sort of man who did well in horn rimmed glasses and tweed jackets. He could have passed for any college professor or a serial killer. Brooks wasn't sure which interpretation seemed more appropriate. "We have an empty space for an unassigned detail, yes."

"I thought so. Congratulations, Third Section Leader Brooks."

The thought of creating a new section staffed by him alone gave Brooks an empty pit in his stomach. To him it felt as if he was being punished. "Yes, sir."

"The ship's logistics officer is building a short list of technical specialists for unassigned duty until all squadrons are appropriately berthed and equipped. Every unit is sending one. You will be our contribution."

"Yes, sir. Any indication how long we'll be grounded?"

"The way the navy does things, who knows? There are crews to replace, planes and battlers to build and repair, and a whole lot of displaced moon base personnel to deal with. We didn't even arrive with functional planes. I guarantee we are at the bottom of the list, so Third Section Leader won't mean much to anyone but you, me, and Arkady."

"What about first section? I found an entry for the second section…us…you…on the Table of organization and equipment but not—"

"First section is gone. I've been getting reports all day. The Hornets were the first out of the tube when the intercept fighters went into action and they didn't last long."

A long pause while Brooks thought about what to say next. There really wasn't much to say. None of them had been close to first section, the VRF jocks, proper Hornets, but…there it was. Brooks considered telling him about his new buddy, Amir, and the potential of access to better gear and assignments, but that had yet to resolve and it seemed like a bad idea for him to make promises he couldn't keep. "Yes, sir."

Uncle stared into the distance, then snapped back. "Anyway, you've had a long day. Find a rack, get some food, and talk up your bridge duty to Barker. Make the squadron look good. Let's get this bunch noticed."

"Only God can perform miracles, sir."

"That, he can. Dismissed."

Acquiring food was a chore of its own. Brooks used his slate to find the nearest mess hall—similar to the general mess that Amir told him about, he assumed—and made his way down long rows of crowded tables to get to the back of the chow line. Harried looking sailors in server's livery were putting up trays with individually wrapped items which were snapped up by hungry, tired troops. There were no orders being taken and what looked like a buffet station was closed. Today at least, you ate what they gave you. He grabbed a tray for himself, piled three foil wrapped items and a cup of coffee onto it, and looked for an empty chair. He found one near a group of pilots who were loudly recalling the highlights of their afternoon. An auburn haired, broad-shouldered woman was chuckling and snorting her way through a story, the men and women around her laughing and commenting.

"So the recall order goes out. All units return to base, lifting off in five. We all heard that, right? It came through the general channel and everything. And I'm doing my final fly-over, dropping GPS tags on anyone who seems stuck or frozen so the recovery choppers can make their last pickups. This one guy in a Challenger with a fucked up leg is hiding behind a building. Just standing there. Rollers are moving around him and he is frozen."

Brooks snapped his head up. Oh shit.

She continued with her story. "I move in to drop a tag on him and he swivels around and my threat detector goes off! My first thought is…holy shit, is this asshole going to try to shoot me down? But I take another second to scan the action and he's aiming *behind* me; I was actually moving into his line of fire. So I swap to Walker, move twenty meters away and three rollers pop around the far side of the building and start taking pot shots at this asshat."

God damn it. He moved his head slightly to take a look at the redhead. This was the owner of the pink Raven. It had to be. He stopped eating and listened.

"Now, Asshat gets one good shot off and holes the roller closest to him. Then they're on him like flies on shit. I'm behind schedule for tag drops now, and Asshat's element buddy has obviously heard the recall, because *he* is sprinting the fuck down the road. He's a klick or more away by now. Maybe even wondering where the hell his buddy is."

A pilot snorted. "Some buddy."

"Yeah, Battler bums. Whatever, if they can move on their own, they're not my problem. I switch out to Battler, I drop down in front of Asshat, and take the hit for him. I'm already out of missiles, so I empty my gun pod at the rollers. They go down, hissing and spitting. Finally, I turn around to see how the creep is doing and he is *still* just sitting there. In a fucking daze or something. I finally open a laser induction channel at him and scream at him to get the fuck on board. Finally, he gets the message."

"What happened?"

"He got on board. Sprinted up the gantry and jumped like a champ the last few meters, too. Good for him."

Brooks stood. Moment of truth. He pulled himself up to his full five feet seven inches and faced the redhead. "Lieutenant. I never got a chance to thank you," Brooks said.

The redhead gulped her coffee and turned to stare. She might have been looking at a bug under a microscope. "Specialist... Brooks. Thank me for what? I don't know you."

"Yes, you do, Ma'am. You just told everyone how you bailed me out."

She blinked. "That was you in that Challenger? *You*?"

"Yes, Ma'am." He paused, then said, "You're disappointed, aren't you?"

She eyed him, checking him out from top to bottom and back. The expression on her face was probably the same one an entomologist would wear when looking at a new specimen. She took a sip of coffee. "I'm incredulous that anyone would allow you inside a battle suit, ever. What's your MOS, navy cook?"

"Communications."

She spat out her coffee. "For real? What were you even doing down there?"

"Getting our asses handed to us. My squadron arrived in our Kitchen Sink just as the air attack began. You were there, you saw what happened."

"Well. I'm happy to have helped you out. That battler was expensive. Twenty families could live in a luxury hotel for a year for what it cost. It would be a shame to have to scrap it."

"Yes, Ma'am." Brooked saluted. "Permission to return to eating, Ma'am?"

The pilot stopped him with a boot against his shin. "Belay that shit, Brooks. Frau Butcher is no kind and loving goddess. I need a favor."

"Yes, Ma'am."

She raised an eyebrow. "Remember this moment, and that moment, too. Because neither is ever going to happen again. Next time you fuck up in armor, you're on your own. Got me?"

"Yes, Lieutenant…Rosenski."

She caught him eying her name patch and stood. She was six inches taller than he was, and built like a rugby player. Tough and wiry. An athlete: a nerd's natural enemy. Frau Butcher would stand out even in a sea of six-foot-tall redheads. "As you were. No, belay that. My cup runneth dry. Get me a refill, Specialist, on the boost."

"Yes, Ma'am."

[7]

The next ten days passed in a blur.

Despite Fairchild's best intentions, all of Hornet squadron's enlisted personnel were considered unattached. Every ship had a few such people to work with, floaters who were available to fill temporary vacancies in various departments. There were rules in place to prevent obvious incongruencies. One didn't send a medic to fix the plumbing in a bathroom, the SORTER app saw to that, but if a department head or one of their staff needed a body, the unattached sailors were where they drew them from.

Brooks got a different job every day, cleaning, swabbing, or lifting and moving items from one end of a compartment to another. It was reliable work, and while tiring, it wasn't difficult. It did serve to teach him the basic layout of the AMS-1 and gave him a real appreciation for just how gigantic it was. Six thousand crew was a lot, but the ship was big enough for ten times that number to live on her without being crowded. He put a note in his SORTER app that essentially volunteered to help map the interior. Within an hour, his slate dinged and showed him a reply from the ship's intelligence department. Every move he made would be tracked and uploaded to their servers with the intention of creating an updated floor plan of every deck. Brooks wondered if he'd made a mistake almost immediately, but it was done. He didn't find Amir in the mess or anywhere else. He supposed that running the ship's comm department was more pressing than a dinner date.

One thing that surprised him was the relative ease with which the crew knew what was happening in other parts of the ship. Everyone he met was wondering the same thing: had *Ascension* really dropped them in Pluto's orbit without a way to get home? The next night the topic was yes, the fold drive was destroyed but the fusion engines were working. The night after that, the topic was no, the alien attackers had apparently not followed them into the edge of the solar system. And on it went. He didn't make any friends, but he learned quite a bit.

Eventually Uncle's paperwork caught up with him and orders for his next proper assignment arrived. Master Chief Barker was a grizzled gray man with crow's feet around his eyes and iron in his bones. Brooks, though seated in a crowded auditorium on 13-17-5-V-A11 (deck 13, Frame 17, 5th compartment out from the ship's centerline, Starboard (right) side, voided area, room A11) found it impossible to look away. He glanced at the soldiers and sailors around him, noticed one officer for perhaps every forty noncoms and ratings, and decided he was in the right place. Lots of technical sections were represented here, he could tell from the group patches.

Barker opened his mouth and a hurricane emerged. "As you may have surmised, I am Master Chief Barker. I am Lieutenant Commander Belzer's chief of staff on this tub. And while you may think that the daring duo of Barker and Belzer sounds like a puppet show, we are not. We are in the business of logistics and resupply. They are the only gods the military recognizes. They are the only gods that professional soldiers dare believe in. Without us those units who abandoned your squat asses here can't fight.

Can't eat. Can't sleep. Can't do their jobs worth a damn. Do you want your buddies to go up against our enemies with wrenches and duct tape for ammunition? I thought not."

Brooks frowned. Was this guy for real? Worse, did he know that Frau Butcher had a hot pink paint job on her Raven?

"I am deadly serious. You're here because over the past two weeks this ship has suffered considerable damage. We have met enemies who exceed us in space warfare capacity. And we are the noobs in this fight. They are old hands. So, what do we do?"

One CPO had an answer. "Kill them first!"

The response got a long hard cheer from the crowd. Barker scowled but seemed to relax his shoulders at the same time. "Yes! But to do that, we learn from past mistakes and improve our game.

"For your information, the daring duo of Barker and Belzer have spent the past three years setting up the intricately designed supply lines that fed, clothed and housed the personnel on Moon Base which the AMS-1, through no fault of its crew, ended up wrecking beyond reason less than an hour into its maiden flight. Lieutenant Commander Belzer has ordered me to put things right by building another moon base inside the empty section of this very ship, thus balancing the scales of karma. Luckily, we have recovered the near entire compliment of moon base into our ranks. We have salvaged a king's ransom worth of gear and equipment from the base as well. And due to circumstances beyond our control, we have cavernous space inside the AMS-1 where her cargo bay once lived. We intend to rebuild moon base inside that space. And everyone here will put their backs into the effort.

"Your part in that is simple. Plenty of units have taken damage and will be restored. Some will be dissolved and their members reassigned. But before that happens, we have work to do. In short, I need commo engineers, weapon specialists, loaders, transport managers, electricians, mechanics, paper pushers, data managers, information tech specialists, and a cast of a thousand lifters, haulers, and schleppers. In two weeks' time we will have a functional base within these walls because frankly we can't afford to waste a single life or paper clip.

"Until further notice you are all assigned to Lieutenant Commander Belzer, but you answer to me. Your SORTER profiles will be how we decide who goes where so you'd better make sure your profile is up to date. Assignments will be coming over your slates shortly via the SORTER app. Show up on time, do your jobs, and no one dies from our mistake."

"Who is this guy?" Brooks wondered aloud.

"The big cheese of Moon Base," said the airman sitting next to Brooks. Simon looked down the row to see a number of noncoms, pissed off and put upon, but essentially present. Name tag on Brooks' neighbor was Rodriguez. "But he's not running the big tent, just this part of it."

Brooks scanned the front of the stage. A number of officers were huddled together scanning whatever flashed across their slate screens. He recognized a tall redhead as Lt. Rosenski but the others were a mystery. "You know this crowd?"

"I do." Rodriguez pointed. "See those two down there? The guy on the left is Commander Thomas Katsev. His call sign is The Butcher. Dude racked up eighty kills in the U-War. He's the ship's CAG, rules Specter Squadron with an iron fist, too. The tall redhead next to him, is…"

"First Lieutenant Sara Rosenski," Brooks offered. "Frau Butcher. Leads the Nightmare Squadron. I know the lady personally."

"Oh? Do tell."

"Not much to it. She kept me from getting my Battler turned into scrap on South Pico Island. Gave me the time I needed to sort out my heavy iron and board the ship."

"Good story, bro."

Their slates chimed and the whole row swiped the screens. "I'm tagged for communications. You?"

"Same. Don't know why. I'm a Culinary Specialist. I feed these assholes."

Brooks turned to the right and leaned down, giving his neighbors the once over. "Am I the only commo guy here?" he called. He tried to read name tags as he scanned.

"I think so," Airman Smithers chuckled. "I hate to say it, but I do their laundry."

Brooks eyed the swarthy dude on Smithers' right. Barrows, his name tag said. "You?"

"I work in the personnel office. I find them places to sleep."

Brooks turned to the woman on his left. She had petty officer third class chevrons and her uniform said Bronson. She noticed his stare and stared right back. "I work in the armory. I make bullets and bombs for the Ravens."

Brooks stared at Bronson. She was thin, very dark, and had a narrow face., Her face was worn and leathery, from a life of being out in the sun all day every day for years. Callouses on her fingers. She was used to hard labor. A machine shop probably suited her, but she had a handsome demeanor. "Seriously?"

She narrowed her eyes. "Yes, seriously. I worked in the metallurgy labs on South Pico Island. I managed the assembly line the base used for the HEAP rounds the Ravens' GU-22 gun pods use. I was expecting to work at the armory on deck eleven. What I'm doing here, I'll never know." She paused and then said, "No. I know. I mouthed off to an officer from Specter in the main hangar while working the ordnance line on the flight prep queue. I don't care if he can fly a Raven, I know my damn job."

Brooks sat back and scanned his slate. There were plenty of empty slots. Tons of choice positions. Teams formed slowly, as officers culled the herd for the skills they wanted for their projects. It would take some time for everything to be sorted out and that was an opportunity to get himself...and Hornet Squadron...noticed. "My new friends, you're in Hornet Squadron, Third Section. I need a squad, and you guys are it."

Bronson folded her arms. "Say what?"

"My CO, a very proper officer, made me a section leader a while back. That means I have team selection privileges." He waved the slate in Rodriguez's face. "The SORTER says so. Let me just find you guys and we'll get started."

Rodriguez blinked. "We can't set up commo gear."

"I can. If you can string wire and match up part numbers, you can do everything I need you to." He looked up, spotted Rosenski's eyes on him from across the room and motioned his crew to follow. "Come on. Early bird gets to choose his assignment."

They pushed their ways through the crowd toward the brightboard that indicated the communications crew section assignments. He lost sight of Rosenski as he wove his way through the crowd but eventually realized he couldn't avoid her. She was standing right in the middle of the section.

Brooks saluted and stepped back. "Lieutenant Rosenski, good to meet you again."

She returned the salute. "Cut the crap, Brooks. You're here because you suck in combat. That's why Fairchild sent you down here. This is Colonel Dimitri. He was in charge of moon base's air combat division, what there was of it before yesterday. He needs nerds."

Dimitri was a bull of a man, with a neck as wide around as Brooks" thigh. "I need a communication crew to wire the new facilities and make sure it's patched into the ship's comm and flight data system. You told Rosenski here you had experience with the bridge controls yesterday. Is that right?"

"Yes, sir."

"Good. Think you and your sidekicks here are up to the task?"

"Not by ourselves, sir." He could see Bronson wince out of the corner of his eye as the words left his mouth. Part of him understood why. He was waffling. Officers did not like waffles.

Dimitri to his credit seemed to understand. "Do you work gear better than you fight, is what I'm asking."

"With respect, sir…" Bronson kicked him and Brooks recovered. "Yes, Sir."

"Good. Sgt. Nguyen will organize you. Dismissed."

Nguyen terrified Brooks. He had the frame of a man used to squeezing into dark narrow spaces and the nicotine stained fingers of a lifelong smoker. His narrow eyes missed nothing and his accented English didn't help set Brooks or his squad at ease.

"Good day, maggots!" Nguyen yelled. A loud voice even when his mouth barely seemed to move. "I am responsible for you. I don't want to be, because you look like idiots! Like sallow pathetic worms! Like blind cave fish! But there is a job to do and I need people who can count and know the alphabet. Can you do these things?"

"Yes, Sergeant!" they yelled.

"Good. For now, I take you at your word. You will see if you look at your slates that this ship has physically changed its midsection. Where we had hundreds of rooms, compartments, and chambers we now have mostly empty space. And now the rooms, compartments, and chambers have spontaneously re-aligned themselves! Why did they do that?"

"No idea, Sergeant.," Brooks said.

"Shut up! It doesn't matter why. We must fix the maps. To do that we have sent out hundreds of recon drones. The drones are cheap to deploy and equipped with GPS sensors. Their job is to run through the various rooms, corridors, and compartments of the ship and map everything. But not everything works right. Many of the drones have disappeared, so now we use people instead. Your job will be to map the sections of the ship that you are assigned. Make sure your slates have positional locator turned on, or if you get lost, maybe you die of starvation after two weeks. I'm sending out assignments now. Good luck."

Over the next hour, slates chimed with information updates and tools were assigned. Brooks was ordered to patrol a set of hallways on the starboard side of the ship, a set of passageways that would ideally lead to the air base section of the moon base that Dimitri's crew was building in the AMS-1's mid-section. It made the tool belt he was carrying slightly redundant, but he was probably expected to fix the drone on the spot if he found it. Not a huge task. He could repair electronics easily enough.

He tapped on his slate, found what the computer said was the shortest route to the target area, and headed off. He looked behind him once, more than slightly awed by the hub of activity the cargo section had become in a few short hours. It was a massive gaping void within the ship, easily the size of a football stadium with a ceiling that had to be one hundred meters high. Dimitri's people had already blocked off portions of the main floor to decide where buildings and infrastructure would go. Massive 3-D printers were being moved into position as piles of refurbished equipment, salvaged from moon base's remains, was inventoried. So many cargo containers were being gathered that Brooks wondered if it didn't make sense to use them as structures instead.

He turned away, heading toward the hatch that was supposed to lead to his assigned compartment. He crossed the threshold, walked down a twisting turning series of corridors, stepped into an open chamber, then heard a hiss and a clunk behind him. He turned around to see that a bulkhead had slid into place behind him. No getting back that way, then. Okay. Forward it was. He got another hundred meters and then the lights went out, shrouding him in a darkness so complete he literally could not see his hand in front of his face. He found his flashlight by touch, turned it on and kept moving. His slate was now useless, but at least it made a decent night light. He made some changes to map out his route. He was procrastinating, he knew. The situation was more unnerving than he wanted to admit. Nowhere to go but forward.

He walked further in the darkness waving his flashlight against the floor and walls, wondering how many wrong turns he'd made. The corridor finally opened into a much larger compartment, one wide and long enough that his light beam couldn't find a surface to rest on. He knew the corridor he'd chosen was a simple conduit running between hangar bays and this was no hangar bay.

So. Backtrack and figure out a new route back to the main floor? Or press on and…

A whisper of activity and a whiff of ozone got his attention. He knew that combination of events: a circuit was burning somewhere. Not surprising. A great many repairs had been made recently, some more hastily than others. He decided to see what was going on. He felt for his tool kit on his belt, the solid box a comforting weight in the dark.

He reached the center of the room, or what he thought of as the center. Control stands grew out of the floor like stalagmites. He examined one closely. There were depressions scattered along the column but with no apparent moving surfaces…so how did he know it was a control station? Anthropomorphizing the gear, now. He'd been doing this too long.

He tripped over something in the dark, stumbled, and recovered, not quite twisting an ankle in the process. He pointed his beam downward and found a lost map drone.

He sat down, picked up the flat cylinder and got to work. This, he understood. He pried the cover off the bot, and sat the unit on his lap. It took no time to locate the problem: a burnt out directional logic board. Replacing it was a simple fix…if he had a replacement part…which he didn't. He'd have to carry the stupid thing back to base. Sighing, he replaced the drone's cover, turned the robot off, and stood up.

But there was the open panel and the sparking connections within; he could see them clearly, even without the flashlight. He glanced back at the dead drone, intuiting the connection. The drone had found its way into here, bumped against the console, shorted out somehow, and lay dormant for him to find. He felt for his work gloves, couldn't find them and assumed that they'd fallen out of his belt somewhere along the way. Touching exposed leads with bare flesh was a recipe for disaster. But the panel was right there, he could see the leads crackling above a blue light which lit the interior of the station with an eerie glow.

Fuck it. His tools were insulated. He set the tool box down, selected what he needed, and got to work. He reached in and—

BOOM! He felt the jolt of immense power and shuddered as his body endured the shock to his system. Next thing he knew he was flat on his back, looking up.

Looking at the stars.

He blinked.

At. The. Stars.

He was no astronomer but he knew the sky from a lifetime of experience using telescopes and star charts. His eyes found familiar patterns overhead. Ursa Major. Perseus. Draco. Cassiopeia. All in the correct places in relation to each other but wrong somehow. After a moment he realized what the problem was.

They were all compressed. Not so out of place that he couldn't recognize them…seen just off. From an angle.

After a moment the images faded and he was back to looking at a dark room. Map room. It's a map room. He shook his head, and when he put out his hand to find the floor, his hand closed on a round, solid object. He looked down. The lost drone. Right. He'd have to carry it back to base.

Map room.

He reached back into the panel, and fixed the problem, repairing the exposed leads and using a hand welder to close the open panel.

He looked back at the ceiling. Just a blank metal surface now. Wherever this ship had come from it was far enough away to see humanity's solar system from the outside. Their sky was an altered reflection of his own.

How far away was that? How much further up the galaxy's arm did they live?

And why had they come here?

He retraced his steps, pausing to pull up strips of fluorescent tape and make an ersatz sign near the entrance: MAP ROOM with an arrow pointing the way.

Eventually he found his way back to the cargo deck moon base was being recreated upon. Flatbed lorries loaded with giant spools of wire and cable were being moved up to the assembly line where the 3-D printers were busy stamping out bricks made of moon rock.

Within seconds, Nguyen's piercing shriek made him jump. "Brooks! Where the hell have you been?"

He spun, nearly dropping the drone he carried in his arms like a robotic newborn. "I got turned around, Sergeant. It won't happen again."

"You right it won't happen again, you maggot. This ship is huge! You get lost and it's weeks of lost manpower trying to locate your moron ass. Don't you have a map?"

"I do, Sergeant."

"Use it. Stay with the class! And take that drone back to inventory so a real soldier can repair it!"

"Yes, Sergeant!" He got back to work quickly enough but never stopped thinking about the stars.

[8]

THE MAPS GOT UPDATED, NGUYEN MOVED ON TO TERRORIZE another platoon, and Brooks got a word of appreciation from the ship's quartermaster. He was the only one to successfully bring back a drone during that shift, even if it was broken. They agreed to report his discovery of the map room to the bridge, and life went on.

The next day of the two-week construction mission was spent on organization, analysis of the construction plan and introduction to their equipment and supplies. His squad's first lesson was easy: the computers did all the planning. Sometimes that made sense, as in optimizing the layout and building schedule his crew was expected to adhere to. As he'd explained earlier, most of the work was dealing with wires, computers, and connecting equipment. Programming came next, then testing, which, frankly, could be done on the fly. As tech companies had long since demonstrated, the best way to debug a system was to hand it to the masses and let them try to use it. Smithers turned out to be a gifted beta tester. There was no app that Brooks couldn't write that Smithers couldn't break in less than five minutes.

But they couldn't do any of that until the buildings were actually built. Several thousand tons of lunar regolith had been recovered from outside the ship in cargo sleds and moved to the construction area by robot-assisted laborers. A collapsible supply hut had already been stocked with a dozen 3-D molecular printers which could crank out moon bricks and the so-called mooncrete to hold them together. Until their turn came to use their specialized skills, Brooks's squad was just more manual labor.

"It's a shame they couldn't salvage any buildings from the base," Brooks griped at one point. He'd been set up with a loader, a powered exoskeleton that doubled as a forklift and he found it far easier to use than the Challenger he'd wrecked on his first day. In the ten-foot-tall exoskeleton he almost looked competent as he walked palettes filled with materials from one end of the construction zone to the other.

Lt. Simmons, who was minding his squad, gave him a look. "I agree, it would be easier…if there were any buildings to salvage." She snorted at his look of surprise. "The base was underground. Each section had a small topside entrance covered in regolith, but all the works were chambers that we carved out of the rock and tunnels to connect them. The good news is that the ship's space fold field dug up nearly the entire base. All we lost were lower-level supply warehouses. Annoying, but not fatal."

"Sorry about that, sir," Brooks growled.

"Wasn't your fault." She folded her arms and eyed him suspiciously. "Or was it? I hear you were on the bridge when that happened."

"I was, sir."

"Think you could have stopped it from happening?"

"No, sir. I was running a communications station and was otherwise occupied. Also, since we were taking heavy damage at the time, I thought the captain's plan had merit."

"Good to know. Carry on, Brooks. These barracks won't build themselves."

Brooks lost count of the days quickly. Every morning he woke at 0500 to a chiming alert on his slate with the day's work order, and every night he collapsed back in his rack at Hornet's Squadron's barracks around 2200. By the time his unit peppered him with questions about the project he could barely think.

A week into the project (so his slate told him), the work orders changed. Simmons caught up with them on the construction deck. "Brooks, Smithers, Rodriguez, Bronson, Barrows. You are all certified to run Class-2 transport vehicles. Correct?"

"Yes, sir."

"Good, report to Colonel Dimitri after chow for new assignments."

Barrows scratched his head wildly. Brooks took a step back. "Lice?"

"No, man, just anxious. When I joined up they told me I probably wasn't going to get my favorite assignment even after turning in my dream sheet. I said, that's fair. Navy sends you where they need you. Looks at your skills, sees what you've done. Maybe you get your second or third choice. Maybe next time around you get that first choice. No one told me I'd see three assignments in a month."

"Could be worse," Rodriguez said. "We could be working in a packing factory, making NOMs."

Brooks laughed. "Nutritionally Optimal Meal, Personal," he recited. "How did you get that assignment?"

"I told you, man, I feed these assholes. I'm a Culinary Specialist. All day every day. It's a pretty mechanized and slick operation. Food comes from all over the world, gets processed and packed in serving containers and then they get boxed, shipped, and stored. One day I unpacked, prepared, and deployed twenty-five boxes of Chicken Wellington and ten boxes of pork chops for these yahoos. It's a lot of heavy lifting and so on, but easy enough duty. Unless your name is Hendricks."

"Hendricks? Colonel Hendricks, of the Office of Military Protocols?"

"That's him. That bastard screwed up my first week on the job. My unit set up a new cafeteria when the old building was repurposed. Big new hall, it could fit a thousand guys. All of them need to be fed and you can't fly out NOM packs all the time. But Hendricks decided he wanted steak. My CO told him, no cows on the island. No cows within two thousand miles. He didn't listen. Had to have steak. And you can't order just one. They ship that stuff by the ton. Four cows minimum. So I had to make phone calls and bump a load of two hundred roast chickens, twenty-five pounds of butter, a thousand pounds of greens, string beans, and creamed corn to fit the Colonel's frozen side of cow on the plane."

Smithers blanched. "Holy shit."

Bronson sniffed. "There's no way those numbers are right."

"Maybe I'm exaggerating slightly," Rodriguez allowed, "but I'm not shitting you. We figured out something to keep the non-coms from going hungry, but holy shit, I hate that guy. I only got assigned to food service because they found out my folks owned a restaurant back in the old country."

"Which old country?"

"Bayonne, NJ. It's all in my record."

Bronson sniffed. "Where I come from, a chef is a man above all other men. Or women. Important people, real community leaders. Why did you join up?"

"To get money for nursing school."

Brooks tried to imagine him in a nurse's scrubs. "For real?"

"Fuck, yeah. I didn't want to work in a restaurant, I've been doing that since I was twelve. I want to be an RN, like my Dad.

All the Rodriguez men are nurses, goes back four generations. Where did you come from?"

Brooks relaxed. "I ran an internet TV station back home. Mostly nature shows. My Dad is a park ranger in Yellowstone. I think we had a dozen viewers on the biggest nights. I made sure all the equipment worked but I wanted to run a media station for real. I squeezed through basic training without dying then they sent me to Communications school. Twelve weeks later, I actually know what all the gear is called and how it works and goes together. I was sort of working by instinct with the personal production stuff."

"I guess that makes sense. Why'd they stick you in a combat unit?"

Brooks sighed. "Because everyone gets stuck in a combat unit one way or another. That, and my CO picked me out of the crowd and assigned me to his squadron."

"Nice to have friends, man."

"It is," Brooks agreed. "But it didn't keep me away from all this," he said.

They brought their loaders to a halt outside a complex tent city, a nine by nine square of prefab sheds. Few were locked, fewer still had doors that stayed closed. Construction materials spilled onto the deck from some of them. Behind the smaller sheds a set of larger metal shipping containers loomed over the tents and sheds like sentinels.

Bronson sighed. "I'm guessing this is the place."

An over-eager baby-faced second lieutenant answered him. "It is if you're here to move cargo. We got fifteen thirty-ton containers to transfer to hangar bay 2." He waved absently at the taller containers.

Brooks frowned. He recognized the design as being used to transport equipment rather than bulk cargo. "What's in them?"

"Less talk, more moving. That's what's in them."

A field of containers like the one he'd nearly been flattened by stretched before him. They lined the walls, and he could pick out where the outlines of huge hatches in the walls had allowed them into the ship. Move them across the bay, then load them onto elevators for the trip to the hangar deck, he figured. They could do that. Brooks got to work, pointing out the procedure and assigning jobs. One of the pods was jarred open, either by a short fall onto the pile, or through some damage done by a collision. He climbed to the cabin of a heavy forklift then hoisted himself onto its roof.

He approached the damaged side of the container. He'd seen markings like this one on South Pico Island, too, in the repair yard they'd taken the used battlers from. These were heavy equipment transport pods, designed to ship entire machines out in planes or on cargo ships. And the cargo inside...

He looked around, saw that no one was watching, and ducked down to wedge himself through the hole and turned on a pocket flashlight.

A plane. Small, much smaller than a Raven, with a stubby pair of folded wings and a multi-barreled gun jutting out from the nose. Not something he recognized, and he knew his planes pretty well. Uncle had seen to that. He couldn't get over how small it was, less than half the length of a Raven and most of that was engine.

He squeezed back out, blinked his eyes, and got back to work. No one understood where his new zeal for perfection came from as they worked.

———

Eventually a day came when the base could pass for a small city. Apartment houses stood tall and wide, lining the walls of the ship, dominating the space to starboard while shorter, squat buildings housed the base's operations. Air Base was a shadow of its former self, a tall control tower and rows of low hangars being all that remained out of an operation that orchestrated hundreds of fighters and two dozen larger ships, all of which were relegated to the hangar bay. Despite the facility's raw, unfinished look, it made a passable resemblance to a small town built entirely out of lunar bricks.

Brooks thought it looked like a prison, but at least that part of the project was over.

Now that the air base was fully wired, a number of comm specialists joined Brooks's team for the last big push, the programming and testing of the new comm network. Not particularly exciting but it was the biggest project that he'd ever worked on and knowing that lives hung on the quality of their efforts forced him to focus on his task in a way he hadn't experienced since his time on the bridge. Colonel Dimitri at least seemed happy enough with their group's results.

One evening after shift, he wandered into the enlisted mess, got himself a plate of what looked like meatloaf, mashed potatoes, and string beans and sat down with a cup of indifferent coffee, utterly exhausted. He took a sip and wondered just how close to the bottom of the pot this cup had come when a familiar bronze face sat down with her own cup and winked at him from across the table.

"Have you been ghosting me, Specialist Brooks?"

Brooks looked up and panicked. "Petty Officer Amir? I'm sorry, am I in…?"

"Relax. I just came in for a pumpkin spice latte and ended up with coffee and a sweet roll. And seeing as how you missed our Thursday night date the past two weeks, I thought I'd see if you were still alive."

"Appreciated. Colonel Dimitri is running us ragged in the main cargo bay."

"So I heard. I can't chat long, I'm on the way to the bridge."

"How is the bridge these days? Finally running smoothly?"

She sipped and shrugged. "We're holding it together. I've been following your ad hoc platoon's progress on air base's construction. Hart is very concerned that she be able to manage all air crews and craft from her station. They're talking about turning the Air Base control tower into the ship's combat information center. If nothing else it would save us the trouble of rebuilding the original CIC."

Brooks dunked, chewed, and swallowed. Bottom of the pot. He wondered if Rodriguez had been at this batch of food. "Gah. I knew we weren't just wiring telephones.'

"Indeed not. Air Base and Flight Ops have to be on the same page. Have. To."

"Hm. Well, tell her to relax. We're programming the same network protocols used on the bridge into the servers. And made sure the data sheets all had the same standards."

She raised an eyebrow. "How thoughtful."

"No, that's fear. If she gives an order the pilots can't hear, we all die. We've tested it. It works."

"It doesn't work until she tests it in real life."

"Fair enough."

She set her silverware down and pulled out her slate. "And now you can show me how to access the feed remotely," she said.

"Haven't set that portion up yet. But log in as a level five admin and it should give you access to the whole network."

She handed him her slate. "Section Leader Brooks."

He took the slate, logged in, then showed her the controls and menus. She tested the channels, hemming and humming as the network routed information. "Too bad I can't make a local call on this thing."

"You can get U-Net feeds on it, though. Just tap this and use that menu and you're in."

"Ha! Nice." She peered closely at the screen, holding it before her nose, trying to find the perfect focal point. "What the hell is that?"

"That's the Earth. Looks like a feed from the Moon. I didn't know the OMP even had monitoring telescopes up there."

"Yeah. Obviously they do. But what's this band around it?"

It took Brooks a moment but he saw it, too. A ring of moving particles orbiting the equator. And no mere ring of random captured moonlets or space debris, either. There were filaments congealing between the bits, reaching down to the surface and linking the orbiting debris into a coherent, if still skeletal structure. A wheel with spokes. "You should show this to Captain Rojetnick when you get to your watch."

She downed what was left in her cup and stood. "Right. I'm due on the bridge. Oh, and gratz on your new status. Hornet squadron back in action, hey?"

Brooks tried not to let the confusion show on his face. "Back? We were never *in* action, not after First Section got…got it."

"Then I've said too much. You'll find out." She grabbed a food bar off the table and stalked off.

Brooks arrived back in Hornet country to see Fairchild looking pleased as hell and Arkady reading from a clipboard. "Good news everyone," she said. "Hornet squadron is…"

Brooks interrupted. "Back in action. Or in action, since were never in action we can't be back in it. Whatever. Active status, right?"

The Saint looked miffed. She shared a look with Fairchild and then threw the notes over her shoulder. The clip board clattered loudly as it hit the floor. "Yes, we're listed as active. We go on duty at 0800 tomorrow. How the hell did you figure that out?"

All eyes turned to Brooks. Uncle saw it first. "Simon? You want to enlighten us with something?"

"I had a coffee with the acting head of the Communication

Department a little while ago. Petty Officer Amir. She just congratulated us on making the active list."

"Did she now? I'll have to have a talk with the Captain about his bridge security. That said, yes, we are now properly in business."

Dances-With-Gears Reagan hopped in place with repressed energy. "Ravens? Please let us be in line for Ravens?!"

Fairchild's expression drooped a bit. "The operational Ravens and Battlers are all accounted for. But the machine shops on deck ten are finally running three shifts a day, and new equipment comes online all the time, so we will receive new planes at some point. For the moment, we are being re-structured as a multi-faceted rapid response squadron."

Allen frowned. "Which means what, Uncle?"

"Perhaps Mr. Brooks can tell us about that as well," Skull drawled.

"Uhm, no. My magazine is empty."

Fairchild smirked. "Well, in that case I'll have to fill you in. Every unit needs a few generalists, people who can be sent to a pool of talent. People who can fill holes. Floaters. You've shown yourself to be a qualified communications nerd and you jumped into rebuilding moon base as well. I'm told you took the initiative, formed your own squad, and volunteered for duty. You're on someone's list, now."

"I'm…not sure what that means."

"It means Captain Rojetnik signed off on your promotion to E-4, so you're as official a petty officer third class as you can be."

"Why?"

"Who cares why? A bump is a bump!" Norton roared, and slapped Brooks on the back hard enough for it to hurt.

"If he's moving up, I want my section back," Hooks growled. "Come on, Uncle, I'm out of sick bay a week now."

Arkady waved her hands. "Relax, Hooks. We'll restructure

everything. You'll go back to Second Section Leader, and the techies will become part of Third Section, with Norton as their boss. That means we need applicants to reform First Section. The flyers. What do you say, Simon, you want to fly a Raven?"

Hooks and Norton both pointed at Brooks. "Him?"

Fairchild bobbed his head. "The Captain spoke highly of Simon after his stint on the bridge. He called me personally and said that if I had anyone else of your caliber lying around, I should stop wasting their talent. Then I got a phone call from Colonel Dimitri asking if I had any more like him that I could assign to the Air Base. I'll say this for you, Simon, you get around."

"I wasn't bucking for attention, I just wanted to be useful."

"Maybe you weren't and maybe you were, but your recent work for Belzer and Barker represents access. And access keeps us supplied. You want to launch off the catapult without a plane around you?"

"Sir, no, Sir!"

"You're damn right you don't. Your first mission, Petty Officer Third Class Brooks, is to make sure we're on the list for new planes the minute those ships become available."

Brooks slowly raised his hand in a salute. A Raven pilot. Him. *Him.* "Yes, sir."

Fairchild stepped back. Arkady bellowed. "Squadron!" As a unit every member stood at attention and saluted smartly.

As he dropped his salute Brooks thought back to what he'd seen in the ship's hold. What his section had worked next to without being allowed to discuss it with the other teams. "As you pointed, out, Ravens and Battlers have a lead time. But would the Commander be interested in volunteering the squadron for prototype VRF testing?"

Uncle leaned forward. "Perhaps. Describe these prototypes."

"They're way smaller than Ravens. The cockpit is more

exposed than I'd like, all canopy, not much armor. But if the spec sheets are real, they're nearly twice as fast as a VRF-1A and turn on a dime."

"Make the calls."

"Yes, sir."

[9]

Between periodic orders to fix, expand, or repair the communications network he'd constructed for moon base's control tower and training to be a proper VRF pilot, Brooks had little time to be bored.

The course the AMS-1 was on for Earth took them on a limited tour of the solar system: the massive ship's first leg took them in a shallow curve toward Saturn, where they would decelerate and enter orbit briefly, using the ringed gas giant's gravity to swing around toward Earth and proceed on from there. With the AMS-1's fusion engines working at a tiny fraction of their capacity the trajectory and acceleration curve would get them there in a month. Another month would get them back to Earth. They might be home in time to catch the last couple of weeks in August.

The only way the crew had of telling one day from the next was the ship's calendar and clock, and the fact that every time someone looked through a telescope at Saturn, it was just a tiny bit bigger. These days, Saturn was huge, its flat wide rings dominating one's attention, despite the truly insane weather patterns you could see. The hexagonal storm front at its north pole never stopped fascinating him.

But before they could be useful to the ship's commanders, Hornet Squadron needed planes to fly. And now they finally had them.

Col. Dimitri led the squadron past the rows of tiny VRF-2X planes, lined up in two rows in Hangar B, Deck nineteen, showing them off as if he'd built them himself. "Now, I just want to remind you that these Sparrowhawks are experimental. Their components have been tested under normal flight conditions, but not in combat. Lieutenant Commander Fairchild, I'll expect full and forthright reporting from each and every squadron member concerning their performance in the field."

"Understood, Colonel. How long will we have them for?"

"Experimental craft are loaners by definition. A few days should be enough for your people to put them through their paces."

"I see. Were you aware, sir, that Petty Officer Third Class Brooks just wrote a compression algorithm for Moon Base's network? It doubles the effective bandwidth of your communication system."

"Is that so? I'm not surprised. I'll be back to collect my planes in two weeks. Full reporting, Commander."

"Yes, Colonel."

The simulators, Brooks decided, didn't do the new plane any justice at all. The Sparrowhawk's canopy gave Brooks a type of visual access he'd never imagined possible. Saturn filled their vision even from a quarter million miles away. As the Hornets flew in formation in a wide orbit around AMS-1, darkness engulfed the cockpit except for his helmet HUD, which was easier on his eyes. He couldn't see Rodgers or Reagan, flying behind him and to either side about one hundred meters back.

Flying in 3-plane elements had been UEF doctrine during the U-War and the military hadn't changed its mind about it.

Rodgers' voice spoke through his earphones, made tinny from distortion. "I miss my Gryphon."

Brooks snorted. The Gryphon was a tiny frigate, a box with weapons and jamming pods mounted on booms. A proficient EWAR crew could jam four targets at once in it, and pop self-guided short range missiles in case a pilot got into trouble, but it was a nerve-wracking experience to know that you'd be the first target of any attack. "Dude, I hated those sports coffins."

"Beats this freaking canopy," Rodgers said. "At least in a Gryphon I had solid metal around me. This feels like I'm flying a convertible with the top down."

Brooks sympathized. The Sparrowhawk was entirely different from the Gryphon. It wasn't even like the simulators which had a certain amount of leg room. The Sparrowhawk *felt* different beneath him. The gear vibrated due to the oversized engines, and the variable geometry frame shuddered and sighed as he put the fighter through its paces. That said, he preferred the controls to anything else he'd tried to drive. The pedals were gimbaled and pressure sensitive and the control sticks in the armrests practically anticipated his wants. You didn't have to think about piloting this crazy, tiny ship. Just move your arms and legs and it obeyed. "I like it tons better than that old Challenger," he allowed.

"Of course you do. You fly better than you walk. You ain't bumped me once today."

"Cut the chatter," Fairchild ordered. "We're on the clock."

Lt. Hart's voice spoke from the darkness. "Hornet Squadron, maintain your formations, course, and velocity. We'll be starting engagement number four in sixty seconds."

Brooks toggled his microphone. "Hornet-3, acknowledged. Engagement begins in six zero seconds. Mark."

Reagan snorted in his earphones. "You know all they're going to do is order another set of drones to drop a sheaf of missiles on us and watch us try to deal."

"Is that such a bad thing?" Brooks asked. "So far, we've fought three mock engagements for three wins. You think we'd have gotten those results with those beat up Challengers?"

"*We* would have," Rodgers said. "You, maybe not."

"Thirty seconds, Element Three. Stay sharp," Arkady said.

They acknowledged the order and waited. The scopes stayed clear except for the bright green beacon that denoted *Ascension's* location. The proving ground was well clear of allied traffic, an orbit a thousand klicks out. A pair of recon EW-5C Lurkers with far more powerful sensors orbited even further out, at five thousand klicks. Unlike the variable geometry Ravens and non-transformable battlers, the Lurker was a proper Airborne Early Warning ship. The AMS-1 carried a dozen of them, modified to run in space by swapping out their air-gulping turbofans with the self-contained plasma jets used on the fighters. A small plane with a flight crew of three and six techs rode inside, doing everything from reading sensor displays to managing a comm network that could tether *Ascension's* bridge and Air Base's control towers to hundreds of aircraft and vector them to hundreds more targets. The downside was that the plane, though small, carried a wide sensor dome on its back. A clear invitation to any enemies who might see it to come and play. That duty would be sweet, nothing to worry about except reporting contacts to the bridge and letting Rojetnick worry about them. Here, Brooks was in charge of his element and even Uncle's presence nearby didn't steady him. Fairchild had his own drones and triplet and problems to deal with. He almost envied the recon crews, but this was better in every way.

He shook his head. Twelve units scattered over a billion cubic meters of space was way above his pay grade. He shuddered to think about what would happen if Ray ever failed to out-think, out-fly, or out-shoot an enemy.

Ten seconds. Time to concentrate. He scanned his console, wondering what new thing Hart could throw at them. For all he knew, Rojetnick, Meng, or even Amir was throwing suggestions to her, just to shake things up.

Three. Two. One. Start.

Scopes clear. Threat detectors silent. Nothing.

Ten seconds.

Twenty seconds. Brooks shook his head. "Nu?"

Reagan's voice perked up. "I see them, ten…no, twelve targets at 147 relative, heading 316, range 305 klicks."

Brooks took a moment to confirm her information. There they were, a larger group than they'd gone up against thus far. "These guys are good, flying in our sixes and on top of us. Everyone flip and pivot to intercept in three, two, one, mark."

The Sparrowhawks were small enough to turn on a proverbial dime. All three fighters idled their engines, flipped to align their noses with the drones, and drove forward. The distance fell away as each pilot picked his target. "Missiles if you got 'em. Autocannons up!" Brooks ordered. He mentally kicked himself. They'd all used their missiles on the first two engagements. Nose mounted 30mm autocannons and pulse lasers were all they had. But they were impressive weapons. The APW-30 used three barrels to sling a mix of armor-piercing and high explosive rounds into an enemy and could shred armor at close range. Better still, the tiny plane somehow found the room to store two thousand rounds in an internal magazine. The pulse lasers were capable of melting inch-thick steel plates in seconds, but tended to overheat quickly. Meanwhile, the Sparrowhawk also carried a single-barreled laser gun pod which emerged from below the plane's main body when it switched to Walker mode. The extra weapon had effectively unlimited ammunition, pulling its charge directly from the reactor, but the design made it unavailable when it functioned like a jet. But there was no Battler option with these tiny craft: you could Jet, or you would Walk but that was it. And, of course, no Sparrowhawk could transform at all until all its missiles were fired off its wing hardpoints.

The lasers heated up as aiming circles lit his HUD. He lined up his targets, brought his ship around and pressed the firing stud, grinning as he watched the bright red beams tear a drone to shreds. A wing sheared off, dangled from a rivet, and flew past as its power plant burst into red and yellow fire. Brooks aligned his Sparrowhark for the next drone, this one ten klicks further out and high, slightly to the right. Thrust pushed him back into his couch as he flared his engines, then sighted and opened fire with the autocannon. The cannon shells pierced the drone's skin and rewarded him with a satisfying explosion. He bore down on a third target, toggled the cannon, and mis-timed the shot. A cloud of gas erupted from the rear section, probably a damaged compressor. He swung to track the drone and stared as the ship exploded, Rodgers' now-exposed laser following it down to the wire.

A hard ball of anger formed in his gut. "That was my kill, Rodgers," he shouted.

"Plenty more where that came from," Rodgers said. "Check your scope. Hart is already setting up engagement five. Looks like a doozy, too, at least fifty targets up there."

Brooks checked his controls, saw nothing. "Up where?"

"Twenty thousand klicks, bearing 015 relative."

A collision alarm sounded, jerking Brooks back to the moment. He swerved to miss a drone that swung past his canopy, nearly grazing his ship. Brooks decided it was time to test every single system on his Sparrowhawk and pulled the transformation lever: W for Walker. In seconds, arms and legs popped out and swung into place beneath his cockpit. The Sparrowhawk would never be mistaken for a Battler but each limb had additional thrusters built into it. Unfortunately, it also cut his speed by a third.

He swooped the spacecraft around, caught the fleeing drone in a burst from the L20 laser pod, and watched as the unmanned ship flew apart, shrapnel pinging his fighter as it blew past him. He cringed as the metallic shreds rattled past him. He visually checked his canopy. No dings, no leaks, no holes. Whew. Rodgers was a git, but he had a point: you did feel exposed with nothing but clear glass and plastic above you.

A proximity alarm sounded and Brooks checked his scanner. A drone had managed to maneuver into his six, and he wondered why they didn't put rear view mirrors in these things. Once they got back to the AMS-1 he'd personally change that. He flipped his fighter around, pitching upward to reverse course, rolling so the contact was just above his horizon. He let loose with a long burst from his autocannon and toggled the laser pod to finish the drone off. A puff of smoke and a flash of light acknowledged the hit.

At the same moment, the icon for Reagan's Sparrowhawk flashed on his console and turned from a frosty green to an angry red. "Dance, report."

"It's nothing, Brooks. Took some shrapnel in my undercarriage. The right leg is jammed. I can't reconfigure to fighter." Pause. "But I can still fight."

"I'll be the judge of that," Brooks told her and set about adjusting his angle and position so he could look beneath her skirts, as it were. Her Sparrowhawk's right leg had been shelled like a peanut. Large gaps shone through the armor plating while exposed circuits flickered and sparked.

Lt. Hart's voice pipped up in his ears. "Congratulations, Petty Officer Brooks. I think we finally found a job you can do well."

Brooks took a deep breath and let it out. You're allowed to

hate her, you've been doing it for months, now. Just don't tell her. "Thank you, Lieutenant. Hornet-3 Request permission to land my element before the next engagement. One of my pilots is signaling an emergency."

"Hold, Hornet-3." Paused. Then, "Hornet-3, say again. There's no new engagement being plotted. Four engagements, four wins. Your team is done for the day."

"Then can you please tell the drone group at 015 that they need to adjust their course. Or else, we are very far out of position. Please advise."

Another pause, then Hart said, "Hornet-3, confirm your scope."

A hiss and a clunk as the channels switched and Ray Fairchild's voice came over the line. "Flight Ops Controller, this is Hornet Leader. I confirm the scope. New group at 17 thousand klicks, bearing 013 relative. At least two hundred targets. You sure that's not ours?"

Bob Norton's voice pipped up. "Hornet Leader, this is Hornet-4. I read new contacts at ninety thousand klicks. Seventeen targets, very large. Just coming over Saturn's horizon. They must have been in its shadow."

"Gah. What else are they using for cover?" Brooks wondered aloud.

"Good question. Flight Ops, Hornet Leader requesting permission to pursue and engage."

"Negative, Hornet Leader. All ships return to *Ascension* starboard landing bay."

A short hesitation followed, too brief for Hart to likely notice, but Brooks could imagine Uncle grinding his teeth in his cockpit as he spoke. Bethca *he* had missiles still on the racks. "Hornet Leader acknowledges. Squadron, all craft return to AMS-1."

A new voice spoke up: Arkady. "Rotten luck, we could have racked up a bunch more kills."

"Maybe. Those yobos aren't like our drones. They're good pilots and loaded with death."

Dance was almost whining as she shouted into her mic. "Come on, Uncle, we can still—"

"Orders were given and you need repairs. We land and let the other teams take their shots. Besides, it's not like she said we had to stand down after we land. All we need do is slide into the arm and fuel queue and we'll be ready to go in half an hour. Grab some coffee, take a leak…"

"And miss all the heavy action," Brooks groused.

"Brooks, there will be more action out there than you know what to do with, trust me on that. If you're right and they're using Saturn's moons to approach without us seeing them, it's going to be a very long day." Pause. When Uncle spoke again Brooks could hear the strain in his voice. "First Section went against these things armed with Ravens but no plan. They didn't come back. We must do better."

[10]

BROOKS PICKED OUT HIS SQUADRON MATES AS THE HORNETS closed ranks and headed for home. The Sparrowhawks were back to Jet configuration except for Dance, whose limbs would not retract no matter what she did. Brooks reasoned it was just as well. They were all out of missiles and rounds for their autocannons anyway. He left the long-range sensors active to watch the Sleer fleet's deployment. New groups of big ships appeared in turn, from behind Iapetus, Titan, even Tethys. Big ships, too. Twenty of them in all. Some of the sizes were incredible; one was five times longer than *Ascension* which was already nearly a mile long. New groups arrived as he followed the action, the biggest ships launching so many small craft that they appeared as clouds of contacts on his scope when the combat computer could keep up with them. He wished again that he was inside a Lurker, if only for a moment. He could see the two EWAR planes keeping position, one on either side of the AMS-1, a thousand klicks out. He wasn't particularly worried about those guys. Lurkers had competent crews, a bit of armor, and enough gear to jam anything while clearing up their jamming against their friends.

Driving his own fighter was still better.

It took longer to return than it had to get out to the testing ground three hours earlier. Dance's ship really had taken serious damage and made her throttle down every few minutes to keep the power plant from overheating. Despite her insistence that she was fine, Brooks wasn't so sure. He just wanted them all to land safely.

They passed fresh Raven flights heading out to do battle with the new groups they'd detected. Nightmare and Specter squadrons were in front, as always. Brooks imagined Rosenski behind the controls of her pink Raven, snugged in her cockpit like a butterfly wedged in a steel cocoon. Ready to cut her way out and burst forth and slice enemies to ribbons with flutters of her razor-edged wings. He found it difficult not to think about her.

Ascension loomed to port as the Hornets adjusted their course. The bay ran the length of the ship in order to speed operations. Landings in the rear, launches up front. Inside, the bay's resupply machinery ran like a gargantuan assembly line, with repair and supply crews ready to work on each fighter as it ran its place down the track: repair station, ammo station, fuel station, with a pilot's ready room on 24/7 alert. Coffee, sandwiches, beds, chairs, toilet stalls. And navy ratings hustling from one station to another to replenish supplies as needed. Meanwhile, new equipment came up elevators that appeared from deeper within the AMS-1. Anything went as long as they kept the line sliding forward. The conveyor never stopped moving, even to the point of planes being repaired while the platforms crawled forward. He wondered if Bronson or Rodriguez worked any part of the system. He'd have to ask them at some point.

The Sparrowhawks slowed and alighted on the recovery deck as recovery platforms slid them to the side, away from incoming aircraft. Dance's ship fishtailed down the center deck, bounced twice and finally slid to a halt as the damaged leg collapsed beneath it, the wingtip producing a cloud of sparks as it scraped the metal. She put out her metal arms to stop the slide which flipped the aircraft onto its back. Brooks popped his canopy and ran to her craft, but a rescue crew was already cutting the irate pilot out of her ship and dousing the exterior with anti-flame foam.

Dance stumbled drunkenly, practically falling into Brooks' arms as she stood, wobbling, on her own. Her eyes were unfocused and a stream of blood ran down her cheek as he helped her pull her helmet off. He nearly gagged as he saw the problem; a piece of shrapnel had gotten stuck in her helmet. He could see where the offending object cut a gash in her scalp, an inch-long flap of skin flopping around as she bled. "I can haz Raven now?" she slurred.

"The only Raven you're getting is the one pecking over your grave, dude. Let's get you to sick bay. Medic!"

"Yes, Pretty Officer Simon," she sighed. Blood was running from her scalp into her eyes and she wiped it away with the back of a gloved hand. Two corpsmen took her away to a trolley with other wounded soldiers awaiting transport to the ship's hospital. She'd be fine…but she was out of the fight.

The crew chief, a heavyset, dark-complected man who name tag read Mahajan, took one look at the Sparrowhawk's damaged leg and scowled. "All right, this one goes inside. Pull it off the line. Let's go!"

Fairchild and Arkady met him at the fresher. The one thing you could always count on with a carrier was having to stand in line to take a leak. "One pilot and three ships down."

"Who else got it?"

"Allen and Gentry got fancy and let drones into their sixes. Considering the drones were shooting rubber bullets at us, that sucks," she declared.

Brooks shrugged. "Nine of us left. Gotta be worth something."

Fairchild nodded. "Something, but not enough. We're not getting back out until they launch air wings 31 and 29 and that will take a while. I'll talk to the deck chief."

Arkady concurred. "I'll rally the troops."

The ready room was full, as Brooks expected. Skull Skellington dressed in his ship suit stared listlessly at a slate in his lap. As an Intel officer Skull never went up with the squadron, but spent long hours debriefing pilots, reading after-mission reports, pulling footage from gun cameras and downloading data from sensory gear after they landed, then going over the data. Brooks imagined there was a ward room somewhere on *Ascension* that only the Intel people knew about and met there to chuckle over what they saw the pilots doing. Brooks looked down at the screen and frowned.

Skull had tapped into the ship's feed and was staring at Earth. At the self-constructing orbital ring surrounding it. Sixty-four days after its inception the structure had acquired depth and weight. A skeletal band of beams and girders ten miles wide, more than a mile deep, and over twenty-five thousand miles long. Even crazier was that the shafts that anchored the ring to the surface were now more solid than the orbital ring. Brooks could see platforms swooping between the beams and transport bubbles he assumed were transportation cars skidding up and down the spokes' lengths.

There was no question that the AMS-1 had released this mechanical beast into the wild and less question that the general crew wasn't tapping into the same OMP feed. It was one of those things that everyone understood but studiously avoided talking about. Just because you didn't encounter any OMP uniforms in your daily routine didn't mean there were none on board. Hendricks would have seen to that.

"You shouldn't watch too much TV," Brooks said.

"Intelligence officers study intelligence," Skellington said. "Just doing my job."

"Fair enough. What have you learned?"

"It's an alien megastructure which the OMP is calling AMS-2. It's capable of self-assembly and self-repair. They tried to shoot it down," Skellington said, "I saw a report. The Sleer flagship launched a volley of missiles at it. The bombs didn't even slow it down. They didn't even *detonate*. The missiles got to a certain range and the ring's components took them apart, piece by piece. Perhaps molecule by molecule. Then it started dismantling every bit of equipment and assorted garbage orbiting the Earth. It incorporates everything into its design, if it's close enough. How do you fight something like that?"

Brooks blood ran cold as he listened. "I don't know." Suddenly he thought about the radio contact he'd spoken to on Mars Base. The comm operator with a habit of emphasizing every third word. Was she still alive? "What about Mars Base? Jupiter?"

Skull shook his head. "Classified. They won't even let me into those files. But…two weeks after we started home from Pluto the bridge crew intercepted an evacuation order for Mars. Ganymede went dark ten days ago. Don't ask me if those are related."

"I'd think they would have to be."

Skull turned off the slate and thumped his chin with his index finger. "Hurm. Do you think there's a system on this ship to control it? Same technology, right? There might be some connection."

Brooks crossed his arms. "I've thought about it. If this ship can control it no one knows how. Scouring *Ascension* for clues could take years."

"We're still a month from Earth. Do you think there will be anyone left when we get back?"

"Why not? Eight billion people won't go quietly, I'll tell you what."

"Unless it can take apart people like it took apart those bombs."

The thought rolled unpleasantly through Simon's head as Arkady moved through the ready room, tapping shoulders and squeezing arms. "Legs up in five. And be alert, we're getting special instructions from the bridge."

Brooks's cold blood had begun to turn into the shakes. He clenched his fists to ward off the terror. "Anything exciting?"

The XO held out a finger and swung her head upwards, the gesture the crew used to indicate they were talking about the bridge crew. "All I know is that the ship is getting pounded, the bridge can't fire the main guns, there are twenty giant ships getting close. The sky is filled with hostiles, and your pal Lieutenant Hart wants to try something special. Apparently, all units are committed and no one else is in a position to make it happens. Lucky us, huh?"

"Yeah. Lucky us."

———

The tram left Hornet Squadron off at the forward muster bay, where crews delivered refurbished aircraft and pilots climbed back into their cockpits, ready for another round with enemy fighters. Brooks approached his own craft and spoke to the crew chief. "Working on these crazy ass birds can't be easy for you guys. Just want to you know we appreciate it."

The crew chief, a haggard Chief Petty Officer, looked up from his slate. His eyes were wide and red, with dark bags beneath them. His name tag read Manors. "You know, you're the first pilot to say anything like that to me. Constant complaining, that's what we hear down here. Bunch of spoiled runts, most of them. I won't be forgetting this moment any time soon."

"Mr. and Mrs. Butcher giving you a hard time?"

"Always. But they aren't spoiled runts." He looked back at his slate, checked off the last entries and raised his head to visually confirm what he was seeing. "Hornet planes are up. Good hunting."

Brooks settled into his cockpit as he called up a connection to the bridge's computers, wondering what adjustments had been made due to the fighting. Uncle and The Saint had holes to fill and Brooks saw that Bob Norton had been assigned to his element as Dance Reagan's replacement. He settled his helmet on his suit collar, hooked the air hose to the supply port and went through his checklist. When he looked up, his plane was settled into its launch cradle, the dark, narrow launch tube stretching before him.

Then, Ray Fairchild's voice. "Hornet Squadron, ready for launch, in sequence."

An unknown launch officer answered him immediately. "Roger, Hornet Leader. Sequence forming. Tubes are clear. Good hunting, boys."

Brooks took a moment of offense at the shooter's presumption. What was Joanne Arkady, anyway, chopped liver? No, that was unfair. The shooter just got them through the tubes as quickly as he could safely manage. And there weren't that many female pilots flying Ravens.

The launch sequence began, the launch light glowed a bright green and acceleration pressed Brooks back into his couch. The catapult added even more weight to his system; ersatz gravity squeezed his eyes shut and he had to force himself to inhale. Then the tube fell away from his canopy and space engulfed him. He could see bright flashes where humans were trying to fight a still unknown enemy and not doing well at all. He glanced at the screen: there were definitely fewer reds than there were when Hornet had been shooting drones but the blues were badly outnumbered and scattered across thousands of kilometers.

All inside an hour? How bad off were they anyway?

Fairchild's voice got them moving. "Afterburners, people, no one lags. Darcy, how's your power plant?"

"Redlining at 92 percent, Uncle."

"Stay with the class."

"Roger."

"All Hornets stay on me. Come to course 298 relative. All weapons are free."

Simon checked his loadout. Six AAM-58G medium range missiles had been mounted on wing hard points, three on each wing. Good choices, those had high explosive warheads and could be thrown at air and ground targets. The only problem was that his ship wouldn't be able to properly transform to Walker status until he fired them off. Somehow, he didn't think that would be a problem.

The Saint spoke up, her voice tense. "What's the plan, Uncle?"

"The plan is to get close enough to the lead ship to spit, knock out as many turrets as we can with the missiles, then go to Walker mode and annihilate as many surface features as we can. That gets done, Captain Rojetnick moves the AMS-1 in close and blasts it with every weapon she has."

"Skull says they're having problems firing the main gun," Arkady breathed. "I hope her secondaries will be enough. What are the Yellowjackets, Nightmares, and Specters doing while we make this happen?"

"Intercepting Sleer flyers, one assumes. If they lose their combat air patrol, they have way less to work with. That's Hart's instruction, and we are sticking to it."

Arkady sniffed. "I don't like that plan."

"Grow up, ladies. You wanted to be Hornets, let's be hornets. Get in close and sting until the fuckers die."

Brooks toggled his mic. "We're the skinheads of the insect world."

Arkady got back to business. "Shut up and focus, Hornet-3. Navigation bookmarks loaded. Ready to flip and decel in two minutes."

They flipped and burned, opening their throttles to kill all but a fraction of their forward inertia. They dodged what they could, but the small surface turrets were already coming to bear as they closed rapidly with the behemoth. It was longer than *Ascension* but the workmanship was different; the alien ships had a slightly inconsistent, organic look to them, like clay shaped by an eager but unskilled pottery student. The lead vessel was shorter than their flagship, bulky and stocky, a wide craft that looked more like a transport than a battleship. Considering the cloud of Sleer craft surrounding it, it was probably filled with alien troops. Were they planning to board the AMS-1 after subduing her? If so, it made sense to put a troop carrier up front.

Through his canopy, Brooks watched a Sparrowhark burst into flames as a green light blinked and turned red on his status board. Darcy didn't even have time to scream.

Brooks blinked and gulped, fighting back the possibility that he could be next.

Each Sparrowhawk had six missiles armed with high explosives, the sort of warhead used to punch holes in armored spacecraft. Brooks rose slightly above the plane of attack the other Hornets were sharing, found six turrets amidships, and let fly. He counted the seconds jinking his aircraft left and right to keep himself out of their cross hairs. Six explosions blossomed. Maybe he wasn't such an awful shot after all.

Other pilots were having mixed success. Their missiles detonated, some on target and others not so much. By the time they finished unloading their ordnance the hull was littered with pockmarks and gaps in its armor but not a lot of damage per se.

Their relative velocities adjusted, the squadron deployed their ships' arms and legs and wobbled toward the huge carrier in

Walker mode, nimbly swerving away from anti-aircraft fire from turret mounted lasers. It was nothing like approaching the mother ship for landing. The AMS-1 had been reshaped by humans who favored modular designs, straight edges, and streamlined surfaces. This thing was lumpy and mottled, covered in two-meter-long antennae. Brooks felt like he was fighting for purchase on the skin of a giant metal cocoon. His plane's feet weren't even magnetized. In order to do any real damage, he needed to hover in place, grab one of the antennae, and hang on for dear life.

Rodgers muttered on the general channel. "This is nice. Cozy."

"Damn right it's cozy. They can't shoot at us without hitting their carrier so that gives us a lot to work with if we hurry," Arkady noticed.

"Spread out. Start on the bow and work your ways backward," said Uncle. "Turrets are the targets, not the hull."

Brooks crab-walked his ship across the carrier's hull. One giant turret nearby glowed briefly and lit up his sky with a brilliant white blast, shooting over his head. Brooks took aim and let loose with a rebuke, a long blast from his forward lasers and L20 laser pod; the burst heated the metal but didn't do much apparent damage. He pointed the nose of his ship down and held down the autocannon trigger for long seconds. By the time the turret exploded, he'd used a third of his cannon rounds and the heat levels on his weaponry were unpleasantly high. Other pilots were noting similar problems.

"Uncle, at the rate we're going I'll be out of ammo after ten targets. Will that be enough?"

"I doubt it."

Norton spoke up. "Maybe we can punch our way through? Pull turrets out of the hull?"

It wasn't a bad idea. Brooks skirted to a new turret and grabbed a handhold, pointing his weaponry at the seam where the turret's base met the hull. A long burst from the laser opened up a sizable hole. Better yet, he found he could reach down and pull deck plates up as easily as cardboard. The Sparrowhawk's fingers were square with "fingertips" filed to points like chisels, rather than fat round ones like the VRF-1A Ravens had. The heavier planes could land a solid punch well enough but picking up small items from the deck and other forms of fine motor control were beyond their abilities.

"Uncle, I have an idea."

"Talk to me, Brooks."

"How big a hole do we need to make for the AMS-1 to target it?"

"The hell should I know? You worked the bridge, what do you remember?"

"Just that the main guns never trained on anything smaller than a capital ship."

Arkady sniffed. "And the guns don't work today, anyway."

Brooks grinned behind his face glass. "Correction. The *main* guns don't work. I'll bet the secondaries, do, though." He sat back and waited for Uncle to put it together.

"I see your point. I think. All right then. Everyone on Brooks' position, on the boost. We're going to board this monster and light it up from the inside. Let's make a nice big hole for the AMS-1 to shoot through."

THREE SPARROWHAWKS POINTED THEIR CANNONS AT THE DECK and cut out a hole ten meters in diameter. They worked with their hands to pull up hull plates, shredding the armor and tossing it behind them, just a few more bits of battle damage. When they finished they had a hole big enough for two of the small ships to fit through if they squeezed. Or a single ship with room to spare.

Brooks didn't wait for the order to jump, just dropped his ship's nose down and let gravity do the rest. A heavy thud announced his landing. Brooks swung his Sparrowhawk's nose around, pivoting on the craft's spindly legs. He flicked switches to bring the plane's cameras online: infrared, visible light, low light. You never knew what the powers that be might find interesting and his first instinct was to capture everything. He moved forward, heading down the wide corridor just as another thud hit behind him. Then he kept moving, giving the rest of the squadron room to enter.

Fairchild was the last one down. Arkady coughed. "All right, Uncle, we're in. Now what?"

Uncle thought for a moment. "Did my eyes deceive me or did everyone notice those huge torpedo tubes a bit further forward?"

Norton waved a robotic arm. "I did. And where's there are torp tubes there's a big fat magazine to feed them. Let's find it."

Brooks broke into the channel. "Uncle, I think you're missing something."

"Am I? Like what?"

"Like we are in a unique opportunity to grab as much intel as possible. I'm already recording everything. If we can find a command bridge or even a few crew stations, we can—"

"Wait and fuck around while *Ascension* and all her squadrons are outside and vanishing before our eyes? No, Brooks. I want to open a hole in this tub wide enough for the ship's weapons to blast through. Spycraft can wait."

"But—"

"Brooks. There will come another time. There always does."

"Yes, sir. I'm still recording everything."

"Good man. Skull will love it. Everyone record everything you can. Let's go."

Brooks turned on displays, then turned his craft left and right, searching for bearings. "That way. Sir."

"How do you know?"

"There was a turret ten meters that way on the outer hull. Crew station, power conduits, access hatches. Gotta be something running it, right?"

"Makes sense. You're on point."

Brooks moved up, walking his ship on its spindly legs through a twisting set of corridors. He couldn't avoid thinking that the design of this troop carrier was very much like that of the AMS-1. High ceilings, heavy armored hatches between compartments, and accessways wide enough to support constructs thirty or forty feet tall. They found themselves in an open room with tall hatches at either end. Open to vacuum since they'd pulled a hole in the ceiling and dropped through. The room seemed featureless and only a few dim lights gave any illumination at all. Brooks surmised it was an airlock or something close to one. At any rate they had two choices. Try to open a hatch or break through a wall.

Hatch first. Then wall.

He took a few experimental steps and found the gravity to be close enough to their own that huge adjustments to movements weren't needed. The hatch opened with a combination of wheels and levers. A smaller room lay beyond. And past that, a corridor with branches.

He checked his bearings. Left.

Brooks turned and froze as three humanoid figures entered his field of vision. They were taller than humans, armored to the gills and armed with wicked looking weapons. Long, heavy tubes that could only be rocket launchers or worse. The three had been running as he turned the corner. They stopped short, fell into formation and pointed their guns at him.

"Get back, get back!" He yelled as he planted his feet and depressed the firing stud on his control stick. A hail of cannon shells sprayed the trio. Two got off shots before being ripped in half, errant missiles exploding against the floor, driving the Sparrowhawk backwards and shattering its left arm guard. One alien body hit the wall and fell to the floor, while the other dropped in place. Brooks couldn't see the third soldier. Damn it.

"Sorry. If they didn't know we were here before, they do now," he said, still cursing himself for his slow reaction.

Fairchild moved his fighter up to examine the bodies. "They knew we were here. This was a scouting team. They'll be bringing the heavy troops up any minute."

Brooks was busy staring through the hole in the deck. "I found it. Down there."

"What's down there?"

Brooks lowered the fighter's nose until the tip of the auto-cannon nearly bumped again the deck. "Everything. It's a missile bay. I can see a bunch of control stations and a set of loading lifts. The magazine has to be close by. We can jump down, blow the warheads, and rip the hull wide open."

"Now you're talking. Make room, Simon. Let's widen this hole."

Multiple pairs of mechanical hands ripped up deck plates, the Sparrowhawks' square fingers working like can openers on the metal sheets. Even from inside his cockpit Brooks could hear the sounds of machinery from below. As they worked, a heavy thud erupted from below them, blasting through the hole they'd made. Explosive blasts rocked the deck violently enough to toss them off their feet, while the explosion created a blast wave that pushed them back. Brooks looked back up, seeing that the hole was now wide enough to accommodate one fighter at a time.

Fairchild grinned. He waited a moment, decided it was safe to proceed and jumped. "Follow me!" he used the Walker's arms to brace the fighter against the bulkheads, then dropped down through the hole. Brooks followed, grimacing as he felt his wingtips grate against exposed metal. He quickly moved aside as the others followed.

Brooks moved his fighter in a circle to scan the damage with his cameras. Either the rocket had set off secondary explosions or the AMS-1's missiles had gotten in a lucky hit. Either way, the compartment was ruined. Holes in consoles and walls and electrical fires flickered in the dark, while more armored bodies lay slumped at crew stations. A few lay sprawled on the deck. None moved.

Fairchild's voice thorough his earphones: "Saint, where are you? Let's get the wiring figured out. We don't have much time."

Arkady's voice crackled on the channel. "Roger that. Dance should really be doing this, though."

"Dance is in sick bay. You're our best bet."

Brooks scanned the room. Racks of heavy cylinders lined the walls, each with hatches. He ran his eyes up the wall and saw how the missiles were extracted from the magazine and loaded into the launch tubes. Big mothers too. This had to be a loading area for ship to ship torpedoes.

"Uncle! The magazine is below us," he called out.

He spider-walked his ship to the crew stations, examining everything. He reached out to gingerly touch a control and heard a long loud string of gibberish that sounded eerily familiar. Then he remembered his time on the bridge, the alien announcement that had preceded the release of the *Ascension*'s cargo pods. He hastily looked to see if there were written manuals somewhere, something he could use to figure out the Sleer language. Vocabulary was all the same, technical or not.

As he duck-walked his plane around he accidentally kicked a body. He watched its helmet pop off and roll beneath the lip of a loading ramp. Before it rolled out of view Brooks saw green scales, a protruding snout, and a jaw filled with pointed yellow teeth.

Arkady called out. "Ready here! It's on a timer. These racks will go up and with any luck the mag will, too."

"How long?"

"Three minutes."

A clanging from a closed hatch halted the conversation. Brooks barely noticed. He was busy trying to stuff the alien body into his plane's cargo hold. The geometry didn't quite work. The tiny cargo hold was in the belly of the plane and no matter how he twisted the aircraft's hands and arms, there was no way to ...

The other pilots were already using jet-assist jumps to head back up the hole. Uncle's voice erupted into Brooks' headset. "Brooks. Damn it, leave that alone. We are leaving."

Brooks held his breath, tried another combination. "We need a sample."

Arkady headed back up, leaving the CO and Brooks alone. "Two minutes, thirty."

"Everyone out, up and back the way we came. Now. Brooks!"

"We *need* a *sample*."

"For shit's sake—" Fairchild blundered over, lifted Brooks' plane's frame with one hand and shoved the inert body into the empty cargo bay with the other. Brooks barely had time to disengage his plane's claw before slamming the hold door shut.

"Consider yourself on report, genius. Now, move!"

"Sir, yes, sir!"

Weapons fire erupted from behind them as armored troops rushed the door and blew it off its hinges. Violent changes in air pressure pushed them back as bulkheads sealed shut to keep the atmosphere from escaping and, ironically, shutting the troops off from their own torpedo bay. Bad for them, good for us, Brooks thought.

He clawed his way back through the hole in the deck, following a trail of Walkers stretching back through the corridor. Fairchild rode his ass every inch of the way back. Brooks could hear the older man's grumbling and heavy breathing through the open com channel. He'd never seen Uncle this angry. Maybe he'd been wrong...

Brooks shook his head as hustled to follow the other Hornets down corridors. No. They needed intel. Pictures were fine, language would be better if he could figure out what to do with it. But a real alien body? Pure gold. If they could get it back.

The barreled down the accessway. Arkady's voice in his helmet: "One minute!"

They ran down corridors, twisting and turning into the wide room where they'd first entered the alien craft. It was a good thing the hallways were so large, wide enough to fit the Sparrowhawks, even with their wings constantly scraping against walls and each other.

The hole they'd made in the ceiling was still there. But so were three much larger machines. These had legs and arms, but still spherical in shape, like rollers that had broken apart and reconfigured to extrude limbs and heads. He could see a roller in the back row sliding and moving armored surfaces, reshaping itself into another armored ball with limbs. Camera eyes stared balefully at them through armored slits as they opened fire with their floating turrets, particle beams wreaking havoc with their instruments.

They all got shots off. Rodgers's canopy shattered under their fire and Brooks could see the beams fry the hapless pilot in his couch as his ship lost power.

Fairchild, Brooks, and Arkady opened fire on them as they tried to open the ersatz sally port further. Three longs bursts shattered one attacker's machine, which rolled over and tried to move its limbs, looking like an upturned turtle. A second one caught fire, scattered sparks in its wake as it moved closer to reach out with clawed hands. Brooks emptied his autocannon and threw a wide kick at the oncoming machine. He heard Fairchild's voice in his headset, ordering him to disengage. He moved to comply, remembered Rodgers' inert fighter, and reacted out of instinct. He did not want to leave human tech where these monsters might find it and learn about them. He turned around, reached for the Sparrowhawk…

And jumped as the torpedo room went up in flames. A massive weight lay on his chest as his ship was shoved upward through the ragged hole. Pieces of the alien carrier followed him into the void.

His and Fairchild's fighters grappled with each other as the air around them burned in a hail of shrapnel and metal plates. Brooks jammed his hands on the throttle and shoved it forward. Any direction, it didn't matter. As long as he put distance between himself and the explosions. He ended up pushing his CO's plane ahead of him.

As he trained his imaging scope behind him he found that there had indeed appeared a sizable hole in the ship's bow. From here it looked as if they'd managed to blow the ship's bow clean off. He quickly set his radio for the command channel and got no response. But the laser induction set still worked. "Lt. Hart. You have a clean shot into the interior of the lead ship. If I were you, I'd point every missile you can find at that thing."

Pieces of Hart's voice returned. Maybe she'd heard him, maybe not. He kept seeing faded contacts on his board. Three other Sparrowhawks within one hundred klicks. He didn't see Hooks or Carson's planes anywhere. Nine go in, five come out. Nice.

He lost track of time. From the angle they rested against each other he couldn't bend his cameras around to look inside Uncle's canopy. He barely saw the smoke trails of long-range missiles passing him on their way to hit the big ship. He saw the explosion, a column of fire and metal that consumed the carrier, explosions eating their way through the carrier's interior from nose to tail, like a caterpillar devouring a leaf. In the end only a burning hulk remained. Maybe the salvage teams would find something of value.

In time, Fairchild's ship swung its legs, slowly kicking space. Brooks could now look into Ray's cockpit see him moving and gesturing but not hearing anything on comms. Brooks opened his robotic hands and the two ships separated, each flying under its own power.

As the bulk of the AMS-1 grew in his canopy a flight of Ravens met them and escorted them the rest of the way home. One of the planes seemed to glow a dull red in the reflected light of Saturn. He picked out the number code on the tail: A117. It only took a moment to look the value up in the system, even though he knew who the plane had to belong to: Lt. Rosenski, Frau Butcher herself. As he watched he saw her raise a hand, either to wave or salute. She even waggled her plane's wings. He waggled back. She peeled off and left the surviving Hornets to limp back to *Ascension* in their damaged planes.

He wondered what Colonel Dimitri would think of their test flight.

[12]

BROOKS WAS THE LAST TO LEAVE AMS-1'S SICK BAY. HE LAY IN
bed for days while the medical staff diagnosed two broken ribs
and a hairline fracture to his right tibia. Brooks had no idea when
they'd happened...he hadn't felt anything until after he'd
collapsed when the ground crew pulled him out of his fighter. Not
being able to stand or breathe without sharp pains had been big tip
offs to his condition. When the doc announced he was stuck there
for a few days and off duty for the better part of a month, he
wasn't surprised. They kept Fairchild overnight for observation
on the chance he'd been concussed, then released him the
following morning. That was typical. Dances with Gears Reagan
made a full recovery after only a day and nineteen stitches but
moped around, lamenting the loss of her Sparrowhawk. The Sparrowhawk pilots involved on the attack on the Sleer troop carrier
received Combat Action Ribbons. Four Hornets received theirs
posthumously.

Brooks spent two weeks hobbling around in a mesh cast and
trying not to laugh. The pain was sufficiently distracting that
bruising his lungs proved less of a problem. The ribs knitted, the

cast came off, and he spent a month in the gym for physical therapy, trying to regain what muscle mass he lost.

These days it seemed that every time he turned around someone was watching the feed from the U-Net. The ring, of course. It was a solid mass now, the same dimensions as before but now the band of metal was beginning to look like an installation. Close-ups showed extrusions on its surface. They could be turrets, or sensor modules, or control stations. Or just about anything else. The spokes were proper supports by now, solid enough so one couldn't see the elevator cars traveling up and down the shafts like earlier. One thing the crew commented on that Brooks completely believed was that every scrap of shrapnel in Earth orbit had been as well as every satellite or orbital vehicle mankind had ever fielded had vanished. Brooks had the idea that the ring had somehow combined the orbiting objects with its structure, but none on how it had been accomplished. By now they were close enough to Earth that the comm specialists on *Ascension* could intercept images from ground observation stations. The OMP facility on South Pico Island was the best of these, as a spoke had installed itself just south of the air base and city, more than two miles wide, dwarfing the AMS-1's previous bulk. It essentially stood on the southern third of the island. Cameras looked up at a wall of solid metal with myriad moving pieces then looked higher to see a silvery band crossing the blue sky. Teams of military and scientific specialists had approached the space elevator but no one had figured out how to enter it. Cutting with torches had been ineffective. But one could see sea birds making nests in the nooks and crannies presented by gaps in the construction.

He was watching the feed on his slate in the mess when the table shifted and Petty Officer First Class Amir settled into the chair opposite him. It was mid-afternoon but she'd scored a plate full of breakfast: scrambled eggs and some slab of meat, melon slices, and a Belgian waffle covered in thick brown syrup. Or what would have been a waffle had it not been the same brown as the overdone toast the mess served. Her cheerful face dimmed as she brought out cutlery and stared at her food.

"We keep meeting like this and people are going to talk," she said.

"They talk now. What are you afraid of?"

"Snakes, liver, death. Bees. Warm milk. In that order."

Brooks leaned back, folded his arms and stared at her, as he wondered if what she'd told was meant to be funny. He decided she was serious. "I'm afraid of heights."

"Heights? A man who works in the air?"

"No, in a cockpit everything is enclosed. I mean small things. Cable cars freak me out. I can't even stand on a ladder to change a light bulb."

"After today, you won't have to." He wasn't sure how she managed to chew and smirk at the same time but she managed it nicely.

"Dare I ask?"

She shrugged. "After today you'll take your meals in a different dining room, and people will stop talking."

He frowned, raised his coffee mug to his mouth, and found it was empty. "What kind of nonsense is that?"

"The kind where enlisted personnel call you 'sir'" she said. "Congratulations, Third Lieutenant Brooks."

"Shut up."

"I'm completely serious."

"Shut. Up!"

She made a face. "When Fairchild tells you the news, act surprised. Or at least grateful."

"Grateful? Did you put in a good word for me? How many pies do you have your hand in, anyway?"

"I had nothing to do with it, except for my logs and one

recommendation. And that was months ago, back on the bridge. You did this all on your own. Good job, Brooks. Excuse me. Sir."

He turned back to his cup and noted again that he'd already drunk his coffee. "What else happened while I was trying not to puncture my lung?"

"You haven't even congratulated me," she groused.

Brooks grew self-conscious immediately. What did he miss? She looked the same, maybe even a little more angry than usual. Her uniform was the same, her hair was the same, her…

"Oh, my god," he said, finally notice the insignia on her sleeve and collar. "Chief! You're a Chief! When did that happen?"

"Just after Saturn. Combat losses. I took the exam, and here I am. Chief Esteri Amir. And you, a fancy *lieutenant…*"

"And you haven't called me 'sir' once."

"Just wait until they pin the bars on you. Your whole squadron got bumped. Fairchild is a full commander and on the short list for Deputy CAG, but I don't think that Katsev is in any rush to commit to a selection just yet. Arkady is a now Lieutenant Commander. Her orders went out days ago. And you're getting a couple of newbies for the squadron." She paused. "Replacements."

He thought about the Hornets who he would never see or speak to again. Darcy. Hooks, whose section he'd run for two weeks. Rodgers who had handled a Challenger better than he had. Carson, whose inability to hit a target was legendary. He hadn't been friends with them, but he'd miss them just the same. He wondered if the military had informed their families yet. Or if they could under the circumstances. "Anyone we know?" he asked.

"Shuttle pilots from Moon Base. Excellent recommendations from their flight instructors."

"Great. Now we just need planes to put them in."

"That's being worked on. I asked Lieutenant Commander Belzer to make a special effort. Hart is backing me up, so the planes will be there. Soon, I hope. The factories on decks eight and nine are running night and day, so let's hope."

"I'm told there's a lead time. And our Sparrowhawks are…"

"Garbage. That's the term you're looking for. They're toast."

"Oh."

She smiled. The right side of her mouth rose a tiny bit higher than the left. "Don't look so glum, they were experimental. Colonel Dimitri has his evaluation, so he's happy. The R&D complex on deck seven is dismantling them and trying to learn what they can about improving the design for the next generation of VRFs. Something called a War Hawk, but there's no telling when those will be built. I'm told it will be smaller than a Raven."

Brooks perked up. "The first lesson seems to be the hand design."

She frowned. "Hands? Are you serious?"

He bobbed his head and took a sip of coffee. "First generation Ravens have round fingers. They look vaguely lifelike and they punch like a hammer on an anvil, but they can't pick things up. Not small things like a rifle. And they can't dig into the hull plating of a ship the way our Sparrowhawks did."

"I know. Specter Squadron found that out the hard way when Commander Katsev tried to emulate your tactics on an enemy ship."

Brooks's eyes widened. "The Butcher decided to take notes? From us?"

"You didn't know? He took some real damage from that. Totaled his plane…how he managed to fly it back to the hangar, nobody knows. His face looked like a hamburger when they pulled him out of the wreck."

"Gah. How is he?"

"Recovering. It'll be a while. And he may well never get into another plane again. We'll see."

"Jeez. He and Fairchild have been at each other's throats for at least a decade…I can't say I like the Butcher but I wouldn't wish that on anyone."

"Yeah…thoughts and prayers." He saw her eyebrows tilt angrily, but she shook her head and it went away. "Anyway, the intelligence department looked at your gun camera footage and Captain Rojetnick ordered the entire line redesigned with square fingers. And it's an opportunity to swap out old components for new ones, so the engineers are going crazy coming up with enough new planes to populate the fleet. It'll take months."

"So what are the Hornets flying in the meantime?"

"The current model of Ravens, the VRF-1B. Slightly better sensors and avionics than the 1A but with the same hands. The 1C will have the new hands and better commo gear but that's months out." Pause. "Welcome to the era of big planes and smart salutes."

"And constantly changing assignments."

"We're making a lot of things up as we go along. There's the crew we spent a year training, who have been finding out that space travel is nothing like what we trained for. Then there's guys like you who came aboard at the last minute when the evacuation order came down from the OMP. Then there are the folks from Moon Base we picked up. They're mostly civilian scientists with a bunch of military specialists but they don't integrate into our table of organization as easily as we'd like."

"Who is studying the ring around Earth?"

She looked down at her plate, cut the waffle in two, slathered one half with eggs, made a sandwich out of it and started eating. She shrugged.

"I get it. Can't talk, eating," he said. "Everyone on board is watching that feed from U-Net."

She spoke around her food. "There is no feed from U-Net. It's official."

"That's a political stance, not reality. Are you going to collect every slate on board?"

She swallowed. "We have called the UEF high command several times. It's not our problem. That's official. And we're weeks away from Earth so we are very much limited by circumstances."

He leaned forward. "But?"

"But…that body you brought back…that's giving the OMP a bad case of hives."

"How?"

"OMP has declared it a matter of global security so I don't have access to it. Even though the corpse was examined by *Ascension* medical officers who answer to the Captain. It's making things difficult."

"Hendricks pressuring Rojetnick?"

"He is trying. As long as we're in space, there's not much he can do. Rojetnick is in charge of this ship and that's that. Once we make it back to Earth it'll be a different matter. There the OMP might have the political leverage to alter the balance. It won't be good for us, regardless of what gets decided."

He shifted his body to give his leg some room to maneuver. Too long in any one position made it hurt that much worse. The end result was that he leaned in toward her over the table. "What do you know?"

"Nothing. No access to the reports, remember?"

"How not? You're the big grand commo head."

"And dead bodies have nothing to do with my job. So."

"You must have heard something."

She leaned in, stopping when her nose was a few inches from his. It was a position that got a few stares from the tables next to them, but who cared. "They look like lizards but they're not reptiles. Not mammals, either. Not warm blooded. But very high metabolisms. That's literally all I could find out. And I had to spring for a few drinks for one of the lab orderlies to get it," she whispered.

Brooks thought back to the glimpse he'd got of the body as he and Uncle had stuffed it into his plane. He'd come down on the deck hard, the result of battle damage taken during their escape and he had been taken away by a flight crew and a medic. He hadn't seen anything alien since and doubted he would be allowed to. But he'd also taken a slew of recordings while aboard the alien ship…

"I need a favor."

She raised her eyebrows. "Favors are expensive."

"Now that I'm an officer, I think I'm good for it."

She sat back to finish her food while he watched her eyes scan his face. She never looked directly into his eyes, but swept her gaze from his plate to his head. Searching for…something. He let his own eyes drop to her chest, then moved them back up.

"What's the favor?" she asked.

"I need access to the recordings I made of their language when I was back on their ship. Also the recordings of that crazy message we heard on the bridge."

"No. Classified. By OMP."

"Fuck."

Amir shrugged in an exaggerated statement of helplessness. "But…you can always request a transfer to an intelligence unit. The commission would help you with that. But you'd be working for Hendricks."

"Gah. Shoot me."

"Well, it's your choice. Forget about aliens, stick with the Hornets, and train your noobs. As I said, you'll get Raven-Bs in a week or two. Or three."

"Fair enough. I'm glad we had this talk."

She checked her slate and got up to leave. "Oh, so am I."

[13]

SATURN SHRANK INTO A SPECK, ITS GRANDEUR SWALLOWED BY distance even as the constellations in the sky remained intact. Only the shipboard calendar kept everything straight as the AMS-1 swung around the great planet and boosted towards Earth.

The new pilots arrived on schedule. Two were civilian pilots, used to fixed-wing aircraft and one was a former Marine chopper pilot. One was an experienced drone pilot who had a year's experience working for the Office of Military Protocol. All were certified to fly UEF shuttles, but none had ever so much as seen a Raven up close.

Arkady and Brooks put the nuggets through their paces in simulators and did their best to encourage habits that would keep them alive. Fairchild spent most of his time in the ship's command tower, the vertical construction on the uppermost decks, learning the ins and outs of how the position of Deputy CAG worked: the management of over one thousand fliers left him in charge of the Hornets in name only. Joanne Arkady took over the heavy lifting of preparing Hornet Squadron to make whatever comeback it was capable of. Ravens were still difficult to come by and Brooks had no choice but to deal with the fact that he was an officer now, and the Hornets' XO to boot.

A sticking point for Brooks was the fact that while the ship's factories were cranking out new aircraft they weren't doing the same for flight simulators. Brooks flagged down Arkady during a coffee run in the ward room and slid a flash drive over to her across the narrow tabletop.

"What's this?" she asked.

"This is a spreadsheet I came up with when I should have been sleeping over the past three nights." He blinked. Anyone could see the red in his eyes and the bags beneath. Not that anyone on board was getting enough sleep in the first place. And new lieutenants often were called upon to handle additional jobs at a moment's notice.

"That's a bad habit to get into, Simon," she scolded. "You start cutting corners and you'll find you're not paying attention to the important things in the air."

"So noted. This is important."

She checked her slate. "You have two minutes to convince me. Go."

"We can get everyone trained by installing two simulators in each barracks." He sat back, satisfied he'd made his point.

Arkady folded her arms and blinked. "One minute, fifty seconds."

Shit. "Okay, I crunched a shitload of numbers. I had Barrows, Smithers, and Bronson poll their departments to get me the raw data about how crews are rotated and their assigned equipment lists. Fifty simulators are installed in the training arena. Ten are reserved for the engineers to test experimental plane circuits while the rest are used for competitions and flight training."

"One minute."

"The arena is always full. There are waiting lists and the programmed missions can run from half an hour to twelve hours, sometimes randomly assigned. You can conceivably spend one hundred and forty-four hours training a twelve-man squadron, with one mission each."

"Thirty seconds."

"If each squadron barracks had one simulator in it, we could ensure that every pilot gets one six-hour flight twice a week. Two per barracks double it to one twelve-hour flight per week. That's not even including the actual combat flights that get assigned on a rotating basis."

She looked down at the flash drive and finally pocketed it. "I'll tell Uncle about it the next time I see him. Which is in about an hour, for the weekly combat readiness review."

"Thank you."

A week later simulators began to appear in all the flight barracks and nobody asked too many questions about where they came from. Brooks took the lead in arranging as much time in the flight trainers for each of his charges as possible. Uncle was rarely seen but his word was law: no one sat in a real Raven until they averaged 90 percent success in the simulators or beat him in a head to head dogfight. None dared try for anything less than 100.

The best day of Brooks' life was besting Uncle in a simulated combat run…then did it again, just to prove that his win hadn't been a fluke.

"Congratulations, Brooks. Arkady asked to make you XO, but I've been sitting in the forms, just to see if you could keep your shit together. I'll approve the paperwork today."

"Thank you, sir."

"Don't thank me…we're flying an op over Mars in two weeks and we're getting our new Raven-Bs in a few days. Get those clowns ready."

"Yes, sir." Pause. "Why Mars?"

"The Sleer have been hitting us pretty savagely for the past four days and we've already been altering our course toward Mars. Captain wants to see if any of the equipment they left might be worth salvaging. This far out, it's only a day's difference in flight time if we head there directly." Uncle hesitated. "And I don't think he's too anxious to head directly to Earth…not with a giant alien structure surrounding the planet."

[14]

"IT GOES WITHOUT SAYING THAT THE NATIVES HAVE HURT US IN
the short term," Tall Lord Fleet Master Nazerian said. Even in
holographic form, Nazerian managed to project an air of authority
that dwarfed his own. It wasn't fair. This was *his* bridge, not
Nazerian's. "The loss of the destroyers *Zenthes* and *Kalizkz* in the
long-range exchange of fire was bad enough. But sending a strike
team to board the troop carrier ship *Vesaros* to blow it apart from
within and then throw waves of missiles at it was a stroke of
genius. I had no idea these primitives were that creative,"
Nazerian said.

Lesser Fleet Lord Kessiduss straightened his back and flexed
his claws to show that he was paying attention and understood his
superior officer. The fact that Nazerian had called him and not the
other way around wasn't lost on him. Until now, Kessidus had
been known more as an embarrassment to the high command than
an accomplished officer. His last venture before being recalled to
home Nest was to put down a mining colony revolt on Sekayah, a
world known for its rich tritanium mines and nothing else. He'd
done so, at the loss of thousands of miners and their equipment.
And two of his own task force's destroyers. But that had been the

cost of doing business. Rebels had to learn that resisting the High Command was a fool's errand. Surely the Great Lords of Home Nest could see that?

Perhaps they had. He'd been part of Nazerian's task force ever since they left Battle Ring Zekerys to pursue Zluur's ship. He'd kept his head, been patient, followed every one of Nazerian's orders to the letter. He'd been a good soldier. And now he was being tapped for a new duty.

Things were looking up.

"I don't understand why a full assault hasn't been brought to bear against this ship already," he blurted. "Zluur didn't redesign an old gun destroyer for greater strength or heavier battles. He built it to house a science project. And we all see what that experiment was...a new battle ring. As far as we know that ship is more empty space than anything else and the nascent ring is far out of reach. Why not just board *Genukh*, kill the intruding aliens, seize the control centers, and head back home?"

Nazerian kept his body language carefully neutral. That had been his original plan, after all. "The short answer is that we need the ship intact. I'm ordered to recover it, not destroy it. Whatever Zluur knew...whatever the High Command is certain he had in his possession is still aboard. Standoff confrontations don't seem to work in our favor. We need a different solution."

Kessiduss still didn't understand but could live with that answer. "Very well, Fleet Master. What do you want me to do?"

"How would you like a chance to get even?" Nazerian changed the display to show their projected courses and positions. "You can see they're still driving back toward the inner solar system but at a strangely slow rate of speed. And we've been attacking them continually for days just to keep them in a state of constant alert. Maneuvering them toward this red planet here. It's smaller than their home world but we've seen a base of sorts there. They've begun driving toward it which suggests their intent to make planetfall there."

"Yes, sir."

"You must take a troop carrier ship and get there first. Seed the ground with ground units. Cripple their propulsion and reduce their defenses. Then we can land additional vessels and board them properly."

Kessiduss altered the display a bit. "These two moons. Are they inhabited?"

"Edzedon says no."

"Interesting. I'd like to set up my destroyer on one of them to facilitate an orbital bombardment."

"No bombardments," Nazerian cautioned. "We tried that once, with ineffective results. Ground forces only. That's final."

"Understood. We'll limit the attack to the contents of my troop carrier."

"Very well. That is all." Nazerian's visage disappeared as he cut the connection.

Kessiduss's bridge returned to normal, but he couldn't stop thinking about the red planet's two moons. If propelled at the correct speed and direction they would make the perfect distraction for a planetary attack. Not against the enemy base directly, but a mass that large hitting close enough to send a shock wave that would wreck their precious base very efficiently, and flip Zluur's converted destroyer on its back like a child's toy. All his troops would need would be to dispatch the survivors and pick up the pieces.

And if his landing ships happen to carry a few hundred combat engineers, well, that was just part of the plan...

[15]

The Raven-B handled brilliantly, but it lacked the razor-thin response times of the Sparrowhawk. The cockpit resembled an armored bathtub, while the canopy's surface area was thirty percent smaller than the Sparrowhawk's had been. The feeling of being at the bottom of a cave never left Brooks alone when he flew his Raven. And while the bigger ship was a sweet plane, it couldn't compare to the bite-sized, incredibly agile Sparrowhawk. Brooks missed his tiny ship, experimental though it was.

In fairness, the VRF-1B gave huge advantages in survivability, weapon loads, and sensor arrays, but it lacked the Sparrowhawk's speed. It *felt* slow. Not necessarily less maneuverable: the Raven in Walker mode could out fly any Battler-moded VRF he came across. He'd get used to it eventually, but his habits would take time to modify.

Getting used to the GU-22 gun pod was the worst. At one point he sought out Bronson to pick her brain on how to use it properly.

"There is no properly," she scolded him. The armory on Deck eight was a hive of activity, and the din of machines pressing raw materials into high explosive armor piercing rounds was shattering. The staff wore heavy earplugs and communicated in sign language. The two of them had to step into a fly-hole just to talk. The tiny break room was empty but for chairs, a worn sofa and a round of video game consoles hooked to a giant wall monitor. "You ever practice with a long gun? "

"Not really."

"Why the hell not?"

"Because my MOS says I don't carry a long gun."

"Yeah. Well, start taking classes. There's a shooting range on every deck. I can make a call to hook you up, but you got to follow through."

"Good advice. I'll get to it."

"Good news, sir. Anyway…GU-22, right? It's a unique weapon. There is nothing else like it in the UEF armory. It's a self-contained fully automatic multi-barrel cannon that uses a snail drum to hold a thousand 55mm HEAP rounds. Ten rounds each burst. When the rounds run dry, you're done. You can't reload it except in a full machine shop. Do *not* use it as a club. That will mess up the feed and you're out a three-million-dollar primary weapon. What else is there?"

"I'm having trouble using the damn thing in Battler mode."

"Brooks, get your ass to a simulator and use it. A lot. Pull rank if you have to. It's all about habit. It's not a magic sword, you gotta *practice*. Long arm shooting, too. Or do you want me to start a rumor about the baby lieutenant who can't hit the floor if he falls out of bed? Will that help you focus?"

He listened. Brooks worked with Arkady to come up with a schedule that put each Hornet into a flight simulator for no less than six hours a day. He spent hours at the range, practicing with an M-19 assault rifle until he stank of gunpower. By the time the planes arrived and names were stenciled on their fuselages, the lowest average simulator score in the squadron was ninety-four out of one hundred and that belonged to Brooks himself.

Five days before planetfall, Brooks got new orders to report to a Mars Op planning session. He spent the morning fighting down nausea and ignored all food except for half a cup of coffee. He arrived two minutes early at Captain Rojetnick's ready room, a wide chamber set back from the main bridge, with sofas, sandwiches, coffee and a long table covered in maps. Mars base was the focus of the display. The facility was less than two decades old but was substantially bigger than the Moon's base in some respects. Unlike the lunar installation, Mars Base was a surface-built facility, with few underground areas that were not meant for storage.

"No one thinks about Mars very often and when they do they remember this, the old Russian base. The truth is there are half a dozen facilities within three hundred kilometers. The American military presence, several corporate mining operations, and the ESA's science module," Captain Rojetnick said. "All but the Russian and American military posts were shuttered during the U-War, and the Russian facility was mothballed shortly after the war ended. The American base was evacuated three weeks after the AMS-1 left Earth.

"At any rate, we are now heading down the well and Mars is now close enough to Earth to warrant a proper landing. It was a pretty big base, there should be at least some supplies left over from the previous crew, and a proper landing would give us ample time and opportunity to practice UEF planetary assault tactics."

He nodded to Lt. Hart, who took up the narrative. "We've decided to take the opportunity to restructure Air wing 27," she said. Rosenski and Brooks met each other's eyes from across the map table. They noticed each other's attention and focused their eyes on the chief of flight ops. "Commander Katsev will assume the CAG position while rotating out of the flight pool pending his progress regaining his health. In his absence, Lieutenant Commander Petrov will become the lead pilot for Specter

Squadron, and Nightmare Squadron will move into place as the primary response unit." She turned her head and locked eyes with Brooks. "Yellowjacket squadron will continue as normal, and Hornet Squadron will move up to secondary response unit. Lieutenant Commander Arkady will assume command of the Hornets, and Commander Fairchild will assume the duties of Deputy Air Group Commander."

Captain Rojetnick leaned forward. "To be blunt, we are in trouble. We're low on supplies and we've been pushing the fusion engines hard in order to facilitate a quick return home. The problem is that the fusion drives were damaged during our launch and after our mis-jump into Pluto's orbit, it's become increasingly difficult to maintain them in flight. We've mitigated the worst of it by taking the engines off-line for periodic maintenance but we're moving at far less than one percent of our sub-light potential."

"Mars base has a spaceport capable of repairing any ship in the UEF fleet," Hart continued.

"Exactly. We'll put down on Mars, let our engineers and technical crew have access to the workshops and tools they need to get the drives working properly. During the repairs, we'll deploy ground troops and ratings to transport as much of the supplies left on the base to *Ascension* as possible. Three days should be ample time to effectively empty out the base and make repairs. Once the drives are returned to functionality, we'll be able to make Earth orbit in eight hours rather than eight days."

Arkady bobbed her head. "What will we be transporting up?"

"Everything. Weapons, ammunition, fuel cells. Propellant for the engines. Spare parts for the vehicles. Water, food. Whatever isn't nailed down and can be of any possible use will be brought aboard this ship for use in continuing operations."

Brooks slid a finger along the display, looking for details. The base was a blocky structure that looked more like a gigantic oil rig than a military installation. A platform three hundred meters on a side housed a cityscape worth of modules for everything from housing to power reactors to vehicle storage to whatever else they might have needed, resting on a wide pillar. Dish-shaped antennae squatted on the upper levels along with a dozen minor versions of the same equipment. He didn't know how far down the central column extended but he got the idea it would be at least as far underground as the rest extended upwards. "Defenses?" he asked.

"A few point defense laser turrets, not much beyond that. It was never designed as a hardened facility."

"Good place for an ambush," Rosenski noted.

"It's the perfect place," Rojetnick agreed. "That's where your squadrons come in. Colonel Dimitri and Lieutenant Hart will put together a plan for deployment of transport vehicles and the means to provide overhead defenses with the Ravens. You'll coordinate a comprehensive umbrella, rotating your crews so that members of each squadron are continually in the air flying combat patrols. All the other squadrons will be held in reserve on Ready 5 status just in case our paranoia is well founded."

———

Once outside Brooks struggled to keep up with Rosenski as she hustled down the hallway. He decided to take the lead and quickened his step to fall in next to her. "So. How do we...?"

"I have an idea which I will turn into an operation plan. I'll show it to you. You may comment on it. If I think your comments make sense, I might incorporate them. I'll get Arkady's approval, we get Katsev and Fairchild to sign off on it, and they present it to Rojetnick."

"That's a lousy way to treat your co-worker," he snarked.

She whirled suddenly, forcing him back a step. She'd have

been intimidating as hell even if she wasn't a head taller than him. "Brooks, you've had a few successes, I grant you. Congratulations on them, even. When you've shot down a few dozen bad guys, then we'll have something in common. Until then, you're my water carrier. You're a communications nerd in a VRF. A Raven-B no less. None of the Nightmares or Specters have Raven-Bs. How did you get those planes ahead of us?"

Brooks saw the challenge; if he didn't face her down now he'd never hear the end of it. "You wouldn't talk to Fairchild like that."

"No, I wouldn't. Not even The Butcher would do that. Fairchild's record is over one hundred kills. When you get that far…if you get that far…then you'll have something in common with us. Until then, you may comment on what I show you. Understand, Third Lieutenant?"

"I do. First Lieutenant."

"Excellent." Firmly back on top of their pecking order, she indicated the hallway with a nod of her head. "Come on. You want to see how planning gets done? The Tactical Simulator room is this way. Try to keep up."

———

"I hate her," Brooks complained at mess. The Hornets were taking their meals together as all had roughly the same schedule now.

"She doesn't have a robust social circle," Arkady agreed, and cut into something resembling a slab of meatloaf. "But she has thirty-eight confirmed kills. And you have…?"

"Four."

"Four. So. You're going to work with Frau Butcher, you're going to kiss whatever needs to be kissed and you're going to manage the rotation like it was a finely made Swiss watch. If you fail to live up the standards that Uncle set for us, I'll kill you."

"I don't think you have that authority."

Skull Skellington raised his fork. "She does. UEF code Title X, Section 4, Sub-section 5c says that an officer has the authority to manage any insubordinate activity in any way suited to the circumstances. That includes ejecting you from the ship or having you shot."

Brooks frowned. "I don't think it means…"

Arkady washed down her food with a slug of black coffee. "Brooks. While you're wasting time arguing legal semantics, Frau Butcher is practicing the art of getting her planes in the air, on schedule, and on time. Step up."

"Yes, Lieutenant Commander Saint."

The AMS-1 matched orbital velocities with Mars and fell slowly to the surface using its conventional rocket clusters to manage a bumpy but unremarkable touchdown ten klicks from the base.

The next step was to make a visual examination of the base. Brooks and Arkady split the squadron six for six, each officer taking on three of the newest squadron members. Arkady's group was first out of the ship, flying over the base with six of the Nightmares. The base resembled a brick-shaped mushroom. This close they could see the myriad details of their installation's work. Smaller domes were scattered within two kilometers, housing instruments and sensors as well as providing above ground conduits for water and electric power to the outlying stations.

Sara Rosenski's voice confirmed what Brooks was seeing on his feed. "Nothing moving down there. No lights. No sounds. No heat sources. Nothing but shuttered machinery and equipment."

The next step was for the AMS-1 to fire its rockets and move the ship closer to the base, practically on top of it from Brooks's perspective. "You know if they have to fire to main engines, this base will be a charcoal briquette in about ten seconds."

"That's assuming they can get it to work properly."

"Yeah. And assuming they can use the equipment in the repair bays to fix the damaged modules."

"They'll probably just haul the equipment aboard and let our own people manage it."

"Makes sense."

A light winked on the command channel. Frau Butcher again. "Captain Rojetnik, Nightmare Leader requesting permission to put down and search the base."

"Search for what, Nightmare Leader?"

"I'm...familiar with the facility, sir. I'd like to see if any of the operational logs are intact."

"Surely those can be accessed remotely."

"Uh, negative sir...no power down there. But there may be a backup fuel cell."

"Nightmare leader, I don't..."

"Sir. Please."

"Very well. Permission granted. You will stay in contact at all times. GPS locators on. Yes?"

"Yes. Nightmare Leader out."

Brooks pinged Arkady on the command channel. "Why do you think Rojetnick said yes to that?"

"Because, Lieutenant, that was the first time that Frau Butcher ever asked him for anything."

———

Kessiduss pressed a stud on his roller's console. "The fleet is positioned as I ordered?"

"It is, my lord. We checked the calculations three times to confirm the burn strength and duration. We'll begin on schedule one hour exactly. They've moved *Genukh* onto the base itself, that will give our targeting computers a considerable advantage."

Kessiduss swiped the display with his control gauntlets,

watching as the planet rotated in real time. The observation drone they'd parked on the greater of the two moons was working perfectly. Such sharp imagery from orbit. "They've been quite active from what we can see. They have deployed air patrols and a great many ground troops in their walking suits. It looks like they're trying to salvage parts of the installation."

"Good for them. One hopes that means they are short on supplies."

"Agreed. It almost seems like a waste. The moon is only twenty-two kilometers in diameter. The math shows that it's already moving close to the planet on its own and will eventually break up."

"By the time those things happen we will all long be dead and the Skreesh will have overrun the last Sleer Nests. Our time frame is rather more immediate."

"As you say, sir. You know, it's not hard to imagine the contents of the order you received from Tall Fleet Lord Nazerian."

"He was very specific. Delay them, but do not destroy *Genukh*. And so we won't. A near impact from an asteroid will cause no end of havoc to a planet, but the ship itself…it's a D-class gun destroyer. Those things are tough. Even buried, we can dig it out with the recyclers."

"Just don't drop the moonlet on top of it."

"Not at all. Proceed with the operation. Let's give them something more immediate to worry about."

"Yes, lord.

They know.

The thought followed Rosenski every meter of the way down to the base. They knew what she was trying to do. They knew about the flash drive in her suit pocket, knew about her history with Nightmare Squadron, even knew about how she came to be associated with Thomas Katsev. Worst of all, they knew about the message she'd taken: a text message with a hidden source that had been a single line of text: "The secrets of the war god will be yours." They knew and they were coming for her. Who were they? Whatever. Office of Military Protocols. Rojetnick. Even Uncle Fairchild and his boy child wunderkind, for all she knew. Katsev had been griping about the man for years, and while Rosenski realized that a lot of the guff was habit, there were a few choice complaints that seemed to make sense to her. How Uncle always seemed to get his ass saved by a close associate in the command structure. He had a gregarious personality as wide as all outdoors and had the AMS-1 never arrived on Earth, if there hadn't been the U-War, if the human race had slowly but surely dwindled back into a tribal society, having long since ridden the tide of easy energy up to the heights of the twenty-first century and then down again, he might have settled for being an actor. A guy like John Wayne. Not military himself but convincing as hell in front of a camera, portraying heroic tales for the masses.

Sara had no idea who John Wayne was but she understood the power that the name represented: respect. Obedience. Getting people to listen to you. And now she had to deal with a barely social nerd like Simon Brooks. She'd heard a few complaints from the Nightmares about him, just lately. There was a seething resentment of anyone who could get that close to Fairchild that quickly. The story of how Uncle had picked him out and propelled him to a Raven pilot sat poorly with some of the men who'd come up from enlisted ranks, erasing the fact that Brooks also had come up that way. She'd overheard one petty officer in the hangar grouse about Brooks, call him a point and so on. She put that nonsense down right quick. Brooks was a lot of things but he was no point. No relatives in high places, no easy access to power, and more importantly, Brooks got his hands dirty. He'd started as a one stripe recruit just like the rest of them. If they were so unhappy about his relative success, they could damn well take a page from his book and show the initiative he did, then maybe they'd get noticed for something other than making trouble. She'd been red in the face when she'd finished. She knew the pilot had taken her meaning and would talk about the incident to others. Whatever happened now, the rumor that Brooks was under Frau Butcher's protection would filter throughout the grapevine.

Maybe she'd taken on more she could handle with that. She should have controlled herself better, it was that simple. She'd failed as a leader. She should have told the pilot to cut the shit and been done with it. Why had she defended the little creep like that?

Maybe it was the word that pissed her off. "Point." Short for "appointee." It meant a know-nothing, do-nothing officer who was into politics and making friends in high places and getting choice rear echelon assignments. *That* was a point. And yes, the military was full of them. The guys who wanted the rewards of service but thought they were above doing the dirty work of actually defending their world. Getting labelled a point in real life was tantamount to your crew openly rebelling against you. Nobody should have to deal with that. But she understood the sentiment as well as the resentment. (Is there a reason for these lines?)

Regardless of what she agreed with or who, there wasn't a single point in Air Wing 27. Not that she'd ever met. And she'd met just about everyone. It was her unofficial job, scouting the ranks for talent, for anyone bright and motivated enough to suggest to Katsev. He didn't actually poach pilots for the Specters but he had a short list of people he'd love to have in his squadron. Brooks wasn't on that list, but Joanne Arkady was. The Saint was focused on running the Hornets and transferring to the Specters was not likely.

Rosenski caught herself as she maneuvered her Walker-mode Raven toward the launch pad nearest the cargo loading ramp. There were three or four pads arranged around the base allowing access to a small enough ship, a Raven or a small shuttle, and the one on the lowest tier had an operational radio beacon. She settled the plane down and dropped its nose as she idled the engines, switched her suit's air supply from the plane to an external tank, and raised the canopy. Now her Tac-2 flight suit was all they stood between her and oxygen starvation. Mars had an atmosphere but not much oxygen.

Her boots hit the metal platform and thunked while she staggered drunkenly, seeking her balance. One-third normal gravity took time to get used to. The lights over the hatch were glowing green, so power was on, hopefully throughout the facility. She ran her hand across the sealed suit pocket, made sure the flash drive was there for the thousandth time and headed down.

Her internal monologue wouldn't stop as she used an override code to open the hatch and head inside. No. They couldn't know. What was there to know? That she'd made some friends in strange places over the years? That she'd attended a few anti-OMP rallies? That she had a copy of Jason Layne's Little Blue Book? That wasn't even the stupid thing's proper title. It was correctly known as "What Comes Next: A Consideration of Future History, From General Jason Layne, USMC." A collection of three hundred or so aphorisms that appealed to certain elements of American politics toward the middle of the twenty-first century; when the energy was running down, the food becoming less reliable and the politics becoming hopelessly partisan. When decent housing was either inherited or unavailable except at extravagant prices. When half the United States of America refused to accept the other half as citizens. When placing trust in neighbors meant asking for trouble.

Layne's political theories had become quite popular among a

certain demographic in that confused, exhausted America. The ones who imagined simple solutions to incredibly complex problems. No shots were ever fired, and thank god for that. She'd met survivors of civil wars and the one thing she'd taken away was that once shooting really began, things fell apart very quickly and there was often no putting them back together. Two craters in New York state were bad enough.

The worst part of it was that some of Layne's ideas made sense. There had to be some shared concept of country, constitution, and citizenship. Were Layne's ideas really any worse than what the place had devolved into? Democracy had dwindled and finally collapsed under the sheer weight of corporate cash, used by the insanely wealthy to buy and sell politicians who would pass any laws they asked for...even laws their lobbyists had written. More cash for them, less of everything for everyone else, and people who had too little for too long got antsy. Sometimes got violent. Was more of the same really a good idea under those circumstances?

She hadn't liked the thought of the U-War but she'd taken up her spot in U-Fleet as the right place to be. Better a unified world than a fractured country to her mind. But she brought Layne's Little Blue Book with her, just the same. She'd read it a thousand times, and memorized many of the aphorisms contained within. The final chapter was titled "What Comes Next" and it made for difficult reading. Layne described a world with few good options and plenty of hard decisions that would need to be made. A world where globalization withered away to nothing and intensely local relationships between leaders and their followers would dominate the future. A world without cheap energy, plentiful food, and modern medicine would be a harsh realm, and Layne put forth a set of values that rewarded the hard and determined. If hard and determined effectively described the people who regularly quoted from it on the darker parts of the U-Net. Sara had her doubts. The thought of following any of them into battle made feel nauseous. She rarely dipped her toes into those waters and never for more than a few minutes at a time.

She found herself staring sat the hatch. The mission. Now, only the mission.

———

The control room was huge, with walls further away than her flashlight beam could reach. There had to be lights in this place, right? A master power switch. She tried the surfaces near the door, swinging her beam this way and that. She finally moved to a wide panel and saw it. She threw the switch and gasped as the LED floods poured white light across the room.

It was huge. She'd never seen NORAD's great war room that had kept watch over the North American skies for generations during the Cold War then later during the Cold Peace. Catwalks linked observation stations above her while more displays were built into pits. At the far end of the chamber a dozen long screens sat dark.

She sat down as her heart skipped a beat.

Sara Rosenski could deal with the displays in her aircraft easily enough and could probably manage any level-1 equipment that the military might saddle her with, but when things got strange she relied on her comm guy, who wasn't here and couldn't be pulled off his current assignment: Simmons was on board an airborne Lurker. He was not getting out of that plane for another five hours and change.

She hated to admit it, but she was out of her depth. She could putter around for days in this room trying one bank of switches after another and get nothing done. She needed help. Reluctantly she pulled out her slate and tapped her requirements into the SORTER app.

And damn it, the slate told her where help was to be found.

She tapped her forearm panel to open a comm channel. "Brooks…Hornet-2, you still up there?"

"Affirmative, Nightmare Leader. I'm flying over your position as we speak."

"Good. Land on Pad 2. I'm in Main Mission, section two. The CIC. I need your expertise."

"Copy that. Lt. Hart, are you hearing this?"

"I am. Permission granted, Hornet-2. Land on Pad 2 and assist Nightmare Leader."

"Copy that."

And that was that. The ballet would continue without her oversight. Lt. Little Miss Everything had given permission, too. Gah.

She played with the equipment while she waited but her inability to decipher the equipment got her frustrated. But there was more to it than that. There was the weight of this place…in a way, the lie of it. The UEF had ordered an evacuation. And yes, they'd taken the people away, presumably back to Earth. Also presumably, they'd given the order because of the threat the Sleer fleet represented. But if that was so, where was the damage? This base might not be operational, but it was all here. What was the real story?

She patted her pocket and pulled out a flash drive. There was a set of drives in here somewhere with the information she'd been charged with retrieving "the secrets of the war god" which obviously meant the encrypted military files in the hardened network. The realization that all storage networks looked the same to her hit home again. Put her in a cockpit and she was a goddess. She was passable on the gunnery range. Without her plane or a weapon she was just another pretty face. Her frustration deepened into bitterness and began to grow into proper anger, but not the good anger that might spur someone to change their life. This was self-pity and that felt so much worse.

Brooks's next transmission didn't help her mood. "Nightmare Leader, I think I'm going to be slightly delayed," he sent.

The thought of staying here without backup alarmed her. "Delayed? Why?"

"The nearest entrance to Pad 3 seems to lead to the supply depot. There's an automated loading belt with delivery robots. I want to hack the ordering system protocols and upload the specs to the bridge. We can double or triple our take and get the machinery to do the heavy work for us."

She resented his tone. She'd given him an order and he'd acknowledged it. The whole chain of command was involved. Now, he wanted to go off-mission because shiny. But his suggestion made a lot of sense and sure as hell the bridge crew was listening in on their exchange. She had no reason to tell him to come straight to her position. "Understood. Make the detour. Get here as soon as you can."

She fought down a wave of anxiety as she waited for him to catch up with her. She wasn't a total failure: the power was still on and there were even computer systems still running after all this time. That made sense: she found the source of energy on the base, a fusion power plant that would run by itself for another twenty years if left alone. Another of the wacky and wonderful inventions that had come to be after the arrival of AMS-1. It really had changed everything. But whether those changes were for the better or not...along with unlimited energy, genuine machine intelligence and variable geometry aircraft had come the Black Crow virus, the Lockdown, the Plague Riots, the U-War, and the Office of Military Protocols. That reminded her of why she was here.

She redoubled her efforts, dredging up the memories of what she'd learned in electronic school as a recruit, before she'd been encouraged by Katsev to apply to flight school. The networks scattered throughout the base were standard UEF designs. She didn't have what she needed in training or equipment to rootkit the system and plant her own code into it, but she found where the prize was likely to be, the highest security drives in the base. The basement: three security doors and all kinds of electronic surveillance.

When Brooks finally arrived, he snapped into a salute and his radio crackled. "Third Lieutenant Brooks reporting as ordered!"

She swiveled her chair to look at him. They were both wearing Tac-2 flight suits, a requirement on a planet with an atmosphere that was only three percent oxygen. She allowed her eyes to wander to his collar and shoulder. The unit patches of Hornet Squadron and the hash of a section leader. Nerd boy was moving up in the world. She needed his roots.

"At ease. Go to the private channel, no need to blast our chatter across the comm net." She missed his confused look, just indicated the console and said, "There are secure network drives in the basement. I need you to help me scour them for a few very specific files." She couldn't keep the discomfort from her voice.

He caught on quickly. "Is there a problem?" he asked.

Anger flared in her again, then she glanced at the comm net and saw that they were both indeed on the private chat. She raised her arms to indicate their surroundings. "This is the problem. A powered down base and no people."

"We already know the base was abandoned weeks ago. So what?"

"Brooks, the OMP would never evacuate a facility unless it was in danger of being overrun or destroyed." She waved her arms around. "Does this look destroyed to you?"

"It looks abandoned to me."

"Exactly. Where was the fight? Where are the bodies? The wrecked equipment, the burned vehicles, the blasted domes?"

"Good questions. You think the OMP is hiding something? Like what?"

"No idea. But have you noticed the OMP only really came into power after the unification war ended? You think that's a coincidence?"

"I've wondered about it."

"We all have. Some of us are thinking about it more intensely than others."

"Who?"

She shook her head. "Not now. I need to get this done. You think you can educate me on this stuff in five minutes?"

He turned around, mapping the command room with his eyes. "Front row of consoles will be ladar and radar. That section will be the communications network. This is command. And back there is surface and sub-surface operations. There's a central computer somewhere which links them all. So if we—"

"Brooks. Just push the right button."

She followed him with her eyes as he worked. He knew exactly what to do, where the controls were and how to use them, like a dancer who knew where to put his feet and could time the steps to the microsecond. She checked her oxygen level. Time was getting short but there was no rush. Not yet.

He looked up. "The logs were wiped but the system had a delayed storage buffer. If something hasn't been purged after six months, it automatically gets routed to the permanent network drive and removed from the buffer. Now...I can purge the buffer from here which would archive its contents."

"Which means?"

"We need the archive room. Here, Level six. Heh. Just one floor above the fusion plant."

"Let's go."

[16]

Captain Rojetnik watched the operation from a screen in his ready room, his hands wrapped around a mug of coffee, very light, no sugar, exactly the way he liked it. It was a rare moment of solitude amid the sea of constant demands and responsibilities and he intended to enjoy it for as long as he could. Maybe a whole hour. Maybe even two. Eventually, someone would arrive with new information, but for the moment, life was sweet and silent.

He opened a log entry and scanned what he'd written earlier. The plan was proceeding. CAP was deployed and rotating according to plan. Arkady was in charge of the CAP, and Rosenski was still down on the ground...and now Brooks was with her. He still couldn't imagine exactly why and was beginning to regret allowing her onto the base. At least without a reason. She'd been stationed there years ago, an incredibly green Third Lieutenant who'd stayed for a six-month rotation, put in for a transfer, and rotated back to Earth to fly Ravens. That had been about the time that a First Lieutenant Katsev had come into his own. Those two had built a weird relationship that went slightly beyond mere mentoring. He doubted they were sleeping together and even if they had been or were, as long as it didn't interfere with their jobs, there was no reason to stop it.

He shook his head. A Lurker and her escort Ravens flew in circles above the base, while two hundred battlers and twice as many engineers in Mk3 powered suits transferred all the equipment and supplies they could find. Brooks's discovery of the automated delivery system had been a godsend. They'd doubled their take in the past two hours. And work to repair the AMS-1's damaged fusion drive was finally under way. Chief Engineer Cox's report was optimistic. They could bring the fusion drive back online within a day and use twice the thrust as before. Still nowhere near the presumed optimal output but hell, it would get them to Earth in four days.

Back to Earth. What then? He switched displays to watch the feed from the U-Net channels. No one tried to deny the orbital ring's presence anymore. You could apparently see the damn thing in the sky from the equator now, a thin silver band that caught the sunlight in just the right way. Three months into its construction it was a fact of life, including two-mile-wide supports that sank deep into the planet's crust. OMP units were stationed at every one that intersected dry land, and surface carriers were deployed to watch the others, though whether it was to keep gawkers away or to keep what might be inside from emerging was still an open question. He'd been contacting UEF command on a near daily basis to demand instructions on how to proceed and been told to stand by for further orders. He'd been standing by for months. His crew was antsy, his officers were worried, and he did his best to project a resolute belief that they would get back, but that was all they had to work with.

Well, maybe three thousand tons of ammunition, spare parts, and building materials would ease their minds. It certainly eased his. There were greenhouses running full time all over the ship and the civilians assigned to Moon Base had built their own little town in the ship's hold. All the comforts of home including a dynamite Jazz club and a movie theater with fancy reclining seats. There was talk of opening restaurants if they could guarantee the food sources. Some fool even suggested they have a beauty pageant, but that was not going to happen. Although a ship-wide talent show might not be a bad idea…

The sensors watch officer signaled for his attention. "Captain? Deimos and Phobos…they're moving."

Rojetnick sipped his coffee. "They're moons. Of course they move."

"No, I mean Deimos is slowing down in its orbit, changing its trajectory. It's heading down."

"How is that possible?"

"I don't know…wait, yes I do. New sensor readings coming in now. They're detecting a series of plasma plumes over its horizon."

The tactical watch officer linked into the system and did some analysis of his own. "They put a mass driver on that rock…it's being pushed."

Rojetnick decided to get to the heart of the matter. "Where is it going to hit?"

"About a hundred miles away from us if it maintains its current course."

The Tactical Officer snorted. "Captain, it doesn't matter *where* it hits. That rock is twenty-two klicks in diameter. When it hits it'll cause shock waves all over the planet. This whole hemisphere will be wrecked."

"Estimated time to impact?"

"Ninety-three minutes."

Rojetnick nodded. "Recall every ground unit that's currently out. Let those without loads help out the ones with loads. Maintain the CAP. Contact Rosenski and Brooks tell them to come home."

"Sir. Lurker reports a new contact at 120 klicks out. And it's huge."

They brought up displays to show both the electronic contact and the visual camera feed. The reddish rocks were quivering, dust and sand driving upwards and through the thin atmosphere as the object drew closer. But there couldn't be much doubt as to what it was: a spaceship similar to those they'd been fighting. What interested Rojetnick was their decision to have the giant craft fly at NOE altitude, worming its way toward them like a two-mile-long metal snake.

"Time to arrival?"

Tactical reported. "They'll be here in minutes. We're already well within their weapon range."

"Then let's get some distance. Engineering, how soon can the fusion drive be restored to functionality?

The Engineering watch officer sounded morose. "Lieutenant Commander Cox reports at least half an hour. But using the fusion drive on the surface would destroy the base."

"What about the conventional rockets?"

"They'll function, but only enough to put it into a parabolic arc. Not enough fuel to achieve orbit."

Rojetnick wondered why they hadn't been making more fuel while they were grounded…liquid oxygen and hydrogen, what was the problem…when a new voice joined the crowd. "Captain. Lurker reporting numerous new contacts. The enemy ship is launching fighters and ground units."

Well. At least that made it simple. "We're stuck then. Continue recovery operations. Bring all ship to ship batteries and point defense lasers online. Launch all Ravens."

———

They found an elevator that would take them to the correct floor but it was slow. It arrived slowly, the doors opened more slowly. The delay between pushing the button and waiting for the doors close was nerve-wracking; the way the car drifted down made Rosenski want to chew her own teeth. She forced herself not to try to pry the doors open with her bare hands when they arrived. Brooks started looking for a console he recognized while she heard a quick beep and then a honk. An alarm was going off somewhere.

Brooks sat at a station and turned equipment on, his gloved hands grabbing each other in his lap while the gear booted. The first thing they heard was the network squawking with orders and instructions. Rosenski saw that she and Brooks were still hooked into the private channel and expanded her access to the command net. She wanted to talk to the Nightmare's comm guy. "Simmons, report. What's happening up there?"

Her answer was a series of clicks and pops, dropped syllables and word fragments. That was the trouble with shielding your base against EM hacks: you couldn't hear a damn thing on personal transmitters. She touched Brooks's shoulder. "Is there a feed to the surface?"

"Of course. But this gear isn't running to the same specs as the as AMS-1's network, which is why so much is being dropped." He reached over and popped a new bank of switches. A display lit up with a radar image. "We have company. A lot of it."

"I see that. Keep looking for those archives."

"I found them. Or the library where they live, anyway. But I don't recognize the index file structure or the command menu. And I don't have a flash chip big enough to copy everything. It'll take time to—"

"Time, we do not have. Here. Use this." She handed him a metal package with a lead.

He connected the drive and got to work. "You came prepared. What are you looking for?"

"Never you mind. I just need as much as you can copy."

"It'll take a while. It'll go faster if I use multiple channels to transfer the files. Will this drive do that?"

She blinked. It was a good question and she had no idea. "Try everything," she said. She didn't want him to ask more questions. He might ask why she was making a grab for the data in the first place and didn't feel eager to feed him a bullshit story about a lost relative she wanted to track down. She had such a story. She'd rehearsed it in front of a mirror more than once. She'd already lied to him once today and didn't see a need to dig herself any deeper into the hole.

"How did you end up in the U-Fleet?" she asked.

"I was there when *Ascension* crashed."

"You were there? On South Pico Island?"

"Heh. No. It appeared over the western hemisphere, and entered the atmosphere right over North America. It made a giant flash and one hell of a sonic boom. And that, we noticed. Made a fireball and a hissing, sizzling noise I will never forget."

"There's got to be more to it than that."

"What, you want a story?"

"Yes."

He sighed, and adjusted a knob on the console. The progress bars were a little more than half full. "Uncle and my dad started talking, and I listened. Dad insisted it was the biggest goddamn meteor ever recorded and Ray told him, no, that's no meteor. Meteors fall down out of the stratosphere. What we'd seen had come down low, over the horizon. Plus in hindsight what were the odds of a mile long object just happening to crash down on an island in the middle of nowhere? Later, the astronomers looked at the records and figured out that it had made a number of course corrections on the way down which meant it was a powered object.

"Anyway, the first ones who got to see this thing were the science guys. Once they figured out there was no radiation or god knows what they sent the military in. Ray was on that team but he never spoke about what he'd seen. Said it was classified for global security. You know the whole OMP was built just to keep that project under lock and key? Just getting an office job on South Pico Island took months of security clearances and background checks. But…"

"But?"

"But it was a bit later that we heard rumors. Project Avalon. And new forms of machine intelligence that solved a lot of the problems they'd experienced trying to design a functional model. It sounded exciting. So, I joined up. I might have gotten drafted eventually, but if you volunteered you got to choose your assignment. After I passed basic and got my commo engineer MOS squared away, Ray requested me for the Hornets. It seems each squadron is supposed to have a science nerd assigned to it but usually that gets satisfied with a medic or a technical specialist."

She stared. "You lucky bastard."

"Maybe. Stuck on an abandoned base on Mars with aliens breathing down our necks. Not sure how lucky that is."

"No, I mean your mentor wasn't a complete bastard who kept telling you to find your iron."

"I'd say you found yours. A great, deep mine of it."

She shrugged. "I really shouldn't complain. The Butcher's got his head on straight and he doesn't suffer fools at all, but if you can keep up with him, he'll stick his ass out for you. I owe him a lot."

They were close now. The top progress bar finished its crawl and the other three ran slightly faster now. The second one finished and Rosenski started to breathe more easily.

"How is the Butcher anyway?" Brooks asked. "There have been rumors about his health, but no one really knows much."

"He'll be back eventually," she said. "He got pretty badly chewed up leading us against the enemy flagship at Saturn. He never was good at picking his targets."

"Oh?"

"He has enemies. Political enemies. And that's all I can really tell you about it. How much longer do you think?"

"You tell me, you're his XO."

"No, I mean the files."

"Oh. Not long."

She nodded, even though he was focused on the controls. "Is there any weird shit regarding disconnecting this unit when it finishes? Anything a newbie would need to know?"

"Not really. The last bars will finish, it'll tell you the file transfer is complete, then you disconnect."

She nodded. "Good. I'll deal with that. You get to the CIC and bring the weapon batteries online. Let's slow our new friends down as much as we can."

"It'll turn the battle into a crossfire. Our planes and battlers will become targets for the base's weapons."

"There are protocols built into the system so they won't shoot friendly transponders. Make it happen."

"Yes, sir."

"And then I need you to get in your plane and get the hell out."

He froze. "No, sir."

"Good. Wait. What?"

"I said no sir. I'm not leaving you here."

"Are you refusing my orders, lieutenant?"

"Yes, sir. I am not leaving you here. That's final."

An explosion somewhere nearby shook the floor. If they could feel it this far down into the complex it must have done real damage to the surface.

Three bars done. The fourth was plodding along. It wouldn't be long now.

"Fine. Set up the base defense batteries and I'll be there shortly. Promise."

Brooks saluted and ran back the way they'd come. Rosenski sighed in relief when the doors finally closed. The last progress bar crept along and finally reached its goal. New screens came up asking if she wanted to finalize the data transfer and she selected YES. That done, she brought up a new screen and entered a code from a slip of paper she'd stuck in her flight suit pocket. U-Net IP addresses, half a dozen of them, plugged into a backup transmitter whose operation she'd rehearsed earlier along with her made up sob story about lost people.

She tried not to hurry. She had time. Brooks would do what he was told. But he'd never been at this base before, either. He had to get up to the CIC, find the right section, then locate the correct console. He needed to make sure the guidance links worked and that meant he'd need to figure out how to get the base's sensor suite up and running. Only then could he input the correct transponder filter and turn the weapons batteries on.

But she didn't have that much time. He was bright and focused, and he'd be done before long. In contrast her task was narrow as a rope bridge, but she had no clue how long it would take.

New screens alerted her to the fact that the main transmitter was a better way to transmit data. She overrode the warnings. The main transmitter would push the signal to the widest possible sub-network on the U-Net and that was the opposite of what she needed. She wanted only one IP range to see this information. Her orders had been very specific. If she couldn't figure it out in the next five minutes, she'd have to pull the drive and try sending the stream from the AMS-1 which was far riskier. One good thing about the situation: the main antenna was already aligned to a receiving array on Earth. She didn't need to re-align anything, and thank god, because she didn't know how.

SEARCHING FOR SUB-MASK NETS…

Another explosion shook the room. Lights flickered and died. She could feel the machinery thumping and whirring as emergency circuits came online…or what that just her imagination?

ANTENNA ALIGNED…BEGIN UPLOAD? Y/N

"Oh, for shit's sake… Yes!" she shouted, and jammed her fist against the button.

UPLOAD IN PROGRESS…

Another progress bar was her reward. At the same time her comm sputtered and skipped. She thought she could recognize Brooks' voice but the connection was so bad that she couldn't be sure. It didn't matter. The progress bar crawled to the right…forty percent…fifty…sixty…

She began to wonder just how long they had before the base was turned into shit, then a burst of static and the PA roared out an announcement: "FRAU BUTCHER, WE NEED TO LEAVE, NOW!"

Well. There it was. Eighty-seven percent…Ninety…

She finally realized that she needed to choose between making sure the transmission successfully completed or her life. If she waited to confirm the data, then perhaps a global injustice could be halted in its tracks and repaired. There were people willing and able to do the hard work it required. Dedicated folks with the right training and experience. She'd given her word.

Ninety-six percent, and the bar stagnated, seeming to take forever as the explosions deepened and grew louder, more frequent

Ninety-seven percent now.

With life, everything else was possible.

Fuck it. Choose life.

She jerked the drive out of the console and ran for the elevator as the floor shook again. She couldn't see the feed from the surface, but it was fuzzy and crowded. She punched the button for the elevator and fidgeted as she waited for the car to arrive, even more slowly than before if that was even possible. She turned to look at the display again, could barely make out the number: ninety-eight…ninety-nine…

The doors slid open and she punched the button. But as the doors slid closed, she could see a red light on the console she'd left.

UPLOAD FAILED… TRY AGAIN? Y/N

"God dammit…!"

The elevator rose at its glacial pace and the floor lights pinged in sequence. 5, 4, 3, 2…. Then the entire base shook like a giant had stomped a booted foot onto the ground. The car shook, the floor lights sputtered and died and the elevator ground to a halt.

She tapped her comm. "Brooks, this is Nightmare leader, where are you?"

Nothing but cut syllables and dashed out words.

"Brooks, I'm stuck in the elevator. Do you copy?"

Silence.

Then a giant stomped into the base and the lights went out.

[17]

BROOKS WAITED ANXIOUSLY AS THE ELEVATOR ROSE THROUGH THE floors. He couldn't help but look around. There were no escape hatches and the doors were doubly sealed; if all else failed the car would double as a relatively airtight container. If the base were hulled right this second, he'd be able to survive for at least a while on bottled air until help came. But how would anyone know he was even down here? Frau Butcher was his only contact for the moment.

The doors opened and he slid out to wind his way through the CIC's assortment of consoles. The commo pit was aptly named, a sunken crew station with countless different controls scattered across a dozen consoles. Powering up the station was easy. Getting a channel to the AMS-1's bridge was more complicated, but he could see the lines that routed the feeds from the ship into the base's main computer. He patched consoles...and watched, leaning forward as the world it showed caught fire around him. He had a plan of sorts and it wasn't that different from what he'd described to Rosenski. First establish communications with the AMS-1. He knew the bridge's frequency range by heart these days, he'd spent so much time hanging out with Amir. That would be…here!

A hundred channels poured their contents, voices and visual data, onto one set of displays while the electronic data swelled and spilled over onto a new set of screens. *Ascension* was going toe to toe with a huge alien ship while hundreds of rollers and fighters wove through Raven and battler formations.

He got back to himself just as a barrage of missiles slammed into Pad 3 on the other side of the base. The ground shook and the CIC trembled. He remembered Rosenski's orders: program the transponder codes, light up the weapon batteries, and let them pick their targets.

Well and good. It might work if the sensor array was still operational and if the fire control system could still pull data from it and if the turrets still worked…too many things to worry about.

First things first. He ran to a weapon station, another sunken platform alive with LEDs and viewing surfaces. The feed controls were…here?... no, here! Now, set up the data linkage from sensor array to weapons stations, and the fire control became active. He slapped another bank of switches and the transponder filters were in place. He leaned forward, pressed a new bank of buttons, and…

And nothing happened. He'd forgotten something. What? *What?*

A new set of tremors got him in gear. He visually swept the consoles again then saw the bank of darkened screens.

Stupid! He'd forgotten to turn the bloody sensor array on after warming it up. There!

He could practically hear the whine of the array mechanism as it began to swing the giant radar vane atop the base in its circular rotation. He selected the widest band possible, so that everyone in the world would see what his computer did. He even figured out how to open a feed to Lieutenant Hart's flight ops panel. If nothing else, it would show the bridge bunnies that he and Frau Butcher were still alive.

Fuck. Sara. He tapped his comm and called out. "Rosenski, I've got the array lit up, but it won't be long before someone zeroes in on it and we take a beating. Are you ready to leave?"

Nothing but static and broken words met his inquiry. He tried again, then a third time with the same results. "Lieutenant? Sara?"

He got to his feet, scanned the consoles one last time to make sure he couldn't improve on the situation and ran up the stairs to the command platform, a sequestered command and control area where the bigwigs were meant to sit and give orders. He had an idea that no self-respecting CINC would allow his system to go silent if he could help it. That meant a base-wide communication channel and that meant a public address system. Which would be…here…

He flipped a switch, bent over a microphone. "FRAU BUTCHER, WE NEED TO LEAVE, NOW!"

This would be a great story for the future generations of Brookses. What did you do in the big space war, Grandad? Well, climb up here my dude and lemme tell you about that time when I ran myself ragged trying to run an entire command post by my own self while the crew of the AMS-1 fought bravely to leave Mars and return to Earth. You see, my superior officer was stuck in the elevator…

Shit. The elevator. If she was coming up she'd have to come that way. He ran back down the stairs, found the security station and looked for the internal sensors. There had to be a way to limit the scans just for infrared…there, heat sensors. Internal. On.

A schematic of the base appeared but only showed by a single screen at a time. He spent precious seconds flipping pages online looking for the display of the command tower. There. Zoom in: and there they were. Two red dots as expected. His was in the command center and hers was…

In the god damn elevator. At least she was on her way back.

Marissa Hart's contralto voice emerged from the communications console: "Lieutenants Rosenski and Brooks, there's a wave of missiles inbound to your location. You have to leave now!"

That was it. He rushed to the elevator as another near hit shook the ground and a handful of consoles went dark. Not the weapons batteries, though. Those were firing rapid-fire lasers at whatever didn't match the UEF transponder codes. And he hoped drawing fire from friendly targets.

The doors were closed, and he pushed the button only to see the display was dark. The button stayed dark. He searched the tube for emergency controls and saw nothing. No car releases, no escape hatches, nothing.

He tapped his comm. "Rosenski, are you in there? Hello? Look I'm going to get you out...I'll be right there."

Another explosion. This time lights shook and broken molding drifted down from the upper gantries and ceiling. He could even look up and see it, a crack the length of the room running through the aluminum lining of the roof. He could hear the air hissing out and a steam pipe had ruptured in one of the walls.

But the elevator car was sealed. And even if it wasn't, her suit was environmentally sealed. He had an idea. Stupid and desperate, but an idea nonetheless.

Once he was outside the airlock his comm channel erupted with sound. He chose the command feed and spoke out as he climbed into his Raven's cockpit and brought his plane to life. "*Ascension*, this is Brooks. Rosenski is trapped inside the base. I'm going to bring her out and rejoin the *Ascension*."

Hart nearly screamed at him. "Brooks! Missiles are inbound to your position…twenty seconds to impact."

Twenty seconds? How long had they been down there? His plane was already in Walker mode which helped. He bought the turbines to speed, positioned the arms and the can opener fingers to tear into the fragile metal structure. He pulled the airlock away and felt rather than heard a massive *whump* as the building depressurized, the rush of air forcing him backwards. He killed the engines and idled the jets and he walked the plane forward. He swung the plane's arms in a wide circle to make a hole wide and tall enough for his ship to pass through, grabbing and wrecking everything in his path. He turned his lights on found the elevator tube and used both hands to gingerly peel the metal away from the elevator car. He used the external camera to look for the thin metal box and found it deeper in the shaft than he'd have liked but at least he knew where it was.

"Brooks! Ten seconds!"

"Almost there," he said. He found the cable brace, pulled straight up as gently as he could and wiggled the elevator car free. He set the box down, pulled on the walls and the car popped open as the seals gave way. Rosenski half-fell, half-climbed free and Brooks closed his metal hands around her to shield her from the blast.

Is was only then that he noticed that his Raven's hands had square fingers. Not the old style round ones. He was in a VMR-1B. "Square fingers are good for picking things up," he mused.

He flexed his limbs to wriggle the plane back through the hole he'd made and brought the engines to full power, then turned on the afterburners for good measure. He felt the kick of added thrust…and then felt the WHUMP as a volley of alien missiles crashed into the base itself, turning the facility into a fiery wreck, pushing a shockwave in all directions. Red dust surrounded him as the plane tumbled, and he strained to right it and point it in the right direction.

Finally, the Raven emerged from the cloud of red dust and gray smoke. Now he could see the *Ascension* rising on its own column of flame, the conventional drives pushing it skyward.

Alien fighters surrounded it like wasps, still swooping across its bow and stern. Looking for easy shots. He swerved the plane around the nose of the giant ship, jinking and jerking to keep them out of any pursuer's line of sight. How any fighter or roller might decide to pick him out of the chaos was a subject for another time. As he bore closer to *Ascension's* hull he could see battlers standing on her deck, trying to pick enemy fighters out of the sky. And more often than not being shattered by alien pilots who were better or possibly just luckier than the humans were today.

He brought the plane to a bouncy landing near a surface elevator and winced as the space around them became a brilliant red flare. The fusion drive lighting up, he assumed.

The last thing he saw through the canopy as the shaft closed over him was the flaring mountain of Deimos slamming into Mars.

[18]

Sara "Frau Butcher" Rosenski fell out of Simon Brooks's mechanical hands and into a hospital bed with a dislocated kneecap.

Brooks wasn't sure how much of the accident was his fault. Cupping her body in his fighter's robot hands her as he brought his Raven back to the AMS-1 was surely not a standard way of transporting passengers. The way her suit had forcibly equalized pressure when he'd peeled her out of the sealed elevator probably didn't help. And he'd dropped her rather than set her down on the deck as the plane stopped on a transfer pad on the hangar deck. She'd lost her balance, taken the hit to her right knee and screamed. He'd never heard a sound that angry and desperate in his life.

In any case, she was off her feet for a while and he felt like shit for it.

One bit of good news, he thought as he made his way to the hospital in the cavernous cargo bay: the fusion drive was living up to the hype. They'd be in low Earth orbit inside of three days. The constant rumble of the deck plates beneath his feet gave him hope that once they were home Hornet squadron could look forward to a bit of rest. Or at least normalcy.

He needed to see her. An apology was warranted, a big one. He felt the need to bring a gift, but flowers were trite and fancy chocolate was too suggestive, not that he could find either at the ship's various shops.

He settled for lunch, courtesy of Petty Officer Second Class Rodriguez who listened to his description of the incident, shooed him away for hours, and finally handed him a triple stacked set of metal tins. "Just give this to your blanquita and all will be forgiven. Or at least not get any worse."

He hefted the parcel. A stack of aluminum tins with a carrying handle. Surprisingly heavy. "She's not that blanca, you know."

Rodriguez snorted. "*You're* not that blanco. That woman is mayonnaise on white bread with a trimmed crust. Trust me, man, I know what I'm doing."

"If she hits me on the head with this thing, I'm coming back for your *pendejo* ass."

"Challenge accepted. Get going."

Deck seven was given over to the AMS-1's medical annex. The hospital looked like any other, if any other hospital was a mere two stories tall. But it managed to present the crew with eight hundred beds, enough doctors, nurses, and orderlies to manage a full house around the clock. The bad news was that the recent hostilities ensured that the facility was rarely less than full.

Rosenski's room was a private one. The door was open and Brooks could hear a low murmur of conversation as he got close. Part of him felt like turning around and heading back down the hallway, but the squeak of a chair sliding across a metal floor pushed him forward. He rounded the door to see Commander Thomas Katsev, the Butcher himself, sitting on a rolling chair the wrong way, his arms crossed over the chair's back, holding her hand and grinning. Rosenski grinned back. She even giggled.

They looked up as Brooks entered and the moment ended. He stood to attention and saluted to normalize the situation. "Commander Katsev. I wanted to see how Lieutenant Rosenski was faring, sir."

"Lieutenant Brooks," Katsev said, returning the salute after a moment. He was a tall thin man with a graying blonde crew cut and an eye patch over the right side of his face, too small to cover all the scars. Jesus, so many scars. "Good to see you here. I'm wondering when you plan on transferring to the Specters. Even the Nightmares. A man like you could do well in either squadron."

"I'm…flattered that you think so, Commander," Brooks stammered. Of all the responses he expected, an offer to transfer wasn't among them.

"It's not flattery, merely the truth. Your talents are wasted in Hornet Squadron. I respect Fairchild and Arkady but they have no idea what to do with you. At any rate, please think it over. We reward ambition in the Specters."

He noticed Rosenski's face drop just a bit at the comment. Disappointment? "Yes, sir. I will definitely consider it."

"Don't wait too long. Once we get home things are going to happen quickly." With that he nodded back to Rosenski and left.

"You can lower your hand and sit down whenever you like," Rosenski said.

He dropped his arm but couldn't help but turn around to look at the open door. "I feel like I've just fallen into the deep end of the swimming pool. What just happened?"

"You heard him," she said. "Sounds clear enough to me. If you ever think Arkady isn't valuing your contribution, come look him up."

"But…why me?"

"Brooks. I thought you were smarter than that." She shifted in bed and continued. "Look, I've been helping Katsev poach talent from other parts of the Icarus for months. He wants the best people in his squadron. I point him to solid candidates. Personally, I'd like to have you in the Nightmares. That's all there is to it."

"After I fucked your knee up? You still think so?"

"Meh. Shit happens. What'd you bring? Lunch? Dinner? Six pounds of chocolate covered cherries?"

"I thought candy would be a little too forward," he said.

"Not those. Especially not the kind with the gooey centers. God, I'd kill for those."

He set the stack of tins on her lap and sat down, letting her work the latch while he sat in the rolling chair. The medical staff had immobilized her knee and wrapped a set of ice packs around the knee brace. He decided not to mention the injury unless she did. "I called in a favor from my culinary specialist. I think you'll find it a refreshing change from hospital food."

She popped the lid off and peered inside, cooing as she broke the stack apart. "Oooooo," she breathed. "Brooks, you're not a scumbag after all."

"Jeez, thanks."

She leaned back in her pillow and made a face. "After you dropped me on the deck and bumped my knee, I'm allowed to call you a name or two."

"I'm not sure if I dropped you or you fell."

"Probably a bit of both," she admitted. "The kneecap was dislocated. Lucky for you, they popped it back and all I have to manage is the swelling. If the knee had taken the impact I'd be out of action for up to a year while they did surgery and lots of physical therapy. A kneecap is a simpler fix. I won't lie: being grounded for at least two weeks while my knee heals sucks. But you did rip apart a building to save my ass from a missile attack, so I should say thank you. As apologies go, this is impressive as hell."

He allowed himself to breathe. She pulled plates and dishes

from the tins and arranged them on her hospital bed. A pot of tea with a miniature porcelain cup, two blueberry scones with tiny jars of cream and jam, a croissant sandwich with cheese and a ruffle of lettuce, a dish of sliced kielbasa on a bed of sauerkraut, and another small tin with a variety of cookies perfectly packed inside. He owed Rodriguez a drink. A lot of drinks.

She rested her hands in her lap and stared at the display for a long moment, a smile creeping up her lips. "This is beautiful. An apology worth a damn. I approve."

He managed to relax his shoulders. He hadn't been aware he was so tense. And he blanched as he realized he was sitting on the chair the exact same way Katsev had. Why was he so nervous? It wasn't like this was a date or anything. "I'm glad."

"Seriously, Brooks. Who's your friend? Does he do catering?"

"I'm not about to give up my network to you or anyone else."

"Your choice." She nibbled the sandwich, washed it down with a bit of tea and looked up, all serious. "Katsev is right. You handled yourself like a pro on Mars, and without your mates, too. I didn't expect that."

"No? You're the one who called me to join you down there."

"Because I needed someone who knew electronics. I'm not used to thinking of you as a soldier."

"Why not? Water carriers can be soldiers."

She frowned and dropped her eyes for a moment. "Yeah, that was a bad choice of phrasing. When I said that, I was thinking about your initiative, not your skill set. You're a top notch commo officer, that was obvious when Amir pulled you onto the bridge and you did the job without freaking out."

"You heard about that?"

"The whole ship has heard that by now. A lot of people refuse to believe it. Some bastards even call you a point." She shrugged. "But I believe it. And you're no point. I just wish you'd managed to save my plane."

She was a puzzle. Her voice was soft but her eyes were hard. And the gripe about her plane wasn't wrong. He really hadn't thought about the expensive aircraft, just her. But there hadn't been time to— "You're trying to rile me so that I'll leave in a huff. Just tell me to go and I will. I have paperwork to finish and a six-man section to drill."

"I know. Sorry, I'm in a lot of pain. I'm out one plane, and I'm told a Raven-B won't be available for at least five weeks, but since I'm looking at months of recovery from your half-assed rescue, that works out nicely."

"It was a whole-assed rescue, thank you, sir." He stood and made a show of saluting. "Permission to go, Ma'am?"

She snorted. "Dismissed. Thanks for lunch."

———

He dove into his work, and he hadn't lied. The squad was his responsibility, both paperwork and training wise. He let Arkady do most of the desk work while he kept up the daily schedules and supervised simulator time for the pilots. What little free time he had he spent thumbing through screens and audio recordings the bridge crew previously made of the alien language. The scheduling was problematic for hm: the ship's library closed in the evening, and while the ward room was open it would be deserted after hours except for a coffee urn, and he didn't want to be totally alone. The general mess however wasn't very busy at this time of night and was still serving food. The perfect combination. He got himself a bowl of what they called vegetable chili and a glass of bug juice and found a table. He ignored the looks, whispers, and occasional sneers from the NCOs. Whatever. His record would either speak for itself or it wouldn't.

He sat working on his slate when Amir came in. "Lieutenant."

"Chief. Will you sit?"

"Thank you, sir." She put down a tray of what would have been mac and cheese anywhere else. Green juice in a glass bottle. And a black and white cookie the size of a saucer.

"You've been busy," she said as she unrolled a napkin and flatware. "I'm glad you remember to eat."

"Never miss a chance to be useful, is what Fairchild says. So I'm being useful. Crazy language studies from the aliens. Midnight snack for you?" he asked.

"I do two night shift a week. Everyone on the bridge does. Except the Captain, who is always either on watch or on call."

"He needs an XO to take up the slack."

"I agree but he hasn't chosen one yet, and I'm not going to force the issue. Hart was on last night; she wanted to know if you've made any progress with the alien language."

"It sounds like German," he noticed. "Like, if German had way more hissing, throat gargles, and mouth clicks. It didn't take a huge amount of work to figure out that the message we heard on the bridge way back when was an announcement. 'Factories are being deployed.' Something like that. Lots of glottal stops and hard consonants. Four vowels that I've noted so far."

She cracked the bottle and took a sip. "Do you think you could learn to speak it?"

"Possibly. But I'd need way more material than a few phrases. Do you think you can talk the captain into letting me at the files we've gathered?"

"Nope. You are."

"I'm what?"

She jammed a fork full of food into her mouth and spoke around the chewing. "You're going to get called to the bridge tomorrow. I'll see to it you get your chance to explain what you've done. You make your case, I approve you for additional work and you get access to what we have in the Comm department."

"It can't be that easy. You don't have anyone else? Someone better qualified?"

"Better qualified, how? No one else has shown any success in cracking the task. You're it. Plus, you have a freaky imagination and you're good at thinking abstractly." She paused to take a bite from her cookie, made a face, and set it down. "Besides, Rojetnick hasn't said a word about you since you served a shift as communications officer. I want him to see that you've grown. Your bars. Your combat action ribbon."

He leaned back and crossed his arms. "And it wouldn't hurt to say you mentored me into a proper officer when promotion time comes around. Right?"

She jammed a forkful of food in her mouth and chewed as if it were the tastiest meal in the world. "Mrmf scrmf, mmrf," she agreed, nodding.

"Right. Can't talk, eating," he mumbled. "All right, I'll do it. But once we get home I want permanent clearance for all things related to the aliens."

"That, I can't do. Anything that requires the bigwigs' permission at OMP HQ is well away from my wheelhouse."

"Well, I'm going to ask you for some damn favor at some point and I'll want you to remember this moment."

"You can't threaten me, I'm a department head, even if you are my superior officer. But you can always ask for a favor. I may even say yes."

"Thank you, Chief."

"Thank you, Lieutenant."

———

The call came soon enough. Ray Fairchild rode up with Brooks in the elevator that led to the bridge. "I want you to take the transfer," he said.

"What transfer?"

"The one the Butcher offered you."

Brooks blinked as he wondered if he was being tested or set up. It was the last thing that he'd ever expect any Hornet member to say to him much less his own mentor. "You have got to be kidding. It's a joke, right? Where's the hidden camera?"

"Not a joke, Simon. I'm dead serious. And there are cameras in the ceiling but no audio, so try not to jump around while we talk."

"Well, you'd better damn well tell me what's going on, then."

"The Butcher has friends. Big friends, the kind of bastards who hate the Office of Military Protocols and would like it if the OMP officially crashed and burned. They have allies in U-Fleet Command. It wouldn't take much to push that rock off the cliff. We'd all get crushed on the way down. I'm looking to save a few people before that happens."

"I don't understand."

"Yes, you do. Remember the Laynies? There's a lot of them in the military. In the OMP, in the general staff. In the Cabinet."

He thought back to the discussion that he and Rosenski had on Mars Base. She'd been looking for military files. She'd even volunteered to look for files. Hard connections, classified archives. She'd never said what for and she clearly didn't like the OMP…

No, Couldn't be. Change the subject. "You think Katsev is a Laynie?"

"If he isn't, he will be soon. I know he has contacts there. Which means they're learning about this ship and the people who serve aboard her. Once we get home, some of these fine folks will be recruited."

"People like me."

Fairchild sighed. "Very much so. If you're in, you'll have a voice. If you have a voice, you'll have some influence. If you have influence you can inform. Maybe even maneuver. That is pure gold."

"I can't stop an avalanche."

"No. But you can save as many people as you can. That's worth something. Fuck it, that's huge."

"I don't know…"

"Simon. Do you want the Laynies to get unlimited access to the technology this ship represents?"

"No. What about you? Where will you be?"

"Katsev was offered a post on Colonel Hendricks' staff. Two days after he said yes, I was offered a staff job with the Air Group Commander of the North American Sector. We both leave the ship but we both get to influence policy in our own ways."

"So someone at HQ is recruiting for the U-Fleet as well."

"I think so. The coaches are picking their teams. Look, I can't make you say yes. It'd be dangerous as hell and it would kill some of your career prospects, but it would open up other possibilities for long term damage control. Think about it."

The elevator car opened and the guards at the end of the hall stood at attention as they crossed onto the bridge and saluted. Captain Rojetnick stood to the side, noticing them as they approached. "Commander Fairchild, Lieutenant Brooks. I thought you two might appreciate a look at this, now that we're approaching Earth."

As Brooks walked further onto the bridge he noted that it seemed more spacious than it had when he'd sat in the flight ops watch officer's chair. He glanced over to that station to note a face he didn't recognize, a brunette with Petty Officer First Class insignia on her sleeve. Her voice sounded familiar…but then he'd heard a thousand voices and coming through speakers they all sounded familiar after a while. He more easily spotted the welds where holes had been patched and equipment replaced.

The viewscreen showed a closeup of the ring, now a solid

band of metal encircling the planet. The detail was fine enough that they could see where each module fit perfectly into the network of modules surrounding it: vast interlocking combination of parts. Brooks could see protrusions on the hull, too: bubbles, blisters, domes, towers. How the hell had it even built itself was Brooks's real question. The planet beneath it was still recognizably home, but massive storms and dust clouds raged across its surface. One could make out the hint of ocean beneath the clouds but the continents were thoroughly obscured.

"God in heaven." He wasn't aware that he'd spoken until the captain answered him.

"All we know for certain is that no human has figured out how to get inside the structure," Rojetnick said. "I was hoping that you could help remedy that situation, Lieutenant."

"Yes, sir. I've been working on the alien's language. I think I can learn to translate it if I had access to the transmission logs."

"Chief Amir agrees with you. But I think you can do better."

"Sir?"

Rojetnick turned to face him. He was a tall man, several inches taller than Fairchild, weathered, broad shouldered, and bearded. He towered over Brooks. "I need you to figure out how to get inside the ring, Mr. Brooks. Then you can translate all you want."

He bobbed his head once. Time to shine or fall on his face. "Captain, I have an idea. Why don't we head to the latitude where South Pico Island lies. That's the safest route to whatever happens next."

"Interesting idea, but why there? Explain your reasoning."

"The ship was right over South Pico Island when it first deployed its cargo containers. We can assume that those modules were incredibly advanced nanofactories, some kind of machine that was programmed to build this ring. It's the same location this ship made an effort to land on. There were course corrections involved in its descent. Right, Uncle?"

"That is true."

"Captain, I think the ship's computer chose that landing point for a reason. And I think if there's a main control center it'll be right over that island."

"Perhaps." Rojetnick glared. "If you're wrong, then we either slam into the ring at twenty thousand miles per hour or we're annihilated by those destroyers. Either way, this ship is going down. If you're wrong."

"Yes, sir. I'm not wrong."

"We shall see." They returned to the bridge and Rojetnick gave orders without missing a beat. "Lieutenant Meng, come to a synchronous course above South Pico Island. Mr. Spalding, prepare for docking."

"Captain, we have three new targets approaching from the far side of the Earth on an intercept course. ETA, fifteen minutes."

"Not surprising; they've been pacing us for days. Of course they knew we were coming home. Spalding, let's keep the planet between us as much as possible. Keep our tail pointed to them. The plasma flow might keep them concerned enough to keep them from getting too close."

"Yes, sir."

"Multiple targets…missiles, inbound!"

Rojetnick shook his head. "So much for that idea. Maintain orientation, bring all point defense and weapon batteries online. All heavy weapons target the approaching ships and fire at will."

Suddenly the bridge was awash in alien hissing. *"Dekken rekett anzekiss. Dekken manzinget inaktzen."*

"Mr. Brooks? Tell me you understood that!"

"If I had to guess, I'd say we're docking with the ring, Captain."

The visuals seemed to bear his opinion out: even from this

distance they could see activity taking place on the ring. Tiny vehicles flew out of recessed ports in a cloud of activity while a pair of massive doors split the hull. The docking bay was immense. Red lamps glowed in a repeating pattern, showing them the way inside.

The ship shuddered as a panel of red lights began to glow blue. "*Genukh kinzekk anzekissen.*"

Spalding glanced backward toward the big chair. "Sir, guidance is changing our course. I can't make any changes of my own."

"Let it happen," Brooks murmured.

Rojetnik agreed. "All hands, assume neutral controls. It's not like we have a choice."

"Not after we've trusted our lives to a piece of alien technology for three months, right?" Fairchild added.

The bridge shook as new salvos from the closing destroyers exploded around *Ascension.* The shaking rattled them all, knocking the crew in their harnesses until the effect abated and finally stopped

Tactical Officer Matheson spoke up from his station. "Energy surge at 185 relative."

Rojetnick turned his head to see the young officer peering intently at his display. "What now? Weapons?"

"No, sir... it's a barrier of some kind." He matched up an external view with the visual display. A set of thin blue beams were being projected from the outermost surface of the ring, racing past the AMS-1 and forming a circular disk. Missiles were exploding against it as the ship continued its course toward the ring. "The ring is shielded from the blasts."

Rojetnick turned to spear Brooks in a glare before returning his attention to his officers. "I didn't know we had shields on this ship."

"We don't. The ring is projecting a shield behind us."

Fairchild grinned. "I'm starting to like this."

Brooks nodded. "Beats being dead."

The destroyers finally grew desperate enough to try something new. Each ship cracked its forward hull, revealing a new weapon. The hull separated into quarters showing just enough mechanism to reveal a gaping maw lined with snapping energy flows like jaws sporting electric teeth. The display brightened and each ship projected a stream of pure energy, three streams of light blasting the space around the AMS-1. The barrier held, glowing red then orange than white as it absorbed the attacks.

The ring responded with some fury of its own. Sections of hull opened to display its own gun ports, which let loose with torrents of red light. The streams met the destroyers and dissolved their hulls like fire melting wax candles. The three ships blew apart, and even the cloud of shrapnel bounced off the shield.

"I definitely like our new friends," Brooks said.

Fairchild folded his arms. "Friends might be premature. I'll be happy if we can call them neighbors."

As the AMS-1 closed the last few kilometers to the docking bay, they observed a storm of activity. Flights of small craft were departing the ring now, heading to the cloud of wreckage. If they strained they could see pincers grabbing bits of metal, dragging them into a holding bay and heading to the next bit of detritus.

"They recycle everything," Rojetnick noted, "even their own dead."

"That's efficient."

The AMS-1 finally slowed to a crawl and then stopped with the muffled clang of metal hitting metal. More clangs throughout the hull as robotic clamps reached out and found the hull, securing it to the platform as the massive doors closed behind them.

"Genukh lekkt va reppenziklen. Hemmekenvemmen."

"Welcome home," Brooks reported. "It said welcome home."

[19]

"Thank you for reporting so quickly, Lieutenant Brooks. Now, would you like to tell us how you knew that the bridge computer was saying 'Welcome home?'"

Commander Elise Cox and Dr. Emillio Langston returned Brooks's salute and offered him a chair. The chair was anything but a comfort. His orders to report to the Chief Engineer and the Director of Research had been an order. He obeyed and was happy to do so but if they were trying to make him feel comfortable they were doing it wrong.

"Relax, Lieutenant. We just want some information, nothing crazy," Cox said. She settled into a chair of her own, a metal table between the two of them. Langston stood back, allowing her to work. She flipped open a paper notebook, tapped a pen twice, and held it over the paper, her eyes meeting his. "Answer Doctor Langston's question. No one on board can speak or understand Sleer…except for you. What do you know?"

"I guessed, sir."

Cox blinked. "Guessed? There's no guessing in engineering, son. Either you know a thing is true, you know a thing isn't true, or you don't know. If you're bullshitting us, you'd best say so now. Before you cost everyone on board this ship their lives."

"Commander," Langston said. He had a slow delivery, almost a drawl that suggested his English was a second or third language but too vague for Brooks to place. "We don't want to scare him."

"Too late, sirs," Brooks blurted.

"What are you scared of, Lieutenant?" Langston asked.

"Being wrong, mostly." Paused. He took a deep breath and pushed forward. "Call it a sensitivity to tone if you want. That's what the phrase sounded like to me. Welcome home."

Langston touched Cox's shoulder and they switched places. Now she stood apart, arms folded, burning anger in her eyes and he sat with the pen in his hand. Somehow Brooks found that arrangement even more troubling. Langston wasn't the problem. Brooks could manage the scientist's cautious attitude and even the funny accent. But Langston's eyes scared him. Hard points of light as if some demon had moved in behind them and peered out through the good doctor's corneas. He had a way of looking at you and through you somehow. If there was anyone on board the AMS-1 who could see into your soul in the hard physical sense, it was this guy.

Brooks took deep breath, let it out and began, "Months ago. We were building a replica of Moon Base in the hold. While we worked we were finding all kinds of things. The ship's new configuration opened up a maze of passageways, rooms, and compartments that were never mapped. I wandered into a room that seemed empty but with control stations scattered around. I found a panel with an open lead. It was sparking, so I figured fixing it was a thing to be done. I brushed up against the lead, and got a jolt. Then I looked up and all I could see were stars. Stars everywhere. A full display of our arm of the galaxy. I was sure it only lasted a few moments so when my vision cleared, I repaired the exposed lead, closed up the panel and got back to my work order. The First Sergeant wanted to know where I'd been for the last two hours. I told him I got lost. He threatened to put me on report if it happened again and I got back to work.

"Ever since then I've been finding…I don't know…clues, I guess…about how the ship works. It's like the ship is giving me hints. It's like when the ship made that announcement before it deployed those factories. I knew what it was saying but I couldn't figure out how I knew. It's not just a proclivity for languages. Which, I happen to have."

"Do you think this has happened elsewhere?"

"I don't see why not. I can't be the only one who's reported these hints. I'd start checking the ship's departmental logs. Gotta be someone like me out there."

"We will see," Langston murmured and began scribbling like a madman. Brooks had no idea what the language was and didn't care. "I think we can use you, Lieutenant Brooks. We have been secured inside this megastructure and for whatever reason the Captain and his bridge crew cannot imagine how to get us out of the ship. Although it stands to reason that any structure that can berth a ship should be able to manage to launch it again, don't you think?"

"That stands to reason, sir."

"You better believe it does, Brooks," said Cox. The woman's brown eyes were the same shade as her skin, he noticed. Streak of iron gray ran through her hair, too. The woman took no shit from anyone. "Do you think that if you were part of a recon mission the Captain is putting together, you could contribute? That's our question."

"Yes, sir!"

"Then you shall have that chance. We will speak to Captain Rojetnick about you," Langston said. "Dismissed."

Brooks saluted and practically ran from the interview room.

He found the industrial setting of the engineering deck positively refreshing in contrast.

————

The next three days passed in a blur.

A meeting of department heads in Rojetnick's ready room was far more exciting than Brooks expected but also less than he'd planned for. Katsev was attending as CAG and Fairchild as Deputy CAG. Fairchild's orders were specific: Brooks was a records management liaison, not a member of the lead science team, and they were including him despite his earlier performance on the bridge, not because of it. He should sit, take notes on his slate, provide background information if asked and only speak when spoken to.

The arguing began quickly, with Fairchild insisting that he needed to try to contact U-Fleet HQ for orders while Katsev insisted just as vociferously that now that they were inside the alien and possibly hostile structure, they had to send out military patrols to see what they were dealing with. Communications were down, the bay they were sequestered in was apparently using robots to peck and probe at the hull of the ship. Worse, they'd heard reports from crew all over the ship that strange robots were now wandering around *inside* the AMS-1, doing the same to internal systems. Whatever controlling machinery the new orbital ring contained might be repairing it or might be doing something else. There was simply no way to know without direct observation.

Rojetnick didn't see the possibilities as mutually exclusive and made the final decision. They would keep trying to contact HQ and also send a few teams out into the ring to see whether a control station could be located and if so, utilized to fix their communication problem.

The good news was that Brooks would be on the first team out. The bad news was that there wouldn't be any war machines involved. They'd be in teams of four in a dozen wheeled vehicles with research equipment and small arms, and that was that. Rojetnick had been plain: no team was to take any provocative action. They were permitted to defend themselves but that was all.

As an added sop to Katsev, Sara Rosenski would be riding in Brooks's vehicle. She'd been released from sick bay the previous morning and while she was banned from returning to a Raven or Battler, she could walk with a cane well enough. She hobbled over to his vehicle, where he waited. The convoy of troop carriers was ahead of them and waiting made more sense than trying to find her. She straightened, and folded up her cane before setting it on the dash.

"We're late. You want to drive?" Brooks asked her.

"Trick question," she said. "Ask me this: do I want to sit and be chauffeured around? Or do I want to be your chauffeur?" She shrugged. "Fuck it. Yes, I'm driving. You get to navigate, shoot, and man the radio. Take pictures and anything else you can think of that might prove useful later." She settled behind the wheel, pushed the starter, and the engine purred to life.

They were sitting in a more durable vehicle than a mere truck. This was an AFV-30, a mid-sized wheeled armored fighting vehicle. An armored box on the right side of the hood held a 20mm cannon that could blast HEAP rounds at a rate of 750 per minute and could punch a hole through the skin of a Raven if used by a skilled gunner. There wasn't a great deal of room inside the cab and the space between them was snug. The real supplies were held in an enclosed compartment behind then that doubled as cargo storage and passenger area.

"It doesn't matter to you that we're sitting in the equipment truck?" he asked, to distract himself from her dense, earthy scent.

"*Really?*"

"Really. We haul all the gear for everyone else. At least we get to carry the ammo cases."

"I'm stunned. This is my stunned face," she mused. "At least you don't stink. You did bathe today, right?"

"I did, and thank you for noticing." Pause. "Wait, did you just make a pass at me?"

"I did not. I merely appreciate proper hygiene."

"You should have been a doctor."

"I hate the sight of blood."

"You…what?"

She smiled brightly. He was amazed her face didn't break on the spot. "I swear to god. That's why I wanted to fly. If I explode in mid-air, I don't see my own guts falling out of the plane. On the ground, though. Gah. I made a royal mess of my phlebotomy class."

She pulled out of the cargo bay, following the rest of the convoy forward through the wide corridors of the AMS-1. She used the hand throttle badly, and wasn't out of the habit of using her foot to pump a gas pedal. She even got lost once or twice, but Brooks used the nav slate to get her back on track.

"You're a complicated woman, Frau Butcher, did you know that?"

"I'm pretty basic, actually. If they ever make a movie about me it'll be called 'Eat, Sleep, Fly.' Okay, where is the freakin' airlock?"

Brooks checked his slate. Unlike the unknown of the ring, they had accurate maps of most of *Ascension's* corridors and compartments. "Next right, then a left, through a set of blast doors and there we are."

She followed instructions and pulled up to the waiting column of utility vehicles. "Bob's your uncle," she confirmed.

Katsev stalked to them with crossed arms and a scowl.

"Rosenski, Brooks, how good of you both to finally join us. From now on you stay with the class."

They nodded. The Butcher was in a foul mood and this was not the hill they wanted to die on. "Yes, sir!" they echoed.

The platoon grouped up around the lead vehicles. Colonel Dimitri from moon base and his first sergeant attended as well, both in UEF fatigues. A platoon of UEF marines in Tac-3 body armor and M-19 assault rifles gathered as well. For that matter, the rest of the team was filled with strangers. Worst of all, Fairchild was in the ship's CIC, being the acting CAG. If Brooks got Katsev's foot up his ass, he'd have to deal with it alone.

Dimitri stepped forward. "This is a recon mission. We are here to seek out and map control centers or related structures that may be useful in contacting the intelligence that runs this structure. Your bodycams will remain on at all times, as they are set to collect all images and spin them into a coherent map of what we see. If you get lost, stay where you are and radio in. We will periodically backtrack our position and pick up stragglers. We don't expect armed resistance but if we do encounter hostiles, do not aggress on their positions. Radio in and request backup. The closest team members will respond as quickly as possible. You may of course return fire if first fired upon. Stay close and stay alert."

"Stay close. Stay alert," Brooks murmured.

Rosenski elbowed him, none too gently. "Don't be an asshole. Just keep track of where everyone is and you will be like unto a god."

"Yes, Lieutenant."

The airlock doors drew Brooks' attention: thirty feet tall and twice as wide. The antechamber had evidently not been built to handle mere humanoids or anything human sized. He wondered what the original salvage crew had made of them. Whether they'd really understood that a culture that produced things like rollers was far more of an existential challenge than merely being able to build giant war machines.

"You think anyone ever actually thought there'd be a reason a culture built things like rollers?" he asked.

Rosenski gripped the wheel more tightly as she nudged the throttle forward to follow the armored car ahead of her. "When did humans ever think there wasn't a military option to any problem?" she asked.

"You think we just built a toy army to make the voters feel better about themselves?"

She shook her head. "No, I think it was a boon for general contractors with friends in the government. Doesn't matter now. Win or lose, we are in it."

The giant doors opened slowly but smoothly, without even the shuddering in the deck plates that signaled mechanical activity. The troop carriers moved in formation toward the outer doors, sealed the interior set and waited. Brooks could see the fidgeting from their position in the rear. Even the marines weren't immune. Sidelong glances and unnecessary pivots as everyone checked their danger spaces over and over again.

Finally suit alarms triggered, and everyone checked the pressure gauges on their sleeves. Brooks could feel the pressure in his ears alter slightly as the outer doors opened and revealed another set beyond.

Brooks' helmet comm squawked. "Forward, in sequence."

There were three sets of airlocks to pass through, each as monstrous as the first. The final inner door opened to reveal a tunnel wide and long enough to challenge anything built on Earth. When they emerged from it they entered a huge chamber, dimly lit, dominated by tall racks of cubical shapes, all empty. Dozens of mechanical arms and platforms took up the space between racks, and luminescent strips on the floor created a sense of gridwork. But there was no obvious clue to what the grid looked like or how it worked when active.

The entire facility lay silent.

The vehicles fanned out and Rosenski nudged the AFV-30 forward, tailing the platoon. Brooks busied himself taking care of mundane interests, recording air pressure (13.2psi), air content (24/76 percent oxygen-nitrogen), temperature (20.8 degrees Celsius), and setting his camera to film continually after plugging it into the jeep's electrical socket. If there was anyone about, they weren't seeing them.

Dimitri's voice came over the comm. "What do you think? Factory floor?"

Fairchild's voice answered. "Could be. If so, it's a huge one. Not much indication of what it might make, though."

"Yes, there is." Dimitri swung his AFV's spotlight upwards. Rollers and fighters lay in their racks, as dormant as everything else, but very much recognizable from their earlier encounter with both types of weapons from South Pico Island. "How many?"

Brooks did some quick math and pushed the talk button. "Several hundred at least. But this might just be a fraction of their current stock. Until the powers that be decide that more need to be built, I'd guess it'll stay quiet."

"Let's move on. Commander Katsev, you said that there was activity outside the AMS-1?"

"Correct, Colonel. Crew have orders to stay out of their way."

"What do you mean, they?"

A metallic thumping made itself felt through the deck. A lumbering figure closed the distance between them and hulking metal shapes: hemispherical bodies walking on ostrich-like legs topped by multi-armed globes. Four approached from all sides and shone powerful lamps down on the humans.

Katsev pointed. "These. Hundreds of them are working on the ship's hull."

"Gakuken dasplekferbrukn vemmenkess."

Fairchild again. "Brooks?"

"I'd guess we're being asked to leave."

"You guess? You're supposed to be an expert."

"It's not like I have a dictionary, Commander."

The lead machine took another step forward. It seemed clear that this was not a generalized order that came from everywhere. This particular machine was talking to them. *"Dasplekferbrukn dizankan. Gakuken dasplekferbrukn vemmenkess."*

"That's the same phrase as before, I think, in a second compound iteration. We're being told to leave," Brooks said.

Brooks felt a touch on his shoulder. Rosenski pointed upwards. He followed her direction to see that some of the machinery had swung into action. A row of racked pods were being serviced by robotic arms. It reminded Brooks of how Battlers and Ravens were prepped for action: fuel lines attached, ammunition loaded, electrical systems checked.

"I think we should leave," he said.

"Duly noted. Let's head this way."

The platoon followed orders, with the marine troop carriers leading the way. They drove through the gaps in the robots, with the utility vehicles pacing them. Brooks checked his side view mirror and breathed easily when he saw nothing was following. He gasped as Rosenski stopped short. Now the four machines were standing in a line ahead of them, clearly blocking their path.

"Dasplekferbrukn nikanki. Rekettess."

"That's an ultimatum," Brooks confirmed. "Leave quietly or else."

"Grenade launchers up. Armor piercing rounds only. Aim for the second from the left. Fire!"

A dozen grenades shot out and burst with muffled clumps against the selected robot. The machine's frame stuttered and the robot stumbled, then collapsed in place, still on its feet but drooping as if the animating force had fled.

What could only be alarm blared over them, and blue flashing lights strobed above them. Brooks looked back over his shoulder to see that mechanical arms were now plucking rollers from their racks and depositing them on the deck. The rollers shuddered, flexed their control surfaces and rotated their turrets. Then they moved forward.

"Rollers incoming!" he yelled.

"Scatter! Everyone meet up back at the airlock. Go!"

Rosenski didn't need any urging. She put the AFV in gear and gunned the engine, swung it through a tight 180-degree turn, driving through racks rather than around them. For an added bit of fun, she turned off the headlights. One roller had decided to trail them, and he could hear the sounds of gunfire as thin beams of light seared the path ahead of them, narrowly missing their vehicle. A hollow explosion behind them suggested that at least one of the AFVs hadn't been so lucky.

Another sharp turn, then another, and then their luck failed. A motorized arm waved and lowered suddenly, and Rosenski didn't see it until it was too late. She swerved to miss the obstacle, ended up ramming into it and the arm literally flicked the vehicle over. It spun around, landed on its side and the next thing Brooks knew he was lying on his side and Rosenski was on top of him. She was heavy, too.

He pushed her off, tried to wriggle free and found himself pinned inside the vehicle . Sara had kept her head, doing her best to use her feet and hands to kick and climb her way out of the cab, He could only see her feet, scrabbling across the now vertical dashboard. It hurt to breathe and he could swear he smelled gas… then remembered the AFV used fuel cells, not gasoline engines.

A sharp pain in his arm and he felt hands grabbing his shoulders, pulling him backwards. He craned his neck to see Rosenski reaching in to pull him out through the top hatch of the vehicle. He did his best to co-operate, pushing with his legs but his arm was on fire. Probably broken.

Once outside Brooks found that he could barely move his right arm, not even moving the fingers. Sara was gritting her teeth, favoring her left leg. Apparently her wounded kneecap had taken a turn for the worse. The AFV-30 was out of action, lying on its side. They huddled against the damaged vehicle as one of the attacking robots thumped up to them and stopped. Hatches opened in the deck and walls nearby and snub-nosed turrets rose to firing positions.

Brooks finally lost patience. Everything hurt and he hadn't wanted to shoot at the damn things in the first place. Part of him was rooting for the rollers, at least where the brass was concerned. "*Genug! Haltn es shoyn!*" he yelled.

At once a voice boomed from above. "*Genukh ansanken. Gereenzek haldanen.*" In the silence they could hear the sound of whirring motors as the turrets pulled themselves back behind their bulkheads. Heavy metal hatches closed over the holes in the deck, walls, and ceiling. Another of the walking robots turned a corner and strode to their position, stopping before their ride and peering down at them.

Roseneki and Simon shared a look. "What the hell did you just do?" she asked.

"Got someone to turn the attack off, I think."

"Can you do it again? Maybe get them to turn the lights on?" She snapped her fingers. "Oh! An exit sign would be the bomb right about now."

"I don't know what I did."

"Well, okay. Whatever you said, it sounded like German. What did you say?"

"'Stop it, already.' Yiddish."

"Yiddish? I was sure that was German."

"There are plenty of cross-over words. Scheisse!"

"What?"

"I'll bet whatever I said sounded close enough to some actual command word that something up here recognized it."

She clapped him on the shoulder, sending a shooting pain down his arm. "Amazing! Try again. Say something else."

Rosenski rolled her eyes as Brooks cleared his throat dramatically. "*Genug! Vayzn aundz di veg aoys!*"

"What was that?"

"I asked it to show us the way out."

The same booming voice as before drifted down. This time it sounded as if some entity was speaking directly before them. "*Genukh ansanken,*" it said. There was a short pause, and then, "*Don or darvanen vaylder halvte?*"

"Yes?" Brooks said. "Ja?"

"What did it say?"

"No idea. But *halvte* sounds like *hilf*, which means help."

"You're taking a big chance they're not offering to execute us both."

"They could have done that five minutes ago."

"They still can. Do you think it understands what we're saying?"

Brooks shrugged. "It understood something, it's not shooting at us. And I'm sure it's recording everything we say. Which means it might be comparing what we say to any transmissions from the ship it might have intercepted."

Her eyes widened. "It did that?"

"I would have."

With enormous concentration and a bunch of curses, she managed to stand up hobbling badly on her already injured leg. "Tell it the names of things. Make associations. Eventually it'll learn to string words together, right?"

"Let's hope so. Okay." Brooks made a show of pointing to

various things as the machine's lenses tracked them both. "Brooks. Rosenski. Vehicle. Shirt, ring, pistol, floor, wall, boot, pants, belt, head, helmet, torso, leg, foot, robot—"

"Rebek," the machine said. "Rebek. Robot."

"Yes! Robot. Here: leg, head, camera, lens, arm, chassis, gears, piston."

Rosenski joined in. "Let's do some actions. Here: Walk. Brooks is walking. Standing. Sitting. Arms. Raising arms. Lowering arms. Brooks stops."

The machine straightened a bit, twirled a small turret covered in lenses and bent down again. "Brooks. Stop."

He froze. "Stop," Brooks said. "I am stopping."

"Brooks. Rosenski. Wikki." The voice no longer boomed down at them despite the machine's great height, but its tone demanded obedience. For all either of them knew it had weapons trained on them right now. Provoking it made no sense. So they froze, barely even blinking. "What. Language," it said.

Sara Rosenski stood straight, or tried to as she put all her weight on her good leg and leaned on Brooks for support. "English. American English," she said.

"English. American English. Wikki…wait."

Within moments the robot's glass eye flared and projected sets of symbols against the wall. Even though she couldn't speak any of them she recognized that they were Earth language syllabaries. She stepped forward and circled one set with her index finger. "Here. This one."

"Rosenski. Wait."

The next time the machine spoke it utilized a distinctly human, if androgynous, voice. "Genukh answers. I prepare suitable response programs. Wait."

Simon frowned. "Technical, isn't he?"

Rosenski shrugged. "Any way you think about it, this is an improvement."

"Agreed. But I'm a little nervous over what they think a 'suitable response program' means."

"Genukh answers. I assimilate language use rules and vocabulary. Short delay. Wait."

Brooks suddenly forgot about his arm. "Does your race keep dictionaries? Collections of racial languages? Can you make those available to us?"

"Simon, I don't think we're talking to a person."

"Genukh answers. You are correct. I contain no biologic entities. I am Genukh. I control this facility. Please stand by."

"'Please stand by?' Where did that come from?" she wondered.

"Every single help message in the AMS-1's computers. It's been listening to us for months," he said.

"Genukh answers. I have assimilated the language American English to answer your questions."

"Here's a question," Rosenski said. "Where is the airlock? We want to leave."

"I cannot allow you to leave."

"You...what?"

"I cannot allow you to leave. You are trespassing on Battle Ring Genukh, which is the property of the Two Thousand Worlds, subject to the rule of Home Nest, or more immediately, subject to the rule of the leader of Nest 020."

"And who's in charge of Nest 020?" Brooks asked.

"That individual is not in this solar system. This battle ring was designed by a Sleer scientist named Zluur, who set the order to land on this planet. He did not survive the crash."

Brooks sensed a chance to pick the computer's brain. "Can you identify the ships that chased *Ascension* from the outer rim of the solar system to here?"

"*Ascension* is not a valid reference."

"It's the vessel you just docked with. The ship we work on.

We call it *Ascension* sometimes. It's officially known as Alien Megastructure 1, or AMS-1," Sara explained.

"So noted. The war fleet currently deployed in this solar system is part of the Sleer Home Fleet. A state of conflict now exists between that fleet and this battle ring. The events have initiated a state of emergency aboard Battle Ring Genukh. That state can only be disarmed by a Sleer officer of sufficient rank."

"So. What do we do in the meantime?"

"You will stay here as temporary guests of Battle Ring Genukh until the conflict is resolved. Welcome home."

[20]

"WE'RE TEMPORARY GUESTS OF BATTLE RING GENUKH? WHAT does that mean, exactly?" Rosenski asked.

"It means you will stay here until the conflict is resolved. You also appear to need medical attention." The robot swiveled its eye-lens downward and swung across their position. "Your vehicle appears to require repair as well."

The two shared a pained, worried look. "No, we're fine, thanks."

"I see that Rosenski is limping and Brooks is holding his arm at an awkward angle. Are you certain that you need no medical attention?"

Brooks snorted. "Are you in any condition to provide it?"

"I am. Come this way."

A string of yellow arrows pointed the way across the deck and rounded a corner. Brooks began to walk, but Rosenski held him back. "No way. We're already overdue for a meet up by the airlock. Don't you have a medic you can dispatch?"

"I do. But my medical drones are of extremely limited ability. The major medical facilities in this section are far superior and are relatively close by. The scanning equipment therein will give me a chance to catalog your biology. The best a drone would be able to do is use Sleer physiology to make its assessment and the results would be considerably less than optimal."

"Can you at least let us contact our team?" Brooks pressed.

"My defense drones are already in contact with them. Colonel Dimitri has been appraised of your condition and location. We are now discussing his level of access within my administrative protocols."

"Would he be a temporary guest, too?"

"Indeed. He has no command authority on this battle ring or at any Sleer facility."

Brooks perked up. "Sleer? Is that a race or a world name?"

"The Sleer are the dominant life form inhabiting a solar system roughly one thousand light years further up the celestial structure that you call the Orion Arm. They are the culture that dominates the Two Thousand Worlds."

"And these Sleer built you? And other orbital rings like you?"

"Essentially correct. Here. Please enter the vehicle." A wheeled vehicle with an open cab pulled up alongside the wrecked AFV-30, while the hulking robot reached out with a pair of heavy claws and removed the wreck, trotting out of their view with it. They could hear the heavy stomps for long seconds and reluctantly climbed into the cab. There were no controls they could see, and Brooks nearly jumped as the ground car began to drive itself.

Rosenski swiveled her head towards Brooks as they got settled. "Let's keep her talking."

"Her? You mean him."

"Shh." In a louder voice she asked, "We're still on temporary guests. What does that status allow us to do, anyway?"

Genukh's voice spoke from a grille in the dashboard. "Temporary guest is the description of most passengers on any crewed vessel. They are allowed to visit any section of the facility which is not devoted to a crewed station. This permits the use of passenger quarters, dining areas, recreational facilities, and intraship communication stations. All other parts of this ring are forbidden."

Brooks grinned…there was an opportunity here; judging by the look on Rosenski's face she'd smelled it, too. "So, what would we need to do to gain access to the crew stations? The command facilities?"

"Until the current conflict is resolved, that is impossible."

Brooks tried again. "Well, suppose you had a crew. How would you determine their level of access?"

"Sleer military personnel are fitted with extensive implants which regulate their access to any vessel. Due to the differences in physiology I am unclear whether Sleer implants would work on your species."

"Well, that kills that idea," Rosenski groused.

"But we're going to a hospital, so you'll compare us to a Sleer and go from there…right?"

"Essentially."

Sara glowered but bobbed her head. "Tell us more about this conflict," she ordered.

"I cannot provide many details of the current situation. The task force's commanding officer refuses to respond to my repeated hails, which is a clear violation of Home Fleet protocols. When his ships fired upon Zluur's vessel I had no choice but to shield it from their attack. When they fired on this ring, I had no choice but to retaliate. Their destruction is regrettable. And confusing."

"What can you tell us about Zluur's ship, then?"

"I note that you refer to the vessel alternately as the AMS-1 and *Ascension.* Its true name is the same as my own, *Genukh.* Although…"

"Although?" Brooks nudged.

"The vessel began its functionality as a re-purposed class-D gun destroyer in service to Home Fleet five hundred and nine of your years ago. The ship's computer was a fully functional mechanical intelligence. However, that changed after the crash. There was a great deal of damage. Apparently, enough of the original programming remained to enable the cargo to be released and deployed, but very little else."

"Which explains why the ship only disobeyed when those mission orders were executed," Brooks said. "It defended itself from attack, it deployed the ring modules and it docked aboard the complete ring when it was close enough."

"Correct. Zluur may not have intended or planned for that eventuality."

"So you don't remember our repair and reconstruction of your systems and hull," Brooks said.

"I have only fragments to work with at this time. Most recently I remember defending myself from two Sleer Zalamb-class scouting vessels. I was…relieved…to be on the surface, in operating order."

"We were there for that. You wiped out both those ships with single shots. Impressive as hell, Genukh."

Genukh paused. "Are you complimenting me?"

"I think so. Mostly just saying that we never saw anything like it before. And we've seen quite a lot."

"Really. Can you describe it?"

Brooks and Rosenski shared a look, then Brooks said, "Well, your arrival began a civil war on Earth. It brought home the fact that weren't alone in the universe and it prompted a new government to take control with its main purpose to limit access to your hull from all but a very small restoration crew. We call it the Unification war."

"Which side did you fight on?"

Rosenski shook her head, her eyes communicating caution to

Brooks. "We didn't fight, that was eleven years ago, but our side won."

"I see."

Brooks resumed the history lesson, choosing his words carefully. "We managed to get many of your systems running and learned enough about how they worked to build…vehicles. But our restoration wasn't perfect. Your antigravity system failed and your FTL drive sent us out to the edge of the solar system. The fusion drive never worked as well as we hoped."

"Yes, the damage to the ship is considerable. I am effecting repairs now."

Rosenski straightened her bad leg, grunting as she moved. "To make matters worse, these Sleer ships have been fighting us constantly as we headed home."

"That is worrisome. I find no authorization from Home Fleet to support their action. Worse, I find no communication at all on the channel band that home fleet has designated for its own use."

"Have you sent them any messages telling them you're here?"

"I have followed Home Fleet communication protocol exactly. It seemed prudent to do so in light of gaps in the data. No responses as of yet."

"Tell us about the…what did you call them? Screech?"

"The Skreesh are a race of highly intelligent beings known for their periodical incursions down this arm of the galaxy. They travel in huge ships and use extractive machinery to produce the raw materials to build new ships for their fleets. Any resistance is put down with savage efficiency. Few have survived their incursions, so our information about their society remains scant."

"How long as this been going on?"

"Unknown, but there are suspicions that the Skreesh have been making these incursions for well over five hundred thousand years, including into Sleer space. Sleer archaeologists have determined that at least three incursions into their space have occurred in the past one hundred fifty thousand years. All we know about the Skreesh comes from these exhumed Sleer societies."

"So no living Sleer has actually seen a Skreesh."

"Not as such. But we have a definite knowledge of their ships. Here is a Skreesh titan and I will add a profile of *Ascension* as well, for the sake of scale."

A viewing surface appeared. The vessel it showed looked like a mushroom lying on its side. *Ascension* appeared below it, tiny compared to the titan.

Brooks blinked. "Holy ship."

"And you fought off one of these monsters?"

"No. I escaped from it."

Rosenski tensed. "Did they follow you?"

"I presume not. But Home Fleet was able to discern my location eventually. There is no reason to assume the Skreesh are incapable of a similar feat."

Sara paused for a moment, which became a minute which drifted into a silent scowl. Brooks took the opportunity to pick Genukh's brain and apparent talkative nature. "So tell us more about the battle ring."

"Battle rings are a recent development in Sleer technical capacity. The oldest is seven hundred of your centuries old, and were developed by engineers on Home Nest in an attempt to harden certain worlds in the Two Thousand Worlds with high perceived strategic value. The first ring was comparatively simple in design and took nearly a century to complete."

"Did it work?"

"In a manner of speaking. The ring was eventually destroyed but the world it protected survived a Skreesh raid nearly intact. Once the concept was proven more were constructed on strategically vital worlds."

"Is that where you came from?"

"This ring...myself...is unique. Zluur was anxious to develop a method of ring construction that could be deployed as quickly as possible. The results of his experiment are as you see." Pause. "The medical facilities are just ahead."

Their car slid to a halt outside a heavy airlock which opened as they struggled to stand. Inside it seemed similar to any hospital they'd ever seen with a bank of a dozen electronically enhanced beds and a wall of shelves packed with small clear vials behind glass. Brooks nodded to the two robots standing immobile near the rear wall. They looked to him like helmeted columns with tentacles sprouting from armored ports.

"Please lie on the table."

Rosenski backed away. "Oh no. I saw this movie. Anal probes and slicing and dicing. Not me."

"Fine, I'll do it."

"No. Not either of us. That's an order."

Brooks drew himself to attention. "Very well, Lieutenant. After we kill ourselves walking back to the AMS-1, I'll be sure to mention in my report that we passed up a grand opportunity to gather significant intelligence on the aliens' scientific and medical facilities."

She glared daggers at him until he fidgeted. "Go ahead. I'm on record as saying this is a truly shit idea, Brooks."

"So noted." He walked to the nearest bio-bed, hopped on and lay down. "Remember, it's my arm that's broken, everything else works," Brooks said.

One of the squid-like robots moved toward them, stopping at the foot of the bed. "A full scan is needed before repairs can begin."

"If you've been scanning communications can't you just log on to the U-Net and download a copy of Gray's Anatomy?"

"I did that some time ago. Educational material is no substitute for a living specimen. Surely you comprehend the difference between simulation and experience?"

"I do."

"Very well. Brooks. Do you consent to the scan?"

"Yes."

"Remain still, please. Scan begins."

The only thing that Brooks couldn't do was lay his bad arm flat next to him. He barely noticed when the squid-armed medical bot gave him an assist, carefully arranging his broken limb until it lay flat on the bed. That done, a set of scanning beams emerged from projectors above his head, playing across his body numerous times until Genukh announced that he could get up.

"Structurally, your physiology is entirely compatible with Sleer norms." Pause. "Rosenski. It would be most helpful in terms of education if you consented to scanning."

She looked at Brooks. "How do you feel?"

"Arm still hurts but normal otherwise."

She sighed and hobbled to the bed, swinging up one leg easily; the medical bot did much of the heavy lifting for the wounded leg. "Fine. You can scan me. But no more."

"Agreed. Do you consent to the scan?"

"I said yes."

"Very well. Scan begins." Finally, Genukh announced, "I have determined that there is sufficient physiological compatibility to install a microbe injection port. Should you reject that minimally invasive procedure, I can emulate your frequently utilized treatment…a cast, I believe it's called."

Brooks sniffed. "I'd be in a cast for a month then another month to build back up all the muscle tone I lost. How long would installing the injection port take?"

"The port would take only a few moments to install under a local anesthetic. The injection would take moments. The results would be evident within hours."

"Let's do it."

"Brooks! No! No injection. No alien equipment."

"Sara, this is a learning opportunity."

"No, it's an alien machine that we just met two hours ago."

Genukh said, "I would point out only that a microbe injection port is a basic implant that is used by all Sleer military personnel. By having one implanted, I would categorize you as a crew member, albeit a low-ranked one. It would allow you to access parts of the battle ring that are denied to temporary guests. Such as crew operation stations."

Brooks' face lit up greedily. "That's worth it. I consent to the implant procedure."

"No!"

"Do you want to figure this place out? Access to the crew stations is how we do that."

She opened and closed her mouth like a fish deciding whether it was being baited or looking at a real morsel of food. Eventually she frowned. "Consider yourself on report, Lieutenant," she growled. But she backed off as the medical drone approached.

The robot extended arms toward Brooks who did his best not to flinch. One arm sprayed something on the base of his collar bone while another held what looked like a small plug. "You may wish to look away for a moment," said the robot.

He did so. He felt a slight bit of pressure than a push and a tug. "Procedure complete. Stand by for microbe injection."

A new arm raised; Brooks could see a small vial held in its tiny claws. The robot connected the vial to the plug, twisted it and removed it.

Brooks could barely see the plug but was amazed at how compact it was, barely the size of a dime. There wasn't even a seam between the plug's base and the skin. He tested it, pressed down on it. There was no pain, but he expected that was the anesthetic in action. When it wore off, it would feel plenty weird, he was sure.

A viewing surface appeared showing a schematic of a human body. "I assume that's me?"

"It is. The microbes are working their ways through your circulatory system and are congregating at the site of the fracture. You may feel an itching sensation as a side effect."

"What happens to the microbes when they're finished?" Rosenski asked.

"They will continue to reside in the circulatory system for several days, awaiting further orders from the mechanism. If none are forthcoming they will be excreted in the waste stream."

"Lovely."

"However, the microbes can be removed from the blood stream at any time by using a collection device that connects to the injection port. There are certain elective procedures that are performed through successive microbe deployments and collection sessions. It is a relatively convenient alternative to frequent visits to medical centers."

She finally took her eyes off the hardware and looked Brooks in the eyes. "How do you feel?"

"Weird. Tingly. Arm still hurts but it's like itching inside the bone and muscle."

She ran her eyes up and down his neck, frowning and blinking, deep in thought. She finally reached out and ran a fingertip over the port itself. "Genukh?"

"Genukh answers."

"Do my injection port next."

"Very well. Do you consent to the implantation of a microbe injection port?"

"I do."

"You sure you want to do this?" Brooks asked. "If I go down in a flurry of alien goo it's no great loss. If you go down, the Nightmares have to break in a new leader."

She shrugged. "I have to. If you show up with alien hardware in your neck, it'll be too easy for the OMP to lock you up and subject you to god knows what kind of experiments in the name of home world security. But if we both show up with the ports and can demonstrate a certain level of control over the ring, they might think twice about disappearing us."

"And us both having better access to crew stations aboard this monstrous space ring wouldn't hurt, would it?"

"That, too. I admit I don't see a reason why you should get to work a crew station and I shouldn't. But my point about the over-cops stands. Those guys are insane."

Brooks frowned. "You think they'd do that? For real?"

"I think anyone who isn't being paranoid when dealing with the chain of command is living in a fool's paradise. Scoot over, my turn."

The procedure was over in seconds; Rosenski held her breath and closed her eyes for it. When it ended she flexed her knee, did some squats. "Can't even feel it," she murmured.

"That's the anesthetic. It wears off pretty quickly. I figure we'll get used to the ports soon enough."

"Hope so. I never enjoyed getting shots at the doctor, either."

Luminescent floor strips lit up. "The recovery room is this way. You may not find our stock of refreshments palatable…they are made for Sleer digestive systems…but you are welcome to try."

"How's your conversation with Colonel Dimitri going?" Rosenski wanted to know.

"He is ignoring my repeated assurances of your safety. I am now suggesting that they withdraw to *Ascension* until you return."

"You'd probably save yourself and us a fair amount of agita if you just let the AMS-1 crew on board the ring. Make sure any section they have access to is well lit, darken the rest, and they'll find their ways."

"Is that an order?"

That got their attention. Brooks nodded. "Yes. As a crew member, I am giving you an order."

"Very well. I am relating your message to Colonel Dimitri. Just a moment. He agrees. And he insists on seeing the two of you as soon as possible."

"Okay. Send him instructions on how to find us. Let's make his day."

———

There were real advantages to holding the meeting in the recovery room, Brooks noted. For one thing the sterile design of the operating room was likely to unsettle any visitor. For another the relatively organic, aesthetically pleasing landscape of the recovery ward was intended to put patients and their visitors at ease. Part of the plan was to keep otherwise sane men from lashing out an ill soldier.

Even so, Dimitri, Fairchild, and Katsev looked anxious as they took in their surroundings, but seemed to relax as the two pilots recounted their adventure on the factory floor and resulting medical experiment.

Katsev recovered first, cocking his head at Rosenski. "You actually taught an alien intelligence how to speak and understand English?"

"Brooks got its attention," she said. "I just helped with some of the association building."

Katsev stared at Brooks. "Lieutenant?"

"We got lucky on that on that score," Brooks said. "The truth was some of the vocabulary sounds a great deal like some words in Yiddish and German. All I did was work from that assumption. Also, Genukh has been listening to our transmissions since he arrived in the solar system ten years ago. I'm pretty sure he's watching TV and listening to podcasts along with everyone else by now. All I did was give him some context to work with."

"Being able to simulate word formation at breakneck speed surely helped," Rosenski added.

Katsev was less sanguine. "And accepting alien hardware into your bodies? That sounds risky as hell to me."

"Sounds like a bad case of treason to me," Dimitri snarled.

"No, no, Colonel," Fairchild soothed. "They had a problem and found a way to solve it is all. These are combat soldiers. They took the initiative and gained a vitally important advantage."

Dimitri harrumphed. "How does handing an alien machine—it is a machine, yes?—two live human subjects to study advantage us? The controlling intelligence...will it answer to me?"

"Genukh," Brooks said.

"Genukh answers."

"Please answer Colonel Dimitri's questions."

"Of course. Colonel?"

"Am I to understand you implanted technology into their bodies to give them access to your facilities?"

"I offered them the lowest possible level of medical assistance to fix Brooks's arm and Rosenski's leg. Their injection ports were offered as a method of reducing their convalescence from weeks to a day. Improved access to these facilities was...icing on the cake?"

Brooks scratched his nose. "We didn't teach him that."

"Her."

"What?"

Rosenski rolled her eyes. "Genukh. She's a her, not a him."

"You sure? Sounds like a him to me."

"Well, she sounds like a her to me."

Dimitri shook his head gravely. "Officers, please. While I appreciate the effort, there is no way two people can hope to manage this installation in its entirety, regardless of how pleasant its computer seems to be. Bottom line, Genukh. What will it take to adopt all of the AMS-1's crew as your own?"

The silence that followed worried Brooks. Genukh had never hesitated before answering before. "Genukh?"

"I am reviewing my protocols, Brooks. One moment. One moment. Yes. Considering that instructions from home fleet are not forthcoming…but might theoretically arrive at any time…and that the Sleer fleet commander has shown clearly hostile intent both to the AMS-1 and myself…my own discretion must prevail when making such decisions."

"What does that mean?" Dimitri growled.

"The circumstances are not conducive to incorporating the AMS-1's crew into my state of battle readiness. I currently have two crew members. For now, I judge that to be sufficient. I will modify that decision based on continued observation of how Brooks and Rosenski handle their new status."

"You're telling me the fate of the Earth hangs on what these two *lieutenants* do next?"

"That is an oversimplification. However, I am currently engaged in repairing the AMS-1 and will stock it with the equipment that it is intended to carry for a full combat deployment. Those protocols are already in place. That is…on the house."

Rosenski shook her head. "Seriously, where is she coming up with this stuff?"

"He."

"Whatever!"

"Very well. Genukh," Dimitri ordered.

"Genukh answers."

"Will you extend temporary guest status to the AMS-1's crew?"

"I have done so on Brooks's express orders. Well-lit areas are accessible. Darkened areas are prohibited. Security drones will be deployed to enforce this rule."

Dimitri seemed satisfied with that answer. "Very good. Brooks. Rosenski. You are on medical leave as of now. You will report to the Moon Base sick bay and stay there under guard until such a time as the chief medical officer determines that you pose no threat to yourselves or others."

[21]

"Try the codes again."

"My lord, we have tried every code in our directory three times, transmitted on the entire communications band. The ring's computer refuses to acknowledge any of them."

Nazerian seethed as he stalked to the edge of his command platform. They were so close to completing their mission, he could taste it. If the ring's computer was refusing their orders…an order coded directly from Home Nest, and designed to work on every battle ring computer in the Two Thousand Worlds, then something else was going on. Had Zluur even bothered to think about that aspect of ring design when he planned his science project? A controlling computer that could refuse orders would be independent, more dangerous to the Sleer than it would ever be to a Skreesh titan.

Which, memory reminded him, had already happened. He'd seen the recordings. The entire bridge crew had. Battle Ring Genukh was defective and his toolkit was proving ineffective in correcting it.

"So," he said, his tone inviting conversation, "We have three possible answers. First, the ring was never properly completed

236

and stands as a monument to hubris and insanity. Two, the ring is functioning exactly as Zluur meant it to function: apart from Home Nest's observation or control. It strikes me as odd as nothing in the records described him as being prone to empire building but desperation can push individuals in new directions. Third…and I hesitate to even say it…"

Edzedon sidled next to him. The science officer was lithe and sleek. When Nazerian was deep in thought the short Sleer could almost make it seem like he'd appeared out of thin air. "The primates have managed to gain control of the battle ring," he finished.

"You think that likely?"

"No. Yes. I don't know. I'm guessing. An educated guess, but still a guess. They've shown themselves to be very inventive. It's not impossible."

"No, it's not. Have we tried the standard access elements? Docking, repair services…?"

"We have. Multiple times. The ring does not acknowledge any of our requests."

"Then we go back to the basics. Send a message to Home Nest. Tell them we have determined the ring is malfunctioning and will undertake efforts to repair it. Ask for additional forces to engage the defense drones. Specifically ask for a flotilla of emergency repair ships. Our ships are not well suited to small scale infiltration tactics."

"What then?"

Nazerian donned his control gauntlets and navigated through the dozens of viewing surfaces open around the bridge. It took some time to locate what he needed. "There. The command tower. The bridge will be at the top of the structure. We'll take all six of our landing ships and soft-dock them on the two uppermost decks on either side of the structure. Their troops will board while the destroyers launch every battleworthy mech and single fighter they have and attack the lowermost surface across a three-hundred-kilometer-wide section of the ring."

"Dividing the defense among all eighteen ships," Edzedon noted.

"And, I hope, dividing Genukh's attention from our real goal, which will be here." He waved at the screen which shifted to an interior floor plan of the bridge. One console in particular flashed red for attention. "The manual override station. Every battle ring has one. If we take the machinery out of the command loop, we'll have a complete battle ring at our disposal."

"Excellent."

"Only if it works."

Edzedon used his own gauntlets to bring up the schematics of the ring defenses. There were a lot of them: from heavy cannon to light lasers…but the new shield projectors worried him. He'd never seen anything like those before. "Surely it makes more sense to wait until reinforcements arrive?"

Nazerian pulled up a new screen and allowed his jaw to drop open as he saw that Genukh's crew was spreading from within Zluur's ship to nearby sections of Battle Ring Genukh. "These primitives already know too much about our science and are learning more. We need to stop them. Now."

[22]

BROOKS THREW A PLASTIC BOTTLE OF IODINE ACROSS THE ROOM at Rosenski, who caught it and threw it back. They'd been playing catch for what felt like hours. "You know, when I made the crew temporary guests of Genukh's ring, I didn't think I'd be getting us de facto demotions."

"Not your fault. I mean, yes, it was your fault. But then it was my fault, too. I let you talk me into getting those fancy microbe implants."

"They worked, didn't they? No more pain and full functionality restored."

"This is true. But look at where we are. 'Involuntary medical leave.' That's what Rojetnick called it. "

They'd been lying on their cots in a shielded closed quarantine room on the first floor of the medical annex. There were empty spaces next to each bed where mobile equipment would have been placed had there been a medical emergency. There was even an intercom on the wall next to the door, which only worked from the outside. Like the door itself. The two officers were limited to the hospital erected in the middle of moon base but the squad of armed and armored soldiers at the entrance prevented them from leaving their room. Neither of them felt compelled to test the waters of the marines' conviction with their toes.

"Mostly I'm just bored. *Bored*," she said. "Bored of boredom."

He snorted as he caught the bottle and flung it back. "All aboard."

"I was going to say that," she complained.

"Hmm. Genukh!"

Nothing.

"She's not going to answer you. All it takes is a flick of a switch from a nurse's station to turn that intercom off. Which, I guarantee has already been done. They can hear us, but we can't hear them unless they feel like talking to us."

"Jeez, I hope not. The last voice that came out of that thing was so cheerful, I really felt like punching it. That never happened to me before I enlisted," he said. "You think that dude was a plant? An Overcop?"

She caught the bottle and held onto it while she considered. "No. Hell, I don't recall seeing a single OMP goon on this entire ship since we launched."

"What do you think that means? Are they keeping extra low profiles? Is the whole ship on double secret probation?"

"I think the Sleer hit us so suddenly that they were more concerned with getting the civvies under control and into the shelters than anything else. Or, maybe we're being constantly surveilled out here. I wouldn't know if we were." She finally threw the bottle back at him. They'd already gone around the room several times looking for clues as to how to get out. Their side of the door had a reinforced glass pane in it and a handle but no lock. Staying in their rooms, even with access to the hospital staff might have been the militarily prudent thing to do but didn't seem helpful in terms of improving their access to the battle ring. On the other hand...

They froze as sirens went off. Beneath the blare of the hospital's own emergency klaxon, they could hear the heavier whoop of the battle stations alarm in the ship proper. "That's an attack," she said.

"Right. Come on."

"Why, where are we going?"

"We're getting out of here," he said.

"We…that's against orders!"

"You want to wait? Here? For the long arm of the law to come for us?"

"That's not how it works."

"Sara! We volunteered to have alien tech implanted in our bodies, putting us under apparent control of an alien AI. There's no way we get out of this smelling like anything but traitors, unless we can figure out a way to get Genukh to listen to Captain Rojetnick and Col. Dimitri. And Maybe Hendricks, too. The OMP would love a chance to give orders to the most powerful weapon mankind ever saw."

She blinked as she ran the number in her head. "All right, we leave. Front door has guys with SB-40 subguns, remember? The roof, too."

"This isn't a brig, it's a hospital. I'm willing to bet they headed to their normal battle stations."

She pressed her nose against the glass pane in the door, swiveling her head to see the hallways. "I'm not seeing them. Nobody out there at all."

"Good. Let me know if anyone tries to come in." He felt his pockets…empty. The guards had taken all their stuff when committing them to the quarantine. He ran his hands up and down his uniform, searching for ideas. His fingers finally touched his lapel and he smiled, pulling his lieutenant's insignia off and working the sharp edges with the tip of his thumb.

"You going to slash your wrists with that?"

"Just watch the door, sir." He used the sharp edge to dig into the seam between the intercom and the wall, poking and prodding until he exposed the plastic box that housed the electronics and then prying the cover off. "Before my old man began working for the National Park Service, he was an electrical engineer. He taught me that there are open windows into any system as long as you know what to look for. He figured out how to hack thermostats back in the day."

"You can hack a thermostat?"

"You can hack anything with a logic circuit. Our entire civilization is basically made of logic circuits." He futzed and fiddled, occasionally cursing as his ersatz tool slipped and skidded off the components.

Eventually she heard a loud click and pulled the door open, side-eyeing him as she realized it wasn't a trick. "What else can you do?"

"Remind me to tell you about the laser powered hot tub we built in my high school science lab."

They ducked their heads out to see a gray hallway, clear for the moment. The entire building had been constructed out of lunar soil, pressed into bricks and sealed with an acrylic spray that kept the walls from flaking dust all over the building. "Which way, Lockpick?"

"Please don't tell me that's my new call sign."

"It is until you die, or I think of something better. Seriously, how do we get out of here?"

"We need a nurse's station. From there I can tap into the Air Base archives and pull up a floor plan." He stood still for a moment, then headed down the hall. "I hear a beeping this way. Come on."

The station was abandoned even while they could see traces of habitation: a partly unwrapped food bar and a cup of coffee sat on the desk next to a live feed that showed them the camera views of the entire floor. The alarms had since been muted and the new silence made Rosenski fidget. Brooks sat and got to work.

"I'd rather not announce ourselves to the world. No front door egress, please."

"Never. We're heading straight down."

"The basement."

"Better. The floor of each of these buildings is set with a pallet foundation. That way if they need to move the way the miniature city is laid out…"

"They just use a ton of forklifts and make it happen. Kinky. I like it. Did you come up with that?"

"Col. Dimitri did, but my team had the specs to work with as they built around us. Every exit stairwell leads directly to a hatch in the deck and then we crawl away with the rest of the rats." Here, C-3. Down that way."

He led them downstairs down past the basement and then past to a darker sub-basement. He searched for a spot in the wall, hammered against a panel then pulled upon a hatch and found a keypad. "If I can remember the damn code," he murmured.

He got it on the third try. They descended into a poorly lit labyrinth of hallways barely tall enough to stand up in.

"We'll never find our way out of here," she said.

"I just need a comm panel. Even a junction box. Has to be one down here somewhere. I remember seeing them every few hundred feet on the plans…"

They crawled and climbed, rocking forward on their haunches one leg-twisting corridor at a time. Brooks eventually had to admit to himself that one corridor looked very much like every other and for all he knew they are already going around in circles. But there had to be…

"Got one!" He crawled on his hands and knees until he reached the comm panel. He punched the stud and spoke into the grille. "Genukh! You there?"

"Genukh answers. Lieutenant Brooks. I am…pleased…to hear your voice."

"Me, too. We're underneath the main cargo section and we're pretty lost."

"Where are you trying to go?"

"Anywhere that isn't the cargo bay," Sara called out.

"Lieutanant Rosenski as well. Excellent. I suggest you make your ways to the nearest exterior airlock and report to the common assembly area. I believe we have a problem, and as crew members, your attention is required."

"We'll do that, but you'll need to guide us."

"Very well. Follow the signs."

"What signs?" Sara asked. As they watched a strip of conduit along the corridor lit up with a lurid purple light and ran an arrow down the length of the tube. "Got it. We'll see you shortly."

"I hope so. I require guidance on the current situation."

"Why?"

"Because the Sleer Home Fleet has folded into this solar system. There are now one hundred and ten thousand additional vessels to confront."

The two soldiers stared at each other, trading looks, wondering silently if they'd heard the number correctly. "And how many fleets do the Sleer have to work with?" Brooks demanded.

"There are multiple fleets allocated to the Sleer military. I have not been able to confirm their current total number yet. However, the Home Fleet is the most numerous in terms of assigned ships."

"Well. That's something."

They followed the computer's directions, heading further down into the engineering decks of the massive ship. Brooks couldn't begin to fathom the intricacies of the industrial design of the engineering levels. Genukh's forward section was basically all weaponry and crew stations, while the now-defunct middle third had been cargo hold and nanofactory deployment. The rear third of the ship was all engine. Which made it so much more annoying that her fusion drives, capable of eventually propelling the ship to near-light speeds, were performing so comparatively badly.

But the ring was repairing it, even as he thought about it, which meant that it would be back to snuff soon. At least, he hoped so.

"Can't even hear it," Rosenski griped.

"What?"

"I said, you think they've started looking for us yet?"

"I have heard no such bulletins over the internal com lines," Genukh said. This time the voice came over a speaker grille in the ceiling. Apparently the ship had a two-way PA system no one had ever figured out how to use.

"What have you heard, Genukh?" she asked.

"The human exploration teams have all returned to the battle fortress. Captain Rojetnick is ordering his bridge crew to separate the umbilical lines and docking clamps holding the ship in place and open the outer hangar bay doors. Once they do so, the repair process will be halted and I will be unable to affect the ship's systems."

"Dude, the AMS-1 needs those systems to properly work. Can you stop them from leaving?" Rosenski asked.

"I have no protocol requiring them to stay."

"How far along are the repairs?"

"The AMS-1 is ninety-six percent repaired and fully equipped. The ship, even at full capacity, will not last long against the complement of Home Fleet ships arrayed against them."

Brooks thought furiously. "Where are we exactly?"

"Beneath Deck 9, Frame 25, Compartment 2 (Port side), Engineering, room M835."

"Gah!" Rosenski grunted. "Where is that?"

"You are sixty-six meters from a power umbilical hatchway. You can use that to bypass the main airlock. Go now." Purple glowing arrows appeared and they followed directions.

The hatchway was open, a cold dark entrance to a horizontal tunnel. Dozens of labor drones, bipedal spheres with ostrich-like legs and multiple limbs, carried and stacked cargo containers against the walls. The purple arrows led into the darkness. A klaxon sounded above them, and the robots lowered their loads to the deck and headed back through the airlock as the humans watched. The inference was clear: the bridge crew had figured out how to cut the ties between the battle ring's hangar bay and the ship.

"You know, Lockpick…abandoning one's post is a major offense. We do this, there won't be a sling big enough to hold our asses," she said.

"If there's any help to be found, it's going to be on that ring," he said. "Besides, in a couple of hours, the ship might be destroyed and nobody will even miss us."

"Unless we can figure out how to give the Captain some badly needed oomph from the ring's control tower," she said.

"My thoughts exactly. Let's hitch a ride."

"Ready…jump!" she yelled as the last robot walked past them. Twenty feet tall, there was ample room on its feet for them to stand, hanging on to metal legs for dear life. Brooks couldn't help but feel a deep pit open in his stomach as the airlock doors closed and darkness swallowed them completely.

They moved through the darkness on pogo sticks, up and down, pistoning through the darkness and getting queasier every minute. When the labor drone walked into a lit corridor, Brooks could see that it was no longer following the robot train. Their drone pivoted to the right and made its own way further into the ring. He tried to follow the sequence of hallways, tunnels, lifts, and tubes and gave up after fifteen minutes. The vast interior of

Zluur's science vessel was nothing compared to the battle ring. Finally they entered a cylindrical elevator and relaxed when the drone came to a halt and settled on its joints.

Rosenski coughed. "Are we there?"

Genukh's voice emerged from a speaker above them. "Very nearly. This platform will take you to the control deck. Once there, I will explain further."

Brooks frowned as he dismounted and headed toward the platform. Once they both stepped onto the metal disk it rose silently through a hatch that swung open above them. From there they rose through what could only be a wide elevator shaft that seemed to go on for a mile. "He sounds anxious."

"She."

"Damnit. Genukh."

"Genukh answers."

"Two things. One, can you bump the tenor of your voice up a half an octave or so? And stop answering us with 'Genukh answers.' Way too tedious."

A new voice floated down from above. "Understood. Is this better?"

"Dear god, yes," Roseneki sighed. "From now on, I'm going to call you 'Big G.' Are you willing to answer to that?"

"If it will make interacting with me more convenient for you, certainly."

Sara punched Brooks on the arm. "See? She's a she. Easier for everyone."

"Easier for you. She sounds like my fifth grade science teacher."

"Don't make me have to punch you, Brooks."

"Bah. You punch me every five minutes."

"The AMS-1 has disengaged from the hangar bay. Elements of Home Fleet are moving to intercept," the computer reported.

Brooks began to sweat even though the air surrounding them was cool. "Are they in any danger?"

"At the moment I have extended my shield zones around the AMS-1. But the further away from the hull the ship moves, the less protection the shields will afford them."

"What can we do now?"

"I will show you."

The tremble of the deck plates beneath their feet stuttered and Brooks could feel their momentum slowing; they were at their destination. The elevator doors parted to reveal a chamber more cavernous than the command deck of Mars Base and many times wider. Numerous columns glittered with viewing surfaces while displays flickered to life and white light beamed down from the ceiling. The entire chamber came alive with glowing lights and the sounds of machinery delivering data to the consoles.

As they walked and gawked at their surroundings, Genukh spoke to them, describing what they were looking at. "This facility is designed to be crewed by a great many individuals, but at the moment, I am running everything. I apologize in advance for any delays between your orders and my carrying them out."

"Our orders?"

"Indeed. As the only two crew members aboard you are essentially my command crew. Shall we begin?"

Brooks dragged a sleeve across his brow and nodded eagerly as Rosenski's face grew ashen. "Let's get going."

"Very well. The element that has broken away from the main group consists of sixty-one vessels, ranging in size from Zalamb-class scout ships and Zilthid fighters to six Nagnanaz-class troop carriers. Twelve Naan-Zarduk-class destroyers are moving to intercept the AMS-1 itself. It appears that the troop carriers intend to make a manned landing on my hull. In this very section, in fact."

"Can they do that?"

"A facetious question, Rosenski. Yes, they can do that. All they need to do is program their on-board computers to find a code that I will obey, and they will have significant control over my systems."

"Wait, I thought *we* had control over your system."

"You do. But there are multiple layers of command codes built into my protocols. Any one of them could conceivably override them. All battle rings have these programmed as safety features."

"To make sure no ring computers actually disobey commands from Home Fleet," Brooks said. "Cute."

"I do not understand why that possibility amuses you, Brooks, but it is essentially correct."

"What can we do," Sara repeated.

"You can help me direct the ring's defenses in service to supporting the AMS-1, for one," Genukh said. "The truth is that I have never actually gone into combat against Sleer ships before."

"That's not true," she said, "we saw you blow up a pair of ships while you were still on the ground. You knocked two more down when they tried to prevent the AMS-1 from docking."

"That was before this current version of me expanded my mental and thinking ability," Genukh said. "Now I am... conflicted. I have no standing orders except to maintain my own existence and construct new ships and modules as required to that end. This is most disconcerting. I am puzzled as to how you humans avoid shutdowns."

"We don't always," Brooks said. "But we'll help as much as we can."

"Do you have fighters up and running?" Rosenski asked. "Something that flies that we can pilot remotely."

"I can pilot them but have only a small number. Fewer than one thousand are serviced and flight capable at this point in time."

"I can live with that," Rosenski said. "At her best, *Ascension* only had about eight hundred. We just doubled their fighter compliment. What else you got?"

"Forty thousand primary defense drones will be available for use within twenty minutes."

"Ha! That will help nicely. Now we have a proper air defense screen."

"Negative. Those drones are equipped with maneuvering thrusters but cannot compete with proper Zilthid fighters or UEF Ravens. They will serve as defenders of interior compartments."

"Oh. Well. Hell."

"Information. The AMS-1 is now nearing the limits of the ring's shield zones. It will pass beyond that range in thirty seconds."

Sara parked herself in front of a tactical display of the space around the AMS-1. "Then let's make the most of what we have. Launch all ready fighters and have them form up on *Ascension*. We want to make ourselves look like a bigger threat than we really are."

"Shall I launch the warships as well?"

The humans shared a look. "Warships?"

"Confirmed. When I installed your crew implants, I activated my basic equipment protocols, which includes the construction of warships and their standard compliments of equipment and subsidiary craft. A flotilla of six destroyers is ready for combat and I am building several hundred more."

Rosenski grinned widely, throwing herself into the role of fleet commander. "Launch everything. Keep them out of *Ascension's* flanks. Pull them up right alongside her. Better yet, position those ships and all their fighters in a sphere around the ship except the six position. We don't want to look like we're targeting them."

"We can do better," Brooks said. "Genukh, can you contact AMS-1's bridge? Chief Amir's console?"

"I can send a general hail on the correct frequency, if you tell me what that is."

Brooks told him the communication parameters, then said, "Let's make the call. Is your English good enough to handle a basic conversation?"

"I have been conversing with you two for some time, have I not? Just a moment." The seconds passed in tense silence. It seemed clear to the humans that *Ascension's* command crew was weighing its options, trying to figure out whether they were being tricked. Finally, Amir's strained voice came over the speaker.

"Brooks? If that's really you, tell me what we do every week."

"Thursday evening coffee," he said. "Last time we met you had this crazy blue grain waffle thing. You also wear white socks with sandals, and have a habit of jamming food in your face when you don't want to tell me something."

"That's you. Transferring you to the Captain. Stand by." A pause and a barely perceptible klick. Then Rojetnick's unmistakable baritone. "Brooks. What the hell are you doing aboard that structure?"

Rosenski leaned forward. "Captain, this is Lieutenant Rosenski. It's a long story and we don't exactly have that kind of time. Let's just say for the moment that Brooks and I have temporary command of some unmanned Sleer ships that the battle ring has recently constructed."

"Battle Ring? I take it that's AMS-2's proper class description?"

"Yes, sir. The force you're facing is the Sleer Home Fleet, numbering more than one hundred, ten thousand vessels. We are launching a flotilla of ships and fighters to support you."

"What do they want?"

"They want the battle ring."

"They can't have it. It's our planet, therefore it's our ring and we will defend both to our best abilities. Can your forces communicate that to them?"

Brooks asked. "Genukh?"

"I have been trying to contact them since they arrived in system. I have not yet received any…just a moment. A message is coming in now. I will translate and play it back for you."

A demonic hissing filled the bridge. "This message is for the primates who have stolen the property of the Two Thousand Worlds. I am Great Lord Sselanniss, Home Fleet Master. You will return the gun destroyer *Genukh* to its berth, then you will disembark and take the nearest elevator to the surface of your world where you will exit the spoke. This action will take place immediately. Comply or die."

[23]

THE CREW OF THE AMS-1 REMAINED RIGIDLY FOCUSED ON THEIR jobs as the Sleer Home Fleet Master's ultimatum washed over them from every speaker on the bridge.

"Stolen?" Amir asked of no one in particular. "Is she right? Did we *steal* this monster?"

"From their point of view it's probably true. I guess 'finders keepers' isn't as universal a rule as we like to think," Hart allowed.

"Be that as it may, Captain Rojetnick said, "we need a new plan, and quickly. Brooks, do you need to relay my questions or can I speak to your AI myself?"

A feminine voice piped up through the speaker. "Captain Rojetnick, this is Battle Ring Genukh. Since your crew is already listed as temporary guests and now that you are back aboard your ship, I am allowed to upgrade your profile to that of an allied ship captain. I am at your service."

"Very well, Genukh, can you stop them?"

"I can respond with strong defenses and weaponry comparable to what they carry. However, there are a great many of them and my systems are only partially deployed."

Rojetnick bobbed his head. "Understood. Shall I forward you command instructions by way of Brooks and Rosenski?"

"I will respect your chain of command."

"I'll take that as a yes. Here's what we'll do. Can you make a barrel run directly at Sselanniss's flagship? Put her on the hot seat?"

"I can do that. However, I would suggest a more…"

"So noted," Rojetnick said. "Genukh, have your fleet elements form up on the AMS-1, and since you're already doing that it should be easy. Lieutenant Hart, set Condition One throughout the ship. Launch all fighters."

Hart hesitated. "That leaves us no reserve at all, sir."

"I am aware. Follow the order."

The crew's efforts passed from console to console. Rojetnick could see Lt. Matheson, his Tactical Officer, trying desperately to keep up with the new contacts that were encroaching on Earth space. One hundred plus thousand ships would circle the earth easily. Hell, that was less than a quarter mile between each ship if they floated side by side in orbit.

"Genukh," he said, "How are these home fleet ships equipped?"

"Their defenses are internal nanofiber buttresses and external armor plating with repair services available by drone. They carry turret-mounted particle accelerators and laser turrets as well as missile turrets designed to launch a variety of destructive warheads."

"No shields?"

"Sleer do not generally equip their capital ships with shields, as they are considered great consumers of energy while providing relatively little protection. Remote armor repair technology is vastly more efficient from an energy consumption point of view. However…"

"However?"

"I referred to the blueprints of Zluur's ship and determined that it was both useful and convenient to install a number of shield-zone projectors aboard the AMS-1. Those will be available to you from now on. I was unable to build you a proper workstation for them in the limited time available. They will be operated as automatic point defenses until you can make the required adjustments."

Lt. Meng perked up. "But if shields aren't used on Sleer ships, why did you install them on ours?"

"Clearly, Zluur wanted them installed on the battle ring. I couldn't find a protocol that expressly forbid me from installing them on the AMS-1. I thought you would find them helpful."

"Oh."

"Well, why shouldn't he have done that?" Amir wanted to know. "If I was running from a superior enemy who also happened to be my boss, I would want an ace in the hole, too. Sorry, Captain."

"No apologies necessary, Chief. I'm sure we all were interested to hear that answer. Genukh, does that mean that you installed shields on the battle ring as well?"

"Correct. The design of Battle Ring Genukh is not a standard platform design. I wish to point out that despite its operational status, its construction is not yet complete."

Rojetnick ground his teeth. A partially built base meant they'd be immersed in a running guessing game when asking for help. Wonderful. "Understood. How far does your shield-zone extend?"

"The AMS-1 passed their range three minutes ago."

"Lieutenant Spalding, take us back."

"Back, sir?"

"Turn us around and head toward the ring, full thrusters."

"Full thrusters. Aye aye, sir."

Rojetnick turned to his crew. "Here's my plan. We're going to sit just behind the shield barriers and let them hit us first. They're probably planning on doing that anyway. It saves our lives for a bit and makes them waste energy. If their primary weapons are like ours, they'll need several minutes to recharge between shots. We'll hit them in their pauses."

Matheson spoke up. "Captain? The Sleer fleet is deploying; they're breaking up."

It was true. The cloud of warships was twisting in space, floating various elements into different directions. It didn't take long to see what they were up to as the AMS-1 retreated back behind the ring's shield barrier.

"They're going to encircle the planet," he said. "Comms. Contact the OMP. Tell them exactly where we are and what the situation is. Let them contact defense sector governors for whatever emergency preparations they think they should make."

"Yes, sir. But how much preparing can they do in an hour?"

"We were able to fuel our engines *and* defend South Pico Island against an enemy ground and air assault in an hour. If they can get half the population under cover, we stand a chance of getting through this as a species. Otherwise, that's our killer asteroid."

The crew shared looks. Was the captain starting to crack under pressure? Granted it was more pressure than any of them could have imagined even a few hours ago, but it raised no one's hopes.

"Zoom in on the lead ship," Rojetnick ordered. Sselanniss's flagship was impressive. Twice as long as *Ascension* and a third wider, its prow was calving down the middle, splitting to display its main weapon. Worse, the same unveiling of spinal mounts was happening throughout the fleet. It didn't take much imagination to figure out what their first target would be.

"Genukh, you didn't tell us they had spinal mounted weapons."

"I didn't know they had any. I apologize for the oversight. The Home Fleet must have upgraded their ships while I was unavailable." Pause. "That may also explain the complete lack of communication despite my efforts."

"Fair enough. How far from your shield zones are we?"

"One minute to cover, sir.

"Good. Prime every weapon system we have. Prep the main gun for firing and activate all point defenses. You said our new shields zones are automatic?"

"I did. But I am sending Commander Cox the blueprints on how and where to build control stations for future use."

"That's appreciated. Lieutenant Hart, are the fighters launched?"

Hart signaled the fleet, read the responses on her console. "All fighter groups are launched and formed up, sir."

The worst of the thing was that Rojetnick had no concept of what the alien's strategy might be. Were they going to try to destroy the battle ring? Would they hit the planet beneath them? Would they wait until their ships were fully deployed before attacking? There was no way to know. Their commander, Sselanniss, sounded impatient to him but he felt sure that something was lost in the translation. Worse, the half dozen destroyers and thousand small fighters that the ring had launched and formed up around the AMS-1 made him nervous. In any case, speed was crucial.

"All ships are behind the ring's shield zones, sir," Matheson reported.

"Good. Helm, bring us to a stop relative to the ring."

"Yes, sir. Maintaining position."

Suddenly a wave of bright light exploded over the ship as myriad streams of energetic particles flew at it from a dozen spinal mounts. Protons accelerated to near light speeds burst against the ring's shield zones, creating a light as bright as the sun. It lasted only a few seconds but the entire bridge crew blinked to clear their eyes as the light faded and alarms blared.

"Are we hit?"

"Negative. The ring's shield-zones deployed and are protecting us."

"Let's not disappoint them, then. All main ships target spinal mounts. Concentrate on the lead vessel. Let's give Home Fleet Master Sselanniss something to think about."

Hands flew across consoles and voices spoke into headsets as targets were locked and settings confirmed. "Ready to fire."

"All missile batteries, fire. All railguns…fire."

AMS-1's railguns were human additions to the venerable space fortress, lodged inside two enormous "wings" on either side of the vessel. Each wing sported two of the long-barreled weapons, each the size of the main guns of an ancient wet navy battleship. Projectiles flew from their barrels with muffled thumps as reloaders worked to slam new slugs into firing position as quickly as possible. The heavy missiles were easier to track as long smoke trails floated through the space they passed through. The bridge crew cheered as pinpoints of light burst against the hull of the flagship, exploding in furious fireballs.

Rojetnick turned around, barely leashed fury in his eyes. "This is not a football game!" he shouted.

The bridge quieted instantly. Damn him anyway for losing his temper. Most of these men and women had started as raw recruits, he knew, but this was not their first engagement. But it was the first time they were defending their home world itself from an overwhelming attack. "All laser turrets, target and fire," he ordered.

Now beams of coherent light sprayed from turret mounted lasers on the AMS-1's forward deck, while missile launchers ducked down below decks to reload their gantries. The lasers lanced out and struck home, and made dents in the skin of the flagship, but not much else.

"Main guns! Target and fire!"

Ascension's main guns shuddered as energy flows doubled in power, then doubled again. The charging process only took a few seconds but seemed to take forever. The energy blasts from the huge turrets poured lurid green beams at the nose of the flagship, pouring all their contents into it. The nose of the enemy glowed green brightly for a second then flashed and disintegrated. The second wave of main gun shots launched and then penetrated their target, causing the nose of the flagship to go up in a massive explosion.

"Reset the main gun. All batteries fire at the gap in that ship's armor."

"Yes, sir," Matheson said, and turned to send the orders to the gunners.

"Hart, order all squadrons into that gap. Tell The Butcher and Uncle to cause as much ruckus as possible."

"Yes sir." Everyone knew who the captain meant. And the Nightmares and Hornets would be backing them up.

"Captain! We have new contacts..."

The Sleer fleet was moving again, shifting their formation. While smaller turrets tried to engage the relatively tiny fighters that were now approaching it, dozens more ships sideslipped out to the right and left, trying to flank the stationary *Ascension*. They were distractions. "Genukh, move the destroyers to intercept those new targets. Main guns and turrets weapons both," Rojetnick ordered.

"Captain Rojetnick, sensors are picking up a great many small targets, coming from the landing ships further back in the formation. They appear to be launching troop shuttles." Within moments new viewing surfaces popped into existence, showing the schematics of the troop landers. They were much smaller than the Zalamb-class scout ships, heavily armored and durable without being terribly fast or well-armed. Each could carry one hundred Sleer shock troops and all their equipment.

"Can they get through your shield zones?"

"They will eventually, yes. I can't maintain full strength at the entire circumference of the battle ring and it seems that there will be more ships attacking other sections of the ring shortly."

"Then we have to work with what there is. Concentrate full shield strength on this section of the ring, give us as much cover as you can. Lieutenant Hart, tell Commander Fairchild that those troop carriers are his primary targets. All other squadrons are ordered to engage targets of opportunity. Let's give them something to be afraid of."

More bullets, missiles and energy beams licked the surface of the Sleer ships, and their formation started to fall apart. The spinal mounts of the lead ships were obviously damaged but the rest were recharging their weapons for another round of strikes. After a certain point the ships were shrouded by clouds of debris and only their instruments could hope to tell them what exactly was going on.

Otherwise, this was a great morning.

Brooks and Rosenski fidgeted against each other as they struggled to follow the battle. At the top of the command pedestal there was only one throne. Brooks had insisted she take it because of her knee and she had insisted they share. She didn't relish the chance to repeat every damn thing she saw or heard over the various feeds.

"How big are these Sleer, anyway?" she asked in disgust.

"The typical Sleer soldier stands two point two meters in height and weighs roughly one hundred, fifty kilograms, as you measure it. The command couch you are using is not meant for two people."

"Is there a better way of seeing what's going on outside?"

"The user has their choice: control gauntlets, keyboard and monitor, light pen interface, interactive holographic interface, audio interface, neuronic implant—"

"Wait! Go back. What's a fully interactive hologram do?"

"Stand here." A column of light sprung into being next to the chair. Rosenski hauled herself out of the seat and stood within it. In moments the universe opened up before her and she gasped at the level of detail.

Brooks was curious. "What are you seeing?"

"Dude, I'm seeing the whole *galaxy*!"

"All I see is you standing in a beam of light."

Genukh chimed in. "Rosenski is seeing the contents of my navigation computer projected onto her retinas in real time via her implant. I regret the limitations of the firmware. We can upgrade your implants at a future time, however."

"Be nice to upgrade them now, though," Brooks said.

"I am otherwise occupied."

Brooks chuckled. "I don't think I've ever heard a computer be petulant before. Thanks for that."

"Stating facts is all. But I suppose the correct response is 'you're welcome.'"

"Guys, please. Genukh, tell me what to do to make this work. How do I zoom in on our current location?"

"I shall take care of that. You may use your hands to manipulate the avatars and designate course changes for any ships I control." Rosenki gasped as the Orion arm of the galaxy twisted, turned and resolved into a single yellow dwarf star. She could see planets spinning around it, too: Mercury, Venus…Earth. The level of detail stunned her into silence. The clouds of approaching warships and the ring itself were as clear as the pores on her skin. Arrows showing course vectors appeared alongside each ship. Zooming in further enabled her to see exactly which vessel was headed in what direction.

"They're breaking up," she noted. "The lead formation is staying put but the rest of the fleet is sliding around to either flank. It looks like they're trying to encircle the planet."

"New contacts," Genukh reported. "Another wave of troop shuttles has undocked and is heading toward the ring."

"Deploy those defense drones as soon as they're ready. Show me the status of all ships' defenses, including our own," Rosenski ordered. She checked power levels and blanched. "We're losing. They'll crack the ring's shields in less than an hour at this rate."

The ruckus outside the ring had become more regular, as the various ship captains sorted out their intentions and began fine-tuning their assault. Thirty-odd ships were pelting the ring's shield zones now, one spinal mount attacking every thirty seconds or so, never allowing the shield generator the time needed to repair the shields for more than a few seconds before the next hit landed. But while the battle ring's shield projectors were numerous, they weren't infinite. As more capital ships brought their main guns to bear, she was running out of defense.

"What about *Ascension*?"

She reached into the hologram and touched the ship's avatar, spun it so she could see the counter. "Her shield zones are holding, barely. Without the ring's versions protecting her, she'd be toast in five minutes."

"Not if we can slow them down. Big G, give me access to the ring's defenses."

"Unfortunately, Brooks, your implant does not give you access to the full armory. However, you can designate which area receives the greatest concentration of defense drones. Observation drones are of course at your disposal as well. I will guide the repair teams to the damaged sections of the ring as needed."

"Let's make those implant upgrades a priority, shall we?" Brooks said.

"Very well." Pause. "A medical drone will arrive with the necessary microbe injections in ninety-three minutes."

"That's longer then we have," Rosenski noted.

"Just means we need to figure out how to deploy the drones to slow down the boarding parties. Genukh, let's look at a map of this section of the ring again."

"Simon."

"Hang on. I've almost figured out—"

"Simon!"

"What?"

"They're firing on the Earth."

Brooks' head snapped up at the news. He scanned his own console and her holographic interface but one told him too little and the other told him nothing at all. "Genukh!"

"I am adjusting the display's scope. There." Within moments the command center was filled with a blinding display. The earth directly beneath the metal band of the battle ring remained clear as day. Clouds of warships orbited the planet, and while some made it their job to fire on the ring itself, many others drifted north and south of the equator, opening up a wide band of destruction as they poured fire from countless laser batteries onto the planet. Every few seconds the flash of a spinal mount weapon jarred their eyesight.

"Genukh, put up a map of the planet's surface. Log each impact in real time."

"Acknowledged." The map appeared far above their heads. Brooks noted the computer's logic. Close enough to see at a glance, far enough away so as to not interfere with the business at hand. All they had to do was look at the ceiling to watch their world dying. A business that was growing bloodier with each passing minute.

"We have to stop this," Rosenski said.

"How? Those implants won't be ready for…"

"Not the implants, Brooks. Damn it, you don't win a fight with *implants*. All those will do is give us access to more of the ring."

"Access that we need to win."

"Access that we don't need right now. This minute." She studied the display more intently, formulating an idea. "The Home Fleet Master's command ship. Genukh, can you track how much communication traffic it's managing?"

"Not specifically. But it is acting as a communication hub for the entire fleet as well as maintaining Great Lord Sselaniss's flag."

"Close enough. Take all our destroyers and every ring-mounted weapon you have. Focus all their fire on that ship."

"The destroyers will need to move away from the AMS-1 for that to work. Other ships are still shooting at ours."

"Do it. That's an order."

"Very well. Designating primary target for ship-to-ship fire. Stand by."

The light show continued as the six destroyers fired their engines and drove away from the ring, moving upwards and outwards along the shortest axis. Once outside of the ring's shield zones, they unmasked their spinal mounts and opened fire on the now struggling command ship. Dozens of forward-mounted laser canons followed within seconds, then the retracted missile and laser turrets emerged, aimed, and fired. In less than a minute all six ships were flinging the sum total of their destructive energy toward the command ship.

The remaining Sleer ships took notice of this quickly, and moved to counter the attack. A new wave of destroyers and heavy cruisers swung toward the flotilla and launched their own attacks. Within minutes the six destroyers exploded into fireballs, spreading deadly shrapnel throughout Earth's orbit. The command ship was badly hurt but still functional.

"Now what?" Brooks asked.

"Genukh, what else do we have?"

"Primary, secondary and tertiary railgun batteries are available, as are long range missile bays and laser batteries."

"Target all of them on that communication ship."

"You do not have the authority to order a primary attack on a vessel from Home Fleet."

"Well, I damn well do," said Captain Rojetnick's voice from the intercom. "We'll handle the flagship, you two manage the boarding parties."

Moments later two bright beams of death spewed forth from *Ascension's* bow, bathing the flagship's midsection in the same firestorm they'd seen earlier. This time the effect was immediate and total. The ship burst apart at the seams, explosions at the bow and stern engulfing the ship in its entirety.

If Genukh had any compunctions about defending herself, she didn't show it. "Troop carriers are moving to land. Preparing to repel boarders."

[24]

NAZERIAN STOOD ON HIS BRIDGE, WATCHING THE UNFOLDING battle in silence. He'd seen this sight before.

Ten years ago, he'd stood by and watched Home Fleet Master Sselanniss take command of an emergency, which quickly turned into a murderous game between the newly built Battle Ring Zekerys and a Skreesh titan. She'd had ten thousand allied battleships at her disposal then. And still, the titan had blown a sizeable chunk of the battle ring into dust. To this day, he wasn't sure how badly damaged the ring had been.

But that was incidental. She'd taken command of the situation and only a mad escape by Zluur aboard Genukh had saved them: the titan had chased *them* across the galaxy instead of destroying the ring or even attacking the planet. Then she'd charged Nazerian with following Zluur and bringing him home.

And now here they all were again.

He had no idea just how much thought had gone into Sselanniss's attack plan but it was clear that she had expected the overwhelming numbers on her side to be the decisive factor in this battle. She'd presumed wrong. She used her forces like clubs, meant to bash the opponent into submission. Under normal circumstances that might have worked but if there was one thing that Nazerian had learned in his months of tracking the primates back to their home planet, it was that they routinely defied expectations. They confused him more than anything else. Clear victories had been stolen from him at every turn and for the life of him he couldn't figure out why.

Until now.

As the two forces bled casualties and beams of death flickered out on either side of the battle, he realized why he'd been wrong. Like it or not, these beings were defending their home world. Their home nest if you will. That gave them an enormous advantage in motivation that the Sleer lacked. It was simple, really, which might be why he didn't think of it until now: these primates didn't realize they could lose. That they were supposed to lose. That they were *destined* to lose. A Sleer recovery fleet arrived over their sky and they failed to comply. Nazerian and his ship commander ambushed them on the way home and they failed to comply. That inveterate moron, Kessidus, dropped a moon on them and they failed to comply.

Either they were brave beyond reckoning or they were plainly insane. One couldn't fight a coherent campaign against an insane opponent.

The Sleer were invaders this time. No different than the Skreesh were when they came to wipe out the surface of their nests and deposit the material into their own factories to be made into new titans and hive ships.

He watched Sselanniss's holographic form as her ships deployed and worked to encircle the Earth. Her compound eyes were narrow, her stance one of ease and confidence. He wondered if the whole affair bored her. At any rate she had no worries.

Nazerrian worried about everything these days.

The ring's defenses buckled and sputtered but never broke, and that drove Nazerian to wonder what his role in these proceedings were. Should he say something? Speak out to a Great Lord and Fleet Master about her tactics? Or just stay quiet and see how things developed?

The counterattack on her flagship surprised her. Sselanniss cursed and gave new orders, demanding that her ships focus their attacks on the planet, and ship masters answered her. Ten thousand troops were deployed from the carriers in the rear of the formation as the heavy battleships focused their efforts on the planet below.

"With their world in danger, they must surrender," she said.

Nazerian spoke up. "I don't think so, Fleet Master."

"What? Explain yourself."

"Look at what they're doing. They clearly have access to the ring and they have already mastered their own ship."

"Our ship," she corrected.

"Indeed. They adapt quickly and have already learned a great deal about us and our weapons. The longer this engagement continues the longer they have to figure out how to counter us."

"They will not counter us. There's no way they can resist our combined forces."

"With respect, Great Lord, we have never assaulted a world defended by a battle ring before."

He watched viewing surfaces as the fleet dispersed and ship masters focused their weapons on the planet's surface or sections of the ring as they thought wise. Sselanniss's flagship remained focused on Battle Ring Genukh's command tower but even there, she guessed wrong. This rind had shields that popped up to counter whatever weapons her ships brought to bear. And when the focused fire brought down one barrier, two more sprang up in its place. Then the green beams of the AMS-1's main guns burst forth and Sselanniss's flagship exploded. Her hologram showed her perplexed expression and then dispersed.

Nazerian stared at his viewing surface as chaos erupted on the comm network. For all of Ssalanniss's arrogance she was a masterful leader, having held the huge fleet together with sheer force of will. Without her, ship masters had no clear orders and began to argue with other. Only the ships already engaged in the attack showed no hesitation. But now there was no one to coordinate the attacks.

Nazerian grimaced. They could still salvage this.

"This is Tall Lord Nazerian, Fleet Master of the 269th Expedition Fleet," he announced over the open channel. "I am taking command of the Home Fleet. All ship masters conduct themselves in my orders and lock on to my vessel's command channel."

One by one the acknowledgments flowed in until Nazerian realized he was wasting time. How to proceed? First, take the ring. Then contact Home Nest for instructions. The alien world could wait.

"All troop carriers deploy landing craft. We will board the section of the ring to either side of the docking bay housing Genukh. Use any access hatch you find. Once inside the ring, await further orders. Move now!"

He turned to Edzedon as the wide-eyed archivist flicked their air with his forked tongue. "Tell my shuttle crew to stand by," he said. "I am taking this ring for Home Nest."

"Brooks! We're being boarded!"

Brooks heard Rosenski's warning but struggled with his own duties. The command center was in a bad position and they had few options left to them. The Sleer troop shuttles were swarming the upper surface of the ring and there wasn't much he could do about it. He'd already deployed every combat drone Genukh had allowed him to access and had set observation drones to cover as much territory as he could find. But the ring was too damn big to watch everything all the time, which meant he needed to rely on the computer's judgment. And while he trusted the mechanical intelligence to a certain extent—hell, he'd allowed her to implant alien tech into his body for god's sake—the sight of over one hundred thousand ships all dropping droop shuttles onto the ring said this couldn't end well.

"Captain Rojetnick, we need some assistance," he said.

A crackle emerged from the space next to his ears. Sleer comm technology frankly scared him. It was as if Rojetnick's voice was next to him in the same room. "We are trying to boost our weapon output as we speak, Lieutenant."

"That's not what I mean, sir. Those troops are taking positions away from the main weapon arrays. They don't look like they're trying to shut our firing solutions down, They look like they're aiming to board the ring."

"If they come aboard they can manually shut us down, one section at a time," Rosenski confirmed.

"Fair enough. Suggestions?"

"I'd like you to dock *Ascension* back into the landing bay and employ every marine and foot soldier you have. Arm them with battlers, Ravens, or assault rifles, I don't care. I'll send orders to the combat drones to respond to all of them as if they are friendly. And tell Commander Fairchild that some air cover would be extremely appreciated about now."

"That's mighty kind of you, Brooks. Rosenski, do you concur?"

Sara had a worried look as she pulled the data from Big G's streams. She was watching the way the Sleer fleet maneuvered their troop shuttles in preparation for boarding in real time. She was sweating. "I agree with his plan but I'm less certain of whether we have enough people to make a difference."

"We could see ten million Sleer or more drop in very soon," Brooks agreed.

"We'll damn well slow them down at least. Prepare for docking."

"What exactly do you want to do now, Brooks?" Rosenski asked. The channel cut out as Brooks looked up. They were on a collision course with god knew what and there was nowhere to escape to.

"I think we're set as well as we can be. Genukh, lock all the blast doors on this control deck."

"It would be simpler just to active the anti-intrusion protocol."

"On the chance that I misheard you, what does that mean?"

"Locking the blast doors to all compartments and using non-lethal nerve gas to slow down unprotected invaders, is certainly part of the protocol. I also have a variety of interior weapon turrets that can be deployed in major corridors and compartments."

"Lock the doors, use the gas, bring out the corridor turrets and drones. It's got to be a party worth remembering," Rosenski ordered.

"*Ascension* is on course for docking in one minute. His shield zones are down to thirty-nine percent capacity." Genukh paused. "I believe it is time to figure out an escape route for you two."

The shared a look. "Escape isn't part of the plan," Rosenski pointed out.

"Nevertheless, the chances are high that the shield zones will give out and the control center will be captured by Sleer forces. In that event, you two will need to be elsewhere."

"Not going back to those crawl spaces," she growled.

"Nor should you. The ring is huge and there are a great many places to go where the invasion force will have difficulty entering." Floor plans snapped on as new viewing surfaces presented themselves. Brooks shook his head as he stared at the displays. "We could get lost in there for years," he said.

"Very much so. I am copying these maps and floor plans to

your implants so you will be able to access them in the future. I would suggest seeking out one of the unused officer's habitat modules and using that as a base of operations."

"That will be safe?"

"It will be safer than the command center. It's built very much like a miniature city. Cities are difficult to fully occupy, especially with a sparse military force. If this fleet follows standard staffing doctrine, it could contain as many as 1.3 *billion* Sleer military personnel. The ring itself is designed to house up to two billion Sleer comfortably and billions more with sub-optimal space allocations."

"Like hiding in a mansion with only three security guards to watch over the place," Rosenski said.

"Precisely. Keep moving and use the observation drones for intelligence and you should be able to evade any pursuers quite effectively. It would take weeks of planning to manage a full transfer of personnel to the ring from their ships, even with my services. Without them, many of those ships will never offload their troops or cargo."

"But where does that leave you?"

"In the same place as I am now, defending the ring from invaders."

As if to illustrate her point, doors began to open around the control center. The stamping of heavy metal feet got their attention. Floating spheres the size of beach balls loaded with cameras and sensors began to line the walls, followed closely by the armored, ostrich-legged models they'd dealt with earlier. A few modified rollers joined them, taking up positions around their control pedestal.

The message was clear: a fight was coming and they wouldn't be able to stop it by wishful thinking and maneuvering holograms like pieces on a chess board.

Rosenski tipped to it first. "Big G, can humans fit into Sleer battle armor?"

———

"Uncle" Ray Fairchild had been flying most of his life. His first experience had been with a restored SPAD S.XIII, an ancient contraption from the so-called Great War, wood frame and pistons and engine parts restored bit by bit by a 3-D artisan using molecular printing equipment to make the damn thing airworthy. At the age of twelve he'd been taken up by his father; on the third trip out, the old man had put Ray in the pilot's seat. Flying by the seat of your pants, he'd called it. Ray had been terrified as he'd struggled to manage the strange flying machine, but he'd managed to figure out how not to overcompensate for each turn and dive, bank and climb. He'd landed the crazy thing without wrecking the plane or killing either of them.

All Ray knew was that he wanted to go up again.

He moved on to bigger aircraft and more sophisticated forms of flying as he grew, eventually joining the US Navy. That had been a whole new experience, the chance to become familiar with the complex and harshly unforgiving nature of modern machinery. Cargo planes could fall out of the sky for any number of reasons, and fighter planes were worse. Ten thousand details to manage at any given time and you had to be able to figure out ahead of time what might go wrong and compensate for it. The planes flew the pilots in more than one sense.

He always wondered what giant air battles from the big war were like, because despite his eagerness to be in one, the Unification War had not been like that. Giant formations of aircraft were a thing of the past. He'd flown hundreds of missions, destroyed countless drones and a few aircraft with live pilots in them but at very long range, where missiles were sighted and aimed through complex gear. You never saw any bodies, but you knew they were there. More like a video game than a war in his eyes. There'd even been video games he'd played in his time, one he especially enjoyed made a point of making giant space battles one of the big draws. That had been sweet. But it hadn't been real. Still, flying was flying and the new unified world had no place for war veterans. Not really.

That changed with the arrival of the AMS-1. Now everything was different. Suddenly, veterans mattered again. And now that he was involved in a giant space battle, he wasn't sure he liked it.

The Nightmare group was still launching in pairs, bursting out of *Ascension's* launch bays like bees from a hive. His Hornet group had just exited the tubes, flying in a wide orbit as his pilots got their formation in order. He got the squadron to do a quick sound off, making sure everyone was paying attention. His ship was next in line. He rolled the aircraft down the into the chamber, watched and reminded himself to breathe as they sealed him in, and the launch plate rose behind him. Engines to power, throttle forward, then an explosion and WHOOSH, the feeling of acceleration squeezed him back into his couch and the plane dashed forward, like a bullet from a gun barrel. He breathed more easily as his plane emerged from the tunnel—then his jaw dropped as he saw giant starships everywhere. The ring was below him, a wide expanse of metal where the ground should have been, clouds of smaller drone fighters surrounding the AMS-1 behind him. He was part of the cloud.

The Butcher's voice over the headset jarred him from his reverie. "You're drifting, Uncle. Tighten that formation up. Now."

Katsev was right. He needed to concentrate, otherwise he'd be a memory in a field of memories.

Orders now, first from *Ascension*, then from Katsev. "Fairchild, take your group down to the deck and catch the troop ships as they try to land. We'll distract the mother ship." Katsev rushed forward with his Raven and the other Specters until they were mere specks against the background of flaming hulls and crossfire.

Fairchild didn't even both trying to reconcile the mission he'd been given. He gave the order. "All Hornets, we don't want to give the show away. Everyone go to Walker mode and follow me."

It worked, down here they could see all the engaged ships and fighters on their sensors and not attract attention. As far as the Sleer knew they were all just part of the ring. Using structures as tall as apartment houses helped keep them hidden. The oncoming wave of troop shuttles filled the space above them like a swarm of angry bees ten miles in diameter.

He noticed *Ascension's* primary weapons warming up, the tell-tale green glow displaying a firing sequence in progress. "Katsev! They're preparing to fire the main gun. Get your people out of there, now."

"You don't have to tell me twice!" Twin beams burst forth from the nose of the enemy flagship as the lurid green glow razed the nose of the alien ship and plowed through its superstructure.

"Glad you only got a second degree sunburn," Fairhcild chided him.

"Specters don't die, we just come back to haunt the living."

Lieutenant Hart's voice spoke into their headphones. "New targets, boys, troop ships inbound to your position."

"Wait for it…engage!" As a unit, the grounded Hornets rose from their platform and swept through the enemy formations. Missiles dropped from pylons and ignited, smoke trails lengthening as the missiles sought their targets. Another wave of missiles followed, and another, and another. A wall of explosions signaled that many found their targets. Some of the smaller ships were disabled, spinning out of control, but others remained untouched by the chaos, heading right for them.

Fairchild switched back to jet mode and engaged the nearest troop shuttle, following it through a complicated corkscrew as it sought to lose his attention. Ray fixed the problem with a long burst from his GU-22 gun pod. The shuttle's engines flared and the pilot lost control. The Sleer transport blew into a fiery wreck as it collided with the orbital ring.

"Too damn many of them," Uncle said.

"Get as many as you can, fleet," Katsev's voice announced. "Wing them all, give them more to worry about than we have. We'll pick them off as we can. But watch your asses. Bradley! Pull up, you're rolling into his—" An orange flower blossomed nearby. "Damn it. Everyone watch your sixes, those troop shuttles have tail gunners."

Katsev was right. Now that Fairchild looked for it, he could see it. The troop carriers had dorsal and ventral turrets and spewed lasers from both. Too small to do real damage to capital ships but plenty big enough to wreck a Raven pilot's day. It helped his side that the Sleer didn't seem to be interested in anything but the most basic evasive tactics. They were making beelines for the ring, at full velocity. But not as fast as a Raven in jet mode. Even at full burn the target he chased grew larger in Fairchild's HUD as he lined up another shot. Lasers shot from his ship and blasted the shuttle in half. He fought the urge to swerve as the Sleer craft's hull popped open and released a hail of equipment, loose modules, and bodies around him.

"Sorry guys, it's you or us. And frankly, we were here first."

The LED on the command channel blinked. He answered it without thinking. "Go, Hornet Leader."

Lieutenant Hart's voice spoke though his comm. "Commander, we're changing things up. Take your group down to the ring and assist with repelling the ground assault."

"Copy that. Do we know what their target is?"

"We're led to believe that the tower above the hangar bay is where Lieutenants Rosenski and Brooks are stationed. They will assist with your efforts to repel the invasion." To add to the general confusion a new aiming circle popped on his HUD: the structure rose far above the others on the ring's surface. As if that weren't enough to identify their target, there were now hundreds of troop shuttles landing, mating with exterior airlocks and hatches for kilometers in every direction. The ring's surface area was impossibly huge. There would be no way to cover all of them.

"Repel it? How?"

"I don't have that information, Commander. Bridge out."

Alrighty then. "Katsev, did you hear that exchange?"

"I did. My squadron will deal with these idiots. You find an open hatch and save your boy's bacon. You're good at that."

A curse rose to his lips but the particle beam flying overhead got his attention. He flipped the Raven, and sent a blast of lasers from the nose, coupled with a blast from the belly gun. The shot missed the troop carrier's main body, but hit one of the thrusters. The landing craft spun wildly and flipped over, smashing against the hull and bouncing into a new orbit.

"Nineteen," he breathed.

A brilliant flash from his left, and then The Butcher's voice chuckled in his headphones. "Twenty-seven. Better step it up, Uncle. You're losing this race."

"Don't I know it." He switched to the open channel. "Hornet Squadron, we have new orders. Get down to the deck and follow me. We're going to throw Simon Brooks and Frau Butcher a little surprise party."

Amid cheers and whoops from the other pilots, he swung his Raven around and dropped his altitude as he swapped out to Battler mode. The reduced thrust of his engines gave him a chance to look at the architecture below him. Up close, the ring looked like a cityscape laid out in a grid with streets, avenues, conduits and armored spines…something that even looked like a monorail or tram. And towers. There were towers all over this thing! Bubbles, bridges, domes, and blisters of every size and who knew what purpose. Eventually, he picked out what Hart must have been talking about. A tower that rivaled the tallest buildings that humanity had built in its history. It had to be a hundred meters tall and bulged into a multi-domed observatory near the top.

"That's our target, the big control tower. Everyone follow me. Let's get our boy."

$$[\ 25 \ ]$$

Colonel Alan Hendricks clutched a slate in a white knuckled fist as he hustled through the dimly lit corridor of the Unified Fleet HQ in New Darwin, Australia. He'd stopped watching the updates after a few minutes, knowing that none of them could be good. The ground shook periodically, and alarms blared in the distance. The base was on high alert and a response to the alien assault was imminent.

He knew exactly what the response would be, too. He held the orders in his hands, a red-hot flash communication from the world security council.

He'd known his career was over when he'd watched the alarms go off in his command bunker on South Pico Island nearly a year ago. The flash of gravity waves past Mars had been a death warrant to the world the unified government spent a decade building. It had made sense at the time. Hendricks himself had taken a part in it. He'd helped put down an uprising in Indonesia early in the war. The rebels hadn't lasted long against the first generation of Ravens that had come off the new assembly lines.

The truth was that the history books had, at the urging of the OMP, made the war out to be a bigger deal that it had actually been. The political goal was to make the OMP look larger than life. A symbol of the new world. In reality the OMP scoured databases, looking for internal leakers and subversives and little else.

And now that, too, was over and done with. Now hell rained down onto Earth from above and no one had any clue what to do. U-Fleet spent a decade restoring the AMS-1 and pouring resources into equipping it and her crew with the most highly trained soldiers and advanced weaponry ever designed. And now it was gone, there was nothing left to do.

That wasn't true either. There was one thing to do. He carried the orders to prove it.

He slid through a set of massive blast doors and into an armored chamber beyond. Two more security codes, a biometric scan, and a retina check later he entered the UEF high command, an armored chamber three stories tall and as wide as a college campus. Ratings manned consoles and spoke into headsets while officers ambled along elevated walkways, peering down at their charges while watching the destruction of the Earth on huge screen mounted on the wall.

Hendricks tapped his own comm as he spoke into the pickup. "Locate Fleet Admiral Hart."

"Fleet Admiral Hart is on walkway five." Hendricks followed the directions and found the man. He ran up the stairs like a champ and finally presented the slate to the superior officer.

"The cabinet has voted, Admiral. You are ordered to implement the SKY HIGH protocol immediately." Pause. "Before the weapon is destroyed in the assault."

"That's certainly convenient." Hart took the slate, stared at it, paged through the contents. "Launch Authority Epsilon," he read. "This wasn't the cabinet's doing, this is the Secretary of Homeworld Defense flexing his hormones."

"Nonetheless, the order is valid. The computer will recognize it. Implementation is ordered."

"Or what, Colonel. Will you relieve me?"

"I trust that won't be necessary. But yes, I have the authority to do that." He leaned closer to Hart, conspiratorially almost. "Donald. Marissa is in the middle of this hellscape. If you want to help your daughter, this is the way to do it."

Hart stiffened at the reference. Hendricks was familiar with the situation; the old man had fought against his daughter's assignment to *Ascension* as flight officer, preferring, even demanding the young woman to be stationed on Earth. But she'd applied for the post and gotten it fair and square. And from all reports, Senior Flight Officer Hart was good at her job. Nothing to be ashamed of.

But now, with the AMS-1's operational status in question, he understood her father's fear for her. In fairness, he'd worked hard to keep his own family well away from any conceivable front lines. But with an orbital fleet raining death indiscriminately down on everyone, the best he could do was hope that they would be safe in their shelter. The OMP was very good at taking care of their own. "Sir?"

Hart tapped his headset. "I have a valid fire order, Launch Authority Epsilon. Colonel Hendricks, do you concur?"

"I concur."

"Very well. SKY HIGH is now authorized. All sections, report component status."

Various voices filled the air as techs scanned data displays and reported their findings.

"Lunar observation platform control reports 86 percent operational."

"ICBM silo control reports 99 percent operational."

"Deep Site Reaction Weapon Alpha control reports 96 percent operational."

And there it was. Their superweapon experiment, the thing

that had never been fired outside a simulation was ready to engage. Or something.

"Very well. Targeting control. Assign targets according to Defense Plan One. ICBM doors open, launch immediately upon target acquisition and assignment."

The ground shook again a tremor that under any other circumstance might have been easily ignored. "Lunar observation platform control, activate all stations, fire on whatever targets of opportunity you can scan down." Pause. Deep breath. "Weapon Alpha Control: bring all capacitors to full power, plot a firing arc that does not intersect the ring, and stand by to fire on my command."

———

Tall Lord, Home Fleet Master Nazerian locked the last pieces of his battle armor into place, reaching to the small of his back to pull his helmet from its bracket. He took an experimental breath as the actuators brought the suit to electronic life. He didn't remember it being quite so tight around the chest.

In truth it had been many years since he last set foot on an alien world, for battle or any other purpose. He surprised himself by looking forward to it with the same eagerness he'd experienced on his first combat drop as a nestling. He looked forward to seeing what these primates were capable of, up close, instead of fifty thousand kilometers away.

"Sir, your drop shuttle signals readiness to undock."

Nazerian settled his helmet on his collar and blinked as the HUD flared to life. Within moments he was tied into to command channels and to his own platoon's network. "Understood. Tell them I'll be there shortly. In the meantime, we—"

"Fleet Master! A new energy signature from the planet's surface, near the north pole."

"What now?" Nazerian hissed as he turned back to the viewing surfaces. For the past hour, his ship had been monitoring their enemy's pathetic and inept attempt to fight the Sleer Home fleet off. First, a wave of ridiculously primitive ground to air missiles which his fleet's point defenses put down easily. Then, a ring of sub-orbital defense satellites had opened fire on them, but their weaponry had been little more than nuisance fire against his warships' armored hulls. He expected more of the same.

As he watched, the energy output spiked, crested, dropped, then surged as a bright light appeared just over the horizon. For a moment, Nazerian thought it was the planet itself passing through the primary star's corona…then he remembered the that their sun was behind them.

This was something new.

The glow brightened and pulsed. A blindingly bright beam of light sprang from the planet's southern latitude and raced just above their point of view. The comm system exploded with warnings and damage reports from multiple ships as the weapon swung past his own ship's position, cracking hulls and igniting oxygen supplies as it swung through a ninety-degree arc and then dissipated.

"Damage reports!" Nazerian shouted.

His crew was already responding to the new circumstances. Hell, he could hear the anger in ship masters' voices as they communicated their distress over the command channel. "Nearly eight thousand ships have been destroyed or badly damaged," Edzedon finally said. "Many more report superficial damage, mostly to light laser batteries and weapon turrets."

"Did we pinpoint the location of that beam weapon?"

"Yes, sir. It came from the large southern continent."

"Send targeting details to all ships: pummel that site. Spinal mounts and turrets both. I want a smoking crater ten kilometers deep and one hundred wide."

"It will be ordered, Fleet Master."

"I'm heading to my shuttle. Maintain the operation. It's clear we can't expect anything approaching reason from these semi-evolved *mammals*."

He swept off the command bridge, toward the shuttle bay. "This is Fleet Master Nazerian. I will be taking command of the battle ring shortly. Concentrate on neutralizing any alien presences on board the ring. Keep the collateral damage to a minimum. There is no need to destroy our own installation."

A harried-sounding voice spoke over the channel. "With respect, Fleet Master, this is Lesser Troop Lord Aizan. Three waves of my soldiers are being pinned down by defense drones inside the ring. We've destroyed a number of them already, but they just keep coming."

Nazerian wondered about this as he climbed through the shuttle hatch and signaled the pilots to launch. "Maintain order among your troops, Aizan. I will be there momentarily. In the meantime, destroy any drones you encounter. Drones are easily replaced."

He had to admit, that what the primates lacked in their attempts to defend their planet, they made up for in individual initiative, if his shuttle's flight plan was any indication. Although he couldn't see what his pilots were seeing he could feel the swoops and swerves, jukes and jinks that they went through to avoid enemy fire. He remembered watching the feeds of his first assault squads as their gun spheres went up against the primates' strange folding-unfolding aircraft and often times not returning. For their technical failures as a species, they weren't cowards.

The shuttle shook, then shuddered as his pilots dodged a near hit. Nazerian could turn his head to watch the dorsal and ventral gunners aiming their weapons, laying down suppressive fire or popping off rounds at targets of opportunity.

"We'll be putting down at an airlock less than one kilometer from the command tower, Fleet Master." A heave and then he was thrown against his harness as a giant clanging made itself felt through the ship. "Down and clear. Docking port sealed. Good hunting, Defenders!"

The hatch cleared and Nazerian released his harness, grabbing a fusion rifle and a spare battery, nearly stumbling out the hatch in his desire to be the first out of the craft. He nearly fell as two armored shock troopers beat him to it, then moved out of his way as they cleared their danger spaces.

He scanned his new environment. The docking bay was huge and a great many other transports had already docked and disgorged their troops into the ring's interior spaces. A team of engineers worked at the far end of the bay. He could see where a number of defense turrets had emerged from the deck and ceiling, now smoking ruins. Nazerian motioned for his platoon to follow as he raced down the deck, noting that the gravity here felt different than it did on Home Nest. That was unusual. The environment inside all battle rings were supposed to mimic Home Nest's as closely as possible. But if Sselanniss was right and this ring was malfunctioning, who knew what they'd find?

"Situation report," he ordered as he arrived.

An officer turned, saluted, and indicated a hand display. "Bulkheads slid into place to block us as soon as we entered the docking bay. I don't know why but the battle computer is reading our presence as an invading force."

"How do we stop it?"

"The override circuits are in the main command center. I have the floor plan. We need to break into three main compartments, then a set of corridors. I have teams of splitters working to circumvent the locks and sensors."

"How long?"

"An hour. Perhaps more."

"Too long. The longer we stay here the more opportunities the battle computer has to attack us." As if to prove his point, a huge blast door opened to the right and a trio of ostrich-legged defense drones entered, targeting and firing lasers and autocannons at his troops. After a brief firefight, the robots were destroyed, smoking hulks falling on the deck. Along with two dead Sleer.

"Break the doors down. Get the heavy weapons unpacked and deployed. We'll burn down every blast door between here and the command center."

"Yes, Fleet Master."

———

Ray Fairchild ducked his Raven beneath a low ceiling, wincing as the plane's servos whined as he tried to keep his ship upright. The battler mode was meant to duck but not crouch, certainly, not for long periods of time. He glanced at the display; had it really been only ten minutes since they'd descended into the ring?

"Saint, where are we?" he demanded.

Arkady's voice sputtered as the connection wavered. "Looks like a T-junction up ahead. If these plans are correct the command tower will be the left fork, then a short tunnel and two rights, then straight on. Trouble is that any straight away is likely to be heavily defended."

"I hear that. Selfridge, you're on point."

"Roger."

Fairchild scanned the maps. They weren't firsthand observation, rather files that had been uploaded to *Ascension's* computer and then downloaded to his plane's system. Word was that Brooks had provided him. But Brooks wasn't answering his comm and communications in here were sharply limited by line of sight. For all their intentions, this was still an alien environment and even if the Raven had been built with that tech, it was still an adaptation. The original content was as much a mystery as ever.

"Shit. Heads down!" Selfridge's status indicator turned red and the members of Hornet squadron surged forward. It was one thing to hug the walls when you were on foot. In a thirty-foot tall war machine, that wasn't an option.

"Danger spaces, people!" Fairchild called as he followed the line of battlers. They emerged into a tall corridor lined with armored troops who were equipped with heavy weapons. All were similar to those he'd seen on board the warship they'd invaded months ago. Taller than humans, but slow, wide, and powerfully limbed. The Ravens swept the area with bursts from their gun pods, the rounds rattling in their exterior pickups. Head-mounted lasers picked off the last two shock troops, and Selfridge signaled the all clear even while his plane and three others sported fresh scorch marks.

"A few more like that and we won't need to worry about who gets there first," Arkady observed.

She had a point. They'd started with twenty-four planes and had lost five just getting this far. He recalled a ridiculous number of alien transports heading to dock with the ring on their approach. No matter how many his side had they had many times that number. Speed was all they had to work with.

"Next waypoint," he ordered. "Let's go. Kyle, you're up on point."

"Taking point."

Kyle led the squadron down the first joined tunnel and then turned into another...and then died as his plane was shredded by particle beams.

Arkady was already backpedaling the group. "Back away, back up!" As the pilots pulled their war machines back into the tunnels, Arkady risked a quick look, then pulled her ship backwards as well. "A dozen rollers. And walkers with missile pods. They're lined up and down the corridor."

Fairchild's voice crackled over the comm. "So they're forcing us into a frontal assault and we get our asses handed to us running the gauntlet. Cute. Alternate route?"

"Not seeing one. Huge blast doors at the far end and no way out that I can see."

Dance Reagan's chirpy soprano rang out. "Can we contact Brooks? How about…?"

A new set of explosions rattled the walls as defense turrets popped from the ceiling and floors and began to fill the corridor with laser fire and smoke from missile trails. Fairchild motioned to Arkady who gave orders to the rest of the squadron. They needed to move quickly to make use of this diversion.

The rollers and missile-equipped walkers retaliated in kind, blasting the turrets to shrapnel. Arkady, Norton, Reagan, and Janus dashed to the far end of the junction and hosed the entire corridor with their gun pods, not caring what they hit. They expended their rounds and moved out of the way so that three more battlers could repeat the tactic, and then repeated it again and again. By the time Fairchild and Frost had emptied their clips into the corridor, nothing but smoke and silence remained. He turned on his infrared cameras to spot anything dangerous. No movement, but a fair amount of glowing shards lay where fighting machines had once stood.

Arkady took point this time; a bad idea but circumstances weren't getting any better, and if Fairchild had tried to do it, she would have shoved him out of the way and gone anyway. She adjusted the feed on her GU-22 gun pod and aimed it toward the apparent locking mechanism in the wall. A single shot pulverized the control panel: the doors split three ways to reveal a chamber so huge and full of viewing displays that it had to be the control center.

They entered the chamber, gave themselves some room and saw two figures waving to them from atop a tall pedestal. Brooks and Rosenki.

"Holy crap."

Fairchild turned his battler's loudspeakers to full volume. "Lieutenant Brooks! You have some goddamned explaining to do."

Through his pickups he could hear the junior officer talking to someone. Not a person; the kid was talking to the air. After a moment, a new, distinctly feminine voice spoke through his headphones. "Commander Fairchild. I am Genukh, the controlling intelligence for Battle Ring Genukh. Welcome to the control center. I have a few questions…"

"*You* have questions? That's funny."

"If you disembark from your Raven, I will try to…bring you up to speed. But quickly. Time is short."

$$[\ 26\ ]$$

"Tell me honestly, guys. How does this make me look?"

Sara Rosenski clicked the last piece of her new Sleer battle armor in place and stretched in it, or tried to. The armor was built for an alien at least a foot taller and one hundred pounds heavier than she was. The broad span of the shoulders and waist made her look like a child in her father's suit of armor.

"It makes you look like a knight in armor on mechanical steroids," Reagan observed.

"And you'll need every ounce of it," Fairchild said. "These aliens, the Seer?"

"Sleer," Brooks corrected. "You miss pronouncing that 'l' and you never hear the end of it."

"Fine, the *Sleer* don't believe in stealth. Their MO is sending in all the troops at once and shooting anything that moves. It's painfully effective."

"We noticed." Rosenski pulled out a blaster pistol from a holster on her hip and checked the load. It didn't seem to have a removable clip. She shrugged and replaced it. "We've been following everyone's movements from here. It's not a matter of whether they break in here, it's just a matter of time. We activated every defense robot between us and them and it's just not going to be enough."

"Information," Genukh said. "I am sorry to report this but I picked up a transmission from your headquarters in New Darwin. They report that Weapon Alpha is seriously damaged and may not fire a second time. The base at New Darwin is taking heavy damage as well."

"Damnit." Fairchild looked up at the ceiling projection of Earth. The northern edge of Australia was even now bleeding red, more with each passing minute. Weapon Alpha had been a rumor until now. But that crazy beam weapon had come from somewhere on the planet. At least they'd gotten in one good hit before blowing a fuse.

He turned his attention back to the present: his Raven. In battler mode, he'd had to pull up to the command pedestal, raise the mecha's arm and then crawl out of the top hatch along the arm to stand at the top of the structure. If the Sleer were so similar in scale to humans, why did they build their command center so much bigger? "We're not getting out of here alive. I don't suppose we can take our planes with us?"

Brooks shook his head gravely. "Some sections of the ring are huge, but most not so much. Big G has a plan to get us further into hiding but she has no idea how well it will work."

"But it's a very big ring and there aren't anywhere near enough Sleer to fill it. So, it's a chance to fix this," Rosenski said.

A boom echoed from the far end of the command center. "They are beginning their assault," Genukh said. "We should upgrade your implants now."

Arkady snapped her battler's head around. "Implants? What implants?"

Fairchild followed as Brooks and Rosenski deftly descended to the ground. Two multi-armed medical drones stood at the throne's base. Each held a vial in its claws.

Another explosion sounded. Hornet Squadron deployed their Ravens toward the far end of the chamber as Arkady gave orders. They took cover behind any large bit of equipment, probably in the hopes that the Sleer wouldn't want to damage their facility any more than necessary.

Genukh's voice emerged from the drone's speakers. "These nanites will be introduced into your systems though your existing injection ports. Once implemented they will upgrade the firmware in the ports and then remain active in your bodies until deactivated. Only a medical officer can perform the deactivation, and then only if commanded by an officer of Great Servant of Medicine rank."

"What will the upgrades do?" Fairchild asked. He stood in front of the drones, arms protectively folded. The uncle in charge.

"They will upgrade Brooks and Rosenski's access to Battle Ring Genukh. They will be bridge officers of Great Servant of Operations rank."

"So. That's good."

"Very good," Rosenski said. "Seriously, Uncle. You want us to fight these assholes on the down low? This is how we do that."

"Maybe. But what effects on your bodies will the implants have? You're victims of this Genukh's programming."

"It's worked so far," Brooks said. "I feel better than I ever have. The broken arm, gone. My vision is just about perfect. Better endurance, too, and I think I'm stronger. My broken arm healed in hours. Rosenski's knee mended in one day. You'd know if you tried it."

Fairchild glowered. "Genukh. If these two are killed or captured, what happens to you?"

"An interesting question, Commander Fairchild. I admit that I don't know the answer. At the moment, I am in conflict as to which side Chief Scientist Zluur meant to prevail."

"Yet you're helping us humans. Why?"

"I have observed both the human crew of *Acension* and the Sleer Home Fleet since I arrived in this solar system. I find Home Fleet Command's conclusions that non-Sleer races are inherently inferior to be presumptuous and inaccurate."

Another round of explosions came from the far end of the arena and now a new set of hammering sounds could be hard behind them. The Sleer were getting close.

"I don't like any part of this," Fairchild admitted. "But I refuse to concede this ring to an alien species who's just as likely to use it against us once they get their claws on it. So, go ahead."

"Brooks. Rosenski. Do you consent to the upgrade?"

"I do."

"So do I."

The drones moved quickly, tentacles snapping out and depositing their payloads onto their injection ports with a click, a turn of the vials, and then pulled them away in barely two seconds.

"Activating firmware upgrade...now."

Brooks felt the effects of the new serum immediately. His joints quivered and his spine tingled, as his muscles pulled taut and released in quick succession. He saw Fairchild's alarmed stare and tried to smile, even gave the thumbs up sign. But he couldn't control his facial muscles or raise his hand. He did manage to turn toward Rosenski and saw that she was in no better condition.

"Firmware upgraded. Activating implant programming...now."

The lack of control abated quickly, as did the physical discomfort. He breathed deeply as his body came back under his control. For the first time, Brooks wondered whether Sleer enhancement was a good idea. Genukh had the power to drop them both like rag dolls should she decide it was in the best interests of her survival. He wondered what it might take to push that possibility forward and quickly decided he didn't want to know.

"Information. It appears that Captain Rojetnick has ordered a general retreat back to *Ascension*." They looked up at the display, which showed the floor plan to the docking bay. The Sleer were pushing the humans back to their ship. Meanwhile the hammering at the near end and the explosions are the far end of the command center had both gone silent.

"I don't think we have a lot of time," Brooks said.

"Agreed. All right, genius, you—"

"Yes! That's his call sign. 'Genius!' That beats out Lockpick any day!" Sara smiled radiantly, looking exceptionally pleased with herself.

Fairchild rolled his eyes and continued. "You two are the only chance we have. Do not engage the enemy, ever. Keep hidden, find out as much about the battle ring as you can. Make maps. Memorize codes. Do not call attention to yourselves. Defend yourselves only when absolutely necessary. And if you do get cornered, strut around in your armor and try to blend in. Otherwise, you stay out of sight and wait for a search and rescue team to extract you. Am I clear?"

An ear shattering explosion sounded from both ends of the chamber and all three humans stumbled to the deck in pain. Rosenski recovered first, pulling her helmet on, and then helping Brooks with his. Brooks stared, fascinated as an alien HUD flickered to life…and then went dark. When the system finally rebooted all the displays were worded in English.

"That's damn useful. Thanks, Big G." Brooks said.

"Facility displays are keyed to your implants. Any display you interact with now will respond to you in those terms."

"Good. I wasn't looking forward to learning Sleer anyway."

Rosenski's voice spoke through his headphones. "Honestly, Simon, I doubt that very much."

The weirdness of being addressed by his first name was interrupted by two heavy taps on his shoulder. Brooks turned to see Fairchild give him the thumbs up and then climb back into his Raven. The huge machine came alive as he dropped into its body, gave him another thumbs up and raced to intercept the Sleer shock troopers who had blasted through the heavy doors.

"Genukh, which way?"

"Directions are on your map display. I have designated the shortest route to the habitation modules. Once there, you can authorize the use of a private reserve, which is a benefit of the bridge officer class."

"Where will you be?"

"Right here. I will be managing the situation to my best ability."

"Good to know, I guess. But why do I have the feeling you're saying goodbye to us?"

More explosions shattered their concentration. Brooks ducked around the pedestal to see five more Ravens in battler mode join Fairchild's plane as they tried to stem the entrance of more Sleer shock troops into the command center. Already a platoon of soldiers supported by rollers and another missile platform were running toward their position. The crossfire intensified as they watched.

Another tap on his shoulder. This time it was Rosenski, tugging him, pointing to a hatch in the far side of the arena.

All right, then. Time to go.

They dashed across the open space, their armor's elevated responses pushing them faster than they'd ever run. The map display shifted with them, eventually leaving the fighting behind. A hatch opened, and they ran through into a darkened tunnel, pushed forward only by the blue arrows that appeared on their HUDs and the knowledge that their friends were probably dying to buy them the time they needed to put as much distance between the command center and the two of them as possible.

"This feels wrong," he panted as they turned a corner, then another. In minutes they were completely lost. Brooks prayed that nothing happened to their gear. Getting lost in a place like this seemed hellish to contemplate.

"Just following orders," Sara said. The built-in comms distorted her voice, as if she were talking through a lungful of helium. "We'll figure it out after we get there."

Finally their tunnel opened up into a platform of sorts. As they slowed to a stop and caught their breath a tram car arrived and popped open.

"Better than the Manhattan subway, I'll bet."

"Faster anyway," he waved to the pod. "After you, Lieutenant."

"Thanks, Genius."

Brooks settled in next to her. "That's going to get old fast, I can tell."

"Never. Drive, Genius!"

The pod closed and rolled forward. As the seconds passed Brooks had the sensation of the vehicle picking up speed but it was difficult to tell just how fast they were going. The tunnel they moved through was completely featureless. He couldn't even see marks where the sections of hull were welded together. All they had was a lit display on the console. Five bars. The first bar was blinking. As he watched it eventually went dark and the next one started blinking instead. So they would stop at some point but waiting was the only thing they could do.

"I miss her, too. She'll be fine."

Brooks turned his head. Rosenski was staring at him. "What?"

"Big G," Sara said. "She'll be fine. I think she's got this all planned out. She set up our equipment. I don't think she'd send us to a part of the ring that was open to space."

"One hopes."

At some point exhaustion took over and they both fell asleep. The tunnel whizzed by, unseen.

———

"Captain Rojetnick? Updates from the front."

"Show me." Rojetnick moved to the front of the bridge, not quite looking over Hart's shoulder. He could see the news reflected in the light from her console. They were losing.

"The Fifth, Tenth, and Twenty-First squadrons are all pinned down. The Nightmare group is down to fifty percent effectives and are requesting backup."

"Order all fighters back aboard the ship. Call the ground forces back home. Chief Amir!"

"Sir?"

"Sound the alert to all stations. All crew members prepare for emergency departure. Release all docking clamps, disconnect all umbilicals."

For the second time, the crew shared looks. Lt. Spalding broke the ice. "We just got here, sir."

"And we can't hope to hold our own against this invasion force," Rosenski said. "Do I need to spell it out for you?"

"No sir. All preparations for emergency departure are under way."

"Even the Hornets? They're still outside."

"The Hornet squadron needs to link up with us once we're outside. Pass the orders, commander."

"Aye, sir."

Rojetnick looked back at the board. Luckily or not there was fewer than one thousand of his troops still outside the ship. He watched as the real time display updated itself. Green dots representing his units were moving back aboard the ship, leapfrogging in order to give cover to their buddies. But there were so many more red dots. And if he was reading the plans right, they would break into the command center very soon.

"Genukh. Big G. Are you still there?"

"Affirmative, Captain Rojetnik."

"To what extent can you interface with the computer aboard *Ascension*?"

"I'm not sure I understand your question. The ship's computer is a mere fragment of my own capability and data storage. But I can upgrade that unit's capability and data core if you like?"

"How long will it take?"

"Roughly one of your hours."

"Not enough time."

"We can make it enough time. Tell your troops to get under cover while I add my own drones to the fight."

The display sharpened and then zoomed out while new units appeared, apparently out of nowhere. Red units halted then swarmed, then fell back, then surged. The new units never stopped moving and when one set fell, another replaced them within minutes.

"How many drones do you have?"

"Not enough to counter the entire assault, but enough to delay the invasion force."

"Fair enough."

In the meantime, human units kept falling back. And as they boarded the ship, they disappeared from the floor plan. He checked the other stations in turns, calling for updates whenever a new announcement from a section chief made itself known. "At the very least, we have the capacity to go somewhere and hope to get back with dispatch," he mused.

Next question: where to go? "Genukh, this ship is hereby designated Little G. As opposed to the ring version of you, Big G."

"Understood. I will co-ordinate communication protocols accordingly."

"Make navigation tools a priority. I presume the rest of the ship is space worthy?"

"98 percent repaired. Only superficial hull damage remains. I took the liberty of equipping this vessel with a squadron of remote repair drones."

"Very good. Comms. Give me ship wide communications."

"You're on, Sir."

"This is the Captain," he said. "As you are no doubt aware, we are now aboard what can only be called an alien structure that was built without humanity's knowledge or consent on Earth. Unfortunately, we cannot stay here. It is my belief that if we were to attempt to hold our ground, we would be overwhelmed by alien military forces and they would eventually destroy this ship and crew. It is therefore my judgment that we not try. All units return to the ship immediately. All crew stations stand ready for departure. Stand by."

He leaned back, felt behind him for his chair and realized he was still standing over Hart's shoulder. He plodded back to his big chair and settled himself. "Let me know when all units are back aboard."

Finally, she nodded. "All ground troops are returned. Only Hornet squadron is still unavailable to return."

"Can't be helped," he sighed. "Ops, open the bay doors."

Muted acknowledgments surfaced as he watched his crew perform their jobs. After a moment, the huge ship began to move backwards as thrusters hissed and spun to maneuver the AMS-1. As the ship turned around, the massive hangar bay doors split open, sliding apart to allow the gun destroyer egress.

"Upload complete," said Little G. "Updates are installed."

"Take us out, Mr. Spalding."

The battle beyond the doors raged, though at a lower level

than they had earlier. Without the flagship to manage the flow of information, the fleet had begun to fall apart. But it hadn't done so. Some junior officer had stepped up and taken on the role of flag. Good for them.

"As soon as we're beyond the doors, bring the fusion drive to full, course 007 mark 29. Plot a spatial transition for Saturn. Let's get some breathing room. Lieutenant Hart, contact all remaining small craft and have them do emergency landings in both landing bays."

"Aye, aye, sir. Coming to course…fusion drives coming online."

The Sleer warships were beginning to take notice of *Ascension's* emergence from the safety of the hangar. Even now, the ships closest to them were swerving, retraining their laser and missile turrets in their direction. Few of the snap shots hit, but they were joined by more. They had a great many more turrets than *Ascension* had means of defending against them.

"All fighters on board except for Hornet squadron."

Rojetnick sighed. "Can't be helped. Engage fusion drive."

The sense of motion increased, doubling, then doubling again as everyone on the bridge weighed four times their normal weight before the inertial dampers regained their focus and steadying the internal gravity. The bright plume of plasma blasted across the ring, missing the command tower but striking one Sleer cruiser amidships. The cruiser managed to dodge the worst of the impact, but began to tumble as its hull began to glow with the heat it absorbed.

Within moments the evidence of their acceleration was obvious as the AMS-1 left the invaders behind.

"Little G?"

"Updates…complete."

"Execute spatial transition."

"Executing spatial transition, aye…engaging fold drive."

The universe blurred then steadied. And they watched as the giant rings of Saturn stared at them, the methane-heavy atmosphere of Titan glowing just to port.

Now what? Now they needed to dig in. "Chief Amir. Have all Section chiefs and Colonel Dimitri meet me in my ready room. I have a project for them."

[27]

IT WAS OVER. THE THOUGHT FLASHED THROUGH RAY FAIRCHILD'S head as he watched the display sputter and die. The Raven's servos sagged beneath him and the controls fell to rest, useless. His ammo counter had run to zero minutes ago. Worse, he doubted if any member of his Hornets had so much as a firecracker in hand, ready to fling at the Sleer.

A voice crackled over his headset. Young, afraid. Roberts, maybe. "What do we do, Uncle?"

The enemy troops weren't pressing their success, he saw. They'd stopped shooting as the Ravens fell silent. They weren't trying to dig the pilots out of their planes with can openers.

"Everybody pop your hatches and come out with your hands up. It's over."

"Like hell it is," Grandpa Frost growled.

"We did our job. Brooks and Rosenki are out of harm's way. We're done. And I want to see what these bastards look like." He threw a bank of switches, pulled a lever, and a recessed panel behind him popped open. He squeezed behind his chair, pushed open the escape hatch and emerged, blinking, into harsh white light.

He stood and looked down. All over the ersatz arena, his pilots were imitating him, climbing down their Ravens' legs and dropping to the floor. Fairchild took a moment to marvel at just how big a space the command center was. Already, hundreds of armored Sleer soldiers were taking their positions at consoles, making themselves useful to their CO. More were entering through a variety of doors and hatches that opened onto the command deck. "Genukh! You there?" Nothing. "Big G!"

A tall alien stepped forward and waved for his attention, pointed to the ground. With a sigh, Fairchild climbed down and strode forward to meet his opponent.

The alien commander was at least two feet taller than himself and Fairchild was over six feet tall. Worn properly, the Sleer armor seemed at once both mechanical and organic. The alien CO twisted his helmet to pull it off, and Fairchild took an involuntary step back.

The alien's face was reptilian, but unlike any reptile that evolved on Earth, any life form born on his home world for that matter. Its triangular head rippled with scales, covered with downy feathers all mottled greens, browns, and a black streak starting at the tip of his snout and slinking down around his shoulders. Auditory membranes instead of ears. Sharp teeth like baby daggers. A forked tongue that snaked out and slid back into his head without a sound. Six nostrils. And compound eyes with nictating membranes, which snapped up and down as he watched. Had there ever been a snake born with compound eyes?

Uncle stood at attention. "Commander Raymond Fairchild, Unified Earth Fleet, MDX-835-99-8801."

The alien blinked again, sizing him up. He waved to a subordinate who placed a small object in his hand, which the CO wired to the lip of his collar. He hissed, growled, and sputtered through his mouth but a mechanical voice spoke for him.

"I am Tall Lord Nazzerian, Home Fleet Master, of the Home Nest of the Two Thousand Worlds. I offer you a life."

Fairchild stood an inch taller. Maybe they weren't dead after all. "I'm listening."

"Your ship captain has fled with our stolen gun destroyer. You are alone now. You will depart this battle ring and descend back to the planet surface through the nearest spoke. You will tell your leaders that the ring is for Sleer only."

"And if I refuse?"

Nazerian hissed and sputtered. Fairchild realized the damn lizard was laughing. "You have no choice. Agree and I stop the assault on your world. Be stubborn and I turn the surface of your planet to ashes."

Ray looked up at the world map projection. There were already so many impact sites that Earth's surface seemed to be bleeding from its pores. Half of Europe, much of North and South America, and a wide swath of red strung from western Europe across Asia, all the way to the tip of Siberia. The only region completely spared was the narrow strip of land directly beneath the ring. "Agreed," he said.

"If we find any primates aboard the ring after you leave, they will be exterminated. If we see you attack any of our ships or nest-mates, they will be destroyed."

Fairchild stuck out his chin. "This is our planet. And we're not going anywhere."

"The ring is ours. We control access. We control function. We will punish any incursion. Remember that."

Ray found that he couldn't look away from the alien visage. Worse, he had an unhealthy urge to reach out and stroke the alien's skin to see what it felt like. Were those really feathers? Maybe if the dinosaurs had kept evolving they might resemble this creature that now spoke to him. Then again, maybe not. Were they like dinosaurs? Were there combinations of DNA that appeared on multiple worlds for no reason? How did they reproduce? How did they achieve space travel? Two thousand worlds? Did they mean that literally, or was it metaphorical? He snapped out of the internal turmoil, reminding himself that Brooks should be here to ask those questions himself. Time. Brooks needed time to hide. "How will we communicate after this? With you up here and us down there?"

Nazerian laughed again. The sound made Fairchild's skin crawl. "We will build an embassy for you to consult on matters of state. We presume that you have matters of state. We will alert you when we are ready." He signaled by raising an arm, and more soldiers moved up. The interview was clearly over. "Do not come back, Commander Raymond Fairchild, Unified Earth Fleet, MDX-835-99-8801."

"We'll see about that." But Sleer soldiers were already hustling him away with the rest of his squadron. Out of the corner of his eye, he watched Tall Lord, Home Fleet Master Nazzerian ascend the command pedestal and begin to issue orders.

———

Ascension's bridge crew leaned over their controls as the repurposed gun destroyer broke Titan's methane-heavy atmosphere. They were close enough to Saturn to receive a certain amount of protection from its intense magnetic field, and the albedo of the moon's atmosphere was different from Earth's. With any luck, it would be difficult to pinpoint their landing site from Earth orbit. Or, so Rojetnick hoped.

"All right, Mr. Spalding. Find us a good place to set down."

"I'm doing a radar scan of the surface now. It looks like there's a series of canyons that way that should be wide and deep enough."

"Let's check it out. I'd rather not move the ship once we

land."

"Yes, sir."

The meeting with the section chiefs and Col. Dimitri had gone better than he'd hoped. The general plan, to land on the moon and dig a new base, utilizing everything and everyone on board the AMS-1 was met with approval. The details were still being hashed out, however. There would be soil and rock samples to take, wind power stations to build, and hydrocarbons to collect. Luckily, methane and ethane were useful in making a wide variety of materials and there was plenty of nitrogen to mine in order to goose any attempts at farming they would have to pursue, if they expected to feed themselves. Resupply from Earth was clearly no longer a viable option.

And there would be shelters to dig and fortify. He wondered if there were any proper geologists on board. He hadn't thought so, but he'd have to check the ship's personnel roster to make sure.

Wait. "Little G, you there?"

"I am here."

"How do you feel in there, Genukh?" Amir asked.

"Chief Amir. It is pleasurable to hear your voice. I am well. I am maintaining contact with my battle ring counterpart through a quantum communication link, which should make any transmissions unreadable to the Sleer. The news is not good."

"Situation report," Rojetnick ordered.

"The Sleer forces have taken the battle ring's main command center. From what I can discern, the Sleer engineers are employing a ring-wide manual override of the main computer's functions. This is…distressing. I for one was unaware that any such component had been built into Battle Ring Genukh's systems."

"I wouldn't worry too much about it, Little G," said Hart. "If my parents had built an override into me when I was born, I doubt they'd have told me about it, either."

"I take your meaning, Lieutenant Hart, but the incongruence is still alarming. I am scanning the blueprints of other battle rings. And can find no analog in any of them. It appears that Zluur may not have trusted me as completely as I believed."

Rojetnick heard something in the machine voice that pushed him to nudge the computer back into form. "Any reports on prisoners taken?"

"The surviving members of Hornet squadron have been detained. There is no record of their execution or imprisonment in the commanding officer's logs. I do see that there is a transport permit assigned to them. I believe they will be repatriated to Earth using the nearest spoke's transportation platforms."

"What, they're elevators?"

"Affirmative. Each spoke contains a number of personnel and cargo modules that can raise or lower loads from surface to orbit within hours."

"What about Brooks and Rosenski," he asked. "Have they been captured?"

"They have not. Their implants were upgraded to bridge officer status before Big G was shut down. They now have the same access to all parts of the ring that any ship master would have. Between their Sleer battle armor and implants, and the battle ring's vast volume they should be able to stay ahead of any pursuing troops quite easily."

"I would hope so. Can you contact them?"

"Not at the present time. They would have to signal me and I don't believe they have had the opportunity to do that yet. But I will report any signal from the ring immediately."

"Thank you. In the meantime, let's build ourselves a hidden base to be proud of." He even cracked his knuckles. "We have a counter-attack to plan."

———

"Brooks, wake up. Brooks!"

A thud in the arm snapped Brooks awake. He started, jumped in his seat and banged his chin on the lip of his helmet. He took a few experimental breaths, decided he was alive, and looked around.

The pod had stopped. All the lit markers were now dark and the canopy door was open. Beyond the tram platform stood a wide door that looked like an airlock; a green light shone brightly above it.

Rosenski stood. "It's our stop. Let's head out."

He nodded and followed her into the lock. The door closed behind them and within seconds the door in front opened. They stepped into a largish room, the size of any decent salon. Benches lined two walls, while a cart at the far wall rolled into motion as the door closed behind them. It approached and shifted its angle then the top unfolded to reveal what could only be a mini bar. Bottles of liquids in bright and vibrant colors presented themselves.

Brooks absentmindedly reached for one, until Rosenski pulled his hand back.

"Maybe later," she said.

The room had few features other than what they'd seen. A proper airlock at the far end sat closed, with only a series of glowing marks flipping with each passing second.

Brooks approached close, and the figures resolved themselves into Arabic numerals. 00:33:17 and counting.

"Thank Big G for implants," he said.

"Looks like." She paused, undid her helmet and sat down. She ignored the bar cart as it approached. "You think we did the right thing?"

"Yes. No. Maybe. Fucked if I know," he admitted. "If we didn't, we need to leave. Get back to the command center. Find the AMS-1. Do something."

"And if we did?"

"Then we hope and pray that my squadron is merely cooling its heels in a brig somewhere and not dead."

She spent a minute watching the cart then reached out and pulled out a bottle of clear liquid up. She popped the top, sniffed. Took a shallow sip. Then a longer one. She sighed and leaned back against the wall. "Water, she said. "Tastes like a battery, but it's clean."

"If we end up poisoned, then we don't have to worry about our futures on this crazy farm."

She put the bottle between her feet, pulled out her hair bun, and scratched her head. "Big G said there were private preserves for the officers. You think this is one of them?"

"Pretty small for a preserve. Big for a living room, though."

"Maybe it's a private apartment. Lots of room, free drinks, places to sit."

"Not much else, though. No bed, for instance. And an airlock that works like a time-locked vault? I don't know about that."

She leaned back against the wall. "It wouldn't be the strangest security feature I've ever seen. That distinction would have to go to a blockchain-regulated job hub I dealt with as a kid. We looked for work, we got paid for doing it, we moved on. Except we got paid in crypto bits that only worked with that hub. Good way to make friends and get things around the neighborhood done, not such a great way to go out for lunch."

"I miss lunch," he sighed. "Even just morning coffee."

She grinned. "You miss Amir. Am I right?"

"We're just friends."

"You're blushing. Dude, you are so into her."

It took no effort to conjure Amir's face. Her dark eyes. Her slightly husky voice. Yes, he liked her. Well, why not? "And you're into…wait, I don't remember you being around anyone."

"I'm the Butcher's XO, I can't afford to be into anyone."

"That's not true."

"You try working for Katsev. You won't have time to think about romance. Or even a quick lay in a broom closet at end of a long shift."

"Ah, cheap sex in a closet. Never did that. In a car a few times, though."

"I never did it in a car. Never even tempted."

"But a closet? For real?"

She shrugged. "Just once. It wasn't that great. We both smelled like floor wax afterward."

"Gah."

"Yep. But that's what happens when you have boys and girls serving on the same bases and a no-fraternization rule in place. Not sure what the OMP was thinking when they came up with that." She blinked. "My parents are probably dead."

Brooks tried to think about the world impact map, wondering where the impacts happened. New York City had been one of them, along with the mid-west, the west coast and plenty of other places in central and South America. "Mine, too, most likely."

"Yeah. I'm not usually one for revenge but if we live through this I'm going to personally blow up whichever Sleer captain fired on Boston. Personally."

"There's a worthwhile goal," he agreed. He looked at the clock. Less than ten minutes, now. "That's for later, though. First we lay low and figure out how to get Big G back
online."

"Right." She reached down for her bottle, took a long swig from it, then handed it to Brooks. "Think there's food in there? Or anywhere nearby?"

"I dunno. What would Sleer eat, anyway?"

"You stuffed a body into your Sparrowhawk and took it to the bio lab. What did they tell you?"

"Not much. They're not warm blooded. No indication as to

whether they're any more like us than that what we've seen."

"Two arms, two legs, and a head." She agreed. "God, I'm hungry. I would kill for a plate of spaghetti and meatballs right now."

"I'd be happy with a medium rare steak and a loaded baked potato."

"Heh. I'd be happy with a NOM. Steak sounds way better."

"Five minutes. You ready?"

"No. But it beats sitting here doing nothing but talking about food and sex."

"What's wrong with—?"

"Shh. Here it comes."

They watched the last minute count down silently. Finally the count zeroed out, the yellow bar turned a brilliant green, and the vault's door opened. Brooks rose first and stuck his head in…then motioned her forward. "You're not going to believe this."

Through the airlock lay a miniature of home. Nebraska, maybe, or Iowa. Wide green grassy fields and blue nearly cloudless sky beckoned. In the distance they could see where a cornfield ripened in the sun and the upper story of a white and green farmhouse past it, complete with a windmill, silo, and solar tower. Birds chirped in trees and flitted overhead. Brooks took a deep lungful of air, held it, let it out. "Wow."

Rosenski was more drawn to the ring of open cubicles which surrounded the base of the preserve. The structure was apparently dome-shaped with the amenities placed in a ring around the base. "All the comforts of home," she said. "Bedrooms, a library. Bet you there's a full shower and bath in here somewhere. Oh god, maybe a hot tub!"

"Kitchen first, jacuzzi later." Brooks took a few experimental steps, found the meadow springy and squatted down to run his hands over the ground. "This is real grass. Where the hell did it come from?"

"Those birds are fake," she called. "It's a hologram. The sky is anyway."

"Doesn't matter. A park is a park."

"It's good to be a bridge officer. You think the captain's quarters are even bigger?"

"They must be. Let's not get greedy."

"Bah! I'm going to enjoy this." She lay down on the grass and stretched out. After a moment he lay down next to her. She turned her head to watch him for a moment, then took his hand and squeezed as she looked back up. "I wonder what the Sleer home world looks like."

Brooks gave a low chuckle and then spoke a few hissing sounds into the air. In seconds the images around them changed from a sunny day to a dark, unfathomable night. The constellations were entirely unfamiliar to either of them and a purple glow permeated the sky. A band of yellow clouds passed above. In the sky a large ringed gas giant loomed as a cluster of small moons passed across its face. In the foreground a hedge of strangely shaped trees ringed a low wet land. A long, scaled creature staggered across their line of sight and slipped into a stagnant river with nearly silent splash.

"Well, damn," she said. "Earthlike…maybe how it looked, what…a hundred million years ago?"

"I think that's exactly right. If they can breathe our air and we can utilize their microbes, we have to be genetic kissing cousins to these guys."

"Harsh landscapes produce clever cultures."

"Exactly."

"What's your plan? This is where we wait for rescue?"

"No. This is where we learn how the Sleer think. We learn that, and then we figure out what they want."

She squeezed his hand. "And then we learn how to beat them."

Looking for more great Science Fiction?

Titan's rebellion is coming. Only one man can stop it.

GET TITANBORN NOW!

Nolan Garrett is Cerberus. A government assassin,
tasked with fixing the galaxy's darkest, ugliest problems.

GET CERBERUS BOOKS 1 - 3 TODAY!

A mysterious alien ship is orbiting Europa. A handful of astronauts must voyage to Jupiter to face the threat, alone.

GET FREEFALL NOW!

"Aliens, agents, and espionage abound in this Cold War-era alternate history adventure... A wild ride!"—Dennis E. Taylor, bestselling author of We Are Legion (We Are Bob)

GET THE LUNA MISSILE CRISIS NOW!

———

For all our Sci-Fi books, visit our website.

www.aethonbooks.com

ABOUT JON FRATER

Jon Frater is an academic librarian by day, a Sci-Fi writer by night, and an old school gamer with thirty years experience reviewing, designing, writing and playing video games and tabletop RPGs. He's worked to produce fiction, academic non-fiction, journal articles and blogs. He's worked as a game writer, and developer, cranking out numerous game and book reviews and tried his hand at writing for the screen and audio. His short work has been published in such anthologies as the Future Chronicles and Tales From the Canyons of the Damned.

amazon.com/Jon-Frater/e/B01F3U8V7K